TREASON

Orson Scott Card

ST. MARTIN'S PAPERBACKS

NOTE: If you purchased this book without a cover you should be aware that this book is stolen property. It was reported as 'unsold and destroyed' to the publisher, and neither the author nor the publisher has received any payment for this 'stripped book'.

Treason was originally published in 1979, in hardcover by St. Martin's Press and in paperback by Dell, in a substantially different form, under the title *A Planet Called Treason*. *Treason* represents a thorough, page-by-page reworking of *A Planet Called Treason*. Almost ten percent of it is completely original.

TREASON

Copyright © 1979, 1988 by Orson Scott Card.

All rights reserved. No part of this book may be used or reproduced in any manner whatsoever without written permission except in the case of brief quotations embodied in critical articles or reviews. For information, address St. Martin's Press, 175 Fifth Avenue, New York, N.Y. 10010.

Library of Congress Catalog Card Number: 88-18213

ISBN: 0-312-92109-8

Printed in the United States of America

St. Martin's Press hardcover edition published 1988
St. Martin's Paperbacks edition/April 1990

10 9 8 7 6 5 4 3

To
My brother Bill, who lent me *Catseye*;
MaryJo, who led me to Bradbury's *Body Electric*;
Laura Dene, who put Asimov's *Foundation* in my hands;
Dale and Maria, who made me read the
Chronicles of Narnia;
and the librarians in
Santa Clara, California, and Mesa, Arizona,
who made it possible to find
Poul Anderson's "Call Me Joe"
and Lloyd Biggle's "Tunesmith,"
Andre Norton's *Galactic Derelict*
and Robert Heinlein's *Tunnel in the Sky*:
You set me to dreaming.
I hope I don't wake up.

Author's Note

A Planet Called Treason was my second novel to be published, and in the intervening years I have learned a little more about how a story can and should be told. The story of Lanik Mueller is one I still believe in, and in preparing this new edition, I left the plain tale alone. What has been changed is the manner of presentation—the tone, the pacing, the clarity. The result is that about ten percent of this volume is new material, with smaller revisions on almost every page. This revision was not an attempt to tell the story of Lanik Mueller as if I were writing it for the first time in 1988—*that* novel, which because of the pressure of time will never be written, would be half again as long as this, with much more time spent on developing other characters and relationships. Instead, this edition retains the simplicity of the original, the story of one young man's discovery and transformation of his world and of himself.

I am grateful to my mother, Peggy Card, who retyped the entire novel from the Dell paperback edition, so that it could be on disk in WordPerfect format for my work on revision; to my wife, Kristine, who read the first draft of the new edition as it came out of the printer, helping me to make this a more clear, consistent, and effective novel than I could have produced on my own; and to my sister, Janice Card, for her excellent work on the revised and clarified map of Treason's inhabited continent.

TREASON

1 MUELLER

I was the last to know what was happening to me. Or at least I was the last to know that I knew.

Saranna realized it when her hand glided up my chest and instead of smoothly cresting the pectorals made lean and hard by hours of sword and javelin and archery, her fingers snagged on a looser kind of flesh. Her hands remembered that same discovery on her own body not that many years before, and being a true daughter of Mueller, with a sharp eye and an uncompromising mind, she knew it all at once, knew all my future history, knew all that was now impossible between us. Yet, being a true daughter of Mueller, she said nothing, nor did she grieve; it simply·happened that from then until I left Mueller, she never touched me, at least not as she had before, not with the promise of decades of passion in our future. She knew, but I did not yet know.

Dinte saw it, too. Watching me as he always does, the second son hoping for some accident to befall me so that he can delay any help that might come to me; searching for some hint of congenital idiocy so he can be named regent after father dies; noting any flaws or weaknesses in my fighting or my thinking, so that when, not if, he betrays me, he can gain some advantage over me—watching me with that kind of eagerness, he had to see the way my shirt moved differently across my chest. Of all the ways that I could be rendered unfit to sit on Father's throne, this had to be the one that he would relish most. Being a poor excuse for a son of Mueller, he immediately became cocky, not naming my affliction, but treating me with the arrogance that even cowards have the grace to display only toward the corpse of their enemy. He knew, but I did not yet know.

Father would not have seen it. There was always too much work for the Mueller to do; he had no time for watching me himself. But he had me watched, by all my tutors and half my friends; especially during the crucial time of puberty, when the greatest danger comes.

We in whom the Mueller blood runs true, our bodies have a great gift: to heal so quickly that scars form before the blood is dry, and to grow back any part of our body that is lost. It makes us very hard to kill.

Our enemies say that Muellers feel no pain, but it isn't true. To them it looks that way because in battle we willingly absorb a dangerous blow that any other man would have to parry to save his life, and while our enemy's sword is buried in our own flesh, we can cut the lifeblood out of him and then walk on to find another enemy to engage, our own wound already healing.

But we feel pain, just like anyone else. Our women faint in childbirth when the flesh is torn. When you put our hand into the fire, the agony burns as hot inside our brain as inside any other man's. We feel pain; what we don't feel is fear. Or rather, we've learned to separate pain and fear.

To other people, pain means that their life is in danger; to preserve themselves, they must have the reflex to avoid that pain by any means they can. But to a Mueller, pain means that the danger is small. Death comes to us only in ways that are beyond pain—the crumbling of senility, the cold hard breath of drowning, the loss of all feeling when the body is severed from the head. A mere cut or burn or stab or broken bone means only that some vigor will be taken from us as our body quickly heals; it means we'll be fed on blood-rare steak and not on radishes when the battle ends.

And the worst fear that others feel—the fear of dismemberment, of losing toes or fingers, hands or feet, ears or nose or eyes or genitals—we laugh at that.

Why is it their worst fear? Because they've come to think of their present shape as their true self, and if they lose that shape, they lose their self, they become a monster even in their own eyes.

But we Muellers have long since learned that our present shape is not ourself at all. We can have many different shapes and still be who we always were. It's a lesson we learn during the madness of adolescence. At twelve or fourteen years of age, we also go through the bizarre jumbling of chemicals that cause others to grow hair in strange places and become machines that can build copies of themselves; with us, though, since our bodies are so powerful, adolescence is also stronger. We bred ourselves to regenerate lost or broken body parts; during the madness of puberty, our bodies forget their proper shape and try to grow parts that are already there. Every young man and woman has waved a third arm tauntingly at friends, danced some complicated step designed to make use of an extra leg or two, winked a superfluous eye, grimaced with three rows of teeth above and four below. I endured having four arms once, an extra nose, and two hearts pumping away before the surgeon took me under his knife to cut away the excess. Our self is not our shape. We can have any shape, and still be who we are. We have no dread of losing limbs. We can't distort or destroy our self through subtraction.

We have other dreads.

All during my adolescence, Father had me watched. Even at the age of fifteen, when my body was only a decimeter or two from a man's full height and my sexual changes should have been complete—complete enough for Saranna to have my child in her already—even then, I could still feel their eyes on me from dawn to dusk, measuring me body and soul, so they could tell the tale to Father in those moments when he had the time to think of me. It's impossible that they missed what was happening to me; Father must have known before Dinte, even before Saranna did. They all knew.

But I didn't know.

Oh, of course I *knew*. I knew it well enough to abandon all my tight-fitting clothing and wear only the looser, blousier clothes. I knew it well enough to find excuses rather than go swimming with my friends, well enough not to snap at Dinte for being even snottier than ever, as if I dared not provoke him into naming what it was I had become. I knew it well enough not to wonder why Saranna wasn't touching me, knew it well enough during that last month not to take her into my bed. And yet I never named what had become of me, not even to myself.

I never even let the thought of my terrible new future come into my head. Except once, with the precious steel sword of royalty flashing in my hand, when I vowed, so strongly that I remember the moment even now as if it had happened only this morning—I vowed never to live without such a sword in my hand or at my side. Even then, I was pretending to myself that my fear was of becoming a commoner, the sort of sluglike semi-soul who never touches iron and who shudders at the slightest cut that bleeds.

"Today," said Homarnoch.

"I haven't time," I said, with that imperious archness that the sons of princes use to remind others of authority they don't yet have.

"The Mueller says."

And that was that. All deceptions were over; all lies that I believed, I'd have to unbelieve all at once. Yet still I put him off, told him I was filthy and had to wash, which was true enough; but I managed to bathe without once looking in the silvered glass to see myself. Clothing hung over all the mirrors, or somehow they had all been set aside, so that in my room I never had to see myself. This was just one more sign that I knew without knowing—until that month I had been as vain as any boy and surrounded myself with glass.

But there was no hiding from the mirror in Homarnoch's sterile surgical den, his place of sharp steel knives and bloody beds, where barbed arrows were cut from soldiers' flesh and gaudy useless body parts were struck from adolescent bodies.

He stood me before the mirror, himself behind me, and cupped both hands under breasts that by now had grown voluptuous. For the first time I was forced to stare at flesh that couldn't possibly be my own. For the first time I was aware of the pressure of someone else's touch. Still, I don't think it was Homarnoch's brusk surgeonly caress that aroused me. That touch was far more strange to me than sexual. I think it was the sight of what had to be someone else's breasts being taken in someone else's hands. I think it was voyeurism. I still didn't believe in what was happening to me.

"Why didn't you come to me at once?" asked Homarnoch. He sounded almost hurt.

"For what? I've grown all kinds of body parts before."

He shook his head. "You're not a fool, Lanik Mueller."

I heard my name, and felt a sick dread. Later I realized that it was the name *Mueller* that caused me fear—not because it was my name, but because so soon it would *not* be.

"It happens even in the Mueller's family, Lanik. Every few generations. No one is immune."

"It's just puberty," I said, willing him to believe it.

He looked at me sadly, and not without affection, I thought. "I hope you're right," he said, but of course he had no hope. "I hope that when I examine you, we find out that you're right."

"There's no need to—"

"Now, Lanik," he said. "The Mueller asks me to give him my answer within the hour."

What my father commanded, I performed. I lay down on the table and willed myself to relax as the knife bit into my abdomen. I had felt worse pain before—the ragged tearing of the wooden practice swords, for instance, or the time an arrow passed into my temple and out my eye—but it wasn't the pain. Or not the pain alone. Because for the first time since earliest childhood, pain and fear burned together within me, and I felt what common men feel that so unmans them on the battlefield, that makes them fodder for a Mueller's hungry sword.

When he was finished, he taped the wound. I already felt the giddiness and tingling that told me healing was under way—these were clean cuts, and all would heal without scars within hours. I didn't have to ask what he had found. I knew from the stooping of his shoulders, the harsh stoicism of his face. I could tell that it was grief and not rejoicing that his dispassionate mask concealed.

"Just cut them off," I said, lightly, jokingly.

He didn't take it as a joke. "It's ovaries, too, Lanik, and if I cut them out, cut out the uterus, they'll just grow back." He faced me then, with the same courage with which a man faces his enemy in battle. "You're a radical regenerative, Lanik. It will never end."

There it was. The name for what I had become. Like my beautiful cousin Velinisik, who went mad and pissed all over everyone with the penis whose growth had monstered her. *Radical regenerative. Rad.* Like everyone else, I had turned away from her, hadn't so much as spoken her name from that day to this. First she ceased to be human. Then she had never been human. Then she had never existed.

At the end of puberty, most Muellers settled into their adult form, and only regrew those parts of their bodies that had been lost. But a certain small number of us never got back under control. Adolescence went on forever, with new body parts growing at random. In such cases the body forgot what its natural shape ought to be; it thought of itself as an endless wound, forever to be healed; as a perpetually dismembered body, with parts forever to be renewed.

It was the worst way to die, because there was no funeral; you ceased to be a person, but they refused to let you become a corpse.

"Say that, Homarnoch," I told him, "and you might as well also say that I'm dead."

"I'm sorry," he said simply. "But I must tell your father immediately."

And he left.

I looked again in the large mirror on the wall, where my clothing hung on a hook. My shoulders were still broad from hours and days and weeks with sword, staff, spear, and bow; and more recently with the bellows at the forge. My hips still slim from running and riding. My stomach ridged with muscle, hard and solid and virile. And then, ridiculously soft and inviting, my breasts—

I took my knife from the belt hanging on the wall and pressed its sharp silver edge against my breast. It hurt too badly—I cut only an inch deep and had to stop. There was a sound at the door. I turned.

A little black Cramer bowed her head so she would not see me. I remembered that she had been taken in the last war (which Father won), and so belonged to us for life; I spoke gently to her because she was a slave.

"You're all right, don't worry," I said to her, but she didn't relax.

"My lord Ensel wants to see his son Lanik. He says immediately."

"Damn!" I said, and she knelt to receive my anger. I didn't hit her, though, only touched her head as I walked to my clothing and put it on. I couldn't help but see my reflection as I left—my chest heaving up and down as I strode out of the room. The little Cramer murmured her thanks as I left.

I started to run down the stairs to Father's chambers. I hadn't learned yet to walk like a woman, smoothing my steps and rolling my hips to avoid needless jostling. After three steps I stopped and leaned on the banister until the pain and fear subsided. When I turned around to go down more slowly, I saw my brother Dinte at the bottom of the stairs. He was smirking, as fine a specimen of budding asshood as the Family had ever produced.

"I see you've heard the news," I said, walking carefully downstairs.

"May I suggest you acquire a halter?" he offered blandly. "I'd loan you one of Mannoah's but hers are far too small."

I put my hand on my knife and he retreated a few steps. I had cut off his fingers and put out his eyes so many times in childhood quarrels that I knew the futility of it—but the knife felt necessary in my hands when I was angry.

"You mustn't hurt me anymore, Lanik," Dinte said, still smirking. "I'll be heir now, and head of the Family soon enough, and I'll remember."

I tried to think of some answer. Some scornful reply, to let him know that nothing he could ever do to me would compare in agony to what had just happened, to what was about to happen.

But to confess that much fear and pain is what you do with your most trusted friend, and perhaps not even then. So I said nothing and walked past him toward Father's private room. As I passed he hummed in the back of his throat, as one does to call the prostitutes on Hivvel Street. I did not kill him, however.

"Hello, my son," said Father when I came into his chamber.

"You might advise your second son," I answered, "that I still know how to kill."

"I'm sure you meant to say hello. Greet your mother."

I looked over to where he glanced and saw the Turd, as we children of Daddy's first wife less-than-affectionately called Number Two, who had moved up into my mother's position when she died of a strange and sudden heart attack. Father didn't think it was strange and sudden, but I did. The Turd's official name was Ruva; she was from Schmidt and had been part of a package deal that included an alliance, two forts, and about three million acres. She was only supposed to be a concubine, but chance and Father's inexplicable passion had moved her up in the world. We were compelled by custom, law, and Father's wrath to call her *mother*.

"Hello, Mother," I said coldly. She only smiled her sweet, gentle, murderous smile.

Father didn't waste time with gentleness or sympathy. "Homarnoch tells me that you're a radical regenerative."

"I'll kill anyone who tries to put me in the pens," I said. "Even you."

"Someday I'll take your treasonous statements seriously, boy, and have you strangled. But you can remove that fear, at least. I'd never put one of my own sons in the pens, even if he's a rad."

"It's been done before," I pointed out. "I've studied a little Family history."

"Then you'll know what's happening now. Come in, Dinte," Father said, and I turned to see my little brother walking in. It was then that I lost control for the first time.

I shouted: "You're going to let that half-assed moron ruin Mueller, you bastard, when you know I'm the only one who can hope to hold this flimsy empire together when you've had the courtesy to die! I hope you live long enough to see it all crumble!" Later I would remember those words bitterly, but how could I have known at the time that this hot-hearted curse would someday come true?

Father leaped to his feet and strode around his table to where I stood. I expected a blow, and braced for it. Instead he put his hands at my throat and I felt a sickening momentary fear that he was at last going to carry out his threat to strangle me. Then he ripped open my tunic, put his hands on my breasts, and pushed them together brutally. I gasped in pain and pulled away.

"You're weak now, Lanik!" he shouted. "You're soft and womanly, and no man of Mueller would follow you anywhere!"

"Except to bed," Dinte added lewdly. Father turned and slapped his ear.

When he turned away I covered my chest with my arms like a virgin girl and spun around, coming face to face with the Turd. She was still smiling, and I

watched her eyes move from my face down to my
bosom—

Not *my* breasts! I cried out silently. Not mine, not
a part of me, and I felt an overwhelming desire to
retreat, to back out of my body completely, let it
stay *there* while I went elsewhere, still a man, still
an heir with the expectation of power, still a man,
still myself.

"Put on a cloak," Father ordered.

"Yes, my lord Ensel," I murmured, and instead of
fading from my body I covered it, and felt the rough
fabric of the cloak harsh against my tender nipples.
I stood there and watched as Father went through
the ritual of declaring me a bastard and my brother
Dinte the heir. My brother looked tall and blond and
strong and clever, though I knew better than anyone
that his cleverness was merely a tendency to be sly;
his strength was not equaled by any quickness or
skill. When the ceremony was over, Dinte sat naturally in the chair that had for so many years been
mine.

I stood before them then, and Father commanded
me to swear allegiance to my younger brother.

"I would rather die," I said.

"That's the choice," Father said, and Dinte smiled.

I swore eternal allegiance to Dinte Mueller, heir
to the Mueller Family holdings, which included the
Mueller estate and the lands my father had conquered: Cramer, Helper, Wizer, and the island of
Huntington. I made the pledge because Dinte so obviously wanted me to refuse and die. Now, with me
alive, he would have to worry constantly; I wondered
idly how many guards he would post around his bed
tonight.

But I knew I wouldn't try to kill him. Removing
Dinte wouldn't put me in his place; it would only
mean a savage dispute over the succession—or worse:
Ruva might be allowed to spawn some hideous off-

spring with half my father's genes in it to take his place. No matter what, a rad like me could never hope to govern in Mueller. Besides, rads rarely lived into their thirties, and it was illegal for them—no, for me—to interbreed with ubermen. I felt a sudden pang as I realized what this would do to poor Saranna. The women would take the child out of her now, and destroy it. She would find herself now the former concubine of a monster instead of the potential first wife of the father of the Family. On the day the women chose me to be her breeding-partner she had set her foot on the road of glory; now the road was crumbling under her feet. Not just my future was destroyed, but hers also.

"Do I see the thoughts of a strangler in your eyes, Lanik?" Father asked. He thought I was still thinking about Dinte.

"Never, Father," I assured him.

"Poison, then. Or deep water. I think my heir is not safe with you here in Mueller."

I glared at him. "Dinte's worst enemy is himself. He needs no help from me to end in disaster."

"I've read Family history, too," Father said. "Every Mueller who was too sentimental to send his radical regenerative offspring to the pens regretted it soon after."

"Then have me killed with dignity, Father." It was as close as I would come to pleading. Yet silently I begged him: Don't let them feed and harvest me, reaping limbs and organs from me the way wool is sheared from a lamb, or milk pulled down from a cow, or silk spun out of a spider.

"I'm too affectionate," said Father. "I don't want to kill you. So I'm sending you on an embassy, a long one and far away, so that I have a reasonable hope of keeping Dinte alive."

"I'm not afraid of *him*," Dinte said scornfully.

"Then you *are* a fool," Father said sharply. "Teats

or no teats, Lanik is more than a match for you, boy, and I won't trust you with my empire until you show me that you're at least half as clever as your brother."

Dinte was silent then, but I knew that my father had written my death sentence in Dinte's mind. Deliberately? I hoped not. But it occurred to me that Father might have decided that the best test for Dinte's fitness to rule was seeing how well he managed my murder.

"An embassy to what nation?" I asked.

"Nkumai," he answered.

"A kingdom of tree-dwelling savage blacks far to the east," I said, remembering my geography lessons. "Why should we send emissaries to animals?"

"Not animals," Father said. "They've lately been using steel swords in battle. They conquered Drew two years ago. Allison is falling easily while we're talking here."

I felt my anger rise to think of tree-dwelling blacks conquering the proud stonecarvers of Drew or the backwater religious folk of Allison. Hadn't we just conquered Cramer, and taught them the true place of blacks in the world by enslaving them? "Why are we sending embassies instead of armies?" I asked angrily.

"Am I a fool?" Father asked in return. "If I wanted mindless bigotry I could call a moot and listen to the nobility."

I found it at once encouraging and painful that he expected me to think like the Mueller and not like some common soldier who had no responsibility. So I answered him truly now. "If they have hard metal, it means that they've found something that the Offworld will buy. We don't know how much metal they have; we don't know what they're selling. Therefore my embassy is not to make a treaty, but rather to find out what they have to sell and what the Ambassador is paying for it."

"Very good," Father said. "Dinte, you may go."

"If these are affairs of the kingdom," Dinte said, "shouldn't I be here to hear them?"

Father didn't answer. Dinte got up and left. And then Father waved a hand at the Turd, who also left the room, waggling her hips insolently.

"Lanik," Father said when we were alone, "Lanik, I wish to God there were something I could do." His eyes filled with tears and I realized with some surprise that Father cared enough to grieve for me. But not really for me, I thought. For his precious empire, which Dinte could not possibly hold together.

"Lanik, never in the three thousand years of Mueller has there been a mind like yours, in a body like yours, a man truly fit to lead men. And now the body is ruined. Will the mind still serve me? Will the man still love his father?"

"Man? If you saw me on the street you'd want to take me to your bed."

"Lanik!" he cried out. "Can't you believe my grief?" He pulled out his golden dagger, raised it high, and jabbed it through his left hand, pinning it to the table. When he pulled out the weapon the blood spouted and pulsed from the wound, and he rubbed the hand across his forehead, covering his face with blood. Then he wept, while the bleeding stopped and scar tissue formed across the wound.

I sat and watched him in the ritual of grief. We were silent except for his heavy breathing until his hand was healed. Then he looked at me from heavy eyes.

"Even if this hadn't happened," he said, "I would have sent you to Nkumai. For forty years we've been the only ones in the world, the only ones we knew about, who had enough hard metals to make a difference in war. Nkumai is now our only rival, and we know nothing about that Family. You have to go secretly; if they know you're from Mueller they'll kill you. Even if you lived they'd be sure you saw nothing of importance."

I laughed bitterly. "And now I have the perfect disguise. No one would ever believe Mueller would send a woman to do a man's work."

There, I said it, gave myself the name that might keep me from ceasing to exist. But I knew that this was just as impossible; Mueller would no more accept a rad as a woman than as a man. Only outside Mueller could I be taken as human. Father might call it an embassy, or even spying, but we both knew that the true name for it was exile.

He smiled back at me. Then his eyes filled with tears again and I wondered if, after all, his love might be for me.

The interview was over and I left.

I saw to arrangements, setting the grooms to tending my horses and shoeing them for the journey; instructing the scullers to preparing packs for my journey; getting the scholars to make me a map. When the work was in motion, I left the castle proper and walked through the covered corridors to the Genetics Laboratories.

The news had spread quickly—all the high-ranking officers avoided me, and only the students were there to open doors and lead me to the place I wanted to see.

The pens were kept brightly lit day and night, and I looked through the high observation window at the bodies endlessly scattered across the soft lawns. Here and there dust rose from the wallows. All the flesh was nude, and I watched as the noon food was spread into the feeders. Some of them looked like any other men. Others had small growths here and there on their bodies, or defects barely noticeable from a distance—three breasts, or two noses, or extra toes and fingers.

And then there were those that were ready for

harvest. I watched one creature as it lumbered toward the troughs. Its five legs didn't move well together, and it flailed its four arms awkwardly, to keep a balance. An extra head dangled uselessly from its back; a second spine curved away from the body like a sucking snake clinging rigidly to its victim.

"Why have they let this one go so long unharvested?" I asked the student who was near me.

"Because of the head," he said. "Complete heads are very rare, and we didn't dare interfere with the regeneration until it was complete."

"Do we get a good price for heads?" I asked.

"I'm not in merchandising," he answered, which meant that the price was very high indeed.

I looked at the monster as it struggled to bring food to its mouth with unresponsive arms. Could it be Velinisik? I shuddered.

"Are you cold?" asked the student, over-solicitously.

"Very," I answered. "My curiosity is satisfied. I'll go now."

I wondered why I wasn't even slightly grateful that my exile at least saved me from the pens. Perhaps because I knew that if I were sentenced to live there, supplying extra parts for the Offworld, I would kill myself. As it was I was still this side of suicide, and so had no retreat from the terrible knowledge of my loss.

Saranna met me in the greeting room of the Genetics Laboratories. I couldn't avoid her.

"I thought I would find you here," she said, "being morbid."

I knew she was trying to cheer me up, trying to pretend that all was still well between us. Under the circumstances, such a pretence was grotesque. Rather I wanted her to grieve for me, to speak to me as if I were only a memory of one who was dead, for that's what I felt then that I was.

I tried to walk past her. She caught my arm, clung to me and wouldn't let me pull away.

"Do you think it makes any difference to me?" she cried out.

"You're being indecorous," I hissed. Several people were looking at the floor in embarrassment, and the servants were already kneeling. "You're causing us shame."

"Come with me then," she said. To avoid causing any more awkwardness for the others in the room I went with her. As we left I could hear the rods being whipped across the servants' backs because they had seen the highborn acting in a low manner. I felt the blows as if they fell on me.

"How could you do that?" I asked her.

"And how could you stay away from me for all these days?"

"Not that long."

"Longer! Lanik, do you think I didn't know? Do you think my love for you was just because you were the Mueller's heir?"

"What do you plan to do?" I demanded. "Go in there with me? Let yourself be harvested, too?"

She pushed herself away from me, horror in her eyes.

"Next time be luckier," I said. "Next time love a human being."

"Lanik!" she cried, and then put her arms around me and pressed her head to my chest. When she leaned against soft breasts instead of hard muscle, she pulled her head away for a moment, then resolutely held to me even tighter.

With her head on my bosom I found myself wondering if I should feel motherly. Didn't she realize that her touch was no comfort to me now, only a reminder of all that I had lost? I pushed her away and ran. I stopped at a turn in the corridor and looked back. She was already slitting her wrists and crying out, the blood dripping onto the stone floor. The cuts were savage—the loss of blood would make her sick for hours, with that many lacerations. I went quickly to my room.

I lay on my bed, looking up at the delicate gold inlay on the ceiling. Set in the middle of the gold was a single pearl of iron, black and angry and beautiful. For iron, I said silently. For iron we have bred ourselves into monsters; the "normal" Muellers able to heal from any wound, and the rads serving as domesticated animals, selling their extra parts to the Offworld for more iron. Iron is power in a world with no hard metals. With our arms and legs and hearts and bowels we buy that power.

Put an arm in the Ambassador, and in a half hour a bar of iron appears in the cube of dancing light. Put living frozen sex organs in the cube, and five bars of iron replace it. An entire head? Who knows the price.

At that rate, how many arms and legs and eyes and livers must we give before we have enough iron to make one starship?

The walls pressed in on me and I felt myself trapped on Treason, our planet forming high walls of poverty that tied us down, that kept us from the Offworld, that made us prisoners as surely as the creatures in the pens. And like them, we lived under watching eyes, Family competing madly against Family in order to produce something, anything that the Offworld would buy, paying us in precious metals like iron, aluminum, copper, tin, zinc.

We Muellers had been first. The Nkumai were second, perhaps. A battle for supremacy, sooner or later. And whoever the victor, the pyrrhic prize would be a few tons of iron. Could a technology be built on that?

I slept like a prisoner, tied to my bed by the immense manacles of gravity on our poor prison planet;

bound to despair by two full and lovely breasts that rose and fell regularly. I slept.

I woke to darkness in the room, and the rasping sound of labored breath. The breath was mine, and in sudden panic I felt liquid in my lungs and began to cough violently. I threw myself to the edge of the bed, coughing a dark liquid out of my throat, each cough an exquisite pain. My gasping brought the breath in coldly at my throat, not through my mouth.

I touched the gaping wound under my chin. My larynx had been cut out, and I could feel the veins and arteries that were covered with scar tissue as they tried to heal, sending blood into my brain whatever the cost. The wound went from ear to ear. But finally my lungs were clear of blood, and I lay on the bed and tried to ignore the pain as my body's vigor surged to heal the gash.

But it wouldn't do it quickly enough, I realized. Whoever had tried so clumsily to kill me would be back to make sure of his work (or her work—Ruva?) and they wouldn't be so careless next time. So I stood, not waiting to be healed, breath still hissing in and out of the open wound at my throat. At least the bleeding had stopped, and if I moved carefully the scar tissue working gradually inward from the edges of the wound would eventually close it.

I stepped out into the corridor, faint from loss of blood. No one; but the packs I had ordered were stacked outside my room, awaiting inspection. I dragged them in. The strain caused a little bleeding, so I rested a moment while the blood vessels healed again. Then I sorted through the packs and combined the most essential items into one bundle. My bow and the glass-tipped arrows were the only things I took with me from my room; carrying the single pack, I made my way carefully down the corridors and stairways to the stable.

When I passed the sentry stall I was relieved to

see that no one was there to challenge me. A few steps later on I realized what that meant and whirled around, drawing my dagger as I turned.

But it was not an enemy who stood there. Saranna gasped when she saw the wound in my throat.

"What happened to you!" she cried out.

I tried to answer, but my body had not yet rebuilt the larynx I had lost, and so all I could do was shake my head slowly and put a finger to her lips, to silence her.

"I heard that you were leaving, Lanik. Take me with you."

I turned my back and went to my horses, which were standing new-shod at the woodsmith's bar. Their wooden shoes clumped softly on the stone floor as they moved. I threw the pack over Himmler's back and saddled the stallion, Hitler, to ride.

"Take me with you," Saranna pleaded. I turned to her. Even if I could have spoken, what would I have said? So I said nothing, only kissed her and then, because I had to leave in silence and could not hope to persuade her to let me go alone, I struck her sharply with the hilt of my dagger on the back of her head, and she fell softly into the hay and straw on the stable floor. If she hadn't been a Mueller, the blow might well have killed her. As it was, I'd be lucky if she stayed unconscious for five minutes.

The horses were quiet as I brought them out of the stable, and there was no further incident as I led them to the gate. The high collar of my cloak hid the wound in my throat as I passed the guards. I half expected to be challenged there, but no. And I wondered why it made so much difference to Dinte whether I was dead or left Mueller. Either way I would not be there to plot against him; and I knew that if I ever tried to return, a hundred hired assassins would wait for me behind every corner. Why had he bothered trying to kill me?

As I mounted Hitler and led Himmler along in the faint light of Dissent, the quick moon, I almost laughed. Only Dinte could have botched so badly the attempt to kill me. But in the moonlight I soon forgot Dinte, and remembered only Saranna, white with loss of blood in grief for me as she lay on the floor of the stable. I let the reins fall and plunged my hands into my tunic to touch my breasts and so remember hers.

Then the slow moon, Freedom, rose in the east, casting a bright light over the plain. I took the reins again, and urged the horses on, so that daylight would find me far from the castle.

Nkumai. What would I find there? And did I even care?

But I was a dutiful son of Ensel Mueller. I would go, I would see, so that Mueller might, with luck, conquer.

Behind me I saw lights come on in the castle; torches ran along the walls. They had discovered I was gone. I could not count on Dinte being bright enough even now to realize that killing me would be pointless. I dug my heels into Hitler's flanks. He galloped off, and I clung to the reins with one hand as with the other I tried to ease the pain of the horse's violent footfalls, each one jarring my chest until I realized that I felt no pain in my breasts. Nor in the wound in my throat. The pain was deeper in my chest and in the back of my throat, and I wept as I sped eastward—not toward the highway as they would surely, knowing my mission, suppose; not toward the surrounding enemies who would be glad to give shelter to a possible tool in their struggle against Mueller imperialism. I went eastward, to the forest of Ku Kuei, where no man went, and so where no man would think to look for me.

2   ALLISON

The well-farmed plain broke into small canyons and grassy plateaus, and sheep began to be more common than people. Freedom was still low in the west and the sun was well into morning. I was hot.

I was also trapped. Though I could see no one on the trail behind me, I knew where the pursuers were, if there were any (and I had to assume there were): to the south and east of me, guarding the borders with Wong, and to the north of me, patrolling the long hostile border with Epson. Only to the east were there no guards, because no guards were necessary there.

Now the plateaus turned to cliffs and ridges, and I followed the eastward trail carefully. The tracks of a hundred thousand sheep had worn these trails, and this one was easy enough to follow. But sometimes the trail narrowed between a cliff rising on the left and a cliff falling away on the right, and at those times I dismounted and led Hitler along, with Himmler following docilely.

At noon I came to a house.

A woman stood at the door with a stone-tipped spear. She was in her middle age, her breasts sagging but still full, her hips wide, her belly protuberant. There was fire in her eyes.

"Off the horse and away from my house, ye dammid interloper!" she cried out.

I dismounted, though I found no threat in her silly spear. I was hoping to convince her to let me rest. My legs and back ached from riding.

"Sweet lady," I said in my most unthreatening, gentle voice, "you have nothing to fear from me."

She kept the spear pointed at my chest. "Half the people in these High Hills have been robbed of late, and of a sudden all the troopers have took their bowen off north or south chasing the king's son. How kin I ken ye've no weapon and plan to steal?"

I dropped away my cloak and spread my arms wide. By now the scar on my neck would be nothing but a white line, which would disappear by noon. As I spread my arms my breasts rose under my tunic. Her eyes widened.

"I have all I need," I said, "except a bed to rest on and proper clothes. Will you help me?"

She moved the point of the spear and shuffled closer. Suddenly her hand darted out and squeezed my breast. I cried out in surprise and pain.

She laughed. "Why come ye to the house of honest folk all dissembling undressed? Come in, lady, I've a pallet for ye, if ye like."

I liked. But even though it had fooled this woman and earned me a bed, I still found myself darkly ashamed of my transformation. I was a wolf, being let into the house because they took me for a friendly dog.

The house was larger inside than it looked from outside. Then I realized it was built right into a cave. I touched the rock wall.

"Ya, lady, cave keeps it right cool all summer, stops the wind good enow in the winter."

"I imagine," I agreed, deliberately letting my voice get even softer and higher. "Why are they chasing the king's son?"

"Ach, child, the king's son's done sommat terrible bad, I guess. Word comes like the wind this morrow early, must be taking all the troopery of this country here."

I was astonished that Father would let Dinte pursue me so long, and openly enough to say it was the king's son they were chasing. "Don't they fear the king's son might come this way?"

She darted me a quick glance. I thought for a moment she guessed who I was, but then she said, "I thinked for a moment here you were having your little fun. Don't ye know not two mile of here starts the forest of Ku Kuei?"

That close. I pretended ignorance. "And what does that mean?"

She shook her head. "They tells it that no man or woman goes into that forest and comes out again alive."

"And I suppose just as few come out dead."

"They don't come out at all, lady. Have a splash of soup, smells like sheep dung, but it's true mutton, killed a ewe a week gone and this be simmering ever yet."

It was good and strong. It did, however, smell like sheep dung. After a few swallows I felt ready enough for sleep and slid from the table, went to the cot she pointed out in the corner.

I woke in darkness. A dim fire crackled in a hearth, and I saw the woman's shape moving back and forth in the room. She was humming a low tune with a melody as monotonous and beautiful as the sea.

"Has it words?" I asked. She didn't hear me, and I fell back asleep. When I woke again there was a candle in my face, and the old woman was gazing intently at me. I opened my eyes wide, and she moved back, a little embarrassed. The cold night air made me realize my tunic was open, my breasts bare, and I covered myself.

"Sorry, wee lady," the woman said. "But a soldier came, he did, looking for a young man of sixteen years named Lanik. I told him none such had been this way, and that only here was me and my daughter. And because your hair is so close-cropped, lady, I had to show him proof ye were a girl, didn't I? So I let your tunic to fall open."

I nodded slowly.

"I thought ye might not want to be known by the soldier, lady. And another bit of news. I had to turn your horses loose."

I sat up quickly. "My horses? Where are they?"

"Soldier found them down the road, a long way, all empty. I hid your things under my own bed."

"Why, woman? How can I travel now?" I felt betrayed, though even then I suspected the woman had saved my life.

"Have ye no feet? And I think ye'll not be wanting to go far now where horses can go."

"And where do you think I'm going?"

She smiled. "Ach, ye've a lovely face, lady. Pretty enough to be a boy or girl, and young, and fair, like a king's child. Happy the woman to have you for a daughter, or the man to have you for a son."

I said nothing then.

"I think," she said, "that there be no place for you now but the forest of Ku Kuei."

I laughed. "So I can go in and never come out?"

"That," she said with a smile, "be what we tell outlanders and lowlanders. But we be knowing right enow that a man can go in a good few leagues and gather roots and berries and other fruit and come out safe. Though odd things do happen there, and a wise man skirts the edge."

I was wide awake now. "How did you know about me?"

"Ye've got royalty in every move ye make, every word ye say, boy. Or girl. Which be ye? I care little.

I only know I have little love for the godlike men of the plain who think they rule all Muellerfolk. If ye be running from the king, ye have my blessing and my arm of help."

I had never suspected that any citizens of Mueller would feel that way about my father. Now it was helpful, though I wondered how I'd feel about her attitude if I were still heir.

"I've packed ye a bundle easy enough to heft," she said. "And fooded and watered it, hoping ye like cold mutton."

I liked it better than starving.

"Don't eat the white berries on oaky-looking bushes in the forest, they'll drop ye dead in a minute. And the fruit with wrinkly bulges, don't even touch that, and be careful not to step on a smoky-yellow fungus, or it'll plague you for years."

"I still don't even know if I'm going into the forest."

"And where else, then, if not there?"

I got up and walked to the door. Dissent was high and dim, with clouds across her face. Freedom hadn't risen yet. "How soon must I leave?"

"As soon as Freedom come," she said. "Then I lead you afoot to the edge of the forest, and there ye stay until just before sunrise. Then off and in. Head east but about a third to the south till ye touch a lake. Then they say the true road to safety is due south, into Jones. Follow no paths. Follow no man shape or woman shape ye see. And pay no heed to day and night."

She brought out woman's clothing from a trunk and held it up to me. It was shabby enough, and old, but modest and virginal.

"My own," she said, "though I misdoubt I ever did fit it on my old corpse, what's swoll up with fat these last year and ten." She laughed, and put it in my pack.

Freedom rose, and she led me out the door and along a path leading due east from her house, and not much traveled by. She chattered as we went.

"What be the need of troopery at all, ask I? They flash a bit of hard metal, dip it in another's blood, and then what? Is the world all changed? Do men now fly Offworld, are we of Treason now freed by all the bloodshed? I think we be like dogs that fight and kill over a bone, and what has the winner got? Just a bone. And no hope of any more after that. Just the one bone."

Then an arrow swicked out of the darkness and into her throat and she dropped dead in front of me.

Two soldiers stepped into the moonlight, arrows ready. I ducked just as one let fly. He missed. The second hit me in the shoulder.

But by then my pack was to the ground, and I buried my dagger in the first man's heart, then kicked the other to the ground. There were ways of fighting that they never taught the troops.

When they were both still I cut off their heads so there was no hope of their regenerating and telling what they knew. I took the better of their two bows and all the glass-tipped arrows, then went back to where the woman lay. I pulled the arrow from her throat, but saw that she wasn't healing at all. One of the oldest branches of the family, then, that was too poor to stay in the chain of genetic advancement that had resulted in masterworks of self-preservation like the royal family, like the royal troops.

And genetic monsters like the people in the pens. Like me.

I gave her grief, letting the blood drip from my hand onto her face. Then I put the arrow that had struck my shoulder into her hand, to give her power in the next world, though I doubted privately that there was such a thing.

The packstraps chafed my wounded shoulder, and

the pain was bad, but I had been trained to endure pain, and I knew that soon enough it would heal, like the wound in my hand. I walked eastward, following the trail, and soon came into the shadow of the black trees of Ku Kuei.

The forest was as sudden as a storm, from the bright light of Freedom into utter darkness. The trees looked eternal, right from the edge, as if five hundred years ago (or five thousand, the trees are that large) some great gardener had planted an orchard just *so*, with the edges neat and crisp along the property line.

The forest had already been like this, though, three thousand years ago when the ships of the Republic (the lying name for the foul dictatorship of the servile classes, said the histories) took the great rebels and their families and dumped them on the useless planet called Treason, where they would be exiled until they had ships enough to come out. Ships, they said with a laugh, with silver the strongest workable metal on the planet.

Metal we could only buy, and then by selling something that they wanted. For centuries upon centuries every Family would put something in the bright cube of their Ambassador; for centuries upon centuries the Ambassador took it—and returned it. Until we stumbled upon a way to exploit the agony of the radical regeneratives.

But some of the Families did not take part in the rush to trade with our captors. The Schwartzes stayed secretly on their desert, where no one went; the Ku Kuei lived somewhere in the bowels of their dark forest, never leaving it and never being troubled by outsiders, who feared the mysteries of the world's most impenetrable forest. The edge of the forest had always been Mueller's eastern border; and only in that direction did my father and his father never try to conquer.

It was cold and silent. Not a birdsound. Not an

insect, though there were flowers enough in the open brush. Then the sun rose and so did I, setting off into the depths of the trees, going east but one-third south.

At first there was a morning breeze, but then that died, and the leaves hung absolutely still. Birds were rare, and when I saw any they were as if asleep in high branches, motionless. No small animals moved underfoot, and I wondered if this were the secret of Ku Kuei—that nothing but plants lived here.

I could not see the sun, and so marked my direction by noting the trees that went in a line, correcting now and then. East and one-third south, I said again and again, trying not to hear it in the woman's voice—why did I grieve for her, whom I did not know?

I walked for hours and hours, it seemed, and still it was only morning from the vague direction of the brightest light, where I supposed the sun must be. Paths ran left and right, but I followed again the voice of the old woman in my memory, saying, "Follow no paths."

I became hungry. I chewed on mutton. I found berries and ate them, but not the white ones.

At last my legs were so weary I couldn't set one in front of the other, and yet it was still day. I didn't understand my tiredness. In my training I had often been required to walk briskly from sunrise to sunset, until I could do it with little strain. Was there, then, some element in the forest air, some drug that weakened me? Or had the healing of all my recent wounds taken more from me than I expected?

I didn't know. I set down the pack beside a tree and slept without waking, long and hard.

So long that when I awoke it was daylight again, and I got up and pushed on.

Again a day of walking, then weariness while the sun was still high. This time I forced myself to go on, farther and farther, until I became a machine. I was alert enough to avoid entangling roots, to pick my way through thick places, to scramble over rocks, to slide carefully down the slopes of hollows and ravines, then clamber up the other side, but I was so numb with the effort just to stay awake that I wasn't conscious of any of this, not really; an obstacle was forgotten the moment it was out of view. I felt as if I had been walking for days, and yet the sun was still high.

At first my weariness in so short a time made me feel a deep dread, that the complex of symptoms that marked a radical regenerative included a kind of general dystrophy—but that couldn't be it, for I had found the strength to go on and on, hadn't I? I wasn't weakening, for surely I had covered some ground, at least. But perhaps rads were plagued with the sudden onset of bouts of almost uncontrollable sleepiness. Yet I *was* controlling it, wasn't I? And the rads in the pens, while they moved with the languor of despair, did not seem to *sleep* more often than other men, or at least no one ever said they did.

Then I had a thought that comforted me a little —that the strange thing that was happening to me might not be a product of the condition of my own body, but rather might arise from the mysterious forest of Ku Kuei. Couldn't it be that the forests exuded some chemical that caused weariness? Or perhaps only the illusion of weariness. Or perhaps a whole complex of debilitating drugs in the air, causing hallucinations, distorting my sense of time, making me long to sleep with as much desperation as a man longs for water after three days without a drink.

That would explain why Ku Kuei had become such a feared and hated place. What if a man could wander in here and find his sense of time so distorted that he thought he had wandered miles in only a few minutes? Overcome with weariness, he might sleep twenty-four hours, then rise again, walk a few more meters, and fall down thinking he had done a day's labor. In only a short time the cumulative effect of all these chemicals could become fatal, either directly, by poisoning the man, or indirectly, by causing him to sleep until he dies of dehydration.

No wonder there were so few wild animals here. Perhaps a few birds acclimated to the poisonous air, some insects whose brains were too small even to be affected. But this would explain why nothing was heard from the Family of Ku Kuei almost from the hour they entered this wood three thousand years before.

Now here I was, caught up in the same natural defenses of this forest, and just as unlikely to win my way to freedom. My sentence had been death after all, not just exile. My flesh would be consumed by the bacteria and small insects of the forest floor; my bones would bleach and, after decades, crumble; I would then become part of the planet we called Treason, contributing to it the only metal that this soil would ever hold, the metal of men's souls. Was mine a soft and yielding element? Or would I be a hard place in the forest floor; would roots soak up from me a metal that would lend vigor to their massive trunks?

These were my thoughts as I struggled to keep myself awake. For a time I think I even dreamed as I walked on, imagining myself to be one of a thousand trees marching forth to do combat with the dangerous black soldiers of Nkumai. And such was my madness that I even saw myself waving vast branches to sweep the swordsmen of Mueller from their feet, then grinding them into powder with my irresistible roots.

I came to myself again, and thought more soberly—though perhaps just as madly—of what this poisonous forest might imply. It made me realize that in three thousand years of life on this world, all we of Mueller had ever thought about was how to get away, how to earn such vast quantities of iron that we might someday build a spaceship and escape. Other Families had spent their efforts trying to convince their Ambassador that they had repented of their ancestors' rebelliousness and wished to be returned from exile—after all, they said in a thousand different missives, *we* are but the eightieth great grandchildren of those who once threatened your pleasant Republic. But all such wheedling letters were returned torn to shreds. Whoever was on the other end of the Ambassador, controlling it, had not learned forgiveness in three thousand years. It made me wonder if perhaps our ancestors' crimes were not in fact far more terrible than they claimed. After all, the only histories we possessed told *their* version of what happened, and in *their* accounts they were completely innocent. But aren't all monstrous criminals innocent in their own eyes? Don't all their victims somehow deserve to die, in their imagination, at least?

Why in all these years had we kept our gaze starward, hoping to escape this world, and so learned almost nothing of the secrets that it held? Before we came it had been studied only enough to learn two things: First, that it was habitable—that, small as it was, Treason was massive enough to maintain us at about a third the gravity of the world where humans had evolved, so we would be strong, could run bounding across the prairies and among the giant trees; and the basic chemicals of life were close enough to ours that while we couldn't profitably eat the native animals, we and our animals could eat enough of the native plants to sustain ourselves, so sending us here was truly exile, and not a sentence of death. And, second, that so little metal was close enough to the surface that it wasn't even worth trying to extract it. It was a worthless world. A world that did not contain within it the material we could use to build a ladder outward to the stars.

But was it truly worthless, just because it couldn't let us build starships? This world was one of the rare ones that had given rise to life. Did we even understand why life arose here at all? Was it really enough to know that we could eat the plant life? Had we no curiosity about the differences between the native life and the chemistry of our own bodies? We had learned enough about ourselves to create monsters like me, but we hadn't learned enough about this world to truly say we lived here. Yet on the eastern border of Mueller there was a place where the very trees had learned enough about *us* to make a lone wanderer die of dreams beneath their shadow.

All these thoughts led to only one conclusion: The certainty of my death. And yet they filled me with a strange excitement, a longing to live long enough to learn more about this world. I had received a great insight. There was another road to freedom besides iron won from the Ambassadors. We had been given a whole world, hadn't we? Could we be free by no longer pressing upward against the prison wall of gravity, and instead turning downward and discovering what lay beneath our feet; outward, discovering the native life around us and learning wisdom from it?

It was that excitement that drove me on. I even wondered for a time if, in the moments before I died, the plants would speak to me, meaning not that they would find voices, of course, but that their poisons would provoke some illuminating vision that would tell me what this world had planned for us interlopers, us strangers. Now as I laid hold on trunks, leaning and staggering my way through the wood, I silently asked the trees to speak to me. Kill me if you must, but don't let me die without having known my vanquisher.

Until at last I could not make my legs go anymore,

they crumbled under me, and it was only early afternoon, if my guess at the sun's place was correct. As I staggered forward and collapsed to my knees, I saw a shimmer of bright blue before me; I had come at last to the lake.

It was not so wide I couldn't see the other shore, far and faint in the haze of vapor rising invisibly from the surface, but it was long enough that I saw no end, either north or south. The sun dazzled on the bright water. And yes, it could only be two o'clock in the afternoon.

I lay by the water and slept, and woke the next day at what seemed to be the very time I had gone to sleep.

I despaired, but also I hoped. For I *had* slept, that was certain. My muscles ached, my legs were rubbery under me, but I could move again, I had the fresh vigor that could only mean I had had, if not as much rest as I needed, at least enough to go on. Above all, I was *awake*. The poisons in the air had not consigned me to die here in my sleep.

Perhaps it was only because I had won free of the trees and collapsed here, where perhaps the open water cleared the air. I felt it was a kind of victory, to have reached this place. I thought back to the map of Treason I held within my head—one of the things that lingered from school days, the map of the world that dated from the first orbital surveys when our ancestors arrived. There were other lakes, strung out eastward of here. If this was in fact the southwesternmost lake, then striking due east would take me to the largest of the lakes, and by skirting the southern shore and following a large river to the easternmost lake, I would be within reach of the borders of Allison.

I knew that the southern tip of the lake was where the woman had told me I should turn south. But Jones was too much in the shadow of Mueller; Dinte

might have spies there, and Father certainly would
—there was always the chance that Father might
have changed his mind and decided the good of Mueller required my death.

My best hope, now that I had proven I could defeat
the menace of Ku Kuei, was to go east, fight my way
through to Allison, only one Family to the west of
Nkumai. There I could complete the mission Father
had given me, and perhaps, by proving my loyalty,
earn the right to go home, or at least to live without
fear of some agent of Mueller coming to remove a
threat to the government.

I went east, toward Nkumai, toward the rising
sun—rising, that is, in former days, when it used to
move across the sky. The journey changed not at all.
The same confusion, the same exhaustion—for in
each march I seemed to cover so much ground that
from the map I carried in my head it should have
taken two full days at a good hard walk, not the few
hours it seemed to take by the sun. I invented dozens
of new explanations or codicils to the old ones; I
wearied of trying to understand, and let imaginary
visions of Saranna draw me forward, remembering
her insane loyalty to me when there was no hope
that we could be together anymore. At least it was
only thoughts of murder that could carry me across
the last stretch of forest without water to break the
poisonous air—I dreamed of killing Dinte; and,
ashamed of such thoughts toward my own brother,
I dreamed of killing the Turd. I imagined that once
she had sustained her mortal injury, her magical spell
would be released, and she would be revealed as a
huge writhing slug oozing along the stone floor of
the castle, leaving a trail of thick pus and ichor and
glistening slime behind it.

I ate what berries I could find, and my pack was
long since empty; my body, which had always been
muscular, now became lean, and my womanly breasts,

which had grown soft and large on the comfortable diet of Mueller, were now tight and spare and hard, like the rest of me. It made it somehow easier to bear having them, knowing that they had to respond to the same urgencies that drove the rest of my body. Scant rations and hard work affected them along with the rest of me. They were a part of myself. They might have been unwelcome when they first appeared, but it didn't feel strange to have them anymore.

Finally I reached the grey-barked slender ragwit trees that told me I was near

> . . . white-tree Allison,
> of dawn and light among the leaves.

Almost at once, with the change of woods, the poisons stopped having their effect on me. I was still weary—as well a man should be, covering a thousand kilometers, what should have been twenty days' journey even for the bounding stride of a soldier in open country, in only a dozen long, terrible marches. I knew then that whatever seemed to have happened to the sun's passage through the sky, I had surely covered the ground I thought I covered—that my exertions were as excruciating as I imagined them to be. Indeed, if I ever lived to return to Mueller, and ever somehow became a person again in Mueller's eyes, the song they would sing of me would surely include this marvelous journey through the poisonous wood of Ku Kuei, covering in what seemed to be a few days by the sun, in a dozen marching periods, what should have taken a man twenty days in open country, well-supplied; what would have taken an army twice that time. If ever a hero-song were sung of me, this journey would be the envoy. So I thought then, knowing so little.

The madness of the journey was over now, anyway; the sun made its normal passage at its normal pace, and I was able, at last, to walk on until dark.

In the morning, a road. I went back among the trees and changed into the girl's clothing that the woman of the High Hills had given me. I counted my wealth: twenty-two rings of gold, eight rings of platinum, and, in case of great need, two rings of iron. A dagger in the pack.

I was unsure what to do next. The last news we had heard in Mueller was that Nkumai was attacking Allison. Had they won? Was the war still raging?

I stepped onto the road and walked east.

"Hey, little lady," said a soft but penetrating voice behind me. I turned and saw two men. Rather larger than I—I still didn't have my full man's weight, though I did have near my height since I was fifteen. They looked rough, but their clothing seemed to be the vestiges of a uniform.

"Soldiers of Allison, I see," I answered, trying to sound glad to see them.

The one with his head in a bandage answered with a sick smile. "Ay, if there yet *be* an Allison, with black inkers loose to rule."

So the Nkumai had won, or were winning.

The shorter one, who couldn't take his eyes off my bosom, chimed in with a voice that sounded rusty, as if for lack of use. "Will you travel with two old soldiers?"

I smiled. Mistake. They had me half-stripped before they realized that I knew how to use my dagger and was not playing games. The short one got away, but from the way his leg was bleeding I didn't think he'd get far. The tall one lay on his back in the road with his eyes rolled up in his head, as if to say, "And after all I lived through, I have to die like *this*." I closed his eyes.

But they had given me my entry into the first town.

"Andy Apwit's mother's garter, little woman, you look half dead."

"Oh no," I told the man at the inn. "Half raped, perhaps."

As he put a blanket around my shoulders and led me upstairs, he chuckled to me, "Half dead you may be, but rape's an all or nothing thing, lady."

"Tell that to my bruises," I answered. The room he showed me to was small and poor, but I doubted there was much better in the town. He washed my feet before he left; an unusual custom, and he was so gentle it tickled unbearably, but I felt much better when he was through. A custom we could encourage the lower classes to adopt in Mueller, I thought at the time. Then I imagined Ruva washing somebody's feet, and laughed.

"What's funny?" he asked, looking irritated.

"Nothing. I'm from far parts, and we have no such gracious custom as to wash feet of travelers."

"Be damned if I'd do it for everybody. Where you be from, little woman?"

I smiled. "I'm not sure what's proper diplomatic procedure. Let us say I'm a woman from a land where women are not used to being attacked on the road —but where they're also not used to such kind concern from a stranger."

He lowered his eyes in humility. "As the Book says, 'To the poor give comfort, and cleansing, and care better than to the rich.' I but do my duty, little woman."

"But I'm not poor," I said. He stood up abruptly. I hastened to reassure him. "At home we have a house with two rooms."

He smiled patronizingly. "Ay, a woman of such a land as yours might well call that comfort." When he left I was relieved that there was a bar on the door.

In the morning I had a pauper's portion at

breakfast—larger than anyone else in the family. The innkeeper, his wife, and his two sons, both much younger than I, urged me not to travel alone. "Take one of my lads with you. I wouldn't have you losing your way."

"It won't be hard, from here, to find the capital?"

The innkeeper glowered. "Do you mock us?"

I shrugged, trying to look innocent. "How could such a question be a mockery?"

The woman placated her husband. "She's a stranger, and plainly untaught in the Path."

"We here don't go to the capital," a boy helpfully informed me. "That's lost to God, it is, and we stay away from such gaudy doings."

"Then so shall I," I said.

"Besides," said the father, huffily, "the capital is sure to be full of inkers."

I didn't know the word. I asked him.

"The black sons of Andy Apwit," he answered. "From Inkumai."

Must mean Nkumai. Victory for the blacks, then. Ah well.

I left after breakfast, my clothing mended very neatly by the innkeeper's wife. The older of the two boys accompanied me. His name was No-fear. For the first mile or so I queried him about his religion. I'd read about that sort of thing, but had never met anyone who actually believed it, aside from burial rituals and marriage ceremonies. I was surprised at the things his parents had taught him were true—yet he seemed disposed to be obedient, and I thought perhaps there was a place for such things among the servile classes.

At last we came to a fork in the road, with a sign. "Well," I said, "here I send you back to your father."

"You won't go to the capital, will you?" he asked fearfully.

"Of course not," I lied. Then I took a gold ring from my sack. "Did you think your father's kindness would go unrewarded?" I put the ring on his finger. His eyes widened. It was enough, then, for payment.

"But weren't you poor?" he asked.

"When I came I was," I said, trying to sound very mystical. "But after the gifts your family gave me, I am very rich indeed. Tell no man of this, and command your father likewise."

The boy's eyes widened even more. Then he whirled and ran back down the road. I had been able to put his stories to good use; and now I had added to the lore of angels who appeared to be poor men and women at first sight, but who gathered glory to bless or punish according as they had been treated. From man to woman to angel. Next transformation, please?

"Money first," said the man at the counter.

I flashed a platinum ring at him and suddenly his eyes narrowed.

"Stole it, I'll swear!"

"Then you'll commit perjury," I said archly. "I was set upon by rapists on one of your fine highways, and I who have come as an emissary. My guards slew them, but were slain in the process. I must continue in my mission, and I must be dressed as befits a woman of rank."

He backed off. "Pardon, lady." He bowed. "However I may assist." I did not laugh. And when I left the store I was dressed in the gaudy, tight, revealing style of clothing that had surprised me when I saw it on women on the way into the town.

"Emissary from where?" he asked as I left. "And to whom?"

"From Bird," I said, "and to whoever is in authority here."

"Then find the nearest inker. Because no white

person has rank here these days, lady, and all the inkers from Inkumai thinks they rules."

My white-blond hair attracted a few glances on the street, but I went on toward the stables, trying to ignore the men who watched me by using the haughty manner of the high-class whores of Mueller as they ignored the men too poor to afford their services.

That was the full circle of my transformation. Man, monster, woman, angel, and now prostitute. I laughed. I would be surprised at nothing now.

I parted with a platinum ring and got no change, but the carriage the stableman was hitching up belonged to me. The capital of Allison was still a good many kilometers on from this town, and I had to arrive in style.

A thundering of wooden horseshoes on the stone road. I opened the door to the stable and stepped outside. A dozen horses at a walk clopped along the road, raising a deafening din. But I had no eyes for the horses. Instead I watched the riders.

They were as tall as I was—taller, in fact, two meters if anything. And far blacker than any Cramers I had seen. They had narrow noses, not like the flat wide ones of the blacks I had known before. And every one of them carried an iron sword and an iron-studded shield.

Even in Mueller we didn't equip our common soldiers with iron until it was time for battle. How much metal did the Nkumai have?

The stableman spat.

"Inkers," he said, behind me.

But I ignored him and stepped out into the street, raising an arm in salute. The Nkumai soldiers saw me.

Fifteen minutes later I was stripped to the waist and tied to a post in the middle of town. I decided that being a woman was not all it was cracked up to be. A fire was blazing nearby, and an iron brand was already glowing red.

"Skinny, this one," said one of the soldiers. He was nursing his elbow. I could have shattered the bone so he'd never have the use of his arm again. I could have put a hand into his throat so he dropped to the ground dead without even time to see his life pass before him. But that would have compromised my disguise. Now, standing bare-breasted awaiting the torture, it occurred to me that my disguise wouldn't last long if my wounds started to heal before their eyes.

"Be quiet," the captain of the troop said in a mellifluous, educated voice. "You knew you were supposed to register three weeks ago. This won't hurt."

I glared at him. "Let me go from this post or you'll pay with your life," I said. It was hard work to keep my voice high and feminine, and to sound like my threat was just bluster when in point of fact I was certain I could kill him in three seconds if I could get my hands loose—thirty if I stayed tied.

"I'm an emissary," I said, for the dozenth time since they took me, "from Bird—"

"So you've said," he answered mildly, and he beckoned to the soldier who was heating the brand. They were too calm. They meant this to be a show to last for some time. My only hope was to provoke them to anger, so they'd damage me too much, too quickly. Perhaps then the punishment would be swift, and they'd carry away what they thought was my dead body.

I didn't have to pretend to be enraged, of course. In Mueller we only branded sheep and cattle. Even our slaves remained unmarked. So when the grinning Nkumai brought the red-hot brand near my stomach, I howled in fury—hoping my voice sounded somewhat womanly—and kicked him in the groin hard enough to castrate a bull. He screamed. I noticed briefly that the kick had torn my skirt. Then the captain hit me in the head with the flat of his sword, and I was out.

I woke soon after in a dark room with no windows—just a small hole in the roof for light and a heavy wooden door. My head ached only a little, and I was afraid that I had been unconscious so long my quick healing would have given away the truth. But no, it had only been a few minutes. My body was still only half healed from the beating they must have given me after I was out.

They were disciplined troops. Even angry, they hadn't tried to rape me—I was still dressed as I had been, stripped to the waist but otherwise still covered. I quickly pulled the torn blouse back into place, still gaudy but no longer dazzling. It was so tight there was no hope of refastening it or even doubling it over, but all my wounds were on my back, and the tear was down the front, so it did the job well enough, serving my need, not of modesty, but of concealment of my wounds.

Someone knocked timidly. "Here to treat your wounds, ma'am," said a soft girl's voice.

"Go away! Don't touch me!" I tried to sound adamant, but probably ended up merely hysterical. Whether the would-be nurse was of Nkumai or Allison made no difference. When she found wounds that looked days instead of minutes old, all bets would be off. Even in the unlikely event that they had heard no rumors of Muellers' regenerating powers, they'd know *something* strange was up. There'd be a complete examination, and even if I castrated myself first, they'd realize my anatomy was at least somewhat confused.

The girl spoke once more, and again I ordered her away, telling her this time that a woman of Bird allowed no foreign man or woman to touch her blood.

Again, I was improvising some sort of cultural fold-erol to meet my present need, but I had studied folk-ways and rituals in school and pursued it somewhat more than the curriculum required—enough to get a sense, perhaps, of what kinds of things were sacred or tabu in other places. Women's blood—primarily menstrual, but extending to all female blood—was more likely to be invested with holiness or dread than even the bodies of the dead.

Whether it was a local tabu about bleeding women or the hysteria in my voice, the girl went away, and again I waited in the stifling room. The tickling of my back told me that my wounds were completely healed now, scabbed or scarred. I began searching for ways to escape without using the door, trying to remember the layout of the village outside the room so I could plot the quickest possible dash for freedom.

The door creaked open on its heavy wooden hinges, and a black man in a white robe came in. He carried no unguent, so apparently I had carried that point. He held out to me another robe, a light blue one.

"Please," he said, "come out."

I took the robe. He turned away and closed the door.

I stripped away the trashy-looking Allison clothes I had been wearing, drew the robe on over my freshly healed back and shoulders, and bound it in front of me. I felt more confident now, less vulnerable. I opened the door and stepped outside, blinking in the light. The man in the white robe stood two paces back from the door.

"I demand that I be set free," I said.

"Of course," he answered, "and I hope that you will continue on your journey to Nkumai."

I made no effort to conceal my disbelief in the sincerity of his invitation.

"I was afraid you'd feel that way," he said, "but I beg you to forgive our ignorant soldiers. We pride ourselves on our learning in Nkumai, but we know very little about nations beyond our borders. The soldiers know far less, of course, than *we* do."

"We?"

"I am a teacher," he said. "And I have been sent to beg your forgiveness and ask you to continue on your way to our capital. When the captain applied for permission to put you to death for maiming one of our soldiers, he told us that you claimed to be an emissary from Bird. To him the idea of a woman on an embassy is absurd. He is from lower down the tree, where a woman's true potential is not always recognized. But I know that Bird is governed by women, very wisely I am told, and I realized at once that your story must be true."

He smiled and spread his hands. "I cannot hope to undo what our officer has, in ignorance, done. He has, of course, been stripped of rank, and the hands that actually beat you have been cut off."

I nodded. That was probably the least they could do and still appear to be serious about punishment. But I also knew that I had done some damage, too. "The man I kicked," I said. "I believe he has been punished enough."

He raised an eyebrow. "He didn't think so," he said. "You must understand—to be castrated by a single kick from a bound woman—he couldn't bear to live with that story in his name."

Again I nodded as if I understood completely.

"And now," he said, "please let me escort you to Nkumai, where perhaps your embassy can still be offered."

"I wonder," I said, "if our desire to procure alliance with Nkumai was wise after all. We had heard of you as civilized people."

He looked pained for a moment, but then smiled helplessly. "Not so," he answered. "We are not yet civilized. But we are at least trying, which is more than can be said of many peoples here in the East. In the West, I am sure, things are different."

At this point I thought I still could back away, slip out of Allison with no further involvement with Nkumai, and from there disappear from Treason, at least as far as Mueller was concerned. But for good or ill I was still determined to complete my mission and find out what they were selling to their Ambassador that gave them iron in greater quantities than our bodies bought for Mueller. So I said words that would reopen the possibility of negotiation. "There are barbarians in all quarters of the world, and perhaps in troubled times one must befriend those who wish to be civilized in order to protect oneself from those who disdain the refinement of law or courtesy."

"Then indeed it will be good for you to converse with those in power in Nkumai," he said. I nodded benignly, then accepted his invitation. Yet as we got in his carriage and started eastward toward Nkumai, I had the sickening feeling that I was caught in a whirlpool, already so far in that I would be sucked down; I couldn't get out now.

We changed horses daily, and made good speed, though still we stopped for sleep more than a dozen times along the way. My guide pointed out botanical and zoological curiosities, and told some stories and legends that made little sense to me at the time, though later became clearer as I learned more of the ways of the Nkumai. He also told stories of battle, and I noticed that each story seemed to end with a homily about how impossible it was ever to defeat the Nkumai in battle.

He was careful, though, not to offend me. I was always given a private room in the inns of Allison, and though guards attended outside my door, they made no motion to restrain or even follow me when I left my private quarters and ventured into the common room, or even outside for a walk. They were clearly there to protect, not confine me.

Then the white trees of Allison thinned out, replaced by taller trees, shooting straight upward hundreds and hundreds of meters. At last the road wound among giant trees that made even the oldest ones of Ku Kuei look slight. We no longer stopped at inns, but instead slept beside the carriage, or under it when it rained, which seemed to happen almost daily.

Then one day in early afternoon the Nkumai teacher signaled the driver to stop.

"Here we are," he said.

I looked around. I could see no difference between this place and any other part of the forest that had seemed so changeless for days of journeying.

"Where is here?" I asked.

"Nkumai. The capital."

Then I followed his gaze upward and saw the most intricate and clever system of ramps, bridges, and buildings suspended in the trees as far as I could see, upward and outward in every direction.

"Impregnable," he commented.

"A marvel," I answered. I didn't comment that a good fire could wipe the entire thing out in a half hour. I was glad I didn't. Because within moments the daily deluge came, and this time I was neither inside the carriage nor under it. We were immediately drenched as if we had dived into the sea. The Nkumai made no effort to find shelter, and so neither could I.

After only a few minutes the rain stopped, and he turned to me and smiled. "It comes like this nearly every day, often twice a day. If it didn't, we might have to fear a fire. But as it is, our only problem is getting peat dry enough to burn for cooking."

I smiled back and nodded. "I can see that might be a problem." Obviously he had guessed at my observation about the city's vulnerability to fire, and wanted me to understand by direct experience exactly how useless a weapon fire would be against them.

The ground was mud six inches deep, which made for very unhealthy walking, and I was surprised they made no effort to corduroy or cobble any sort of path besides the road; but then we found a rope ladder and swung up into the air. I didn't touch the ground again for weeks.

3 NKUMAI

"Would you like to rest?" he asked, and for once I was glad that I appeared to be a woman, because the platform was an island of stability in an absurd world of swinging rope ladders and sudden gusts of wind. The Mueller's son could never have admitted he wanted to rest. But a lady emissary from Bird lost no face by resting.

I lay down on the platform so that for a few moments I could see only the still-distant roof of green above me and pretend I was on steady ground.

"You don't seem very tired," my guide commented. "You aren't even breathing very heavily."

"Oh, I didn't want the rest because of the exertion. I'm simply—unaccustomed to such heights."

He casually leaned back over the edge of the platform and looked at the ground. "Well, we're only eighty meters off the ground right now. A long way to go."

I stifled a sigh. "Where are you taking me?"

"Where do you want to go?" he countered.

"I want to see the king."

He chuckled, and I wondered if a lady of Bird was supposed to consider it an affront to have someone laugh in her face. I decided to be slightly annoyed. "Is that amusing?"

"Of course you don't really expect to see the *king*, lady," he said.

He said this with a smirk, but I had had plenty of practice at putting down those who dared to condescend to me. I knew how to make my voice sound like it had been aged all winter on ice. "So your king is invisible. How amusing."

His smile dampened a little. "He doesn't meet with the public, that's all I meant."

"Ah. In civilized countries, emissaries are extended the courtesy of an audience with the head of state. But in your country, I imagine foreign embassies must be content with climbing trees and visiting each other."

His smile was gone now. The condescension was all going the other way, and he didn't like it. "We don't get many embassies. Until recently, our neighboring nations have regarded us as 'tree-dwelling apes,' I believe is the term. Only lately, as our soldiers have begun to make a little noise in the world, have emissaries begun arriving. So perhaps we aren't acquainted with all the customs of 'civilized' nations."

I wondered how much truth there was to that. On the great Rebel River plain, every nation had exchanged embassies with every other nation ever since the Families first divided up the world. But if Nkumai had turned outward enough to go a-conquering, surely they had also learned how to deal with emissaries from many nations.

"We have only three emissaries right now, lady," he said. "We had several others, but of course the emissary from Allison is now a loyal subject of the king, while the emissaries from Mancowicz, Parker, Underwood, and Sloan were sent home because they seemed far more interested in our Ambassador than they were in promoting good relations with Nkumai. Now only Johnston, Cummings, and Dyal have embassies here. And since we're quite economical with living space, we've had to house them together. We're a backwater of the world, I'm afraid. Very provincial."

And you're overdoing it a bit, I commented silently. But however unsubtle he had been, I had got the warning well enough. They were alert to what most emissaries were probably looking for, including, most particularly, myself. So I would have to be careful.

"Nevertheless," said I, "I am here to see the king, and if there is no hope of that, I shall go home and tell my superiors that Nkumai has no interest in good relations with Bird."

"Oh, there's a *chance* that you can see the king. But you have to make application at the office of social services, and where that will lead you who can say." He smiled faintly. We were not friends.

"Shall we go?" he suggested.

I advanced warily to the rope ladder that still swung gently in the breeze, moored loosely to the platform by a thin rope tied around a low post.

"Not that," he said. "We're going another way." And he took off running, away from the platform along one of the branches. If you call them branches—neither of them less than ten meters thick. I walked slowly to where he had climbed up the branch, and sure enough, there were some subtle handholds that seemed more to have been worn than cut into the wood. I clumsily got myself from the platform to the place where my guide waited impatiently. Where he was the branch had leveled out a little more and now rose more obliquely up into the distance, criss-crossed by branches from other trees.

"All right?" he asked.

"No," I answered. "But let's go on."

"I'll walk for a while," he said, "until you're more

accustomed to the treeway." Then he asked me a question that seemed out of place, after so many days' travel together. "What's your name, lady?"

Name? Of course I had prepared myself with a name, back in Allison—but the occasion had never arisen when I was required to use it, and now it had slipped my mind. I can't remember even now what name I had chosen before. And since my confusion by now was obvious, there was no way I could simply make another one up without arousing his suspicion. So again I resorted to a pretended custom to cover my momentary need. I sincerely hoped the government of Bird did not choose anytime soon to send a real emissary, for I doubted such a woman would wish to follow the script that I had improvised. And if Nkumai was as efficient as Mueller, and sent spies to learn more about a nation that had sent an embassy, my little fabric of lies would soon unweave itself.

"Name, sir?" I said, now covering confusion with haughtiness. "Either you are no gentleman, or you do not think me a lady."

He looked momentarily abashed. Then he laughed. "You must forgive me, lady. Customs vary. In my land only ladies *have* names. Men are called only for their duties. I am, as I told you, Teacher. But I meant you no disrespect."

"Fine," I said, forgiving him curtly. The game was becoming amusing, trying to assert some superiority over him in a situation in which I couldn't help but be inferior, just as I imagined a genuine female diplomat might find herself forced to do. It almost let me forget the fact that though the path we followed was no more difficult than climbing a steep hill, this hill happened to be a thick tree branch that sloped away quickly on both sides, and if I were to stray from the path I would soon find myself hurtling downward. I dared not look and couldn't guess how far, but, perversely, couldn't resist trying to find out, either. "How many meters to the ground?"

"At this place I would say about a hundred and thirty, lady. But I'm really not sure. We don't measure it, much. Once you're high enough to kill yourself falling, it really doesn't matter how far the ground is, does it? But I can tell you how much higher we have to go."

"How much?"

"About three hundred meters."

I gasped. I knew trees could grow to phenomenal heights on Treason—hadn't I walked through Ku Kuei?—but surely that high up the branches would be too weak and slender to support us. "Where are we going? Why so high?"

He laughed again, and this time he made no effort to conceal his enjoyment at my dislike of heights. Perhaps his way of getting back at me for the little trouble over names, and all the other slights that I had offered him and his country during our trip. "We're going," he said, "to the place where you're going to live. We thought you'd appreciate visiting the very top. Few outsiders ever have."

"I'm going to *live* at the top?"

"Well, we couldn't very well keep you with the other embassies, could we? They're men. We are *somewhat* civilized. So Mwabao Mawa has consented to take you in."

Our conversation was interrupted as he lightly trotted across a rope bridge, only occasionally using his hands. It looked easy, particularly since the tread of the bridge was wooden. But as I stepped on it, it swayed, and the farther out I got, the worse the swaying was. At the apex of each swing, I could see the trunks of the trees dropping down to a ground so distant that I couldn't be sure exactly where it was, in the heavy shade. At last I lost control and vomited, perhaps at the midpoint of the bridge. But then I felt better and made it across the bridge without further incident. And from then on, since I was already utterly disgraced, I made no further attempt to pretend not to feel fear—and found that it therefore became easier to bear. My guide, Teacher, was more helpful, too, and led me at a slower pace. I was more than willing at times to lean on him.

And as we finally got to the level where the leaves grew, giant fans as much as two meters broad, the realization sank in that even if I found out what Nkumai was selling to the Ambassador for iron, it would do us little good. How could the landbound, plains-dwelling men of Mueller ever invade, let alone conquer, a people like this? The Nkumai would only pull up their rope ladders and sneer. Or drop deadly rocks. And the fear of heights would surely incapacitate other Muellers besides me. We may have schooled ourselves to separate fear from pain, but falling was another matter entirely. Besides, I had no way of knowing whether a drop from such heights might do more damage to a Mueller than his body could heal in time to save his life. Fish might as well launch a war against the birds as Mueller fight Nkumai here in their home trees.

Unless, of course, we found some way to train Mueller's soldiers to deal with heights. Perhaps they could practice on artificial platforms, or in the tall trees of Ku Kuei. I might have pursued this idea further, if I hadn't been constantly distracted by the need to pick a footing that wouldn't plunge me headlong to the earth.

We finally walked gingerly along a narrow branch to a rather involved house—though in fact I would have considered it simple back in Mueller. Teacher spoke softly, but penetratingly, saying, "From the earth to the air."

"And to the nest, Teacher. Come in," and the husky

but beautiful voice of Mwabao Mawa drew us into the house.

The house was basically five platforms, each one not much different under foot from those I had already rested on, though two of them were quite a bit larger. However, they had roofs of leaves, and a rather complicated system of gathering all the roofwater into barrels in the corners of the rooms.

If they could be called rooms. Each platform was a separate room. And I could detect no hint of a wall anywhere. Only curtains of brightly colored cloth hanging from the roofline to the floor. Breezes opened the walls easily.

I chose to stand in the center of the platform.

Mwabao Mawa was, in a way, disappointing. She should have been beautiful, from her voice, but she was not—at least not by any standard of beauty I have ever known—not even by Nkumai standards. But she was tall, and her face, however unlovely, was expressive and lively. When I say tall, the word does not convey: in Nkumai, nearly everyone is at least as tall as I am now, and in Mueller I am much above average. At that time, of course, I was not yet at my full height, and since among the Nkumai, Mwabao Mawa was towering, I saw her as a giant. Yet she moved gracefully, and I didn't feel intimidated. I felt, in fact, protected.

"Teacher, whom have you brought me?"

"She won't give me a name," Teacher said. "A gentleman, it appears, does not ask a lady."

"I'm the emissary from Bird," I said, trying to sound impressive without sounding pompous, "and to another lady I will tell my name." By then, of course, I had chosen a new name, and from then on throughout my stay in Nkumai, I was Lark. It was the closest I could come to Lanik and still be plausible as a woman from Bird.

"Lark," Mwabao Mawa said, making the name sound musical. "Come in."

I thought I already was.

"In here," she said, instantly trying to soothe my confusion. "And you, Teacher, can go."

He turned and left, trotting easily along the narrow branch that had so frightened me. I noticed that he obeyed as if Mwabao Mawa had great authority, and it occurred to me that perhaps a womanly disguise was not the handicap here that it had been for me in Allison.

I followed Mwabao Mawa through the curtain she had entered from. There was no path—just a space about a meter and a half across to the next room. Miss the jump, and meet the earth. Not exactly a record-setting leap—but competitive jumping in Mueller offers no further penalty for missing the goal than the scorn of the observers.

This time the wallcurtains were subdued and darker, and the floor was, thank heaven, not one uninterrupted plane. It sank in two steps to a large center arena, which was liberally sprinkled with cushions. When I stepped down, I found that my eyes were willing to believe that I was surrounded by real walls, and I relaxed.

"Go ahead and sit," she said. "This is the room where we relax. Where we sleep at night. I'm sure Teacher showed off all the way up here—but we're not immune to fear of heights. Everyone sleeps in a room like this. We don't like the thought of rolling off in the middle of a dream."

She laughed, a rich, low laugh, but I didn't join in. I just lay back and let my body tremble, releasing the stored-up tension of the climb.

"My name is Mwabao Mawa," she said. "And I should tell you who I am. You'll doubtless hear stories about me. There are rumors that I have been the king's mistress, and I do nothing to discourage them, since it gives me a great deal of petty power. There are also rumors that I am a murderess—and those are even more helpful. The truth is, of course, that I'm nothing but a consummate hostess and a great singer of songs. Perhaps the greatest who ever lived in a land of singers. I'm also vain," she said, smiling. "But I believe that true humility consists of recognizing the truth about yourself."

I mumbled acquiescence, content to enjoy the warmth of her conversation and the security of the floor. She talked on, and sang me some songs. I remember almost nothing of the conversation. I remember even fewer details of the songs, but, although I understood no lyrics and detected no particular melody, the songs carried me off into my imagination, and I could almost see the things she sang of —though how I knew what she was singing of I don't know. Though terrible things have happened since, and I myself silenced Mwabao's music, I'd give up much to be able to hear those songs again.

That night she lit a torch outside her main door and told me that guests would come. I later learned that a torch meant that a person was willing to receive guests, an open invitation to all who might see the glowing in the night. It was a measure of Mwabao Mawa's power over other people (or, less cynically, their devotion to and delight in her) that whenever she put the torch outside, it was only a matter of an hour before her house was full, and she had to douse the outer light.

The guests were mostly men—not uncommon, either, in Nkumai, since women rarely traveled at night, being generally burdened with the care of children, who didn't have the balance for safe walking at night. The talk was mostly small, though by listening carefully I learned a bit. Unfortunately, Nkumai courtesy forced the guests to spend as much time talking to me as they spent talking to each other. It would have been nicer, I thought at the time, if they had shared Mueller's custom of letting a guest sit in silence until he wished to join a conversation. Of course, Nkumai's custom keeps a guest from learning as much; I was certainly kept from learning anything I thought significant that night.

I learned only that all her guests were men of education—scientists of one kind or another. And I got the feeling from the way they talked and argued that these were men little concerned with science as Mueller used it, as a means to an end. Instead, science was the end in itself.

"Good evening, Lady," a small, softspoken man said. "I'm Teacher, and I'm eager to be of service to you."

A standard greeting, but at last I gave in to my curiosity and asked, "How can you be named Teacher, and also three other men in this room, and also the guide who led me here? How can you tell one another apart?"

He laughed, with that superior laugh that already irritated me and which I soon learned was a national custom, and said, "Because I'm myself, and they are not."

"But when you talk *about* each other?"

"Well," he patiently explained, "I hope that when men talk about me, they call me Teacher Who Taught the Stars to Dance, because that's what I did. The man who guided you here this morning—he's Teacher of True Sight. That's because he made that particular discovery."

"True sight?"

"You wouldn't understand," he said. "Very technical. But when someone wants to talk about us, he refers to our greatest accomplishment, and then everybody who matters knows who he's talking about."

"What about someone who hasn't made a great discovery yet?"

He laughed again. "Who would want to talk about such a person?"

"But when you speak of women, they all have names."

"So do dogs and little children," he said, so cheerfully I could almost believe he hadn't intended to be insulting. "But no one expects great accomplishments from women, at least not while they're fully engaged in the work of conceiving, bearing, and rearing children. Don't you think it would be coarse to speak of a woman by referring to her greatest gifts? Imagine calling someone 'Blanket Dancer with the Huge Buttocks' or 'Cook Who Always Scorches Soup.' " He laughed at his own joke, and several others, who had been vaguely listening in, suggested other titles. I thought they were hilarious, but as a woman I had to pretend to find them insulting, and in fact I was a bit annoyed when one of them suggested that I might be called "Emissary with the Freckled Breasts."

"How would you know to call me that?" I asked archly. I was annoyed to discover how easily it came to me to sound arch; all I had to do was imitate the Turd's speech and then raise one eyebrow—which I've been able to do since childhood, to the amusement of my parents and the terror of the troops under my command.

"I don't *know* it," answered a man named Stargazer—the same name as two others in the room. "But I'd be willing to find out."

It was something I hadn't really been prepared for. Rapists on the road I could cope with by killing them. But how does a woman say no to a man in polite company without offending? As a king's son, I was not used to hearing women say no. As Saranna's lover, I had lately not been used to asking, anyway.

Fortunately, I didn't have to answer at all.

"The Lady from Bird is not here to find out what's hidden under your robe," Mwabao Mawa said, "especially since most of us know how little it conceals." The laughter was loud, especially from the man insulted, but they moved away from me for a short time, and I was allowed a few moments to myself, to observe.

There was, amid all the chatter of science and court gossip—more of the latter than of the former, of course—a detectable pattern that amused me. I watched as one man at a time took Mwabao aside for just a moment of quiet, unheard conversation. And one of them I overheard. "At noon," he said, and she nodded. Little enough to generalize on, but I was willing to believe that they were making appointments. For what? I could think of several obvious purposes. She might be a whore; though I doubted it, both because of her lack of beauty and because of the obvious respect these men had for her mind, never leaving her out of their conversations or ignoring a remark she made. Or she might really be a mistress of the king, in which case she could be selling influence—though again I doubted it, because it seemed so unlikely that an emissary would be placed with a woman who had that kind of power.

A third possibility was that she was somehow involved with a rebellion or a secret party, at least. This didn't contradict either fact or logic, and I began to wonder if there was something there that might be exploited.

But not that night, at least. I was tired. Though my body had long since healed from the strain of climbing to Mwabao Mawa's house—and, for that matter, from the beating of the Nkumai soldiers only a short time before—I was still emotionally drained. I needed to sleep. I dozed for a moment and woke to find the last of the men leaving.

"Oh," I said, startled. "Did I sleep so long?"

"Only a few moments," Mwabao Mawa told me, "but they realized it was late, and went. So you could sleep."

She went to a corner, dipped her hand into a barrel, and drank.

I would have done the same, but as I thought of water a horrible realization came over me. In prison I had had privacy to eliminate wastes, and while traveling with Teacher he had delicately let me take care of those needs on the other side of the carriage, forbidding anyone to watch. But alone here in the house with another—another?—woman, there might be no such fastidiousness.

"Is there a room particularly for—" For what, I wondered. Was there a delicate way of putting it? "I mean, what are the other three rooms of your house used for?"

She turned to me and smiled slightly, but there was something other than a smile behind her eyes. "That I will tell to those who have a practical reason for such knowledge."

Didn't work. And worse, I had to watch as Mwabao Mawa casually took off her robe and walked naked across the room toward me.

"Aren't you going to sleep?" she asked me.

"Yes," I said, not bothering to hide how flustered I was. Her body was not particularly attractive, but it *was* the first time I had ever seen such a large woman undressed, and that, combined with her blackness and my long deprivation, made her exotic and intensely arousing. It made it all the more urgent for me to figure out a way to keep from getting undressed myself, since my modesty was essential to my survival in a nation which took me for a woman.

"Then why aren't you undressing?" she asked, puzzled.

"Because in my nation we don't undress to sleep."

She laughed aloud. "You mean you wear clothing even in front of other women?"

I pretended to speak as if I were from a nation whose customs exactly coincided with my present need, though in fact at that time I did not yet know of any such place. "The body is one's most private possession," I said, "and the most important. Do you wear all your jewels all the time?"

She shook her head, still amused. "Well, at least I hope you'll take it off to drop."

"Drop?"

She laughed again (that damned superior laugh) and said, "I guess a soiler would have a different word for it, wouldn't you? Well, you might as well watch the technique—it's easier to show it than to explain it."

I followed her to the corner of the room. She grasped the corner pole and then swung out, through the curtain. I gasped at the suddenness of the way she lurched out over the vast distance to the ground. For a moment I wondered if she had leapt out into space and flown away; but there were her hands, still gripping the pole through the curtains, and she sounded calm as she said, "Well, open the curtain, Lark. You can't learn if you don't look!"

So I opened and watched as she defecated over empty space. Then she swung back in and walked over to another water bucket—*not* the one she had drunk out of—and cleaned herself.

"You've got to learn quickly which bucket is which," she said with a smile. "And also—don't ever drop in a wind, especially in a wind with rain. There's nobody directly below us, but there are plenty of houses off at an angle below my home, and they have strong opinions about feces on their roofs and urine in their drinking water." Then she lay down on a pile of cushions on the floor.

I hitched up my robe until the skirt was very short,

and then grasped the pole tightly and delicately tip-
toed through the curtain. I began to tremble as I
glanced down and saw how far below me the few
torches still burning seemed to be. But I bowed—or
rather squatted—to the inevitable, trying to pretend
that I was not where I was.

It took a long time to convince my sphincters that
they should relax, not clench up in terror. When at
last I finished, I came back and walked awkwardly
to the water barrel. For a difficult moment, I wondered if I was at the wrong one.

"That's the one," came Mwabao Mawa's voice from
the cushions on the floor. I inwardly winced to think
she had been watching me, though I hope I showed
nothing on my face. I cleaned myself and lay down
on another pile of cushions. They were too soft, and
soon I pushed them aside and slept on the wooden
floor, which was more comfortable, though something in between would have been nicer.

Before I slept, though, Mwabao Mawa asked me
sleepily, "If you don't undress to sleep, and you don't
undress to drop, do you undress for sex?"

To which I just as drowsily replied, "That I will
tell to those who have a practical reason for such
knowledge." Her laughter this time told me that I
had a friend, and I slept peacefully all night.

I awoke because of a sound. In a building where
there is not only a north, south, east, and west, but
also an up and down, I couldn't tell where the sound
was coming from. But it was, I realized, music.

Singing, and the voice, which was distant, was
soon joined by another, which was closer. The words
were not clear. There may have been no real words.
But I found myself listening, pleased by the sound
of it. There was no harmony, at least nothing that I
could recognize. Instead, each voice seemed to seek
its own pleasure, without relation to the other. But
there was still some interaction, on some subtle—

or perhaps merely rhythmic—level, and as more voices joined in, the music became very full and lovely.

I noticed a motion, and turned to see Mwabao Mawa looking at me.

"Morningsong," she whispered. "Do you like it?"

I nodded. She nodded back, beckoned to me and walked to a curtain. She drew it aside and stood on the edge of the platform, naked, as the song continued. I held on to the corner pole and watched where she was watching.

It was the east; the hymn was to the imminent sun. As I watched, Mwabao Mawa opened her mouth and began to sing. Not softly, as she had yesterday, but with full voice, a voice that rang among the trees, that seemed to find the same mellow chord that had originally been tuned into the wood, and after a while I noticed that silence had fallen except for her music. And as she sang an intricate series of rapid notes, which seemed to bear no pattern but which, nevertheless, imprinted themselves indelibly in my memory and in my dreams ever since, the sun topped a horizon somewhere, and though I couldn't see it because of the leaves above me, I knew from the sudden brightening of the green ceiling that the sun had risen.

Then all the voices arose again, singing together for a few moments. And then, as if by a signal, silence.

I stood, leaning on the pole. It occurred to me that once I had shared Mueller's delusion that people with black skins were fit only to be slaves. One thing, at least, I had learned from my embassy here, and one thing I would take away: a memory of music unlike any other ever known in this world. I leaned there, unmoving, until Mwabao Mawa closed the curtains.

"Morningsong," she said, smiling. "It was too good an evening last night not to celebrate today."

She cooked breakfast—the meat of a small bird, and a thin-sliced fruit of some kind.

I asked; she told me that the fruit was the fruit of the trees the Nkumai lived in. "We eat it as soilers eat bread or potatoes." It had a strange tang. I didn't like it, but it was edible.

"How do you catch birds?" I asked. "Do you use hawks? If you shot a bird, it would fall forever to the ground."

She shook her head, waiting to answer until her mouth was empty. "I'll have Teacher take you to where the birdnets are."

"Teacher?" I asked.

As if my question had been his cue, a moment later he was standing outside the house, calling softly, "From the earth to the air."

"And to the nest, Teacher," Mwabao Mawa answered. She walked out of the room, on to the next room where Teacher would be waiting. Reluctantly I followed, making the short jump to the other room, and then, without even a good-bye, followed Teacher away from Mwabao Mawa's house. No good-bye, at first because I had no idea how women who barely knew each other should say it, and then because she was already gone from the curtain before I finally decided to turn and say something.

Up was terrible; but down was infinitely worse. Coming up a rope ladder, you reach the platforms with your hands first, pulling yourself to security. But going down you have to lie on your stomach and extend your feet downward, hunting for a rung with your toes, knowing that if you go too far you won't be able to pull yourself up.

I knew that achieving my purpose in Nkumai depended on my ability to get from place to place, and so I refused to let my fear rule me. If I fall, I fall, I told myself. Then I ignored my peripheral vision and trotted along after Teacher.

He, for his part, didn't try to show off as much today as yesterday, so the going *was* easier. I discovered that maneuvers that were difficult and frightening when done slowly were much easier—and much less frightening—when done quickly. A rope bridge is steady enough when you lightly run across it—but when you walk timidly it sways at every step.

When Teacher took a suspended rope with a knot in the end and swung easily from one platform to another, across an abyss that no one in his right mind would ever cross, I simply laughed, caught the rope he threw at me, and swung across just as quickly. At the other end, I pretended that I had jumped no farther than across a small stream, and let go, landing on the platform on my feet. It wasn't hard after all, and I said so.

"Of course not. Glad you're learning so fast."

But as we trotted along a sloping branch, it occurred to me to ask, "What would have happened if I hadn't reached the other platform? If my aim had been wrong, or if I hadn't swung hard enough?"

He didn't answer for a moment. Then he said, "We would have sent a boy down from the top, swinging all the way, to get the rope back to one platform or another."

"Could the rope support two people, doing that?" I asked.

"No," he answered, "but we wouldn't do it right away."

I tried not to think of myself swinging helplessly over nothing as dozens of Nkumai waited impatiently for me to let go and drop (though that word no longer had the same meaning for me) so that they could get their highway working again.

"Don't worry," Teacher said at last. "A lot of those swings have a guy rope on them, so they can be pulled back."

I believed him at the time, but I never saw a swing with a guy rope. Must have been in another part of Nkumai.

Our first stop was at the Office of Social Services.

"I want to see the king," I said, after explaining who I was.

"Wonderful," said the ancient Nkumai who sat on a cushion near the corner pole of the house. "I'm glad for you."

That was all, and apparently he meant to say no more. "Why are you so glad?" I asked.

"Because it's good for every human being to have an unfulfilled wish. It makes all of life so poignant."

I was nonplussed. At this point in Mueller, if I had been in Teacher's position, taking an emissary to a government office, I would have ordered that such a recalcitrant official be strangled on the spot. But Teacher just stood there, smiling. Thanks for the help, friend, I said silently, and proceeded to ask if this was the right place.

"For what?"

"For getting permission to see the king."

"Persistent, aren't you?" he asked.

"Yes," I answered, determined to play the game by his rules, if necessary, but to win whatever the rules might be.

So it went all morning, until finally the man grimaced and said, "I'm hungry, and a man as poor and underpaid as I must take every opportunity to put some meager snack into his belly."

The hint was clear, and I took a gold ring from my pocket. "By chance, sir," I said, "I was given this as a gift. But I couldn't bear to own it, when a man such as you would make so much better use of it."

"I couldn't take that," he said, "poor and under-paid though I am. Yet part of my work is to feed those even less fortunate than I, in the name of the king. So I will accept your gift in order to pass it along to the poor."

Then he excused himself and went to another room to eat lunch.

"What do we do?" I asked Teacher. "Do we go? Do we wait? Did I just waste a perfectly good bribe?"

"Bribe?" he asked suspiciously. "What bribe? Bribery is punishable by death."

I sighed. Who could understand these people?

The official came back into the room, smiling. "Oh, my friend," he said to me, "dear Lady, I have just thought of something. Even though I can't help you, I know a man who can. He lives over there, and he sells carved wooden spoons. Just ask for Spooncarver Who Made the Spoon You Can See Light Through."

We left, and Teacher patted me on the shoulder. "Very well done. It only took you one day."

I was a bit angry. "If you knew this Spooncarver was the one I had to see, why did you bring me *here*?"

"Because," he said, smiling patiently, "Spooncarver won't talk to anyone who wasn't sent by Officer Who Earns Foreign Exchange."

Spooncarver Who Made the Spoon You Can See Light Through didn't have time to see me that day, but urged me to return tomorrow. As I followed Teacher through the maze of trees, he showed me a birdnet being strung among the trees. "In a week or so it'll be fully in place, ready to unfurl. It looks thick enough while it's rolled up, but when it's unrolled among the trees, the net is so fine it can hardly be seen." He showed me how the gaps in the net were just wide enough for a bird's head to pass through, and just small enough that unless the bird withdrew its head exactly backward, which was impossible for most birds, it would break its neck or strangle. "And at the end of the day, we draw up the net and distribute the food."

"Distribute?" I asked.

Then I got a lecture about how in Nkumai, everything belonged to everybody, and no money was ever used because nobody was ever paid.

However, I learned quickly that in fact everybody was paid. I could go to Spooncarver, for instance, and ask for a spoon, and he would readily agree, promising it to me within a week. But at the end of the week, he would have forgotten, or had so much other work to do that he just couldn't get to mine yet. He would keep promising and keep putting me off, until I did him a favor of equivalent value—out of the goodness of my heart.

Mwabao Mawa's favor, which won her living, was that every now and then she stood at the edge of her house and sang morningsong, or eveningsong, or birdsong, or who knows what else. It was enough— she was never hungry, and often had so much food and so many possessions she gave many things away.

The poor were those who had nothing of value to give. The stupid. The untalented. The lazy. They were tolerated; they were fed—barely. They were not, however, considered to have any importance in life. And they all had names.

I was in Nkumai almost two weeks, long enough that the life was beginning to seem normal to me, when I finally got to see someone who had real power. He was Official Who Feeds All the Poor, and Teacher actually bowed slightly to him when we entered his house.

But the interview was pointless. Small talk, a discussion of Nkumai's social conscience, questions about my homeland. I had long since invented my own idea of what Bird was like, since I had no other way of answering the questions so many Nkumai put to me about the country. After all the empty chat, he invited me to dinner a few days hence. "When I burn two torches," he said. I left unsatisfied.

I was more unsatisfied when Teacher laughed at me and said that it looked like my climb upward through the government had reached an end. "What favor will you offer *him*?" he asked. I didn't point out that he was tacitly admitting that I *was* bribing Nkumai officials after all. I just smiled and showed him one of my precious iron rings.

He only smiled and pulled open his robe to reveal a heavy amulet of iron hanging from his neck. The sight of so much iron wastefully used, for mere decoration, made my skin tingle.

"Iron?" he said. "We have so much of that. Iron would do with Spooncarver and Birdmaster, but with Official Who Feeds All the Poor?"

"What kind of gift would he appreciate?"

"Who knows?" Teacher answered. "No one's ever given him one that did any good. But you should be proud of yourself, Lady. You spoke to him at all—which is more than most emissaries have been able to do."

"How wonderful," I said.

I insisted to Teacher that I knew the way back to Mwabao Mawa's house without his help. At last he shrugged and let me go alone. I covered the space quickly, and was pleased to see how well I was doing at traveling among the treetops. I even took a few moments to climb some unmarked branches, for the fun of it, and though I still avoided looking down, I found it a pleasant challenge to conquer a difficult approach. It was nearly dark when I got to Mwabao's house and called to her.

"Come into the nest," she said, smiling. At once she served me supper. "I hear you got to Official Who Feeds All the Poor."

"Someday you have to let me cook you a dinner such as we have in Bird," I said, but she laughed. So I asked her, "Why did you take me in, Mwabao Mawa, if there was never any intention for me to see the king?"

"King?" she asked, smiling. "Intentions? No one has any intentions at all. They asked who would let you live with them, and because I have food enough to spare, I offered. They let me."

I was angry at her, even though I was eating her food. "How can you of Nkumai expect to deal with the world, if you refuse to allow emissaries to see your king?"

She reached out her hand and gently stroked my cheek, to which no beard had come. "We don't refuse you anything, little Lark," she said, and smiled. "Don't be impatient. We Nkumai do things our own way."

I pulled away from her hand, deciding that it was time I let someone see me in a rage. "You all tell me that bribery is forbidden, and yet I've bribed my way through a dozen interviews. You all tell me that you all share everything, and no one has to buy or sell, and yet I've seen purchases and sales just like bartering peddlers. And then you tell me that you don't refuse me anything, but I've met with nothing but impediments."

I stood and walked from her angrily.

She didn't say anything for a while, and I couldn't turn and say more, or I'd lose something, lose the moment of impact. It was an impasse, until she began to sing in a little-girl voice, a voice nothing like the one she used for her real songs:

> Robber bird hunts for berries,
> But only catches bees.
> She says, "I know how to eat and sleep,
> But what do I do with these?"

"One follows them," I said, my back still turned, "until one finds their honey." Then I faced her, and said, "But what are the bees, Mwabao Mawa? Whom do I follow, and where is the honey?"

She didn't answer, just got up and walked out of the room—but not toward the front room where I had often been. Instead she went into one of the forbidden back rooms, and because she didn't say anything else, I followed.

I found myself—after a short run along a branch not even a meter thick—in a brightly curtained room lined with wooden boxes. She had one open, and was rummaging through it.

"Here," she said, finding what she was looking for. "Read this." She handed me a book.

I read it that night. It was a history of Nkumai, and it was the strangest history I had ever read. It wasn't long, and there were no stories of war in it, no records of invasions or conquests. Instead it was a list of Singers and their life stories, of Woodcarvers and Treedancers, of Teachers and Housemakers. It was, in fact, a record of names and their explanations. How Woodcarver Who Taught the Tree to Color Its Wood got his name. How Seeker Who Saw the Cold Sea and Brought It Home in a Bucket earned his. And as I read the brief stories, I began to understand the Nkumai. A peaceful people who were sincere in their belief in equality, despite their tendency to despise those with little to offer. A people who were utterly at one with their world of tall trees and flitting birds.

And as I read in the light of a thick candle, I began to sense contradictions. What could such a people possibly have developed to sell to the Ambassador? And what caused them to come down from the trees and go to war, using their iron to conquer Drew and Allison, and perhaps more by now?

As I thought these things, I began to think of other contradictions. This was the capital of Nkumai, and yet no one seemed aware or even interested in the fact that a war had just been won. There were no

slaves from Allison or Drew making their way carefully among the trees. There was no sudden wealth
from the tribute and taxes. There wasn't even any
pride in the accomplishment, though no one denied
it when I mentioned their victories.

"You're still reading?" Mwabao Mawa whispered
in the darkness.

"No," I said. "Thinking."

"Ah," she answered. "Of what?"

"Of your strange, strange nation, Mwabao."

"I find it comfortable." She was amused; her voice
hinted at a smile.

"You've conquered an empire larger than most other
nations, and yet your people aren't military, aren't
even violent."

She chuckled. "Not violent. That's true enough.
You're violent, though. Teacher tells me that you
killed two would-be rapists on a country road in
Allison."

I was startled. So they had been tracing my travels.
It made me uneasy. How far would they go? I should
have said I was from Stanley, at the other end of the
world from Nkumai—but only Bird had women for
rulers. Then I remembered that a tall black Nkumai
could no more get through Robles or Jones to make
inquiries in Bird than I could jump from Mwabao's
house and land running.

"Yes," I admitted. "In Bird women are trained to
kill in secret ways, or men would soon have power
over us. But Mwabao, why have the Nkumai gone
to war?"

It was her turn to be silent for a moment, and then
she said simply, "I don't know. No one asked me. I
wouldn't have gone."

"Where did they find the soldiers, then?"

"From the poor, of course. They have nothing to
offer that anyone wants. But I suppose the war has
allowed them to give the only thing they have. Their

lives. And their strength. War is easy, after all. Even a fool can be a soldier."

I remembered the strutting, too-brave men of Nkumai armed with iron and quick to abuse the cowering populace of Allison. Of course. The worst of Nkumai, those used to being despised by all, at last in a position of power over others. No wonder they abused it.

"But that isn't what you want to know," said Mwabao Mawa.

"Oh?"

"You came here for something else."

"What?" I asked, feeling that sickening fear that children feel when they are just about to be found in hide-and-go-find.

"You came here to find out where we get our iron."

The sentence hung there in the air. If I said yes, I could imagine her crying out in the darkness of night, and a thousand voices hearing her, and my being cast off the platform into the darkness that led to the ground. But if I denied it, then would I be missing a chance, perhaps the only chance to learn what I wanted to know? If Mwabao was indeed a rebel, as I had suspected, she might be willing to tell me the truth. But if she was working for the king (her lover?) she might be leading me on to trap me.

Be ambiguous, my father always taught me.

"Everyone knows where you get the iron," I said easily. "From your Ambassador, from the Watchers, just like everyone else."

She laughed. "Clever, my girl. But you have a ring of iron, and you thought it had great value"—did she know *everything* I had said and done these two weeks?—"and if your people are getting iron, in however small a quantity, you must be eager to find out what *we're* selling to the Ambassador."

"I've asked no one any questions about such matters."

She chuckled. "Of course not. That's why you're still here."

"Of course I'm curious about many things. But I'm here to see the king."

"The king, the king, the king, there you go like everyone else, always chasing after lies and empty dreams. Iron. You want to know what we do to get iron. Why, so you can stop us? Or so you can do it yourselves, and get as much iron as we?"

"Neither, Mwabao Mawa, and perhaps we shouldn't speak of such things," I said, though I was sure she would go on, was eager to go on.

"But that's where it's all so silly," she said, and I heard a mischievous little girl in her voice. "They take all these precautions, keep you imprisoned either with me or with Teacher all day, every day, and yet it's so impossible for you anyway, either to stop us or to duplicate what we do."

"If it's impossible, why do you worry?"

She laughed—giggled, this time, like a child—and said, "Just in case. Just in case, Lady Lark." She stood up suddenly, though she had already undressed for bed, and strode out of the room, back toward the room with the chests of books and other things. She was after other things. I followed her, and arrived just in time to catch a black robe she threw at me.

"I'll leave the room so you can dress," she said.

When I got back to the sleeping room, she was waiting—impatiently, walking up and down, humming softly to herself. When I came in, she came to me, and put her hands on my cheeks. Something warm and sticky was on them, and she giggled when she looked at me.

"Now you're black!" she whispered, and proceeded to decorate my hands and wrists, then my ankles and feet. As she painted my feet, she ran one hand up the inside of my leg, past the knee, and I stepped back abruptly, frightened that in playfulness she might find out not-too-playful facts.

"Careful!" she cried out. I looked behind me, and realized that I was standing right at the lip of the platform. I stepped forward.

"Sorry," she said. "I won't offend your modesty again! Just playing, just playing."

"What's going on?" I asked. "Why are you doing this?"

"I can travel at night like this," she said, spinning her naked body around in front of me, "and no one sees from very far away. But you—lily-white and hair so light, Lady Lark—you they could see from six trees away." She pulled a snug black cap over my head and took me by the hand to the edge of her house.

"I'm taking you," she said, "and if you like what you see, you must do me a favor in return."

"All right," I said. "What's the favor?"

"Nothing hard," she said, "nothing hard." Then she stepped off into the night. I followed.

It was the first time I had tried to travel in the darkness, and suddenly my old panic returned. Now on the broad branches I was too frightened to run— what if I veered only slightly from the path? How could I see to jump with the swinging ropes? How could I hope to keep my footing anywhere?

But Mwabao Mawa led well, and on the hard places she took my hand. "Don't try to see," she kept whispering. "Just follow me."

She was right. The light, which was only starlight and the dim light of Dissent, did more harm than good, diffused as it was by the leaves. And the lower we got, the darker it became.

There were no swings. For that I was grateful.

And at last we came to a place where she told me to stop. I did, and then she asked me, "Well?"

"Well what?" I responded.

"Can you smell it?"

I hadn't thought to smell. So I breathed slowly, and opened my mouth, and tasted the air through my nose and tongue, and it was delicious.

It was exquisite.

It was a dream of lovemaking, with a woman I had wanted forever but never hoped to have.

It was a memory of warfare, with the lust of blood and the joy of surviving through a sea of dancing spears and obsidian axes.

It was the essence of rest after a long journey at sea, when land smells welcome and the grain waving on the plains seems to be another sea, but one you could walk on without a boat, one you could drown in and live, and I turned to Mwabao Mawa and I know my eyes were wide with astonishment, because she laughed.

"The air of Nkumai," she said.

"What is it?" I asked her.

"Many things combined," she said. "The air rising from a noxious swamp below us. The falling fragrance of the leaves. The smell of old wood. The last vestiges of rain. Spent sunlight. Does it matter?"

"And this is what you sell?"

"Of course," she answered. "Why else would I bring you? Only the smell is much stronger in daylight, when we capture it in bottles."

"Smells," I said, and it seemed funny. "Smells from a gassy swamp. Can't the Watchers synthesize it?"

"They haven't yet," she said. "At least they keep buying it. It's funny, Lady Lark, that mankind can speed between the stars faster than light itself, and yet we still don't know what causes smells."

"Of course we know," I said.

"We know what different things smell like," she answered, "but no one knows all that travels from the substance to the olfactory nerves." There was no arguing that, since I didn't yet know olfactory from occipital.

Another thing she had said intrigued me. I picked up on what she said about men traveling faster than light. "Any schoolchild knows that's impossible," I said. "Our ancestors were brought to Treason in starships that took a hundred years of sleep to arrive."

"So mankind was crawling then," she said. "Did you think they would stop learning, just because our ancestors left them? In three thousand years of isolation, we've missed the great things of humanity."

"But faster than light," I said. "How could they have done that?"

She shook her head, a faint grey in the grey of night moving faintly. "I was just talking," she said. "Just chattering on. Let's go back."

We retraced our steps. We were halfway up a rope ladder when a voice above us whispered faintly in the night.

"Someone's on the ladder."

Mwabao Mawa ahead of me froze, and I did the same. Then I felt the rope jiggle slightly, and her foot came down near my face. I assumed we were going down, and would have descended at once except that her foot twisted and hooked under my arm, stopping my descent. So I waited until she climbed down the opposite side of the ladder to be at the same height as me—her feet on the rung below mine, and so her lips not far below my ear.

The sound wouldn't have been audible three feet away. "First platform. Wash face. Going to visit Official Who Feeds All the Poor. Two Torches."

So we went on climbing, and reached the first platform, which by chance—a lucky chance, too, since it was not common—had a barrel of water. I washed my face as silently as possible, while Mwabao Mawa kept climbing up and down the same three meters of rope ladder, so that anyone observing the strand in the night wouldn't know we had stopped.

I got my face as clean as possible, and also my hands and feet. Then I climbed on the ladder behind her.

"No," she whispered, and then we were both standing on the platform, as she demanded, quietly of course, that I give her my robe.

"I can't," I whispered.

"You're wearing clothing underneath, aren't you?" she asked, and I nodded. "Well, I can't be caught naked on the treeways. I can't."

But still I refused, until finally she said, "Then give me your underclothing." I agreed to that, and reached under the robe to strip off the pants and halter. The pants were too tight for her hips, but she struggled into them anyway. The halter, however, fit nicely—one more sad proof of exactly how buxom I had become.

I had a worse realization, however, at the same time. The halter, as I slipped it off my shoulder inside my robe, had snagged on something on my shoulder. There should have been nothing there to snag on. Which meant that something new was growing.

An arm? Then I had less than a week before I'd have to cut it off, and it wasn't in a good position for me to get at alone. How could I go to an Nkumai surgeon (*were* there any Nkumai surgeons?) and ask him to remove an extra arm?

But the momentary alarm that gave me turned into relief as I realized that of course I didn't have to stay here for a week, or even another day. I had all that I needed, all I had hoped for. I could now make a great show of leaving Nkumai in disgust at their failure to let me see the king; I could return to my father and tell him what the Nkumai sold to the Ambassador.

Smelly air.

I might have laughed, except that we were climbing the ladder again. And as I realized how close I had come to laughing, it occurred to me that whiffs of Nkumai forest air above noxious swamps could be dangerous. Self-restraints that I could normally count on, disciplined reflexes that had always been sure, didn't function as well here, not this night.

Finally we reached the platform where the guards were watching.

"Stop," said the sharp whisper, and then hands grabbed my wrist and pulled me toward the platform. Unfortunately, I wasn't ready for the movement, and it was only with luck that I kept my feet on the rope ladder. As it was, I hung over the abyss, my feet on the ladder and my one arm suspended in the firm grasp of a guard.

"Careful," said Mwabao. "Careful, she's a soiler, she might fall."

"Who are you?"

"Mwabao Mawa and Lady Lark, the soiler emissary from Bird."

A grunt of recognition, and I found myself being pulled toward the platform, until my shin struck the edge. I stepped clumsily onto the wood, falling to one knee.

"What are you doing, wandering in the dark like this?" the voice insisted. I decided to let Mwabao answer. She explained that she was leading me to meet with Official Who Feeds All the Poor.

"Nobody has torches out now," said the voice.

"He will."

"Will he now?"

"Two torches," she insisted. "He is expecting a guest."

Whispers, and then we waited while quiet feet scampered off. A guard—or two, I realized, as the breathing patterns broke up—stayed with us, while another ran to check. It wasn't long before he returned and said, "Two torches."

"All right then," said the voice. "Go on. But in the future, Mwabao Mawa, carry a torch. You are trusted, but not infallible."

Mwabao mumbled her thanks, and so did I, and we were on our way again.

When two torches shone in the distance, Mwabao Mawa said good-bye.

"What?" I said, rather loudly.

"Quiet," she insisted. "Official must not know that I brought you."

"But how do I get there from here?"

"Can't you see the path?"

I couldn't, so she took me closer, until the dim light of the torches illuminated the rest of the way. I was glad that Official didn't have the same penchant for narrow approaches that Mwabao did. I felt safe enough following the path in the dark, as Mwabao Mawa slipped off into the night of the trees.

I came to the door and said, very softly, "From the earth to the air."

"And to the nest, come in," said a soft voice, and I stepped through the curtains. Official sat there looking very, well, *official* in his red robe in the flickering light of two candles.

"You came at last," said Official.

"Yes," I said, and added truthfully, "I'm not very good at traveling in the dark."

"Speak softly," he said, "for the curtains conceal little, and the night air carries sounds a long way."

So we spoke softly as he asked me questions about why I wanted to see the king and what I wanted to accomplish. What could I say? No need to see the old boy now, Official, already got what I wanted. So I answered all his questions, until at last he sighed deeply and said, "Well, Lady Lark, I've been told that if you passed my screening, I was in no way to impede you from further approach to the king."

Yesterday I would have been delighted. But tonight—tonight I just wanted to take my deformed body with the new arm it was growing and get out of Nkumai.

"I'm grateful, Official."

"Of course you don't go straight from me to him. A guide will come and take you to the very highly placed person who gave me my instructions, and that very highly placed person will take you higher."

"To the king?"

"I don't know exactly how highly placed this person is," Official said, not smiling. How could they conduct government this way, I wondered.

But a boy appeared when Official snapped his fingers, and led me off another way. I followed gingerly, and this time there was a swing—but the boy lit a torch at the other end, and I made it, though I landed clumsily and twisted my ankle. The sprain was mild, and it healed and lost its soreness in a few minutes.

The boy left me at a house which had no light, and he told me to say nothing. So I waited in front of the house, until finally a low whisper said, "Come in," and I went in.

The house was absolutely dark, but once again I was asked questions, and once again I answered, not having any idea who I was speaking to or even where, precisely, he was. But after a half hour of this, he finally said, "I will leave now."

"What about me?" I asked idiotically.

"You'll stay. Someone else will come."

"The king?"

"The person next to the king," he said, even more softly, and left through the gap in the curtains I had entered by.

Then I heard soft steps in another direction, and

someone came in and sat beside me. Close beside
me. And then chuckled softly.

"Mwabao Mawa," I said, incredulous.

"Lady Lark," she whispered back to me.

"But they told me—"

"That you would meet the person closest to the
king."

"And it's you?"

She chuckled again.

"So you are the king's mistress."

"In a way," she said. "If only there were a king."

That one took awhile to sink in.

"No king?"

"No *one* king," she answered, "but I can speak for
those who rule as well as anyone. Better than most.
Better than some of *them*."

"But why did I have to go through all of this? Why
did I have to—bribe my way up to you? I was with
you all along!"

"Softly," she said. "Softly. The night listens. Yes,
Lark, you were with me all along. I had to know that
I could trust you. That you weren't a spy."

"But you showed me the place yourself. Let me
smell the smells."

"I also showed you how impossible it was to stop
us, or duplicate it. Near the ground, Lark, the air
smells foul. And your people could never climb our
trees, you know that."

I agreed. "But why did you show me anyway? It's
so useless."

"Not useless," she said. "The smell has other effects. I wanted you to breathe that air."

And then I felt her hand pull the cap off my hair.
She gently pulled at a single lock of it. "You owe me
a favor," she said, and suddenly I felt my own death
approaching.

Her breath was hot on my cheek and her hand was

stroking my throat when I finally thought of a way out of this. At least a way to postpone it. Perhaps the perfumed air was enough to loosen the sexual tabus of the people of Nkumai. Perhaps it would have been enough of a dose to weaken a normal woman's inhibition against making love to another woman. But I had no inhibition against making love to a woman, and my body, too long deprived, reacted to Mwabao Mawa's offer as if it were extraordinarily opportune. Fortunately, my inhibition against dying was very strong, and the air hadn't weakened it a bit. I knew that if I let things go on to their natural conclusion it would lead to discovery of my odd physique. It occurred to me that Mwabao Mawa would not be quite so open-minded about finding a man in her bed as she expected me to be about finding a woman in mine.

"I can't," I said.

"You will," she said, and her cold hand slid inside my robe. "I can help you," she said. "I can pretend to be a man for you, if you like," and she began humming and singing a soft, strange song. Almost immediately that hand inside the robe became rougher, stronger, and the face that kissed my cheek felt rough and whiskered. All of this seemed to happen through her song. How did she do it, I wondered, even as another part of my mind gratefully noticed that her pretence at maleness would probably help quell my desire for her.

Except that my breasts reacted like any woman's, and I began to be very afraid as the song became too rhythmic, pulled me more deeply into a trance.

"I mustn't," I said, and I pulled away. She followed. Or he? The illusion was powerful. I only wished I could do the same, and fool her into thinking I was a woman no matter what evidence her hands and lips and eyes might find. But I couldn't. "If you do," I said, "I'll kill myself afterward."

"Nonsense," she answered.

"I haven't been purified." I tried to sound desperate. It wasn't hard.

"Nonsense," she said.

"If I didn't kill myself, my people would," I said. "They will, if this happens and I haven't been purified first."

"How would they know?"

"Do you think I would lie to my own people?" I hoped that the huskiness and trembling in my voice sounded like offended honor instead of the rank terror I actually felt.

Perhaps it did, for she stopped, or rather paused, and asked, "What is it, this purification?"

I made up a jumble of religious ritual, half stolen from the practices of the people of Ryan and half a product of my need for solitude. She listened. She believed me. And so I made another journey in the dark, and found myself alone in Mwabao Mawa's room, the one with the chests and boxes. My purpose there, she told me, was to meditate.

I stayed there for a morning and an evening and a night.

I had no idea what to do. Mwabao was in the other room, the one we had shared for two weeks, humming softly an erotic song—one that kept me almost constantly aroused.

I toyed with the idea of cutting off my genitals, but I couldn't be sure how long regeneration would take, and the healed wound of castration would not be taken for the anatomy of a woman.

I also thought of escape, of course, but I knew perfectly well that the only escape route lay through the room where Mwabao Mawa cheerfully waited. I cursed again and again—very softly, of course—wondering why I had the miserable fortune to end up imprisoned in a woman's body with a lesbian for a jailer and hundreds of meters of gravity serving as the bars for my cell.

At last I realized that my only hope, thin as it was, was to escape, not as a woman, but as a man. Tomorrow night, in the darkness, if I painted myself black I might elude the guards. If I didn't, and I was taken, all I'd need to do is fall. Drop, I thought ironically. And my identity as a Mueller would be safe.

Getting past Mwabao? Simple. Kill her.

Could I do it? Not so simple. I liked her. She had breached diplomatic protocol, but she had done me no real harm. Also, she was well-connected; she would quickly be missed.

So I wouldn't kill her. A knock on her head, a breaking of bones, that should be enough. It should silence her for long enough, or at least immobilize her. Though truth to tell, I had no idea how hard I'd have to hit a normal person to knock her unconscious without killing her, how many bones to break without crippling her for life. With Muellers, it was never an issue. And I had never heard of a Mueller striking a foreigner without the intent to kill or maim. Still, I'd do my best to leave her whole.

All that remained was to hide who I was. The blacking of my skin could come later, after I finished with Mwabao. But the other preparations would be good for shock value.

I began searching quietly through her boxes, hoping to find a knife. With it I would cut off my breasts. They'd grow back, of course, but by tonight the scar tissue would only have turned back into normal flesh, and the breasts would still not have begun noticeably to grow. It was the closest thing to a change of sex that I could hope to accomplish, I realized bitterly.

I didn't find a knife. Instead I found several more books, and a moment's curiosity led me to a half-hour's concentration.

It was a history of Treason. I had read *our* history of the planet, of course, but this was more complete in some ways. In some very important ways, and I began to realize that I had been almost completely fooled. And yet it was so obvious.

What Mueller's history left out, and what Nkumai's history dwelt on, was the entire group. It was an account of not just one family, but all the members of the conspiracy who were exiled to this metalless planet as a horrible example to the rest of the Republic of what happened to people who tried to establish a government of the intellectual elite. The long-dead issues that had brought the Families here always seemed laughable to me, and still do. Who should rule whom? The answer was always, eternally, "I should." Whoever "I" might be, "I" would seek power.

But the Nkumai history went over the roster of names. I hunted for Mueller, and found it. Han Mueller, a geneticist specializing in the hyperdevelopment of human regeneration. I found others. But of course the one most interesting to me at that moment was Nkumai. Ngago Nkumai, who had adopted a pseudo-African name as a gesture of defiance, had made his name in the development of theoretical physical constructs of the universe. Making new ways of looking at the universe that would enable men to do new things.

It all came together at once, each part so flimsy that alone it proved nothing, but all the events of the weeks I had spent in Nkumai fit so well that I couldn't doubt my conclusion.

The smelly air above the swamp was nothing, was a decoy, was Mwabao Mawa's device for getting the slim, pretty blond girl from Bird into bed. But other things were true. There was no king, for instance. Mwabao had told the truth: a group governed this place. But it was not a group of politicians. It was a group whose profession was the same as the founder, Ngago Nkumai. They were scientists who made up new ways of looking at the universe—scientists who invented things like True Sight and Making the Stars Dance. They used Mwabao Mawa as their liaison with what official government workers Nkumai had. Whom did they use as liaison with the army? With the guards? It hardly mattered. And why did all the common Nkumai believe there was a king? There undoubtedly had been—or perhaps there still was a figurehead. Again, it hardly mattered.

What mattered was that Nkumai wasn't selling smells to the Ambassador at all. It was selling physics. It was selling new ways of looking at the universe. It was selling, of course, faster-than-light travel, as Mwabao Mawa had so blandly let slip and then covered so well. And other things. Things worth far more to the Watchers than arms, legs, hearts, and heads that were carved off the bodies of radical regeneratives.

Each Family would, if it had any hope of creating anything to sell to the Ambassador, try to develop what its founder had known best: Mueller, human genetic manipulation. Nkumai, physics. I looked up Bird and laughed. The original Bird had been a wealthy socialite, a woman with few marketable skills and abilities at all, except her knack for bending others to her will. The matriarchy was her only legacy. In the competition for iron that gave them no advantage. Yet, like all the others, she had passed on to her Family her knowledge of what she was best at.

I closed the book. Now it was even more urgent that I escape, because *this* particular discovery could be the key to a Mueller victory over Nkumai. And I could—I was sure of it—train a Mueller army to be able to fight in the trees. And we could—I had hope for it—win a victory and capture at least some of those minds, or at least control their Ambassador and block them from using it. After all, the basic population of Nkumai was ill-equipped for fighting, but the basic population of Mueller was raised to the knife and the spear and the bow. We could do it.

We *had* to do it. Because Nkumai was getting metal faster, and when they had enough of it, they would have the technology to build a ship and get offplanet. Not a sleepship, but a ship that traveled faster than light itself. They would get off Treason—and Mueller had no hope of that. Then, once the Nkumai had reached the Republic and settled old scores, they would come back with all the metal their ships could carry, and then no Family could hope to stand against them. They would rule.

I had to stop them.

I put away the book and searched again for a knife. I was searching when the curtains parted and five Nkumai guards came into the room.

"Our spies just got back from Bird," one of them said.

I killed two and maimed another. They couldn't subdue me. They had to strike a blow to my head that would have killed an ordinary man. It did so much damage that I was unconscious for hours.

4 LANIK AND
    LANIK

I awoke lying on a platform so small that with my head on the platform my feet dangled off it. I felt rather than saw that I was still dressed. It was beyond belief that they had not discovered my body's secret—surely they had searched me for weapons—yet I still felt some hope that a sense of generous modesty had preserved the secret of Mueller.

Two Nkumai guards were standing nearby. When they saw that I was awake, they quickly threaded their way to me along narrow branches. We were so high that leaves were thick around us, and I could see patches of sky. The branches were so slender that my platform bounced wildly as the guards walked toward me.

When they were standing on the branch that passed under my platform, they reached out hooks and snagged two ropes dangling from even higher, thinner branches. On the ends of the ropes were the most ingenious manacles I had ever seen. Instead of the clumsy and quick-to-rot wooden manacles we used in Mueller, these were made of glass bound in rope. Two half-cylinders of glass were slipped around my wrists. They did not quite meet on either side. Then the rope was tied tightly around them, held in place by a groove in the glass. When the guards were through tying the ropes, the glass half-cylinders met tightly.

As a parting gesture in our wordless interplay, the guards jerked the manacles on my arms. The guard on the right pulled the manacle down, toward my elbow. The other pulled his manacle up, toward my hand. The pain was sharp and immediate. I looked at them in surprise. They smiled grimly and left.

Around my right forearm and around my left hand the manacles had cut deep enough to draw blood. The glass had been ground or chipped to have a sharp edge. It was easy enough to get out of these manacles—as long as you were willing to lose half a hand in the process, and even if you were, it would make climbing down from the tree rather difficult.

The manacles were also tied just far enough apart that I couldn't strike them against each other or anything else, not even my head. There was no way to shatter them. Furthermore, because they were tied to branches with a great deal of spring, when I pulled them down, they had a tendency to spring back, cutting me. As it was, there was such constant tension on them that any movement at all sliced me a little. I couldn't lie down—couldn't even kneel.

They didn't want me to get away, and they didn't want me to enjoy staying with them. I've visited with hosts like that before and since, but none who were so obnoxious about it.

I looked around. It was early evening—the sun was still visible, low amid the leaves to the west, shining under the clouds that were rolling in from the northwest. I must have been out for hours.

My platform rested on a single branch—but it was connected to or rested on many others, making one intertwining network. I bounced lightly on my platform. Immediately the guards felt the movement and looked around.

There were other platforms near me, none occupied. Farther away I thought I could see someone else standing in manacles, but I couldn't be sure. Leaves kept me from seeing very far.

It began to rain. I was immediately soaked, and here, where fewer leaves and branches could dissipate the storm, the heavy drops battered me savagely. Worse, it fell with such force that every gust of wind jerked and jiggled the branches, and it felt like the first time I had walked on a rope bridge— worse than seasickness. During the rain I could see that the guards huddled under two small roofs, watching no one.

My plan formed quickly and easily, but it would only get me away from this prison area. How I would get to the ground alive—and from there, how I would get through the forest to safety (and where was that?)—those were matters too arcane to be investigated right then.

"Lady Lark," said a distant voice I recognized. Mwabao Mawa was making her way along the network of small branches. The guards stood and nodded to her as she approached me.

"Mwabao Mawa," I said. "I've changed my mind. I'd rather continue living with you after all."

She pursed her lips, then said, "We've had the full report from our informants. They're a rather treacherous pair—mercenaries from Allison—and they had the mistaken notion that we'd continue to pay more and more for every bit of information they eked out. I hope you don't have any such mistaken notion, Lark, or whoever you are. We will do no bargaining, except for your life."

I smiled, but I'm sure I didn't look particularly jovial.

"Lady Lark, you are not from Bird. Not only that, but the absurd stories you told us about that Family's culture were so far from the truth as to imply that you have never even been there. Nevertheless, it's obvious from your accent that you *are* from the Rebel River plain. It's also plain from the iron coin you used that you are from a Family that uses money. And since the iron could not have come from us, it must have come from some other Family that has something to sell to the Ambassador. Who is it?"

I smiled more widely.

"Oh well," she said. "I can guess with confidence that you're from Mueller. Precisely who you are I will know within a week, from more reliable spies than the pair of Allisons we used before. Let's get to more practical things. What are your people selling to the Ambassador?"

"Air," I answered, "from the swamps at the mouth of the Rebel River."

She glared at me. "I truly did like you."

"And I truly did like you," I responded. "My liking for you, however, ended night before last, when I found out how widely our sexual tastes diverge." An out-and-out lie—we both liked women.

"I still like you, Lark," she said. "I'm not a sadist, and you aren't here out of spite. So you'll understand if I don't stay to watch."

When she was gone, the guards came and lifted me into the air. I thought at first they would simply drop me, letting the manacles do the work. But apparently not—if they accidently cut off a major portion of my hand, manacles couldn't hold me anymore. Instead, as I was in the air, they spoke for the first time and urged me to take hold of the ropes, which were now slack enough for me to do so.

I held on to the ropes as they swung my feet forward. In that position I couldn't let go of the ropes without slashing my wrists on the manacles, and the ropes were tied to such bouncy branches that I couldn't get leverage to kick at the guards. They proceeded to carve up my feet, in a delightful criss-cross pattern about half an inch deep, getting to bone in several places. It was agonizing, of course, but I had gone through worse in training. Still, I knew what was expected of me and moaned and screamed. I must have given a convincing performance, because they soon stopped cutting, lifted me again, told me to let go of the ropes, and set me gently down.

On my feet, of course, and the manacles still forced me to stand. I thought of what happened to spies in the dungeons of Mueller, and decided that in that aspect of civilization, Nkumai and Mueller were about even. Mueller had a higher technology for inducing pain, but Nkumai understood how to evoke despair.

Thinking about that, I forgot to scream for a moment or two, but once I remembered that I was supposed to be suffering, I moaned a lot. They went away.

In half an hour the simple cuts on my feet were gone, and the pain and the tickle of healing quickly ended, too. However, the trouble with healing so fast was that my would-be tormentors would surely notice it, and there would be no further need for me to hide what it was that Mueller sold to the Ambassador.

I began to pray for rain. Or at least wish for it, since my pantheon didn't include anyone in charge of weather.

It came an hour after nightfall. The clouds rolled across the sky, blotting out the stars and the light of Dissent. The wind came up, bouncing the platform around. That was my signal to begin; with the branches already bouncing, they wouldn't notice *my* movements.

I began pulling against the manacles, to slice off part of my hand. The hardest thing was keeping the pressure on the manacles strong enough in the right direction so that the two outermost fingers on each hand were ripped off by the glass, and not the thumb. I needed the thumb for climbing.

There was a horrifying moment when both hands came free at once, right when a gust of wind jerked the platform under me. I fell flat on my face—but luck was kind to me that day, and I fell on the supporting branch rather than into empty space.

I lay there for a moment, dripping blood from my maimed hands, as the rain began to pour.

Only a few minutes left until the storm died down. Between the clouds, the rain, and the darkness of night, I could see nothing at all. Yet I had to move, had to get away from the prison before my motion became detectable again. The pain was nothing, but conquering my fear of falling and my fear of moving in the darkness was the hardest thing I ever had to do in my life until then, with the greatest personal risk. Even now as I think about it, I wonder at what kind of madness caused me even to attempt it. But I was still young then, and life didn't have quite the high price on it that it has now.

The wood was slippery, and I crawled and climbed and staggered far faster than was safe. I tried to stay on the branches in the direction they forked from, knowing that eventually I would find a thicker branch with firm footing. I mostly kept my eyes closed, feeling ahead of me with my hands, because even in the pitch darkness, as long as my eyes were open my mind kept wanting to see, and tended to panic when it couldn't.

Once I came to a platform, and was afraid for a moment it might be occupied. It wasn't, and from that platform to solid wood was only a matter of moments. I still didn't get up and run, however. I had no guide, and the wood was slick. But it was a relief not to be tossed back and forth, and I let myself descend into the darkness.

The rain stopped. The wind stopped. And just as I sighed in relief, the path I was following suddenly became very steep, and I lost my hold and fell. For a moment I thought that this was my death; but almost immediately I landed on a platform.

"What the hell!" said an angry voice as I got up from the platform. I had knocked somebody down.

"What in the world is falling from the sky these days?" asked a woman's voice, amused.

I doubt they were amused when I took them apart. I had no time to be gentle and persuasive. But I don't think I killed them. Their instincts and my desires coincided far enough that neither of them came close to falling off the platform and, once I had immobilized them, I took a moment to search them for anything I might be able to steal. I had some vague notion of pretending to be a thief, to throw off the chase.

The man did have a knife, and I took it, along with an iron amulet the woman wore around her neck. Even then I had a vague thought that I might need money once I got away from Nkumai—as if I had a reasonable hope of doing that. Then I found a rope ladder that began at the platform, held my breath, and let myself over the side and down into the darkness.

I descended silently, listening for any tell-tale noise that might come through the night air, telling me that my escape had been discovered, but the night was silent. A dim light began to filter down to my level as the clouds moved away and Dissent came higher into the sky.

As I passed a platform that connected with a rope bridge, I toyed with the idea of getting off the ladder. But I decided to go down at least one more level, putting as much vertical distance between me and my pursuers as possible.

It was a bad decision. I had no sooner passed the platform than the rope ladder began to swing violently, pendulum-fashion. And then it began to rise. They had found me.

My reflexes on the treeway were still slow. It took me a moment to decide to turn around on the ladder, get on the other side, the same side as the platform. By then I was a good three meters above it, and rising fast. I couldn't wait to get the range. I jumped backward when a dead guess told me I should.

I landed on my back and slid in the direction of the grain of the wood, filling my back with splinters. I had so much momentum that I slid right off the platform and down the steep beginning of the rope bridge.

It's one thing to run madly down a rope bridge and up the other side. Sliding down headfirst on your back offers far less control. I spread my feet to try to stop myself by hooking on to the ropes on either side. Unfortunately, my right leg caught first, jerking me in that direction. The side ropes stopped me from falling, but my impact had enough force to tip the entire bridge to the side, spilling me over.

I caught the ropes, and my grip held with a sickening jerk. The bridge was virtually upside down where I hung—and the situation became worse as the wooden treads fell out of position. One of them struck me in the shoulder, and by reflex that hand let go. I held with the other, and quickly recovered my grip. But I could see no way of righting the bridge—it was not like a boat that had capsized. There was no water to support me while I turned up the bridge; in fact, the only way to right the bridge was to let go. And that wouldn't help a bit.

I toyed with the idea of going back, hand-over-hand, to the platform I had left because it was much closer than the other side. But I knew that it wouldn't be long before my followers, undoubtedly guards, were on that platform—and besides, they controlled the only other escape from it, the rope ladder.

So I began to go hand over hand toward the other end of the bridge. I was grateful for my thumbs. Even though the bleeding from my amputated fingers had stopped, my hands were still sore, and not at their strongest as they tried to heal. But I had a grip. At first, at least. After a while I had to twist an arm into the ropes to help support my weight. It slowed me down more, but I still made fair time.

Toward the end of the bridge, the position of the main hawsers forced the bridge to a more normal level, despite my body weight, and I gratefully pulled myself up onto the treads.

Then I felt a bouncing that was not caused by my own motion—someone else was coming along the bridge. Now that it was upright again, they'd make good time, except in the section where the treads had fallen out. And sure enough, I heard a cry of surprise and a sudden lurching of the bridge. Did the man fall through, or catch himself in time? I had no way of knowing; even in the dim light I couldn't see more than two meters ahead of me.

Two meters was enough, however, for me to see that the platform I was approaching was occupied. However, they were obviously not part of the chase—both men were facing away from me. I had no time to waste, and there was no longer any point—if there ever had been—in trying to mask the fact that I was escaping. The knife I had stolen found one man's heart as he turned around to face me, even as the other man fell forever into the night from a sharp kick I landed on the small of his back. He made no sound as he fell.

Pulling the knife out of the Nkumai, I looked around for another escape, and discovered that I was at the crotch of a main trunk and a major branch, not two branches. There was no downward slope—only the straight-down plunge of the trunk. The branch led upward—not the direction I wanted to go. And the bridge was still bouncing with my pursuers' travel. If they hadn't been slowed by the missing treads, they would certainly have reached me by then, accustomed as they were to travel in the dark.

I thought of cutting the rope bridge, but the hawsers were far too thick and I didn't try.

Instead, I decided to go up the branch and hope it led to a route I could use. I was starting the climb when I noticed what the two Nkumai had been working on: a birdnet.

They had been securing the end—the rolled-up net swung out taut into the darkness. At least one other point was secure—and that might be enough.

I tested their knots—they were tight. Then I slithered out feet-first onto the thick roll of the netting. It was rough, and provided enough purchase that I didn't fall, or even swing over to hang from the bottom. And as I crept backward along the net, I cut the strings that held the net in a roll.

When I reached the next tie point, I tested, and found to my relief that the net was tied at the point beyond. I could hear—not very far away—the sound of footsteps reaching the platform I had just left.

Cutting every string as I passed, I continued backward along the net. I could see the net unfolding, falling open along the route I had just traveled. Would my followers try to follow my path along the net? With it open, they would find it considerably harder. Or would they cut the net? It wouldn't hurt me— there was a tie point between me and them. And it would make pursuit impossible.

I could almost hear them trying to decide in the darkness and stillness of the Nkumai night.

How far would the net go down? How far, for that matter, had I descended? What good would it do me to unroll the net if, once I clambered to the bottom, there were still a hundred meters between me and the ground?

The net was long, and when I reached the seventh tie point, it occurred to me that guards would probably be waiting at the platform where the net ended, ready for me to back into them and return to captivity. So I laboriously turned around on the net. It was harder, going face first, but I felt more secure about the chances of surprise. And it was a good thing I did. I was at the ninth tie point when I felt a jiggling on the net. It couldn't be coming from behind me—I would have felt it long ago if someone were pursuing me along the route I had followed. All my training in logic was not required for me to conclude that someone was coming in front of me.

I kept slicing knots in the strings as I proceeded forward. And at the next point, I decided to end my journey along the net. Just beyond the tie I began slicing the net itself. Each string cut easily, even five or six strands together, but there were hundreds in the rolled-up net. And I was so involved that I didn't see my enemy until he was nearly with me.

He had not been cutting knots, of course, and so the net was still thick beneath him, while under and behind me the net fell away, leaving me on a much thinner and so less stable strand. I was halfway—or more—through cutting the net, but he had a knife, too, and I prudently decided that fighting him had a higher priority than cutting string.

That battle was rather one-sided. In good condition on level ground—even on a level platform—I'm sure I could have killed him easily. But on a net, high above the ground, in darkness only faintly relieved by dim and dissipated moonlight, and weakened by loss of blood and the still throbbing amputation of my fingers, I was not in the best of shape. Worse yet, the normal advantage of a Mueller—that we didn't mind a few mortal wounds in the process of battle —didn't apply now, since any weakening would force me to let go of the net and plunge so far to the ground that my chances of healing in time were pretty slim.

Worse yet, it was clear that he wasn't trying to

capture me alive—apparently they thought my corpse would be useful enough, even though it couldn't be interrogated. The brief battle would have ended summarily when he finally pressed his knife into my bowels, if the top of the net hadn't been within reach.

He passed the knife back and forth in my belly, and the pain was strong enough to make me gasp. We could absorb a few simple cuts, but it wasn't part of the Mueller battle training to stand there while the enemy gutted us like a fallen deer. I cut down at his arm and struck flesh, but a moment afterward his hand was back, the knife again stabbing to disembowel me. It was clear that such a trade-off—his arm for my guts—would quickly end with me falling. So instead of attacking him I hacked wildly at the net above, where I had already been cutting. Pain and desperation gave me greater strength, or else the time was actually longer than I thought, but the net soon snapped, and my enemy gave a grunt of surprise as the two halves of the net broke apart, falling away from each other and down. He silently disappeared into darkness, leaving me alone, swinging on the dangling net.

It was now open along the entire remaining length, and I clung to the thin mesh by fingers and toes. The air was cold on my open abdomen. Something hot and wet brushed by my knee, and I realized that some intestine had fallen out.

Disguise of my true sex was hardly important now, and I cut off my black robe at the shoulders, to free me for a scramble down the net. Naked now, and becoming numb to the pain, I began to climb down my remnant of net.

I felt like a crippled spider on a broken web. More than once a strand gave way and I had to grasp for another handhold. Constantly the thin mesh cut into my fingers and toes.

After an eon of descent my foot found nothing under it.

I had reached the bottom of the net, and under it was air.

How much air? Fifty centimeters? Or two hundred meters?

I had no idea how high I had been when I started. Because the net had been cut, the bottom corner, where I now dangled, was lower than the net would have been in its regular open position. The ground might be a single step below me.

But what choice did I have? Weak as I was, my bowels open and dangling, blood still seeping from an impossible jumble of half-healed wounds, I could neither climb up again nor hang on much longer. My only hope of survival was to let go of the net. If the net was low enough, I might be able to land with enough bones intact that I could scramble away in the darkness and find some place to hide while my belly healed. If the net was too high, then they'd find me on the ground in the morning whether I jumped or tried to hang on a little longer.

While I hung there, trying to make a decision, the net began to tear. My weight was too much for a net designed to be invisible to birds. I heard the rapid popping of strands for a moment, and then, my fingers still gripping the strings of the net, I tumbled downward into the black air.

I fell free for a long second. I couldn't even prepare myself to roll on impact, since I couldn't see the ground. I landed on my back, the breath knocked out of me by the impact. And because I hadn't let go of the net, I got tangled up in it, meter after meter piled on and around me.

I was alive.

For just a moment I lay there, almost stunned, tempted by the welcome release of unconsciousness. But I refused. The fact that I had lived to get to the bottom of the Nkumai forest made me determined to try to make good the escape. How long would it take the Nkumai to reach the bottom, going by ladder? And once down here, how long would it take them to reach me? Not long, I decided, and struggled free of the net.

I left some intestine with the net, and the gut still connected to me tried to lurch forward out of the gaping wound with every step I took. Only a hand constantly pressed to my belly held it in. I staggered off in a direction that would take me, I hoped, to the sea. I had lost all conscious sense of direction; I hoped that my unconscious northsense would lead me aright.

Even though my mind was not functioning well, I remember making at least some attempt to hide my trail. I found a brook, and pausing long enough to rinse my wound, the cold water striking my bowel like a club, I followed it downstream a long way. The drinks I occasionally took seemed to refresh me, until the sickening moment when the water reached the disrupted gut. I soon gave up drinking.

I was too mind-numbed to realize what it meant when the sound of the brook got so loud. When the waterfall tumbled off into darkness, I fell with a huge splash into the river below. Again I almost lost consciousness there, and might have drowned except that the current was swift and I was able to keep awake and afloat long enough to reach the other shore. In the river I lost the knife I had managed to keep in the fall. I cared little about that at the time, and slept on the far side of the river, in plain sight on the bank.

I woke with the sun shining dimly through the leaves at the top of the forest, and stayed awake long enough to crawl into some thick brush, where I couldn't be seen from above.

I woke again in darkness, panting with thirst, and though I remembered the agony of the last drink I had taken, I knew that to have any hope of healing, I had to have water in my body. I slid painfully down to the river, my intestine trailing limply behind me, and drank the murky water there. It did not turn to torture in my bowel; apparently my Mueller body was coping even with that massive a wound, and had closed a connection somewhere that let the water through. The connection had bypassed much of my former intestine, however. It still slopped and dragged in the grass and dirt, I was too tired to try to clean it.

Again in daylight the sun roused me. This time I heard talking and calling. Feet ran by on the other side of the river. The Nkumai, so silent and sure in the high trees, were not good at reading groundsigns, or they would have immediately spotted the place where I crawled to the river to drink the night before. I remained quiet and unmoving in the thicket where I lay hidden, and my pursuers soon passed on. I slept again, and again that night I slid down to the water and drank. It felt like the dangling intestine was larger and more awkward to drag with me than before, but it probably felt that way because I was so weary, and so I slept again.

The water was not pure. I began vomiting early that morning, and from the first I was puking blood. I didn't open my eyes, just writhed in agony and panicked as I feared that my fever would lead to delirium, and delirium would call my would-be killers.

I don't know how many days after that I was feverish and unconscious. But I was vaguely aware that I recovered strength enough to walk, always in a stupor, staggering through the forest. Only the ignorance of the Nkumai saved me—I wasn't aware enough to be careful. Perhaps I walked at night. Perhaps they had given up the search. I don't know. But I moved from the river to cleaner brooks, and drank;

the trees were an endless brown blur; the sun was merely a bright spot in the green from time to time; I knew nothing of what was transpiring.

And I dreamed that as I traveled I was not alone. I dreamed that someone traveled with me, someone to whom I spoke softly and explained all the wisdom of my fevered brain. I dreamed I held a child in my arms. I dreamed I was a father, and unlike *my* father, I would not, *did* not, disinherit my worthiest son because of some crime beyond his control. I dreamed, and then tried one day to set the child down so I could drink.

But the child would not leave my arms. And gradually, as I struggled to push the child away, I realized that birds were singing, the sun was shining, sweat was dripping from my chin, and I was not asleep.

The boy was whimpering.

The boy was real.

I remembered now how the child had cried out in hunger. I remembered now how I had deliriously crooned to him as I walked along, how we had slept snuggled together. It was all so clear—except where he had come from.

It took little investigation to discover. He was joined to me at the waist by a bridge of flesh. Gut to gut, and his food must have been whatever strength he could draw from my body. His legs dangled to within a foot of the ground when I stood erect; his head was only a little shorter than my own; and as I looked into his eyes, I realized they were mine.

Radical regenerative. I could heal anything. And when half my guts were torn away, connected to my body only by arteries and veins, my body just couldn't decide which was the real me, which part of me to heal. So it healed both halves, and I stood looking into the eyes of my perfect duplicate, who smiled timidly at me like a stupid but sweet-tempered child.

No, not a child. He had grown quickly, and a faint

down of hair around the cheeks and lips hinted at
oncoming adolescence. He was thin, starved; his naked ribs protruded. So did mine. My body, unsure
which of us to save, had raided my body to give
strength to his, and now struggled for a balance.

I did not want a balance.

I remember the monstrous rad I had seen lurching
toward the troughs in the laboratories, and imagined
myself there, ready to be harvested. But I had created,
not a mere head, but an entire body. And when I was
ripe for the plucking, and they cut the bodies apart,
which would be me, and which would they send?

At this moment there was still no doubt which of
us was the original Lanik Mueller. I had breasts; I
had a tiny arm growing out of my shoulder, already
with fingers that clasped and curled. It had not grown
at all since I escaped from the Nkumai prison; I
bitterly congratulated my body on having its priorities straight, healing my gut wound before bothering
with a surplus arm. Good job.

Was the new me alive? Human? Intelligent? I didn't
think to ask. I only knew that I would not live with
two of me.

I was naked and had no knife. But the connection
between us was still only the thin folds of tissue,
rich with arteries, that had kept him alive during his
gestation.

It. That had kept *it* alive. If I let the creature become *him* in my mind, then it was only a short shift
to thinking of him as me. As it was I could hardly
bear thinking of *me* as me.

Its hair grew as mine did, the same curls and twists,
wild and tangled. I tore at the hair, tried to push it
away. Of course it could not go. But it could not stay,
either. It was myself, exactly myself, as I had been
only a few months ago, before my body had changed
to make room for a woman who did not belong there,
a woman they insisted was myself.

Without a weapon, the operation of severance was filthy and painful. The creature awoke as I hacked at our connection with a sharpened stone. It wept, tried feebly to stop me. But it did not speak.

We both bled as the skin broke, as I ripped us apart, as I carved my freedom from the burden of bearing myself.

At last we were separated. My body was weak from having created him, but with all the strength I had I brought the stone down on his head, again and again. Its head. It stopped crying, and the broken skull poured brains. I was sobbing from the exertion, from seeing myself die. I threw down the stone and fled into the forest.

I ate what I could find, trying to gather strength. I saw no more signs of my pursuers—they must have given up the hunt long ago. But that didn't help me escape. If they found me again, my fate would be quick. From where I was, all directions led deeper into Nkumai territory—all but one. From the sun's position I calculated a rough northwest and headed that way.

Travel was hard, for I wasn't strong, but at least now I was conscious. I took the trip in easy stages, each day a little closer, following a brook to a river, the river to, eventually, the sea.

Of course, there was an Nkumai city by the river-mouth, but it was in the trees, except for a few buildings by a rough wharf. They were not sea people, I realized; they had not adapted as we of Mueller had. I remembered the huge fleet that had sailed out the Sleeve from Mueller, carrying thousands of troops that conquered Huntington in less than a month. From Nkumai no ships would sail.

But ships from other lands might come. And such a ship was my only hope of getting out of Nkumai and eventually getting word to Father about what the Nkumai sold to the Ambassador.

I waited until night, then walked under the Nkumai city to the sea. I kept to the border of the forest and walked a couple of kilometers up the coast from the wharf. I could watch for ships from there, and if I could still swim as well as I used to, I could get aboard with no trouble.

Secure in my hiding place, I slept.

I woke at midday, panting and sweating. I had dreamed that I—but it was not I, it was the child-self I had killed in the forest—I dreamed that I had come to kill me, and I had wakened as knives flashed, as both I and my mirror image stabbed deep and found each other's hearts.

I vaguely remembered being wakened from the dream by a cry, and wondered if I had called out in my sleep. But when I crept from hiding and looked toward the sea, I saw a ship passing near shore, and the cries were coming from men who were trimming the sails.

The ship put into the port, and for the two days it stayed I tried to calculate how I could attract the attention of the sailors without calling the Nkumai from the city to find me.

I found a rotted branch and tested it in the water. It would float. Even if I was too weak to make the distance, I would have the branch to support me. The water was cold on my naked skin, but as I saw the ship pull away from the wharf and turn northeast, toward me, I splashed out into the water, and then, lying on the log as if I already needed it, paddled awkwardly out past the gathering breakers into the gentle swells of a calm sea.

Someone on the ship shouted, "Man in the sea! Man!"

I raised a hand and waved.

In a short time I was picked up from the water, and sat shivering under a blanket in a small boat heading for the ship.

"Thank you," I said.

One of the oarsmen grinned. Not a particularly genial smile. And the rudderman said, "Fine. Take you to captain."

"What nation are you from?"

They seemed reluctant to answer. I wondered whether they had understood.

"What Family? What Family does your ship come from?"

Grudgingly the rudderman replied, "Singer."

The island people from the great North Bay, who had been conquering in Wing when I left Mueller. The emissary from Wankier had asked my father for troops, knowing his nation would be next, but he had gone away with our sympathy and little else. But at least these sailors were not Nkumai, and they had enough humanity to pull me from the water. I might live.

The captain looked little kinder than his crew, and after I was taken aboard, he spent little time in interviewing me. "Nation?" he asked, and because I thought it prudent not to tell the truth, I said, "Allison. I just escaped from an Nkumai prison camp."

He nodded reflectively, then made a motion. A few sailors came and tore the blanket from me.

"My God," said the captain, "what are those bastards doing to prisoners these days?"

I didn't answer. Let him think what he liked, I thought defiantly. But I was afraid.

"Which is it? Man or woman? Which is real?"

"Both, now," I said truthfully, and he shook his head.

"Impossible," he said. "This makes things very difficult. How will I know how to price you?"

Price me? And then I remembered something else the Wankier emissary had said. That Singer had a thriving business going. In human flesh.

"Amusement," another officer said. "Put him in a cage and charge money."

"Good," said the captain. "And I think the best market is Rogers. They have circuses. Drop him."

The command had barely been given when I was picked up and carried to a hatch. They opened it and thrust me down. I landed heavily. The hatch closed above me.

There was no light. There was little air. But I was alive. It hadn't occurred to me to resist. What mattered was that I had value to them; only the dead have no hope.

But Rogers was at the southwest corner of the continent. The trip would take months. Would it then be too late for me to get my information about Nkumai to my father? I didn't know. And it didn't matter. There was little enough I could do about it until I got out.

Had they noticed the extra arm growing from my shoulder? In the bright sunlight, perhaps not; staring at my breasts and genitals, they were distracted. But now the arm flexed involuntarily, tickling me on the back. It was going to be a long trip.

5   MONSTER

It was hard to amuse myself, locked alone in utter darkness, stark naked, with about two square meters of floor space. Sleep took up a large amount of my time, of course, but was hardly restful—it was impossible to straighten my body all at once. As the ship sailed north, cold seeped in; as it went south again, the cell became a sweatbox, with not just my body but also the walls dripping with my sweat. The smell of salt was always with me.

Yet it could have been worse. While I did not see the sun for nearly five months, I was fed, and I learned to appreciate the subtle flavors of wormy meat and moldy bread. The bucket was lowered to me each morning, filled with water; each evening, filled with food. When I had emptied the bucket, I refilled it, determined to keep the cell as clean as I could without being able to see. I think they rinsed it in seawater before putting my food and drink in it again. Even the cruelest farmer takes care that his cattle don't get sick.

There *were* sounds. My only contact with other people came from noises above me, below me: the cries of the men in the spars, the snapping of sailcloth in the wind; the morning and evening prayers as the crew sang and chanted hauntingly, and some men wept their confessions to the captain; the curses, the quarrels, the jokes, the fumbling attempts at seduction by men who had been so long at sea that other men began to look beautiful to them. I came to know all their names. Roos and Nose-up had a running quarrel that sounded like friendly banter to me, until one night someone had a knife and Roos died right over my hatch. The blood dripped through before they washed the deck, and I heard Nose-up plead for mercy before they hanged him by his thumbs and fired arrows into his limbs until he bled to death. Funny—he wept and begged until the first arrow. Then he seemed to realize that this was exactly as bad as the pain would get, that they could do no more to him. He began to tell jokes and throw gibes at the archers, and just before he died he told a sentimental story about his mother that had most of the men somber and some shamelessly in tears. I think that was when they finally let him die, by giving him an arrow in the heart. A strange people, at once cruel and kind, strong and weak, and so quick to change from one extreme to the other that I could not predict what they would do.

Except the captain, who was an island of strength amid the confusion. He was a father to a shipful of children, hearing their complaints patiently, mediating their quarrels, forgiving their sins, teaching them their tasks, and making all but their most trivial decisions for them. I marveled at him, for I rarely heard him angry, and then only momentarily, for effect; he never wavered, never broke. I always knew his footsteps on the deck. Step, step, step, in perfect rhythm. It was as if even the sliding deck held firm for him, and he did not have to compromise with the rolling sea. He reminded me of my father, and I longed to go home.

But there is a limit to how much sympathy a slave can have for his owners. After a while the darkness caved in on me, and I resented having to wake up, resented having to go to sleep, and above all dreamed of sunlight. I was a horseman, not a seaman. My idea of travel is with surging flesh between my legs, or my own feet slapping the ground underneath me, not bounding from side to side and up and down and back and forth with the roll, pitch, and yaw of the boat at sea.

Besides, the effects of my visit among the Nkumai were not over. The massive regenerative effort of my body that resulted in the creation of my erstwhile double did not end with the amputation. Instead, my body seemed determined to regenerate every part of me. Within a few weeks of the start of my captivity, the arm sprouting from my shoulder was long enough and developed enough that I could scratch my back with it as it dangled. Other limbs quickly sprouted, other growths began. And while there was plenty of food to sustain the growth, I had no chance for exercise; all the energy I took in only had one outlet. Growth.

The heat had been unbearable for days when I finally realized that I was losing my mind. I found myself lying in the grass by Cramer River, watching the light fishing boats skim upstream with the wind. Beside me was Saranna, her robe falling open carelessly (though I knew she was aware of just how much arousal each centimeter of exposure produced), her finger tickling me unbearably while I pretended not to feel it. I saw all this, I was doing this, while wide awake, curled in a ball on the floor of my steaming hot prison.

I was doing this while the fifth leg to grow from my hips began twitching awkwardly, beginning to come to life. That was the reality. The sweat dripping on my breasts. The darkness. The destruction of my body. The loss of freedom.

This is how the rads in the pens endure it, I realized. They live another life. They are not wallowing in dirt or grass, feeding at troughs—their bodies are sound and whole again, and they lie by riverbanks preparing to make love to a lover who, in reality, dares not now remember that they live.

But as soon as I realized that such madness was my only means of escape, I determined not to use it. I determined, instead, to keep my mind awake in this present reality, unbearable as it was.

I have a good memory. Not a phenomenal one— I can't conjure up written pages one by one—but I began to use my time to put together all I had learned while reading history in Mwabao Mawa's farthest room.

Mueller—genetics.

Nkumai—physics.

Bird—high society.

These stuck easily in my mind. But again and again I forced myself to go back, let the trance of madness take me somewhere useful, until I remembered others. Not all, but others.

Schwartz, lost to all human contact on the desert—she had been a geologist. Wasted on this world without hard metals.

Allison—theology. Much good it had done them.

Underwood—botany. And now in the high mountains, what flowers did his children hopelessly grow?

Hanks—psychology, the treatment of the mad. No help for me.

Anderson—the useless leader of the rebellion, whose only gift was politics.

Drew—dreams and their interpretation.

Who had found what to export? I didn't know. But surely in my father's library were the books that would tell what I couldn't remember; books that would fill in the gaps and give us hints of what projects were secretly being worked on in other Families. Some, of course, would have given way to despair, having nothing that on this world could possibly be of value to the Ambassador—the engineers, for instance, Cramer and Wizer. They had been easy to conquer, farmers now, having forgotten lore that could never be put to adequate use on this world. And Ku Kuei, a philosopher whose ideas obviously had no wide audience in the Republic—he had never lived to found a family. Perhaps in his wisdom he determined that his last act of rebellion was to disappear, to die, so that his children would not be prisoners on Treason forever.

But iron had come at last to Nkumai and Mueller. Physics and genetics. They with ideas, we with products. Our products would never run out; would their ideas? It didn't matter, not if they were getting paid so much iron for each idea that they could overwhelm us quickly.

I would never make it to Mueller in time.

Resist it though I did, I doubt I held off the madness altogether. Because I remember, as if it were real, a creature like myself who came and laughed at me in my cell. He could have been Lanik as I remembered me from mirrors in my early adolescence, except that the side of his head was bashed in and his brains kept sloughing out. Yet he carried on a pleasant conversation and only at the end did he try to kill me. I strangled him with four arms, tore him apart. I remember it clearly.

I also remember my brother, Dinte, visiting me. He cut me into little pieces, and each grew up into a little Lanik, so small at adulthood that Dinte had great fun smashing them with his boots. Perhaps I screamed then—Dinte fled when someone beat on the hatch above me.

Ruva came, too, her mouth full, but bragging to me as she chewed that she had got my father's testicles at last, had got them and was chewing them up, and I was next. She had a hideous little boy with her, wearing a mockery of my father's face; at the age of—what, ten?—he still drooled. His wet chin shone in the light. Yet I knew it could not be real, because there was never light in my cell except a dazzle for a moment as the bucket was lowered or raised.

And an old woman from the high hills of Mueller kept bringing me arrows until I was half-buried in them.

These mad waking dreams I remember as clearly as I remember my father teaching me to cut down a man from horseback or giving me grief and wiping the blood on his face as he told me my fate. In retrospect I have learned to distinguish which of my memories were real from those that could not have been. At the time it was not so clear.

One day I heard a new sound. It was not unusual in intensity, but I realized I was hearing new voices. The ship had not put into any port. No one had come alongside. Obviously, then, they were letting slaves out of the cells and onto the deck. This meant we were nearing port—atrophied muscles must now be awakened so the slaves would make a good showing in the markets of Rogers and Dunn and Dark.

But that first day no one let me out, and I wondered why.

By the second day I reasoned that because I was not to be sold for labor, it didn't matter if I seemed strong. I was to be a freak. I wondered grimly what my owners would think of me now. A new nose was growing alongside and partly joined to the old. On the left side of my head, three ears protruded from my shaggy hair. My body was a hodgepodge of arms and legs that had never been taught to walk or grasp. They thought they had a curiosity before. I would be a one-man circus now.

Above me, other slaves were walking, could see, could feel the sun and the wind. And I could not.

I began shouting. My voice was unaccustomed to speaking, and my mind had lost its command of words. I made little sense, I'm sure. But gradually I increased in volume and my feeding hatch popped open.

"You want your ass kicked up your chest?" asked a voice I knew too well, though I had no idea who owned it.

"I'll do the ass-kicking!" I yelled back. My voice didn't have quite the effect it used to have on training fields when I maneuvered cavalry troops without the help of a caller. But it did well enough. Instead of a kick, I got another voice.

"Listen, Trash," he said, "up to now you've been a model slave. Don't start giving us shit except in your bucket, if you know what's good for you!"

"Take me out!"

"No slaves on deck."

"There are ten slaves on deck right now!"

"They're farmers. You're a sideshow."

"I'll kill myself."

"Naked? In the dark?"

"I'll lie on my back and bite my tongue off and drown on the blood!" I shouted, and for a moment I meant it, though I knew perfectly well that my tongue would heal too damn fast. I must have sounded crazy, though, because a new voice came. It was the captain.

He spoke softly, and the threat in his voice was clear. "There's only one reason we ever let a slave on deck out of turn. It's for punishment."

"Punish me! Just do it in sunlight."

"The punishment usually begins with removal of the tongue."

I laughed. "What do you do for an encore?"

"We finish up by cutting off your balls." He meant it. A eunuch would fetch as good a price as a breeding slave. But that's only a mildly frightening threat to a man who already has three pairs of testicles. Maybe it was the testosterone that had given me an over-large shot of courage.

"You can fry them and feed them to me for breakfast! Let me out!"

It wasn't entirely courage, of course. I knew my main value to them was as a freak. No one wants to see a freak that's been mutilated by men. Nature's mutilations only, please. They wouldn't harm me. In the meantime, the thought of another slave being on deck when I was stuck in a hole was the most outrageous provocation I had yet had in my life.

Still, I was surprised when they gave in and tossed ropes down to me. I took them and held on with four arms as they pulled me up.

I was more surprised at the intensity of their reaction, though I should have expected it: They had put a man with a large bosom in that cell, or a woman with a prick. They pulled out a monster.

I couldn't see anything. The light was too dazzling, and it was hard enough finding my balance on legs that had not really stood up in months. Some of my legs had never borne weight at all. I couldn't walk —I could only lurch from one side to the other, struggling for equilibrium.

They weren't helping. Their screams were deafening, and I kept hearing the word *devil* and other words whose meaning I couldn't guess, except that the sailors were terribly frightened. Of me.

I knew an opportunity when I saw one.

I roared. They answered with a uniform shriek, and I made some fumbling steps toward the loudest group of screamers. I was answered with an arrow in my arm.

I am a Mueller. The pain didn't stop me, and as for the arm, I had several others just as good—two, in fact, that were much better, since they had injured an arm that I didn't use much. I kept on advancing.

And now the terror had turned to awe. An arrow had not made the monster pause.

The captain was shouting. Orders, I supposed. I squinted against the light to try to see. The ocean was dazzling blue. The ship and everyone on it were invisible, shadows that flashed until I had to close my eyes again.

I heard someone coming, felt the vibration of the footsteps on the deck. I turned awkwardly, met the rush. It was then that I discovered I had grown an extra heart—his wooden knife found the one I was used to, and it didn't stop me. I only knew weaponless warfare with my two original arms, but rather than let the sailors notice that fact, I got my extras into the act. They made me fumble at it, but it only delayed me a moment, and in this case delay was rather to my benefit. I took my attacker apart and threw pieces of him to the waiting sailors. I heard vomiting. I heard praying. I heard freedom.

The captain's voice again. But this time conciliatory. It was unnerving to hear him humbled. I felt ashamed, for a moment, of having weakened him.

"Sir, whoever you are," he said, "remember that we saved your life from the sea when we brought you aboard."

I only squinted at him and waved my arms. I could vaguely see that he stepped back. They were afraid of me. Had good reason to be. The wound in my heart had already closed up. Oh, what fun we radical regeneratives can have in a pinch.

"Sir," he said, "whatever god you are or whatever god you serve, we entreat you—tell us what you want, and we'll give it to you, if you'll only go back into the sea."

Back into the sea was out of the question. I was a good swimmer—with two arms and two legs. I had more ballast now, and a bit less coordination.

"Set me on the land," I said, "and we'll be even."

If I had been thinking well, or if I could have seen better, I would have attempted to tyrannize them a little longer and get to more friendly shores. But I couldn't see, not until I was in the prow of the long-boat, with six petrified crewmen jerkily coming to life whenever the swain commanded them to row, then turning back to stone, their eyes riveted on me. That was when my sight came clear—but my back was to the shore.

We touched bottom, and I clumsily lifted myself over the prow and splashed through the water. Only when I found dry land did I look up and see where I was.

I turned as quickly as I could, to see the longboat already nearly at the slaveship. There would be no calling them back. I had just cleverly forced them to help me kill myself.

I stood naked on a beach a few hundred meters broad. Behind it rose the craggy, rough slopes of stone and sand that was called by Mueller's sailors "Sand-wash." Behind it was the bitterest desert in the world. Better to surrender to an enemy than run aground here, where there were no paths, where boats never stopped, and where walking inland only took you deep into the unknown desert of Schwartz. Nothing lived. Not even the scrub brush of the wastes on the west shore of the Sleeve. Not even an insect. Nothing.

It was afternoon. The sun was hot. My skin, white as the clouds from my long confinement, was already burning. Without water, how long would I last?

If only I had kept my mouth shut in my cool, shaded, well-watered cell. If only I had said things to dispel the crew's fear.

I walked because there was nothing else to do. Because old stories told of huge rivers in the center of Schwartz that sank beneath the desert before they escaped into other lands. Because I didn't want my skeleton to be discovered right on the shore, as if I hadn't had guts enough to try to do *something*.

There was no wind.

By nightfall I was already breathlessly thirsty, excruciatingly tired. I had not got to the top of the rise; the sea looked ridiculously close. With so many limbs, I wasn't much of a climber. I couldn't sleep, so I forced unready and unwilling muscles to take me farther in the darkness. The darkness was welcome, and cold came to the desert, bringing relief after the heat of the day. It was summer, or might as well have been, but the night was colder than I had thought possible in such a place, and I kept moving even after I wanted to sleep because movement kept me warmer.

When the sun rose, I was exhausted. But I had reached the top, and could look forward and see endless dunes of sand, with mountains in the distance here and there; I could look back and see, far in the distance, the bright blue ocean. There was no ship in sight. And on land, there was no shade—nowhere I could rest for the heat of the day.

So I walked, arbitrarily picking a mountain as my goal so that I would have one. It seemed to be as close as any, and as impossible to reach. I would die today, I suspected; I was fat from lack of exercise, weak from lack of hope.

By afternoon I merely concentrated on moving forward. No thought of life or death now. Just step. And step again.

That night I slept in the sand, with no insects buzzing around my head because no insects were foolish enough to try to survive where I was.

I surprised myself. I woke up, and walked on. My point of death was farther off than I thought. But surely not much farther. My shadow was still on the morning side when I reached a place where the sand gave way to stone and a rough outcropping of rock. Whether it was a shoulder of a mountain I was too incurious to care. It gave shade. And as I lay down in the shade my heart stopped beating and I gasped for breath and discovered that death was not so bad after all, if only it would come quickly, if only it wouldn't linger, if only I didn't have to lie there for an eternity before I was free to go.

6   SCHWARTZ

He leaned over me, and my eyes could not focus. But he was a man, not a nightmare of Dinte or the Turd or even myself.

"Would you like to die?" he asked in a young voice, a serious voice. I considered the alternatives. If living meant another day on the desert like the ones I had already spent, the answer was yes. But then, this person, this hallucination, whoever he was, was alive. One could live on this desert.

"No," I said.

He did nothing. Just watched me.

"Water," I said.

He nodded. I forced myself to rise, to lean on two elbows as he took a step away from me. Was he going for help? He stopped and squatted on the rock. He was naked and carried nothing with him—not even a water bottle. That meant water was close. Why was he waiting? It should be obvious I couldn't pay him. Or did he consider me, in my monstrous shape, not human? I had to drink, or I would die.

"Water," I repeated. He said nothing, didn't even nod this time. Just looked at the sand. I could feel my heart beating inside me—beating vigorously and well. It was hard to believe that just a short time ago it had stopped. Where had this boy come from?

Why didn't he get water? Did he plan to watch me die, for sport?

I looked at the sand where he was staring. It was moving.

It shifted sloppily to the left and right, then caved in in small patches, falling down, slipping into something, splashing softly, collapsing, until a circle about a meter and a half across was filled with softly swirling water, black water that blinded me with reflected sunlight.

He looked at me. I awkwardly lifted myself (every muscle aching except my strong, youthful heart) and pulled myself to the water. It was still now. Still and cool and deep and good, and I plunged my head in and drank. I came up for air only when I had to.

At last I was satisfied, and I lifted myself and then let myself drop on the sand beside the water. I was too tired to wonder why sand should come up water, or how the boy had known it would. Too tired to wonder why now the water seeped down into the sand and left a dark stain that soon evaporated in the sun. Too tired to answer clearly when the boy looked at my body and asked, "Why are you like that? So strange?"

"God knows I wish I weren't," I said, and then I slept again. Slept this time not expecting death but expecting, somehow, through a coincidence of having been found right beside a spring in this waterless desert, to live.

When I woke again it was night, and I had forgotten the boy entirely. I opened my eyes and saw his friends in the moonlight.

They were silent, sitting around me in a circle, a dozen sun-blackened men with sun-blonded hair, as naked as the boy had been. Their eyes were on me, unmoving. They were alive and so was I and I had no objections.

I would have spoken, would have asked them to shelter me, except that I was sidetracked. I noticed my body from the inside. Noticed that there was nothing to notice. Something was terribly wrong.

No. Something was terribly right.

There was no pulling on my left side where three legs tried to balance two. There was no odd arching of my back to compensate for all the limbs resting awkwardly under me as I slept. There was no pinch of air painfully being drawn in through an extra nose.

From the inside, all I felt were two arms, two legs, the sex I had been born with, a normal face. Not even breasts. Not even that.

I raised my left hand (only one!) and touched my chest. Rounded only with muscle. Hard with muscle. I slapped myself on the chest, and my arm was alive and strong.

What was real? What was the dream? Had I not been confined in a cell on a ship for several months? Was that, too, a hallucination? If it was, how had I come here, I wondered. I could not believe that I was, again, normal.

It was then that I remembered the boy and the water that had come from the desert. This, too, was a dream, then. Impossible things were happening as I died. Dreams of water. Dreams of a whole normal body. These were the dreams of a dying man. Time was being extended in my last remaining moments of life.

Except my heart was beating too strongly to ignore. And I felt as full of life as I had before I ever left Mueller. If this is death, give me more, I thought.

I asked them, "Did you cut them off?"

They didn't answer for a moment. Then one asked, "Cut?"

"Cut," I said. "To make me like this. Normal."

"Helmut said you wanted them off."

"They'll only grow back."

The man who was speaking to me looked puzzled. "I don't think so," he said. "We fixed that."

Fixed that. Undoing what a hundred generations of Muellers had tried to cure and couldn't. So this was what Schwartz had come to. The arrogance of savages.

I stopped myself in mid-contempt. Whatever they had done, it shouldn't have worked this way. When something was cut off a radical regenerative, it grew back, no matter what. Radical regeneratives grew back every impossible limb and added more until they died of sheer mass and unwieldiness. Yet when they cut my limbs off and my breasts and all the other extras, the wounds had healed without a scar, normally.

My body was in its proper shape, and when the boy had stared at the sand, water had risen, and I had drunk of it. Their seeming arrogance—could it, after all, be mere confidence? If what I was seeing and feeling was real, these people, these Schwartzes, had something too valuable to believe.

"How did you do it?" I asked.

"From the inside," the man answered, beaming. "We only work from the inside. Do you want to continue your walk now?"

It was an absurd question. I had been dying of thirst on the desert, a helpless monster, and they had saved my life and cured my deformity. Now did they expect me to wander on through the sand, as if I had some errand that their intervention had delayed?

"No," I said.

They sat, silently. What were they waiting for? In Mueller, a man didn't wait a minute before inviting a stranger—particularly a helpless one—into his home for shelter, unless he thought the man was an enemy, in which case he let off an arrow at the first opportunity. But these people—waited.

Different people, different customs. "Can I stay with you?" I asked.

They nodded. But they said nothing more.

I became impatient. "Will you take me to your home, then?"

They looked at each other. They shrugged.

"What do you mean?" they asked.

I cursed in my mind. A common language all over the planet, and they couldn't understand a simple word like *home*.

"Home," I said. "Where you live."

They looked around again, and the spokesman said, "We're alive now. We don't go to a certain place to live."

"Where do you go to get out of the sun?"

"It's night," said the man, incredulous. "We're not *in* the sun."

This was getting nowhere. But I was surprised and gratified that I was physically up to the challenge of conversing with them. I would live—I was whole and strong and talkative again, that was plain.

"I need to go with you. I can't live here on the desert alone."

Several of them—the ones who seemed oldest, but who could tell?—nodded sagely. Of course, they seemed to say. There are people like that, aren't there?

"I'm a stranger to the desert. I don't know how the hell anyone survives here. Perhaps you can take me to the edge of the desert. To Sill, perhaps, or Wong."

A few of them giggled. "Oh, no," the spokesman said, "we'd rather not. But you can live with us, and stay with us, and learn from us, and be one of us."

But no visits to the borders? Fine, for now. Fine, until I knew how to survive in this hell where they seemed to be so comfortable. In the meantime, I was delighted to live with them and learn from them— the alternative being death.

"Yes," I said. "I'll be one of you."

"Good," said the spokesman. "We examined you. You've got good brains."

I was amused and slightly offended. I was the product of the finest education the most civilized Family in the West could provide, and these savages had examined my brain and decided it was good. "Thanks," I murmured. "What about food?"

They shrugged again, puzzled. It was going to be a long night. I was too tired to deal with this. It would all go away when I woke up for real in the morning. Or when I finished dying. So I lay back and slept again.

I was still alive in the morning.

"I'm with you today," said the boy who had found me. "I'm told to give you what you need."

"Breakfast," I said.

"What's that?" he answered.

"Food. I'm hungry."

He shook his head. "No. You're not."

I was about to take his head off for impertinence when I realized that, despite having eaten nothing for days before, I wasn't hungry at all. So I decided not to belabor the point. The sun was already hot, and it was barely dawn. My skin, which was fair and burned easily at the beginning of every summer, was already browned and able to endure the direct sunshine. And another day had come with my body as it should be. I jumped up (had I ever felt this good upon rising?) and leaped from the rock where I had slept into the sand below, bellowing at the top of my voice. I couldn't help myself. I ran a large circle, then awkwardly turned a somersault in the sand, landing sprawled on my back.

The boy laughed.

"Name!" I shouted. "What's your name?"

"Helmut," he answered.

"And my name's Lanik!" I called back. He grinned broadly, then jumped down and ran to me. He stopped only a meter off, and I snaked out a hand to trip him. I was not used to men anticipating my attacks, but Helmut jumped in the air the exact fraction of a centimeter required to make me miss him. Then he lightly jumped over me, tapping my hip with both feet before I could react.

"Quick little grasshopper, aren't you?" I said.

"Slow as a rock, aren't you?" he answered, and I lunged at him. This time he let me engage, and we wrestled for fifteen minutes or so, my weight and strength making it impossible for him to pin me, his speed getting him out of my grasp when I had him in holds no one had ever been able to resist before.

"We're a match?" he asked.

"I want you," I said, "in my army."

"What's an army?"

In my world, up to then, that was akin to asking, "What's the sun?"

"What's wrong with you?" I demanded. "You don't know about food, about breakfast, about armies—"

"We are not civilized," he said. Then he flashed a broad grin and took off running. I had done that as a child, forcing governors, trainers, and teachers to chase wherever I went. Now I was the follower, and I scrambled after him, up rocky hills and skimming down the faces of sand dunes. The sun was hot and I was pouring with sweat when I finally ran around a rock he had passed only a moment before, to have him jump on my shoulders from above. "Ride, horse! Ride!" he shouted.

I reached up and pulled him off—he was lighter than his size would indicate. "Horses," I said. "You know horses?"

He shrugged. "I know that civilized people ride horses. What's a horse?"

"What's a rock?" I answered, in exasperation.

"Life," he answered.

"What kind of answer is that? Rock is dead if anything is!"

His face went dark. "They told me you're a child, and so I, who choose to be a child, should teach you. But you're too stupid to be a child."

I am not used to being called stupid. But in the last few months I had had ample reason to realize that I would not always be treated like the best soldier in Mueller, and I held my tongue. Besides, he had said *choose*.

"Teach me then," I said.

"We begin," he said instantly, as if he could teach me only as soon as I asked, "with rock." He ran his finger delicately along the face of the rock. "The rock lives," he said.

"Yeah," I answered.

"We stand on his skin," he said. "Underneath he seethes with hot blood, like a man. Here on his skin, he's dry. Like a man. But he's kind, he'll do good to a man, if the man will only speak to him."

Religion again. Except—and it nagged at me, though I tried to put it out of my mind—they had cured me.

"How do you—uh, speak to rock?" I asked.

"We hold him in our mind. And if he knows we're not rock killers, he helps us."

"Show me," I said.

"Show you what?"

"How you talk to the rock."

He shook his head. "I can't show you, Lanik-e. You must do it yourself."

I imagined myself in animated conversation with a pebble and consigned myself to the madhouse, where I had so recently been. Reality was still up for grabs to me, and I wondered if it was I who was hearing wrong, not he who was speaking foolishly. "I don't know how."

"I know," he said, nodding helpfully.

"What happens when you talk to the rock?" I asked.

"He listens. He answers."

"What does he say?"

"It can't be said by mouths."

I was getting nowhere. It was like a game. Nothing could be done for me unless I asked for it, and even then if I asked in the wrong way, I wouldn't get it. Like food—only as soon as I thought of it, I realized I still wasn't hungry.

"Look, Helmut, what kinds of things will the rock *do*?"

He smiled. "What could a man need from rock?"

"Iron," I suggested.

He looked angry. "The iron of this world is hidden far below the surface, where men can never go."

"A path up a high cliff," I said, hoping to soothe him by taking his mind off my first suggestion. The sheer rock face beside us was formidable—I had wondered, briefly, how Helmut scaled it.

Now he was staring intently at the rock, as he had stared at the sand when I first met him. And as I watched him, I heard a faint rustling sound. I looked around, and sand was pouring from a small pocket on the face of the cliff—in a spot where no pocket had been. The sand stopped. I reached over and brushed it out, put my toes in it, and raised myself. I reached up, could find no handhold above me.

"Hold still," said the boy, and suddenly sand fell away under my fingers, making a handhold. It was as if a hundred small spiders had suddenly erupted from the rock, and I pulled my hand away, brushed off the sand.

Helmut clicked his tongue. "No. You *must* climb. Don't reject the gift." He was serious. So I climbed, new handholds and footholds appearing where I needed them, until I was at the top.

I sat, breathless; not from the climb, but from what could only be magic. Helmut stood far below, looking up at me. I was not ready to come down. My hands were trembling. "Come up!" I called.

He did not use my handholds. Instead, he went to a face where the cliff was smooth and unbroken, and crawled quickly up it. His toes had little contact with the rock—just his knees and hands. I leaned over the edge watching him, and felt a terrible vertigo, as if gravity had switched directions and he was on level ground, while I clung, incredibly, to a cliff.

"What *is* this place?" I said, or rather whispered, when he reached the top and sat beside me. "What kind of people are you?"

"We're savages," he said, "and this is the desert."

"No!" I shouted. "No evasions! You know what I'm asking! You do things that human beings simply can't do!"

"We don't kill," he said.

"That doesn't explain anything."

"We don't kill animals," he said. "We don't kill plants. We don't kill rock. We don't kill water. We leave all beings alive, and they also leave us alive. We're savages."

"How can you kill a rock?"

"By cutting him," he said. He seemed to shudder.

"Rock is pretty tough," I answered, feeling superior again. "It doesn't feel pain, or so I've heard."

"Rock is alive," he said, "from the skin to his deepest heart. Here on the surface, he holds us up. Some of his skin he sheds and peels as we do, in sand and gravel and boulders. But it's still part of him. When men cut the rock, it no longer falls where it should; they take the rock and make false mountains of it, and that rock is dead. It's no longer part of him. It's all lost to him until, over the centuries, he can break it back into sand. He could kill you all, by sneezing," said Helmut angrily, "but he doesn't. Because he respects even evil life. Even *civilized* life."

Helmut did not sound like a child.

"But he *will* kill," said Helmut, "if the need is great and the time is right. When the civilized men of Sill decided they must own more of this desert, they came with armies to kill us. Many women lived there, the peaceful sleepers, and the men of Sill killed them. So we held a council, Lanik, and we spoke to the rock, and he agreed with us that this was a time for justice."

He stopped. "And?" I prodded.

"And he swallowed them."

I imagined the horsemen of Sill out in the desert sand, suddenly finding the grains heaving and sifting under them, their horses sinking, their footing impossible, the sand closing over their heads as they screamed and choked and swallowed sand and were swallowed by sand until their bones were rubbed clean.

"Sill has never sent an army into the desert again," said Helmut. "That was when we knew we were savages. Civilized men don't value rocks above men. But then, savages don't kill sleeping women. Do they?"

"Is this true?" I asked.

"Did you climb this cliff?"

I lay back and stared into the blue sky, where not a cloud passed. "How? Why do *you* know how to communicate with the rock—" I couldn't finish. It sounded stupid.

"You're ashamed," he said.

"Damn right," I answered.

"You're a child. But the rock is easiest to speak to. It's simple. It's large. So large that you can grasp it easily. Our children learned this first."

"Learned?"

"When we had children. Now that no one dies, why should we add to our numbers? We have no need. And some of us have chosen to be children forever, so that the older ones can be amused, and because we would rather play than think deep thoughts."

If someone had told me this while I was safely enwombed in the castle at Mueller, I would have laughed. I would have sneered. I would have hired the man who told me as a clown. But I had climbed the cliff. I had drunk the water. My body had been healed.

"Teach me, Helmut," I said. "I want to speak to the rock."

"Carbon is subtle," he said. "It holds to everything, and builds strange chains. It's softer than the rock, but it can make small lives, where rock can only live in a huge ball that spins around the sun. It's hard to speak to the carbon. It takes many voices to be heard by stone so subtle."

"But you spoke to me?"

"We found the place that had gone wrong. It was on your longest chains, and we taught them how to lie differently, so that they only heal what has been lost, and not what is still whole. We thought at first that you were like us, that you could speak to the carbon, because your chains were different. We didn't have this healing in our bodies—we had to heal every scratch, one at a time. We liked what you had done, and so we changed each other, too, and now we all heal like you do."

So much for the secret of Mueller, I thought. "Why hadn't you done it before?"

"We don't do very much to the carbon chains. They're subtle. They can cause problems. There are only a few changes we make. But to pay you for the healing change you taught to us, we gave you the life change."

It was near dark, and we still perched on the pillar of rock; the cliff was our only exit to the sand below. "What's the life change?" I asked.

"Civilized men kill because they have to, to live. To get energy, they have to murder plants or animals. With killing so common, they have no respect for life at all."

"And what do you do?"

"We're savages. We take our energy from the same source as the plants." And he pointed to where the sky was still light from the sun, which had dipped below the mountains to the west.

"From the sun," I said.

"That's why you aren't hungry," he said.

He talked on into the darkness, and I understood what Schwartz had achieved. A geologist, in a geologist's paradise, and her children after her, with a profound respect for rock, an ever deeper understanding of rock until they awakened, not the earth itself, but that part of their minds which could grasp the structures and change them. The language was mystical, but not a mystery. They understood even DNA as the experts of Mueller couldn't grasp it.

Yet the price of their knowledge was savagery. They could use no tools, make no homes, write no language. If they all died and archaeologists came to this desert, they would find nothing but corpses, and marvel that animals with human shape could be so utterly unintelligent.

"How can I learn to speak to the rock?" I asked.

Helmut's voice came from the darkness. "You must leap from this cliff in the darkness."

He was serious. But that was impossible. "I'll be killed."

"That's been known to happen," Helmut said. Was he amused? I couldn't see his face. "But you must do it soon. Dissent rises in a few minutes."

"Why will killing myself help me talk to the rock?" I tried to make a joke of it. Helmut was too serious.

"You've done killing, Lanik," he said. "You must hold yourself for judgment to see if you were innocent of malice. If the sand receives you gently, the rock will make himself known to you."

"But—" I said. I stopped because I couldn't say that I was afraid. Why should I be afraid, when I wasn't sure, even now, if I fully believed all this?

No. I knew that I was afraid because I *did* believe, and I was unsure whether I was innocent of malice. I had relished the prospect of warfare, and while I had never killed a man in battle back in Mueller, I had killed one man on the Singer ship, two soldiers of Mueller before I entered Ku Kuei, two soldiers of Allison as I left; I had surely killed others in escaping from Nkumai. Those killings had been forced on me, to defend myself, but hadn't I relished the feeling of triumph and power afterward? Was that somehow different from loving to kill? Beyond that, I had approved of my father's strategies of war and longed to be the Mueller and better his achievements. Wasn't that longing for domination still in my heart? I was a truly civilized man. I couldn't believe there was any chance that the sand would, as Helmut put it, *accept* me.

"I should tell you," said Helmut, "that there is no other way down from this tower of rock."

"What about the handholds?"

"They're already gone. You'll jump, or you'll stay here forever. And you have to jump now, in the darkness, before Dissent rises, or your jump will surely be your death."

"You don't leave much to chance, do you, little boy?" I was angry—I had been trapped.

"I'm a boy in spirit, Lanik, but I was old when your father's grandfather first learned not to piss in the family drinking water. And I tell you that I believe that if you jump, the sand might well receive you. But you have to have enough trust in yourself to leap. If you know that you're a murderer, you might as well stay here. You won't die if you stay here, you know. You won't starve to death. You'll just be alone here, forever."

I stood. I knew that the edge of the tower was only a few meters away in any direction. But I couldn't take the step.

"Lanik," Helmut whispered, and his voice was young and innocent again. "Lanik, I believe the sand will hold you." A cool, gentle hand grasped the inside of my thigh as I stood, trembling, because of what I had to do. "I want the sand to hold you."

"So do I," I said.

"Then jump while it's still dark."

He took his hand away and I walked briskly toward the edge and suddenly my step was in the air and I was no longer in Schwartz, I was in Nkumai and I had stepped wrong in the darkness and now I was falling endlessly through the silent trees, and everything else was a dream, all these months were a dream and I had fallen in Nkumai and was going to die and I refused to scream but let the wind rush by me and twist me in the air as my stomach rose to my throat and my bladder would not be constrained and death was a thousand knives of soil below me that would carve and break me when I touched them and then I landed in the soft embrace of the sand, which gently parted and sifted and swirled around me, splashed around me warmly, and closed over my head. There in the embrace of the sand I felt the throbbing heart of the earth, felt the rhythm of the currents of boiling rock beneath me, and heard in the most hidden place in my ears a strange song of eons of itching torment, trying to find a comfortable way to settle down and sleep, while continents danced back and forth on my skin and oceans froze and fell. And while I heard the song of this largest dance, still I could hear the small melodies of shifting sand and falling stones and settling soil. I heard the agony of rock being cut and torn in a thousand places on the surface of my skin, and I wept at the thousand deaths of stone and soil, of plants that thinly held to life between the stone and the sky.

Armies thundered on my skin, death in every heart, with dead trees carved to make tools to build more death. Only the voices of men are louder than the voices of trees, and though a million stalks of wheat whisper terribly together as they die, the death scream of a man's mind is the strongest cry the earth can hear. I felt blood soak into my skin, and I no longer wept; I longed to die, to be free of the incessant crying.

I screamed.

The sand sifted by my ears and swept between my legs, and as it pressed against my face I separated myself from the self whose ears had heard for me, and I asked (without words, for there is no mouth that can shape that language) for the sand to lift me to the surface.

I rose through the warm sand and it broke above me. I spread my arms and legs upon the surface of the sand, and it bore me. I had fallen, it seemed, from the pinnacle of rock to the heart of the earth, and now I coasted on the surface, floated on the still wave of sand.

I smiled, and Helmut stood over me, smiling also.

"Did he sing to you?"

I nodded.

"And he found you clean."

"Or cleaned me," I said, and then shuddered to remember the screams of the dying. I looked at the tower of rock I had fallen from. It was no more than two meters high. My eyes widened, and Helmut laughed.

"We raised it up to make your testing place," he said. "If you hadn't jumped yourself, we would have crumbled it and made you fall."

"Nice folks," I said, but I was too full to be bitter,

and it didn't surprise me when Helmut knelt and touched my chest and then embraced me. He wept on my skin, the water standing in drops that soon evaporated. "I love you," he whispered, "and I'm glad that you were received."

"So am I," I said, and we slept, his cool skin pressed against mine as the sand had pressed, not to arouse or satisfy, but to express; and as we slept we dreamed together, and I learned Helmut's true voice, and I loved him.

I could have stayed in Schwartz forever. I wanted to. They wanted me to. I learned quickly, and while they had repaired the most obvious signs of my radical regeneration, my body was still determined to be unusual. There is a part of the brain that holds the function that lets the Schwartzes speak to stone; as I learned to use it, my body developed it, let it grow. My skull bulged a little upward of and behind my ears to make room, and the spokesman finally told me, "You are beyond us now."

I was surprised. "You do things I can't dream of doing."

"Together," he said. "Alone we aren't as strong as you."

"Then make yourselves like I am."

"There are secrets that the carbon chains can keep even from us."

That was that. Yet it didn't occur to me, not for weeks, that this gave me an advantage that would set me free. For the simple reason that I didn't want to be free of them.

When I spoke to the rock, I learned many things that brought me to myself. The wars were continuing, and as I learned to endure the agony of the many deaths, I also learned to study the wars and see where the battles were being fought. When I talked to the rock, the earth's skin became my skin, and I learned to feel where the cries were coming from. The battles at first were on the plain between Allison and the headwaters of the Rebel River. Then the battles moved to the hill country of Robles, and northwest to the confluence of the Myron and the Rebel where the Rebel River ceases to be called Swoop and begins to be called Mueller. And then the war was in Wizer, a land my father had conquered, and that meant that the Nkumai had swept all before them and were at the borders of my country.

It didn't matter now that I knew the secret of the Nkumai's iron. It didn't matter that my father had sent me away and my brother, Dinte, wanted to kill me. I was no longer a radical regenerative, and I was twice the soldier my father was and by far a better general than Dinte. I was needed, if my Family was to endure.

At first the thought of going to war was repugnant to me, but my Family's need tore at me, and I began to ask the rock. I asked whether one life could be more important than another, and the rock said no. I asked whether it was right to end one life, if, by ending it, many others could be saved. The rock said yes. And I asked if loyalty meant anything to the forces of the universe, and the rock wept.

Loyalty? What but loyalty made the rock respond to the call of the Schwartzes? The earth understood trust, and I asked if it was good for me to go back and lead my Family. And the rock said yes.

This conversation was not the product of one night's sleep under the sand, however. It took many nights and many sleeps, and the months passed before I knew that I could go home; that I must go home.

"You can't go home," said the spokesman.

"The rock spoke to me and told me I should go."

"The rock told you it was good for you to go. Good for you. Good for your family. But not good for us."

"Good for the earth."

"The blood soaks into the earth the same no matter who wields the civilized tools," said the spokesman. "If you go, it will be good and it will be bad. I can't let you go, *we* can't let you go; you've taken all we have to teach and now you'll use it to destroy and kill in the name of loyalty."

"I swear I'll never use what you've taught me to kill."

"If you kill, you'll use what we taught you."

"Never."

"Because now every man who dies at your hand will scream into your soul forever, Lanik."

It was something to give me pause.

When the warfare moved to the lowlands of Cramer, not three hundred kilometers from Mueller-on-the-River, the capital, I could wait no longer. Helmut and I were playing in the pinnacles of a knife-like ridge of mountains, doing acrobatics a thousand meters above the sand, when I pulled the rock out from under him and he fell.

The rock caught him on a ledge a hundred meters below me and far above the desert.

"You bastard!" he shouted.

"I have to!" I shouted back. "If you warn the council, they can stop me!"

"You said you loved me!"

I did. I do. But I said nothing. He tried to crawl up the rock. But I forbade the rock to hold him, and I was stronger. He tried to make handholds in the rock. But I was stronger. He tried to throw himself from the ledge to the sand below, but the rock would not let him jump because I said so. And I was stronger.

The ridge pointed northwest, and I went northwest. When it ended, I plunged down into the sand, and ran all day and all night, forbidding my body to sleep. I went by the fastest way any Schwartz could travel, and because none was faster than I, no pursuit could overtake me.

It took eight days. I slept while running, for my mind had to have sleep even when my body didn't. At last I reached a place where clouds skitted through the sky and where occasional clumps of grass poked from crevasses in rocks, and I was out of Schwartz. It should have been a relief, and I was glad enough to see green instead of the endless yellows and greys and browns of the desert, but I regretted leaving, so much that I stopped and turned around and almost started back.

I remembered my father's face. I remembered him saying, "Lanik, I wish to God there were something I could do." I heard his voice plead, "The body is ruined. Will the mind still serve me? Will the man still love his father?"

Yes, you land-hungry bastard, I thought. You're up against something you're no match for. And I'll come. I'm coming.

I turned back around and headed north into the high country of Sill.

The land had been wasted by war.

Burnt-over fields were accented by the shells of houses and piles of ashes that had once been humbler huts. I walked kilometers of ruin, in what had to be marginal farmland at best, this close to the desert. What purpose could be served by such destruction? No great military objectives lay nearby. All it could achieve was the starvation of the people. The land had been murdered. Tortured.

Yet I knew the people of Nkumai (as well as anyone could know them in their endless intertwining lies) and such destruction wasn't in their nature, not the people who stood at the lips of their treehouses and sang the morning. Even their endless, fumbling bureaucracy and the hypocritical denial that they bought and sold for profit—these were more symptoms of good intention than of deep-seated corruption. Besides, greed would have left these fields intact. Only vicious, mindless hate could make someone want to destroy the land instead of conquering it.

But who could hate even the simple-mindedly violent people of Sill? My father had let them alone, even when he conquered their two neighbors, because for all their boisterous village life and boasting and raiding, they were ultimately harmless.

I got angrier the farther I walked.

At last I reached land that was watered by rivers and irrigation, and here there were people working to rebuild the canals. New houses were going up, makeshift homes to keep the rain off. I had lost track of seasons—the rains would be coming soon.

Only now did it occur to me that I was naked, and nudity was frowned on in this part of the world. The idea of clothing seemed foreign to me—I had been without it for a year, at least, ever since I fell from the birdnet in Nkumai. But how does a man get clothing when he has neither friends nor money, and people stare at him and avoid him when they see him coming?

The problem was solved for me. I slept, this time with body as well as mind, in the grass growing along the bank of the River Wong, and when I awoke three women were staring at me. I moved slowly, so as not to alarm them. "Greetings," I said, and they nodded. So much for conversation, I thought. "I mean you no harm," I said.

They nodded again. "We know."

I guess in my unclothed condition it was no secret I wasn't in the mood for rape. I couldn't think what to say to them next, except the obvious. "I need clothing."

They looked at each other in puzzlement.

"I don't have any money," I said, "but I can promise you I'll pay you within a month."

"Then you aren't the Naked Man," one of them murmured.

"Is there only one?" I asked.

"He walks through the fields from the desert. Some say he will take vengeance on our enemies."

So I had been noticed, and word had spread. Not at all odd that such people would take the mysterious and make of it a solution to their problems. "I'm the one," I said. "I came from Schwartz. I'm going to find the army that did all this."

"Will you kill them?" whispered the youngest, who was far along in pregnancy.

"I will stop them from killing," I promised, wondering if I really could. "But in the meantime, I need clothing. It's time for me to dress."

They nodded, and walked away. They were in no hurry, and in the gently rolling countryside they were soon out of sight. I plunged into the water to wait for them, and amused myself by lying on the bottom of the river, watching the fish. Everything was ravaged above the surface of the water, but in the slow current of the River Wong the fish never noticed.

I realized I had been underwater a long time, surfaced, and began breathing again. No sooner had I brought my head into the air than a woman nearby screamed, and answering shouts brought others on the run. Again I realized I had fallen into the trap of thinking and acting like a Schwartz. I had to stop doing things that other people couldn't do.

"He was under there all this time," the woman was saying to the two-score people who crowded around her, glancing frequently at me, where I stood in the water. "He was under there all the time and I was here for an hour, for a whole hour."

"Nonsense," I said. "I couldn't have been under there for more than fifteen minutes."

They looked at me with respect and awe (and not a little fear) and the pregnant woman held out an armful of clothing. I walked out of the water, and they stared at me, as if they expected something unusual. I almost laughed to remember the way the sailors on the Singer ship had reacted to the way I looked before the Schwartzes cured me. If they could see me now—in full possession of the sort of power the sailors had only imagined me to have before. Yet the way these people looked at me reminded me of my shyness about nudity when I was young and in Mueller. I dressed quickly, not waiting for my skin and hair to dry.

"Thank you," I said when I was dressed.

"We are honored," said a man who seemed to be in charge—an old man. I realized that there were no men of arms-bearing age.

"Your sons are all off to war?"

"There is no war anymore," the headman said.

The pregnant woman agreed, soberly. "For Sill, there is no war."

"There is no Sill," said the headman. "We're Nkumai now."

I looked at them, all nodding in agreement. "Is that so? Then what enemy do you want me to kill?"

They were silent. Until one old woman cried out bitterly, with tears in her eyes. "Nkumai! Kill the Nkumai! For God's sake, if you have any power at all—"

Others took up the cry. "Kill the Nkumai! For our sons, for our homes, for our land, kill the devils!"

I could hear the song of hate and death in their hearts, and I nodded softly and walked on.

"What's your name!" the pregnant woman shouted after me.

I turned and called out, "Lanik Mueller."

To my surprise, the crying and shouting died quickly. Some looked terror-stricken. Some wrinkled up their faces in distaste, as if I had made some obscene joke. Other faces simply froze, expressionless. Then they all silently left me and went back to their homes. Only the old woman addressed any kind of message to me. She spat in the dirt.

It could only have been my name that turned them from friendship and hope to hatred and fear. But what could my name mean in a place like this? In Mueller my name had been well enough known, being the heir apparent, but why should my name be familiar in Sill? I'd been gone for a year, throughout the whole war. I pondered the question as I headed north again, bearing a little west, on my way to Mueller-on-the-River. Could Dinte have hated me so much he spread stories about me as a traitor? Or blamed some atrocity on me? Impossible to believe that Father would let him do such a thing. Had I been gone so long that Father was no longer the Mueller? I could make no sense of it.

There were patches here and there that the Nkumai had missed, places where the green was deep and the harvest would be good enough; the people would not starve. As I ran, however, I saw no one. Had the word spread ahead of me? Were people avoiding the journey of the Naked Man? Or was it the name of Lanik Mueller they shied from? Neither seemed impossible. Fast as I was traveling, rumors could pass me; how else could the survivors of Sill have heard tales of the Naked Man, when I had traveled all day and most of the night? The stories of Rumor as an evil bird that flies faster than sound must be true.

It was a good thing I didn't get hungry. As I passed wheatfields and vegetable gardens my mouth remembered the taste and I wished for the food, but I had no need for it and didn't stop. Besides, if I *had* been hungry, no one was there to share food with me, and I was not yet ready to be a thief in a land where there would be little enough to eat this year.

The River Sill was two days behind me when I finally saw another person. Or persons. I felt the pounding of hooves before I saw them. They were coming from the north, from Mueller. And when they came into sight, I recognized the banner of the Army of the East. The commander would be Mancik, my godfather.

But Mancik wasn't with them, though the commander's banner was there; thus I knew that he had died. If I'd had a knife, I would have given him grief, but I had no weapon, and after a few moments I had other things on my mind.

I didn't know the commander, nor did I know the soldiers who leapt from their horses and bound me. I consented to the binding partly because I was confused and partly because I was outnumbered. There's a limit to how many body parts even a reformed radical regenerative can renew. And they looked willing to take me apart.

"I'm told to bring you to the capital alive," said the commander.

"Then I won't hinder you," I answered. "That's where I was going."

This apparently made them angry. Two soldiers struck me at once, and I was dazed for a moment. "I'm Lanik Mueller," I said, spitting out the words, "and I won't be treated like this!"

The commander looked at me coldly. "We know who you are, and after the way you've treated this land, any way we treated you would be far kinder than you deserve." He looked for a moment, grimly, across the wasted fields. "Of all the traitors who have ever lived, Lanik Mueller, there must be a special place in hell reserved for you."

"I've been to hell," I said. "It's a better place than this."

"What if you burn like you burnt these fields?" called a soldier. There was a murmur of bitter assent.

"I didn't do this," I said, perplexed that they could think I did.

"Didn't do it!" shouted a man. "I saw you dangling a torch yourself, ahead of all your inker troops!"

How could I even protest against a charge so absurd?

"Enough talking," said the commander. "He's going to claim he was insane or some such nonsense. No one will believe him, he'll get the death that such a man deserves, but there'll be no glory in it for us, having found him. The damage is already done beyond repair, and killing him won't undo any part of it."

It was a strange thing for any commander to say, and yet it had a strange calming effect on the men. They had none of the hearty lust for battle that I had seen in the army all my life. But the commander's words had stirred in them some silent, desperate courage. All did their work quickly, wordlessly. They threw me over a saddle, strapped my legs to the stirrups, and left me to find my balance as best I could with bound arms on a galloping horse. They rode madly across the fields, as if they hoped (and I'm sure they did) that my horse would fall, would shatter me, would crush me into the ashes that had once been grain. Or perhaps they thought of me no more, and merely rode, machines of flesh astride these heaving horses, empty of thought, empty of anything but the knowledge of desolation.

As I rode, what else had I to do but think? Somehow I was blamed for all this devastation, and not just by strangers, but by the men of Mueller—the ones who once had loved me, if not for myself, then as my father's son. This was not something Dinte's lies could accomplish, nor could Ruva have persuaded anyone to think of me that way, nor any other jealous enemy. The man said he had seen me. *Seen* me, and though I know it was impossible, I could not doubt his honesty. It wasn't just my name that was hated here, it was my face.

Thinking of hatred, thinking of my own face, I saw an image of myself before my eyes, and it was not a memory of my face as I saw it in mirrors. Then I knew the answer, knew why it was that every accusation they made against me could be true and not-true all at once. I also knew that no matter how convincingly I told my tale, they would never believe me.

The slap of hard leather boots rang out in the stone halls of my father's palace. I was dragged in brutally and thrown down on the floor. I had seen the scene before, but from the other point of view, as men accused of treason were prepared for trial. The trial was a mere formality. The charge was so serious it was never brought unless guilt was certain.

Yet my thoughts kept wandering. As they marched me through the corridors, held me in the small cell while the court assembled, I kept looking at the dead stone of the walls, realizing how much death this place had cost the earth. If I said as much to anyone, it would be taken as madness. Living stone? But I spoke in my mind and sang the song of the rock, and felt the resonation. Far under the castle, the stones were listening. They would hear, the living stones would know, if my blood were shed.

The punishment for treason is drawing and quartering the living man. Women are decapitated first. It's grisly, but I had always thought of it as a fine deterrent.

I arose from the floor and stood.

"Kneel!" shouted Harkint, the Captain of the Guard (he used to race me on horseback through the streets of the city). I turned to him and spoke coldly, dramatically, because trials, like most of royal life, are theatrics, and I couldn't help but play my part. "I am royalty, Harkint, and I stand before the throne."

This quieted him, and now the court settled into the steady business of hate and fear.

My father looked old. It was for his sake I had returned at all. Now he looked weary and sick at heart. "Lanik Mueller, there's little point in a trial," he said. "You know and we know why you're here. You're guilty, so let's end this shabby business."

Every delay is a promise of life; and even though I knew there was no chance that they'd believe me, still I had to have my say. Perhaps it would be many years before my innocence was proven, but there would be some then who would remember that I had told the truth this day. "It's my right to hear the charges against me."

"If we listed them all," said my father, "I couldn't stop the people here from killing you with their hands."

"Say them briefly then, but name my crimes, since I don't know what they are."

My father's face wrinkled in distaste at what he thought was a feeble lie. "You shame yourself," he said. But he looked at the herald, and old Swee called out in a ringing voice:

"The crimes of Lanik Mueller: Leading the Nkumai armies into battle against the armies of Mueller. Destroying fields and homes of citizens of Mueller and dependent Families. Betraying the secret of regeneration so that our enemies now hack the bodies of our soldiers to pieces on the field, so they die. Plotting to undo the succession and take the rightful heir from the throne." Swee looked bitter and the gathered court shouted in outrage as each charge was read.

"I didn't do any of this," I said, looking my father in the eye.

"You've been seen by a thousand witnesses," said my father.

A soldier stepped forward in rage—a commoner, since he had lost his arms and neither had grown back. "I saw you myself," he cried, "when you cut off both my arms and made me come here to tell the Mueller that you planned to drink his blood!"

"I never did that, never said it."

Father answered contemptuously. "There are others who knew you who saw you leading the Nkumai armies. We've heard enough now. You're guilty, and I sentence you to—"

"No!" I shouted. "I have a right to speak!"

"A traitor has no rights!" shouted a soldier.

"I'm innocent!"

"If you're innocent," cried my father, "every whore in Mueller is a virgin!"

"I have a right to be heard, and I will speak!"

They fell silent then, perhaps because my voice still had some power to command; or more likely because they drew some bleak satisfaction out of watching me struggle vainly for my life. Still, useless as the effort was, I tried to tell them the only explanation that would fit what they had seen, and what I knew I had and had not done. Half of what I said was speculation, but as far as I knew then, I was telling the truth.

I told them that I had gone to Nkumai, but my subterfuge had been discovered only moments after I found the secret of what they sold to get iron. I told them of my escape, my disembowelment, and of the echo of myself that had been regenerated from my own gut. I described my imprisonment on a Singer ship and how the Schwartzes had cured me (I said nothing of how, or what I had learned about the living rock of our world), and how I had come as quickly as I could to warn my father of the danger.

As to the person who claimed to be me and fooled others into thinking he was, I could only guess that he was my double; that he had not died, but had been found by the Nkumai. "I was careless. I should have destroyed the body. But I wasn't thinking clearly then, and most Muellers would have died from such wounds." They must have trained him, I speculated, and he would have had all my inborn abilities. No wonder people believed he was Lanik Mueller—right down to the genes, he was.

I explained everything I could think to explain, and then I stopped talking.

What effect had all my talking had? Little enough. Most of the people were still hostile, openly disbelieving, eager for my death. But here and there, especially among the older men, there was a face that looked thoughtful. And when I looked at my father, I knew (or did I only wish to know?) that he believed me.

I was no fool. I realized that whether he believed me or not, he had no power to save me. He couldn't have acquitted me, not that day, not before that audience.

I had hardly noticed Ruva and Dinte before, but now they both came up to confer with my father. It startled me to see them as allies—hadn't Dinte hated her as much as I did? But allies they were, and of course they had noticed the change in Father's expression that had told me of his belief in my tale. Now they would try to undo any good my speech might have done for me. Ruva kept whispering to father, while Dinte stepped forward and spoke loudly, for all the court to hear.

"Apparently you think we're fools, Lanik," he said. "Never in all the history of radical regeneration has anyone formed an entire duplicate of himself."

"No rad has ever had his guts torn out and strewn across the countryside, either."

"And then you say the Schwartzes cured you. Desert savages, and they can do what none of our geneticists can manage?"

"I know it's hard to believe—"

"What's hard to believe is that you could tell us all this with a straight face, dear brother. No one has ever come out of the Schwartz Desert alive. No one has ever done any of these heroic deeds you claim to have done. What people *have* done is see you at the head of the enemy's army. I saw you myself, when I was commanding the Army of the South in Cramer, and you waved to me and shouted some obscenity. Don't pretend you don't remember."

"I'd hardly be the first to shout an obscenity at you, Dinte," I said, and to my surprise there were a few chuckles in the court. Not enough to hint that I had any friends. But enough to prove that Dinte had some enemies.

Now my father interrupted. "Dinte," he said, "you're being undignified." There was contempt in my father's voice. But there was some other emotion when he spoke to me:

"Lanik Mueller, your defense is implausible and the testimony of a thousand men is unarguable. I sentence you to be drawn and quartered alive on the playing field by the river tomorrow at noon and may your soul if you have one rot in hell."

He got up to go. How much did I want to live? Enough to sacrifice all dignity and cry out after him, "Father! If all this were true, why in the name of God would I have given myself up to you?"

He turned slowly and looked me in the eye. "Because even the devil gives some justice to his victims, when they're beyond all help."

He left the court. The soldiers took me then, and because I had been sentenced to die they spent the afternoon and evening torturing me. Since Muellers heal so quickly, we can bear exquisite injury and still not die. Of that night I'll say no more.

7 ENSEL

I wasn't bleeding anymore, but I was still in pain, and more painful was the memory of the hatred of the soldiers. I knew only a few of them, but those had always been kind to me, and some of them had been my friends since I was a child. Now they delighted in my pain, wanted me to suffer, and still it was plain that to them, nothing I went through could equal the punishment I deserved. Their loathing stung, worse because I didn't deserve it and yet had no hope of proving my innocence.

So I lay in darkness in the dead stone cell where they at last let me rest until my death the next day. My wounds were healing quickly enough, leaving me exhausted; but soon enough I would be whole. Father had given me a night and morning of life before I died. I determined to use the time, not preparing for death, but trying to think of a way to escape.

I admit my thinking wasn't good. I had come too recently from Schwartz, and still found myself as maddeningly disdainful of normal concerns as they were. No one had fed me since I came to Mueller, but I wasn't hungry. No one had offered me water, but I felt no thirst. And since I could ignore pain as it subsided, what was there to remind me that I had to act quickly, act immediately if I was to save my own life?

Save it for what?

My purpose in Schwartz had been to come warn my Family. The warning was a little late, and no one wanted messages from me now anyway. Worse, they had locked me in a prison of dead stone, so I couldn't even speak to the rock and sink into the soil and escape.

I could kill myself, of course, but my natural aversion to that was abetted by the fact that I could not bear to be guilty of adding that much pain to the earth. Rock bears enough murders without the scream of the self-murderer's death.

There was a patter of light footsteps outside the door of my cell. The bar lifted, and the door, with difficulty, swung out.

"Lanik," said a voice in the darkness. I knew the voice at once, could not believe that I was hearing it. And then Saranna was holding me and weeping. "Lanik, they even put out your eyes."

"They're growing back," I answered. "It's so good to be home."

"Oh, Lanik, we've been so afraid for you!"

She spoke to me as if I had never been away, as if nothing had changed. Her hands fit exactly on my back, in places where ancient habit said that hands that size belonged. She held me with a pressure that I had last felt yesterday (had last felt a year ago) and her breath, her skin as her cheek brushed mine, the scent of her, even the wild wisps of hair tickling my nose—

I held tightly to her because for a moment she took away the nightmare of the last few days and months and years, and I was Ensel Mueller's son Lanik, heir to the throne and a happy young man. Damned happy. Damned.

"Why did you come?" I asked.

"You have friends, Lanik. Some of us believe you."

"Then you must be insane. There's nothing believable about my story."

"I have known you long enough to know when you tell the truth. I don't want you drawn and quartered tomorrow. Come with me."

"You don't think you can get me out of this prison, do you?"

"I can with help."

She held my hand and led me through the corridors. She squeezed once when we reached steps going up, twice when the steps went down. We were as soundless as feet can be, and I, for one, didn't breathe. It was easier that way. My eyes were healing well; already they had their round shape; but it would take time for the nerves to heal properly, for vision to be fully restored. It was frightening to be blind and moving, like that dark night crawling along wet slick branches in Nkumai. That night I never knew what lay ahead. Nor did I this night—but tonight someone held my hand and led the way. Tonight I trusted my life, not to my instincts, but to a woman whom I had always thought of as being a little flighty. Loyal, of course, and wonderfully exuberant in making love, but not dependable. I was wrong, obviously. We met no one on the way.

We stopped.

"What are we waiting for?"

"Quiet," she said, and I was quiet. After a few minutes I could hear the distant shuffle of footsteps. An old man, I decided from the sound. And then he was close and I felt arms going around me and an iron grip holding me and hot tears on my neck.

"Father," I whispered.

"Lanik, my son, my son," he said, and I wasn't afraid anymore.

"You believe me."

"You're my single hope." Always the old bastard regarded me as *his* hope, as if he had first claim on my loyalty, before even myself. Well, he did.

"Four much smaller hopes tomorrow," I answered.

He only held me tighter. "There are times when an honest ruler has to abdicate, and this is that time. They won't cut you up. I knew you'd never betray me, not permanently, anyway."

"Not even temporarily," I said. "But now let's get moving before somebody notices that you're holding court down here."

"We can't go yet," Father said. "We have to wait."

"Why?"

"Changing of the guard at dawn," he said. "We hope they'll be distracted."

"The guard? You're afraid of the guard? Can't you just hide me and command them to let you through?"

Saranna answered. "It's not that simple. Your father doesn't command the guard."

"Well, who the hell does?" I whispered.

"Ruva," said Father.

I raised my voice. "The Turd rules in your palace!"

"Quiet. Yes, she does, she and Dinte. They were plotting it before you left the palace, and once you were gone they made their move. I could have blocked them, I suppose, but I couldn't afford to kill my only heir, as I thought, and so I went along, pretending I didn't notice how my prerogatives were usurped, how my friends' offices became sinecures and the real power seemed to gather in much younger hands."

"My mother tried to warn the court," Saranna said. "I had to sign her death warrant."

"Why did you sign it?" I asked.

"For the reason I signed yours," said my father. "She escaped and is living in exile in the north. In Brian, I believe. Her agents smuggled out half the Family fortune. It stopped when Ruva found the leak."

"I see," I said.

"When we heard you were commanding the Nkumai invaders, I was overjoyed. I used my influence, such as I have, to put our stupidest commanders, including Dinte, in the key positions. I opened the doors to the enemy. Thinking, of course, that you were coming to liberate me and the people from that ass I had the misfortune to marry and that child your mother claimed was also mine."

"It wasn't me."

"I knew it couldn't be you when we heard how the armies were destroying everything. You're too wise for that. I knew it was a fraud. But then there were so many witnesses." He sighed. "I betrayed my own Family, thinking I was opening the door for my son to save me from my wife and our monstrous little whelp Dinte. Now the enemy ravages from Schmidt to Jones and it's only a matter of time before they cross the river and take this city. They'll surely do it soon. The rains will make the river impassable in a few more weeks." Suddenly he wept again. "I dreamed of your homecoming, Lanik. Dreamed that you'd come in triumph and lead these people into battle. *You* could have led my army to defeat the Nkumai. They must have known it. That's why they destroyed the people's love for you. Now we can only run."

"Good enough," I said. "Let's start running."

"The changing of the guard," Saranna whispered.

"No," I said. "Dinte and Ruva are surely watching you. They probably left me unguarded just so you'd try this and get yourselves killed. You'd better go back upstairs, both of you, and pretend you had nothing to do with this."

"Not this time," Saranna said.

"We have to leave with you," Father said. "Things are intolerable here. We have a few hundred loyal men that I've already assigned to duty in the north. They're expecting us. They'll rally to us."

"To you, you mean. Not a soul alive would rally to me. But we're not going to wait for the changing of the guard."

"Then we'll be caught. Every gate is watched closely."

I could see the flicker of Saranna's torch now. My vision was returning. "I'll create a diversion. The postern gate."

"It's heavily guarded."

"I know. Take me near there, but keep me out of sight. I can see faintly, and I should have full vision soon, but in the meantime I couldn't defend myself against a gnat. Once I'm there, you two be ready to spring for the water gate. I'll join you there."

"Blind?"

"I know the way blindfolded. And by then no one will be looking for me."

"What kind of diversion can *you* create?" Father asked doubtfully.

In answer I opened my shirt and showed them my chest. "Do you remember what grew here when you sent me away, Father?"

He remembered.

"It will never grow back. The Schwartzes cured me, as I told you. If they could manage *that*, don't you think they could teach me other things as well?"

Saranna's hand brushed down my chest, like the dream I had lived through a hundred nights on the Singer ship.

"Let's go," I said.

They led me up the stairs and ramps and corridors that would take us to the postern gate. They left me in the window well over the palace door, where, if I could have seen, I would have scanned the courtyard before the postern gate in the palace walls. As it was I could see shapes, dimly; though torches were only bright sparks of light, I could see the flames dance.

There was so much dead rock around that I was hampered, but I soon found the voice of the rock. Much was new; the soil, unlike the sand, had too much life in it. It was a barrier, not a channel. But at last I found the voice of the living rock. I explained my purpose, I asked for help, and the rock complied.

I couldn't really see it happen. I could only hear the grinding of dead stones as the earth heaved under them and cast them from their piles onto the ground. There were shouts as the men from the postern gate ran to the breach in the wall. The earth kept heaving, and some were thrown to the ground. Others foolishly ran too close to where the walls were dancing, where great blocks of stone toppled from their place and crashed into the earth.

I lowered myself from the window and walked the other way, toward the water gate.

Saranna and Father and four soldiers leading seven horses waited in the shelter of a wall.

"What did you do?" Father asked, in awe. "It was like an earthquake."

"It *was* an earthquake," I said. "Just a little one. Big ones take a committee." Then I strode toward the gate. In the gathering light of predawn I could see again, though things were blurry, and with relief I noticed that the gate was unguarded—the soldiers had run off to the breach in the wall.

Unguarded, and so we passed through, Father and Saranna first, and then the soldiers. Which is why I was last and still unarmed when Dinte emerged from the shadows.

I saw the glint of torchlight reflected in steel. "How unequal we are," I said. "A mark of your courage."

"I wanted to have no doubt of the outcome," he said.

"Then you should have picked a different target," I answered. It was a simple thing to make sweat and oil seep out of his hands, so the hilt became slippery.

He trembled; he couldn't hold the sword; it slipped out of his hand, and he looked at it there on the ground, horror in his eyes. He tried to pick it up. It slid again from his fingers. He rubbed his palms frantically on his tunic, leaving dark stains. Did he think he could dry his hands that easily? He tried again to pick up the sword, this time with both hands. He cradled it, then tried to lunge at me; I easily slapped it out of his hands. And this time it was I who picked it up.

It would have been pure justice if I killed him, but he was screaming for help and he was my father's son, so I merely slit his throat from ear to ear and left him silent and bleeding on the ground. He'd regenerate and recover, as I had from the same wound more than a year ago. But at least he'd know that next time when he came for me, he'd have to bring some friends.

I passed through the gate, still holding the sword, and mounted the horse they held for me. I said nothing of my reason for delay. If Father had heard Dinte's voice, if he guessed what had happened inside the gate, he said nothing about it.

We rode north all day, and at night came to a military outpost that had once guarded Mueller's northern frontier in the old days, when Epson had been powerful and Mueller a peaceful farming Family with some strange breeding practices. The outpost was run down, but a quick count made me estimate three hundred or more horses, which meant there'd be as many men at least.

"Are you sure they're friends?" I asked.

"If not, we haven't much hope anyway," Father answered.

"Either way, it would be better if you had this sword, and not I."

I handed it to him. He looked at it and nodded. "Dinte's."

"He'll recover," I said.

"Too bad," Saranna said gruffly.

"Maybe he'll do us a favor and die on his own," I said. But I was sure the wound was one he could recover from.

Then we were at the outpost gates and the soldiers let us in and cheered Father, and he explained (very roughly) that it was an imposter and not I leading the Nkumai. I don't know how many believed him. But they were courageous men and loyal to Father; most cheered and none protested.

"You're brave," he told them, "brave and worthy, but three hundred men are not enough." He ordered them to go back to their homes and bring as many loyal men as they could find. Wisely, he urged them not to mention that I was with him. Let them rally to the king, not to someone most would surely think of as a traitor.

As the three hundred soldiers rode out to bring an army to us, we changed horses for the fifth time that day and rode on north into the darkness.

"You must have been planning this for months," I said.

"We weren't planning on *you*," Father said, "but we knew that sometime soon I'd have a crisis with my dear younger son and would have to be free to call on the loyal troops. We planned for contingencies."

Dissent had already set for the second time that night when we finally stopped at a farmhouse well off the road. The house was right at the bank of the Sweet River. The wind was cool out of the eastern hills that led to Ku Kuei. The fire in the hearth was hot and fierce, and the host forced us to eat soup before he'd let us go to bed.

The bodyguards slept on the ground floor. And when the host showed me to my room, Saranna was already on my bed, waiting for me.

"I know you're tired," she said. "But it's been a year."

As she undressed me I looked out the window onto the rolling wheat-covered hills to the east, where the sun rose out of Ku Kuei, and I felt the breeze playing across my body while Saranna tickled me (nothing forgotten, not even now), and I smelled the reek of horseflesh in my own clothes and the fresh white-wash the host had used a week ago, and it was good to be home.

After three weeks it was clear that ours would be an unnoteworthy rebellion. We had eight thousand soldiers, loyal to the core and some of the finest fighters in the kingdom. But Father's treasury fed them and armed them to no avail: Rumors came, which soon were verified, and we knew our cause was lost. Dinte had signed a treaty with the Nkumai. Now there were 120,000 men against our tiny army. Father and I might have been better generals, but there are limits to what a general can do.

What hurt us worst, however, was the fact that the Nkumai, apparently from the day I was captured, had put their duplicate Lanik into cold storage and started publicly declaring that I had indeed been with them, but had been captured by Mueller forces and was now a defector with my father's army. And as soon as they started that story going, they ended the policy of wasting the land, claiming that the destruction had been entirely my idea and they were grateful to be able to quit.

It did nothing to make me popular or my story of a twin believable, and troops weren't exactly flocking to my banner. We tried to conceal the fact that I was with Father, but some stories can't be kept secret.

So there we were with eight thousand men, a full treasury, and not one choice except to run away. Of course the Nkumai and dear Dinte chose that moment to join forces on the north side of the Mueller River and head straight for us.

"We'll die heroically," said Harkint, who still didn't trust me.

"I'd rather live," I said.

"We know your preferences," he answered coldly.

"I'd rather all of us lived. Because it won't take long with Dinte in command before people start clamoring to have Father back."

"It wouldn't take long *now*, if you weren't with us," said another soldier, and a murmur of assent came from the others gathered in the large room of the house. Father frowned at him, but the soldier was right. I was Father's chief liability. Lose me, and he'd be able to raise more of an army. Maybe ten, fifteen thousand more. Still not enough.

"I have a plan," I said. "And it will work."

The next morning we set out along the Sweet River. We made no secret of our direction and we traveled at a leisurely pace. The river ran southwest, and anyone with half a brain could guess we were heading for Mueller-on-the-Sea, the great port on the Rebel River delta where the fresh water spewed out into the saltwater Sleeve. Strategically it was vital, and the fleet, if we could reach it first, would take us to Huntington, where the troops would still be loyal to Father and, not having seen the devastation, might not hate me as much. There we could wait and prepare an invasion.

This meant, of course, that Dinte and the Nkumai would race us for the fleet and get there first. I had no objection. After all, even if we got to Huntington safely we would be permanently in exile; with the Nkumai getting both our iron and their own, there would be no resisting them. So when we reached the point where we had to leave the river no matter

where we were going, since the river jogged to the
west, I ordered our army to begin a doubletime race,
not southwest for Mueller-on-the-Sea, but southeast
for the Great Bend of the Mueller River, where we
would be free to go eastward, gathering strength among
the recently conquered and none-too-docile popu-
lations of Bird, Jones, Robles, and Hunter. It wasn't
the world's likeliest or safest plan, but it was the
best I could think of at the time.

We didn't bother galloping—we went at the wagons'
best pace, which was still a good deal better, with
each wagon lightly loaded, than Nkumai's army of
former tree climbers could make on foot. I could only
hope that the enemy had got far enough westward,
in the wrong direction, so that we could reach the
bend before them. If we did, they'd never overtake
us heading east, and we'd live to fight another day.

And if they did reach us, I had still another plan,
but it was for the time when we had nothing left to
lose.

As we rode southeast, there was little for me to
do. Father knew his men and no one was eager to
take orders from me. Instead I thought, and the subject that most often came to mind was the imposter,
the all-too-true Lanik who was now out of a job.

It was an interesting speculation, what his life had
been like. His creation had been bad enough for
me—but for him, the first stirrings of consciousness
began with someone who looked exactly like him
trying to bash in his brains with a rock. And then
what had the Nkumai put him through, believing
he was me, before they finally caught on to what
was happening? If I had been haunted by him before,
in dreams, now he haunted my waking hours as I
pictured the hatred they must have taught to him.
You're a monster to the men of Mueller, they must
have told him. They'll kill you if they ever know

who you are. But if you work with us, we'll install you on the throne and you can show them that you are someone to regard, with fear if not respect.

Had he actually led their armies? Perhaps. Were my memories transferred to him along with my body? If so, he would be a match for me on any battlefield, since he'd know my moves before I made them. Surely they'd keep him with them for that purpose if no other.

Whatever role he had actually played before, he was once again betrayed, unceremoniously dropped from any important role. Perhaps they've already killed him, I thought. Or perhaps he's feeling as hopeless as I, knowing that there is no one more hated than he in all the West, and yet truly deserving none of the hatred at all.

I thought of Mwabao Mawa and wanted to strangle her.

No murder, I told myself. No killing. I have heard the song of the earth, and that is stronger than hate.

At such times I would ride off from the army, several kilometers ahead, and lie on the soil and speak to the living rock. Since I feared that I couldn't control myself, I let the rock control me, restore me, bring me peace.

"They've set the Cramers free and they're taking Mueller slaves," one soldier who joined our army told us in horror. The reaction was electric—many of our soldiers had families in West Mueller, where the Cramers might be creating havoc with no one to defend our people. I was not surprised that our numbers began diminishing as soldiers slipped off to head southwest. I was even less surprised when most of our scouts failed to return. Still, we had to try to hold our army: I insisted that Father stop asking for volunteers for scouting missions.

We were only thirty kilometers from the Great

Bend when the most important information of all came from someone we had never thought to see again.

"Homarnoch," Father whispered as he saw the man madly driving a wagon along the road we had just come down. "Homarnoch! Here!" he cried, and the old doctor was soon beside us. We called a rest; the soldiers stopped on the road.

"No use," Homarnoch said. "I've killed a brace of horses coming to tell you. The Nkumai didn't take your bait. They only sent Dinte and his force to Mueller-by-the-Sea, and when you turned southeast the rest of them were ahead of you all the way. Not five kilometers off they're waiting for you. They've been at the Great Bend for days."

Father called his commanders and gave them orders to have our men prepare for a much faster march.

"We'll fight them and win," Harkint insisted.

"We'll escape and survive," Father answered, and Harkint went off in a rage.

While the preparations were going on, Homarnoch told us how and why he had come. "They were going to take everything—all our work for thousands of years. I wouldn't have that. Not those tree-dwelling apes."

I didn't bother telling him that those tree-dwelling apes had given faster-than-light travel to the rest of the universe.

"So I poisoned the rads," Homarnoch said.

Father was shocked. "Killed them!"

"They were five tons worth of iron on the hoof, Ensel, and I couldn't let the inkers have that. So I poisoned them. Not even their fingernails'll be worth a gram of iron in trade."

I said nothing, but remembered a time when I had had five legs and an extra nose and still believed I was a man.

"I also got the library. The essential records. The

theory. It's all in that wagon," he said, "and I burned the rest. With Dinte's men in charge of the city, nobody even thought to keep me in."

"A master stroke," Father said. Homarnoch beamed with pride.

"Having the books with us doesn't answer the real question," I said. "What do we do now?"

"Harkint wants to attack," Father said with a wry smile.

"Harkint's a heroic ass," I answered. "But I can see why he wants to do it. There's nowhere else to go. Dinte's men are between us and the sea, and there's nothing in the north but Epson. They won't be inclined to provoke Nkumai by taking us in."

"Dinte's no match for us."

"He outnumbers us five to one. With odds like that they don't need a competent commander."

We sat in silence. Homarnoch mumbled something about needing to check the horses. And then Harkint came back. The troops were ready. "And what I want to know is, are we going into battle or running from it?"

"Running," Father said. "The question is, which way."

Harkint snorted. "I never thought the day would come when the Mueller would be a coward. I've followed you through everything that's gone wrong, including harboring this Class A bastard"—meaning me—"but I'll be damned if I'll turn tail and run from a fight. And there's others that feel like me."

If he'd had any sense of the theatrical, he would have stormed off then. But he hadn't. So Father answered. "Go through the troops then, Harkint, and ask for all who want to go with you. But tell them that the Mueller is withdrawing, and asks all men to come with him. You tell them that, and take all those who'll go with you."

Harkint nodded and left. I began scratching out a rough map of Mueller and the surrounding territories.

"South and west is out of the question," Father said. "Everyone in Mueller would kill *you*, and everyone in Helper, Cramer, and Wizer would kill *me*."

"And north is impossible," I answered, "because Epson is too weak to protect us, and too strong for us to force them to take us in."

"And we can't reach the East because Nkumai's army is in the way."

"How desperate," said Homarnoch lightly, looking over a sheaf of papers as he returned and stood a few meters off. "We have no hope. Let's throw ourselves in the river and drown."

It was time for me to broach my final, desperate plan. "There *is* a direction we haven't tried."

Father wasn't slow. "Ku Kuei. But there are too many legends about the forest, Lanik. The men wouldn't go in."

"I've been through the forest. Not just around the edges. Through it."

"And they'll follow you anywhere."

I laughed.

"Even if we got them in there, Lanik, what would we do? Nkumai rules the East, and the Singer armies are ruining the far north. What do we do in Ku Kuei?"

"Survive. Dinte can't last forever."

"You're serious about us going there, aren't you?" I could see that he was as afraid of Ku Kuei as anyone. Hadn't I been? And hadn't strange things happened in the trees, time seeming not to move, my body wearying beyond all expectation? Still, it was our only hope.

"There are legends about Schwartz, too," I said. "Yet I went in and came out again, alive."

"Do you think there's still a Ku Kuei Family in there? Do you think they might have something valuable to offer?"

"The forest is strange and dangerous, even maddening. I met no one in there, Father, and I don't expect to find anyone to help us this time. But even a faint hope is better than no hope at all."

Father chuckled. "Lanik, I think such mad hope is the way you show despair."

His amusement meant that he was softening. I pushed harder. "Would Dinte follow us into Ku Kuei?"

"Dinte? He believes all the legends. He closes his windows at night. He won't cross water under a cloudy sky. He sings when the shadow of another man's horse touches him. He's a fool."

"The Nkumai are not fools," I said, "and they don't go into Ku Kuei either. Forests are their native habitat. Ku Kuei scares everybody till their snot freezes. So if we can keep from panicking ourselves, we'll be safe."

More than we had expected chose to follow Harkint into battle. We formed the rest into a double column all the same, and began to march northeast. It was not a pleasant leavetaking. Some of the troops with us called abuse at Harkint's men for abandoning the Mueller. Harkint's men cried coward in return. The march was dismal as we went on our way, only five thousand men or so, with deserters dropping off all along the way. I couldn't blame them, but forced those I caught to get back in line. They didn't mind. They knew they'd get away in an hour or so, when no officer was watching.

We came to the fork in the road where escape to the north would mean following the main way left, while the smaller road east could only take us to Ku Kuei. Father's speech was impressive. But we lost two thousand men right there, just as word reached us that Harkint's forces had been slaughtered within a few hours of our having left. The Nkumai were close behind us, and they had rested for days while waiting for us at Great Bend—they were fresh and we were not.

We filed hopelessly up the narrow road leading through the rough eastern hills. There was little desertion now; in these hills, the best source of food was our wagons, and deserters would have little hope of surviving with the enemy so close behind. Besides, the men who were still with us now were the hard core of Father's supporters. The kind, we thought, who would die before they'd abandon him.

"I'm toying with an idea," Father said to me as we headed the column along the twisting road. "My idea is to pick a good spot here and go down fighting."

"That's a stupid idea," I said cheerfully.

Father smiled. But it was a grim smile. "I'm realizing, the closer we get to Ku Kuei, that I'm a bit superstitious, too. Are you sure you got through there safely?"

"I'm here, aren't I?"

"You're here, but what does that prove? Lanik, my son, I'm a blathering old man, but unless I'm mistaken, you knocked down a wall of my palace without so much as a small rock or a catapult."

"I learned some things in Schwartz."

"Lanik, I don't doubt you. But don't you realize that what is possible for you might not be possible for anyone else? *You* might be safe enough in Ku Kuei, but what makes you sure any of the rest of us will live?"

"Anything I learned, I learned in Schwartz. I was an ordinary boy when I went into Ku Kuei, and I came out weary but unchanged."

He sighed. "What are we going to do in Ku Kuei?"

"Survive." What other plans did he expect me to have?

The road veered north, and in the distance to the

east we could see the trees of Ku Kuei begin. There was not so much as a path leading toward the forest—it wasn't the usual direction for travelers to go. So I picked out what looked like a reasonably good route, and started overland.

The troops didn't follow.

Not that they said anything, or rebelled. The front ranks just sat there on their horses, watching me, not speaking, not moving.

Then Father left the road and came after me, his horse at a slow walk, and one or two others started, too. But while Father came on until he joined me, the others reined in and stopped a few meters from the road.

Father turned to face them. "I won't command any man to come," he said. "But that's where the Mueller's going, and all the Mueller's true men will come with him. Stay with me and you will live as long as I do."

I don't know whether Father's little speech would have been enough to persuade them by itself. Much more convincing was the flight of arrows that sailed toward our column. The aim was not good—the distance was too great for accuracy. But the message was clear: the Nkumai had flanked us, and the entire length of our column would soon be exposed to enemy arrows.

Father cried out, "To me, Mueller!" and then whispered loudly to me, "Lead, dammit!" I took off at a totally unwise canter over broken ground; my horse and I were lucky, but others were not, and many horses spilled their riders before they reached the shelter of the woods.

The trees were tall, but the branches were often low, and it was hard to pick a clear path. I had to dismount, and that meant that our forces would also have to pause at the forest edge, exposing themselves to Nkumai archers as they waited for those ahead of them to move under the trees. We lost more than two hundred men there; but when I had led us two hours into the forest, the rearmost men called ahead that the Nkumai pursuit had withdrawn.

The urgency of flight was over, but we couldn't stop there. The trees were so dense that no decent forage for the horses could grow. I decided to lead the men on to the shores of the narrow lake where I had first stopped. There the trees broke into enough meadow to keep the horses for a few days, at least.

Our passage through the forest was silent. I didn't look behind me at the men—it would have made them even more nervous to know how nervous I was about them. I kept waiting for our strength to fade while time seemed not to pass, as had happened to me before. This time, however, nothing was happening to our endurance, but the very silence of the forest despite the steady tramping of the horses' hooves and the soldiers' boots was unnerving. It was as if the sounds were swallowed up in the silence, a bit of ourselves stolen away by the trees and not reflected back to us.

We spent a hard night in the forest. The ground was soft enough, and there was plenty of food in the saddlepacks, but by morning hundreds of men had disappeared. Gone off into the night or turned away first thing in the morning, but gone. We knew they had merely deserted (and more than a few who had stayed were no doubt wishing they had gone, too), but the feeling that men could simply vanish in the night did little to promote calm.

We lived out of our saddlebags, and it took us more days than I thought possible until at last we found the lake. Hadn't I reached this place—exhausted, yes—but after only a single day of running? Sunlight poured down and birds skirted the edge of the water and the horses grazed openly on the meadow and I thought we had made it to safety. I counted the men.

Fewer than a thousand. And with this we hoped to return to power in Mueller.

The men bathed in the lake, splashing each other with water like children. They laughed loudly. They were safe now, and had no urgent need, neither men nor horses. Father and I decided to leave Homarnoch in charge of our peaceful, happy troops, and go off searching for a place where we could camp, and build huts, and plant crops. Unspoken was the faint hope that in the process we might also find the Ku Kuei, if any such people lingered here.

Saranna clung to me and told me I mustn't go. But Father and I left her anyway, and went searching through the forest. It seemed wise at the time.

8 KU KUEI

It could have been a holiday in one of the Sweet River woods. Father walking briskly along (he isn't old at all, I realized) and I following only a little behind, watching as his hands reached up to touch leaves and branches, down to pluck grass or flowers, out in wild gestures as he talked. Once I had thought those gestures were flamboyance, showing off—or worse, a way of striking out, reaching out to control me and everyone else around him, to beat us into submission. That was when I was a child, though. Now I saw that the waving, slashing, jabbing of his arms was a sign of exuberance. His body wasn't large enough, didn't move swiftly enough to contain all his life and joy.

Ironic, then, that I realized this only now, when his joy was so out of place. It should have been contagious, but to me it seemed forced. Now instead of wanting to laugh and move and shout along with him, I wanted to weep for him. I would have, too, except that it would shame him. There were things that could be wept for, like long-lost sons come home, but for the losses a Mueller didn't weep. Didn't even give grief for the loss of a kingdom. My father was still alive, but already I mourned for him, because his true self was the Mueller, the ruler, the man so large that only a kingdom could contain him; and now here he was, confined into the space of his body, his kingdom a strange forest and a few men who loved the memory of what he was, and so continued to serve this shrunken remnant of himself. Ensel the Mueller was dead. But Ensel Mueller insisted on being alive, on carrying a kind of greatness with him even in defeat.

I had always expected to inherit the kingdom from him. To step into his place when he died; to *become* him. I thought I was capable of it. But now, following behind him through the forest, I realized that while I might have become the Mueller, had things worked out differently, I was not yet large enough to take *his* place, because when he died he would leave so many places empty, places that I barely knew existed, roles that I would never be large enough to fill.

We left the lake soon enough, without event. I was beginning to wonder if what I felt before, when I passed through Ku Kuei mad with weariness, was mere illusion. But then it began again, just as it had happened when I passed through Ku Kuei before. We walked and walked, and still the sun was high in the sky, hardly seeming to move; Father got hungry and we ate, and the sun had not moved, and we walked on until we were tired, and the sun had moved only a little, and at last we had walked until we were utterly exhausted and couldn't walk anymore, and it might have been noon.

"This is ridiculous," Father said wearily as we lay in the grass.

"I find it consoling," I said. "Now I know that I wasn't insane when this happened before."

"Or else that we both are."

"This is just what happened to me when I came here before."

"What, you got weak and gave out after only a morning's walk?"

"That's what I thought, only now I'm not sure." I had learned some things about the world since I last passed through Ku Kuei. That stargazers in tree-tops could imagine ways to make men fly faster than light between the stars. That naked savages in the desert could turn rocks into sand. Were we wearing out early? Or was the sun merely a little slow in her travels? "We see that no matter how tired we get, no time has passed, so we think we must be wearing out early. But think—doesn't it feel as if we've been traveling forever? Maybe our bodies are fine, and it's time itself that's gotten a little sluggish."

"Lanik, I'm too tired even to understand you, let alone think about what you said."

"Rest, then," I said to Father.

Father drew his sword and lay on his left side, so his right hand, which held the sword, would be free to move into action the moment he awoke. He was asleep in a moment.

I also lay on the grass under the trees, but I didn't sleep. Instead I listened to the rock. Listened through the barrier of living soil and the voices of a million trees, and heard:

Not the voice of the rock, but rather a low, soft, almost unthinkable whisper, and I couldn't under-stand. It seemed to speak of sleep, or could that have been my own mind? I tried to hear the cries of the dying (though usually I tried to shut them out) and this time I heard, not a crush of voices crying in agony together, but rather distinct, low calls. Tor-tured, but slow. Tortured and hating and fearing but endlessly delayed and separated and distinct, and against their rhythm my own heart was quick, rac-ing, panicking, and yet I was at rest and my heart beat normally.

I let myself fall into the soil, which gave way only reluctantly until I was down, resting against the rock. Stones slid away behind my back; deep roots slithered off to let me by; and then harsh rock gave way and cushioned me gently and I heard:

Nothing unusual at all. The voice of the rock was unchanged, and what I had heard near the surface was gone.

I was confused. I hadn't merely imagined what I heard before, and yet now, next to the rock, all was as it had been in Schwartz a few weeks before.

I rose again, listening all the way, and gradually the song of the earth changed, seemed to slow, seemed to separate into distinct voices. The earth, too, seemed more sluggish to part and let me by. But at last I was on the surface, my arms spread, floating as always on what could only seem to me to be a slightly-thicker-than-normal sea.

Father was standing, watching me, the expression on his face indescribable. "My God," he said, "what's happened to you!"

"Just resting," I answered, because there was little else to say.

"You were gone, and then you rose up out of the earth, like the dead coming back out of the grave."

"I forgot to tread water," I said. "Don't worry about it. I had to find something out. I—Father, in Schwartz I learned to do some things. Things that could never be exported through an Ambassador, because they're a way of—thinking, and talking to—things that other people never think of talking to."

"I'm afraid of you, Lanik. You aren't—you aren't human anymore."

I knew what he meant, but still it stung to have him say it. "That issue was decided when I sprouted tits and Homarnoch declared me a rad."

"That was—"

"Different," I said, finishing his sentence. "Because then I was less than human, and now you think I'm more. But neither one is true, Father. I was human all along, either way. This is just one thing that can happen to a human, one thing that a human being can do. Not a god, not a devil. A human."

"How do you know?"

"Because I'm a human, and I can do it."

"You were gone for nearly an hour it seemed, forever it seemed, Lanik. How did you breathe?"

"I held my breath very tight. Father, forget what you saw me do. Let me tell you what I *learned*. There's something about the soil here. Something that slows things down, or makes it seem that way. It's as if—I don't know. As if there's a bubble, enclosing us and the earth and trees around us in a sphere, and inside that bubble, time goes slower. Or no, that doesn't work. It's as if time goes *faster* for us. We walk farther, we do a day's worth of walking, and yet to the world outside, only a few minutes have passed. While we're inside, all the rest of the world seems to go slowly, but it doesn't. It's the same as always."

"If we really walked as far as it feels like, that's one big bubble."

"Unless it follows us around."

"Why didn't it happen for the army?"

"Maybe we had too much momentum or something. I don't know. But look at the sun." It was only a little past the zenith. "And we're already through for the day."

"I'm rested now," Father said. "Felt like I had a long nap, and I woke up and you were gone, not a footprint or anything, just gone. I didn't dare leave, for fear I'd lose you again. I waited forever it felt like."

"I was gone a few minutes, that's all," I said. "But I spent those minutes outside the bubble."

"I don't know about bubbles," said Father, "but I'm rested now." So we went on.

By the sun it was only midafternoon; by my own reckoning, I had done two days' walking since morning when we reached another lake. It was one whose southern edge I had skirted on my earlier journey. Now we stood on its western shore, and the far shore was so near we could see it easily. If it was the far shore, that is. Because it seemed to disappear to the north and south, we supposed we might be looking at an island or a peninsula.

I hadn't slept when Father did, but his rest had done him little good. He was staggering like a drunk, and I was so weary that each step was a separate effort, a triumph of will. "I don't know about you," I told Father, "but this is my limit. This is where I stop."

We slept almost before we lay down.

I awoke in darkness. I had never seen night in Ku Kuei on my first journey, and the night before, with the army, I had had other things on my mind. Now I watched the sky. Both Dissent and Freedom had risen, and at this time of year they were near each other. I lay there, still weary with sleep, letting my mind wander, when it occurred to me that Dissent should have passed Freedom by now.

Instead, there was almost no detectable motion.

Could Ku Kuei have developed a way to slow the sun and the moons? No, or we would have seen such things from Mueller, too. What was going on was not real, it was an illusion, a local phenomenon. Not a change in the earth or sky. It could only be a change in us. A change that didn't happen when the army was with us; a change that happened only when we were alone.

"For once Dissent has learned his place," Father said. So he was also awake.

"You noticed, too."

"I hate this place, Lanik." He sighed. "A beggar

loves any coin. But I'm beginning to think I would have been happier with Harkint."

"Up to a point, you probably would."

"What point?"

"When they cut your head off and it didn't grow back."

"It's a problem with Muellers," Father said. "We never can believe that death is permanent. I heard once of a man who couldn't think how to get vengeance on his enemy, short of killing him, and he didn't want *that* much vengeance. So he challenged the man to combat and beat him, and while his enemy was lying on the ground, faint from loss of blood, he cut off his arm and sewed it on backward. He liked the effect so well, that he did the same to the man's other arm, and his legs, too, right at the hips, so that the man's buttocks were facing the same direction as his face. And of course he had a tail. It was a perfect vengeance. When all had healed, his enemy spent the rest of his life watching himself shit, while he never knew whether he was lying with a pretty girl or a plain one."

I laughed. It was the kind of tale told by the huge fires in Mueller-on-the-River during the wintertime. The kind of tale that men now lacked the spirit to tell, even if they had the wit.

"I'm never going back, am I, Lanik?" Father said. And the way he said it, I knew he didn't want the truth.

"Of course you are," I said. "It's only a matter of time before the Nkumai collapse under their own weight. There's a limit to how much land a Family can absorb."

"No there isn't. I could have conquered everyone."

"Not without me, you couldn't," I said, belligerently enough that he laughed. It was the same laugh I heard from him when I was a child. I thought of the time I challenged him to single combat when he ordered me to go to my room for my impertinence. He had laughed like that, until I drew sword and demanded to be met with honor. He had to cut my right hand almost off before I was content and would submit.

"I never should have tried," he said. Tried what, I wondered, until he finished his sentence: "Doing anything without you."

I said nothing. He had been forced to send me away, a year or so ago; I had acted with little enough choice since then. A year ago? It was yesterday. It was forever. In the darkness I felt as if I had never been anywhere but here, staring up at the stars.

Father was also looking at the stars. "Will we ever reach them?"

"With long enough arms."

"And what will we find if we get there?" Father sounded vaguely sad, as if he had just realized that he would never find something he had carelessly mislaid a long time ago. "If we of Mueller got enough iron and somehow built a starship and went out among the stars, what would we find? After three thousand years, would they greet us with open arms?"

"The Ambassadors still work. They send us iron. They know we're here."

"If they ever meant to let us off this planet, they would have come here years ago and taken us off. Whatever sins were committed, they were paid for a thousand times before I was born, Lanik. Did I rebel against the Republic? What threat am I to them? They have weapons that would let one man stand against all of Nkumai's armies and win. While I'm an aging swordsman who once won seventeen archery matches in a single day. I'll wear all my medals and surely they'll bow." He chuckled dismally, and the chuckle twisted off into a sigh.

"When you cut their arms off, they don't grow

back," I said. "So we do have an advantage over them there."

"We're freaks."

"I'm cold," I said, but the clouds stayed frozen in their places near the horizon, and no wind blew.

"No wind," I said. "They've slowed it all down. Look, Father. Across that inlet, see how the grass is lying over? As if a wind were blowing. And yet they stay that way."

Father seemed not to notice.

"Father," I said. "Perhaps we ought to go on."

"Where?" he answered.

"To find the Ku Kuei."

"Off like Andrew Apwiter, then, trying to find the third moon, a moon all of iron that will save us from hell. There *are* no Ku Kuei. The Family died out years ago."

"No, Father. This isn't a natural occurrence, this bubble of time. It follows us everywhere. Since we're not doing it, it must be that it is being done *to* us, and that means that someone is doing it, and I mean to find them."

"So maybe there *are* some Ku Kuei. If we were going to find them, we would have found them already."

"They can't live without making some sign, Father. Without living in some *place*."

"And have we enough years in our lives to search every meter of the forest, hoping for a Ku Kuei dropping or some hair snagged on a low-hanging branch? They can do strange things with us, and yet we never see them. I call it magic. I give up and I call it magic and the magicians have no need for us and no help for us and I should go back to my people and die. At least then they'll remember me as the king who fought until he died, and not as the Mueller who ran away into the forest and was eaten by the trees of Ku Kuei."

"Father—"

"I want to sleep again. I only want to sleep." He rolled on his side, turning his back to me.

I lay there looking at the stars and wondered what kind of people the Ku Kuei would be. On this world, they could be anything, I thought. As a child growing up in Mueller, I had thought nothing about us was strange. Every child learned his lessons with the threat of isolation or dismemberment if he failed his subject, since pain made no difference even to our children. Every child's cuts healed a moment after he fell. That was, I thought, normal. But now I knew otherwise. Tree people who answer the questions of the universe, desert people whose minds reshape stone. On Treason, strangeness was normality, and those who really *were* ordinary were doomed to be forgotten or overrun.

We came to you, I said in my mind to the Ku Kuei, we came to you because there was nowhere else to turn and we hoped for mercy from those who have no need to fear justice.

No one answered my thoughts. No one had heard.

How loud must I shout before you'll notice me, I thought. What must I do to get your attention, even for a moment, however long moments are around here?

The lake reflected the moonlight. Near us the water shimmered a bit, but the shimmering faded and beyond, the lake was still, waves frozen in midfall. And I knew how I could get them to notice us.

After all, water changes were the first that I had seen in Schwartz, when the water pooled so I could drink, then dissipated when I was done. Once again I lay still and spoke in my silent voice, called out to the earth under me.

The earth sensed my great need, perhaps, or perhaps my powers were stronger than I had thought. But the rocks responded, the earth under the lake loosened, flowed, and the lake sank quickly. When I was through only enough water was left to contain the fish, a scattered group of ponds and marshes, and the lake was gone.

"Sir," said a voice behind me.

"How quickly you came," I answered, not turning around.

"You've stolen our lake," he said.

"Borrowed it."

"Give it back."

"I need your help."

"You come from Schwartz."

"No one comes alive out of Schwartz," I said.

"We come alive out of every place we choose to visit," said the voice. "But no one ever knows that we were there." He giggled.

"I'm from Mueller," I insisted.

"If you can make a lake fall into the earth, you come from Schwartz. What else did you learn there? In Schwartz they don't kill. But we aren't Schwartzes, and we're willing to kill."

"Then kill me, and say good-bye to a lake."

"We owe you nothing."

"You will, when I give your lake back."

Silence. I turned around. There was no one there.

"Sneaky little bastards, aren't you?" I murmured.

"What?" Father asked, waking up. "What the hell happened to the lake?"

"I was thirsty," I answered. I didn't like the fear in his eyes when he looked at me. "We had a visitor. He actually spoke to us."

"Where is he?"

"Gone to fetch company to throw us out, I imagine. In the meantime, look at Dissent and Freedom."

Father looked, and saw what I had seen: Dissent moved across the face of Freedom, and the leaves in the trees whispered in the wind.

"Well," he said. "I should go to sleep more often."

We waited on the edge of what had been the lake. But we didn't wait long. Dissent was only a thumb past Freedom when four men came thundering through the underbrush and stood angrily around us. "What the hell!" shouted one man.

"Want to swim?" I asked.

"What right do you have to attack us like this? What harm have we done you?"

"Besides playing with our sense of time?"

They looked at each other in consternation.

"You fooled me on my first trip. But the second time through I caught on a little."

"Why are you here?"

So Father and I told them, and they listened with inscrutable faces. They were all dark-skinned and tall and fat, but there was strength under the fat. They showed no expression as they listened to our tale.

When we were through, they studied our faces for a while until finally the tallest and fattest, who obviously was in charge—do they choose their leaders by the kilogram, I wondered—said, "And?"

"And we need your help."

"So? Is there some reason we should give it?"

Father was perplexed. "We need it. We're doomed unless you help us."

"That much is plain. But what difference does that make to us?"

"We're fellow human beings!" Father began, but was wise enough to know when to quit. They thought the idea was amusing, anyway.

"I have a good reason why you should help us," I said. "If you don't, you don't have a lake. Mosquitoes breed pretty readily in ponds like these."

"So I promise you everything you want, and you refill the lake," said the leader. "All I need to do is kill you, and there goes our agreement. Plus, we keep the lake. So why not fill the lake and go away, back where you came from? We don't bother you, you don't bother us."

I was angry. So I removed the soil under their feet and slid it sideways. They fell heavily. They tried to stand up again (and they were quicker than I thought their bulk would allow), but the soil kept dancing under their feet, until at last they gave up and sprawled on the ground and yelled for me to stop.

"For a moment," I said.

"If you can do that," the leader said, pulling himself upright and brushing off his clothes, "you hardly need our help. For all my talk, you know, we don't have any weapons. We don't need them. We haven't killed anybody in years. Not that we have any moral objection to it, though, so don't think you're out of trouble."

"It would be lovely," I said, "if we could have the earth swallow up our enemies. But rocks don't play with mass murder, so I can only do certain things. Demonstrations. Lake drainings. Pratfalls. Not practical against an enemy. But we don't need you to fight our battles. What we need is time."

They giggled uncontrollably. They laughed. They roared until tears rolled down their cheeks. A clown could retire in five years of working here, they were so easily amused. Finally the leader said, "Why didn't you say so? If time's all you want, we have plenty." Which sent them into spasms of laughter again.

Father looked uncomfortable. "Are we the only sane people in the world?"

"Perhaps they think we're grim."

"We can give you time," the leader said. "We've been working with time for years. We can't go into the future or past, of course, since time is one-dimensional. ("Of course," I thought, "everyone knows that.") But we can change our own speed in relation to the general timeflow. And we can extend that change to our immediate surroundings. It takes one of us for every four or five people we want to change. How many do you have?"

"Less than a thousand," Father said.

"How specific," the leader answered, twisting up his mouth as if he were about to launch on another barrage of laughter. "You are right down to the last decimal, aren't you? That would take less than two hundred of us, wouldn't it? But less, of course, if you bunch up, if you share each other's time. So maybe we can do it with as few as fifty."

"Do what?" Father asked, suspiciously.

"I don't know," the leader said, grinning broadly. "Give you time, of course. How long until all your enemies are dead? Fifty years? If we work hard, that means you have to stay in a small area for, say, five days. Is that too long? It's harder the faster we make the time pass for you, but if you need a supreme effort, we can give you a hundred years in a week."

"A hundred years of what?"

"Time!" He was getting impatient with us. "You sit here for what seems to you a week, while outside our forest, a hundred years have passed. You go out, all your enemies are gone, nobody's looking for you, you're safe. Or am I wrong? Do your enemies live exceptionally long?"

Father turned to me. "They can do that?"

"After this last year," I said, "I believe anything. They made us think the moons had stopped."

The leader shrugged. "That was nothing. We had a child doing that. Let us get volunteers to help you, and while we're gone, you fill the lake."

I shook my head. "When you come back, I'll fill the lake."

"I gave you my word!"

"You also told me that it wouldn't bother you to kill me after your word was given."

He smiled again. "And maybe I still will. Who

knows? Very chancy world, you have to get used to it." Then, abruptly, he and his friends were gone. They didn't turn and walk away, they were simply not there. Now, though, I could guess: Time was suddenly quicker for them, so they could leave faster than our eyes could register their passage.

"I'm old," Father said. "I can't cope with all this."

"Me neither," I said. "But if it means we can survive, I say let's give it a try."

There were only thirty of them, after all, but the leader assured us they were probably enough, and we set off with the lake restored to its pristine beauty behind us. "Maybe now we kill you," said the leader when the lake was full, but then he laughed uproariously and gave me a huge hug. "I like you!" he shouted. All the others laughed. I didn't get the joke.

"Quicktime," said the leader, but to my surprise nobody hurried. Then I realized they meant that their time would pass quickly, while the outside world plodded on at the normal rate. It was early morning when we reached the place where the army was camped, but we had stopped and slept twice on the way, and in all our expedition had taken five days of our time, while to our army it would only be twenty-four hours or so. This time Father and I realized how hard we must have driven ourselves before. The Ku Kuei weren't sluggish, and we were weary enough each time we lay down to rest; Father and I had made the same journey with only two sleep periods.

It was a fine journey, all done in less than twenty-four hours from the time we left the army, if only the army had been there when we got back.

From a kilometer away, it was clear something was wrong. We were skirting the shores of the long lake, and we could see far ahead along the meadowland. But where smoke still rose from the camp-fires, there were no large herds of horses. No horses at all. Nothing.

Except corpses, of course. Not too many, but enough to make the story clear. Homarnoch, who had insisted on bringing his wagon into the forest, troublesome though it was, lay dead in front of the wagon's charred remains. Even a Mueller can't regenerate burns over the entire body—but to make sure, they had cut his head off after his death. The other corpses were similarly taken care of.

This we took in after only a few moments at the camp. I looked for Saranna, calling her name. Yet I hoped she wasn't there—better to imagine her alive among the deserters than dead, here. I went on calling for her, and soon the Ku Kuei joined in the search for living among the dead. It was the leader who called to me. "Lake-drinker!" he shouted. "Someone alive!"

I started toward him.

"It's a woman!" he shouted, and I came faster.

Father was kneeling beside her. Her arms and legs had been cut off, and her larynx had been cut out. Her body was regenerating, but not all that quickly. She was not a rad. She still couldn't talk.

The Ku Kuei leader kept demanding to know how she had healed so quickly and why she hadn't bled to death, until Father told him to shut his fat mouth for a minute. We fed her, and she looked at me with an expression that tore at my heart, and the stumps of her arms reached out to me. I held her. The Ku Kuei, puzzled, watched.

"I guess this means you won't be needing us," said the leader, after a while.

"More than ever," I said, even as Father said, "That's right."

"Now which of you do I believe?" he asked.

"Me," I insisted. "We don't need thirty men for

our army. But there's nowhere we can go now. The three of us. My father, Ensel Mueller. Saranna, my —wife. And my name is Lanik Mueller."

"We've fulfilled our part of the bargain," said the fat Ku Kuei. "So we're rid of you. Shall we carry you to the edge of the forest?"

I had little patience. I moved the ground under him. He landed heavily on his backside and swore.

"You have the instincts of a bully," he said angrily. "May your children all be porcupines! May your gall bladder be full of stones! May your father be found to have been sterile all his life!"

He looked so serious, so intense that I couldn't help but laugh. And when I started laughing, the leader broke into a grin. "You're my kind of fellow!" he shouted.

It didn't take much to get ahead with the Ku Kuei.

They carried Saranna back with them, amazingly careful for such huge, malproportioned people; but they stopped to rest oftener than Father or I needed, and while Father eagerly ate the immense snacks they constantly offered to share with us, I didn't bother eating. Instead I stayed with Saranna and fed her. We had been traveling for hours on our second day after leaving the camp when Saranna finally spoke.

"I think," she began huskily, "that my voice will work again."

"Oh no!" shouted one of the Ku Kuei. "A woman speaks, and silence is banished from the forest!" The remark brought immense peals of laughter, and several of the Ku Kuei were lying on the ground, unable to sit up because either the laughter or the meal made it impossible for them to remain upright.

"Saranna," I said, and she smiled.

"You weren't gone very long, Lanik."

"Too long, it seems," I said.

"They left me alive to tell you what they thought."

"The only good thing that's been done in a month."

"They were sure you had gone off to kill the Mueller. They knew you planned to bring the terrors of Ku Kuei back to destroy them. They hated you. And so they left."

"Killing on the way."

"Homarnoch forbade them and threatened to kill the first man who left. There were a great many who intended to be first, and so Homarnoch killed no one. Some of the men tried to defend him. They died, too."

"And you."

"They were quick. They wanted to make sure I couldn't travel easily. They thought it would stop you and the monsters from pursuing them."

I looked at the thirty-odd Ku Kuei, sitting like small mountains or snoring in the grass. "Monsters," I said, and Saranna laughed, but the laughter soon turned to tears, her voice sobbing thickly.

"It feels so good to have a voice to cry with," she murmured when the tears had subsided.

"How are your feet?"

"Better. But the bones aren't hard. Tomorrow I can walk a little."

I unwrapped the bandage the Ku Kuei had improvised around her legs. "Liar," I said. "You're not even halfway down the shin yet."

"Oh," she answered. "I thought I could feel my toes."

"That's the nerve regenerating. Haven't you ever lost a leg before?"

"My friends didn't pull pranks like that. And I always behaved in school." She smiled.

"All right, we're going, hup hup, hurry, we haven't much time!" shouted the leader, and the others laughed loudly as we started going again. I silently longed to kill the next man who laughed.

The city of the Ku Kuei was in the middle of the lake, on the island we had seen from the shore. If you can call it a city. There were no buildings, no structures of any kind. Just forest, and grass that was rather thoroughly tramped down in a few places.

What was remarkable were the people. The children, mercifully, were thin, but the adults made me suspect that kilo for kilo, the Ku Kuei were more than half the mass of human life on Treason. The impression I got—and I never had any reason to change it—was one of incredible laziness. No one seemed to do anything that he could avoid doing. "Come hunting with us," many of them said to me, and once I went. They would put themselves into quick-time and walk up to the prey and kill it while it stood motionless, still in normal time. When I suggested it wasn't sporting, they looked at me oddly. "When you want to run a race, do you cut off your feet?" one of them asked me. And another one said, "If I cut off my feet, does that mean I never have to run another race?" Paroxysms of laughter. I went back to the city then.

Yet for all their laziness, their determination to be amused at everything, and their utter unwillingness to take any commitment seriously, I came to love the Ku Kuei. Not as I had the Schwartzes, for I had also admired them; I loved the Ku Kuei as immense self-propelled toys. And they, for some strange reason, loved me, too. Perhaps because I had found a new way to force someone to take a pratfall.

"What's your name?" I asked the man who had led our would-be rescue party.

"What do you think, Lake-drinker?"

"How should I know? And my name's Lanik Mueller."

He giggled. "That's not a name. You drank the lake, you're Lake-drinker."

"You're the only one who calls me that."

"I'm the only one who calls you anything," he said. "And how's Stump?"

When I found out he meant Saranna, I left him. He couldn't understand why I was angry. He thought the name was appropriate.

I suppose the months I passed in Ku Kuei were a sort of idyll, like my time in Schwartz. But in Schwartz I was still exuberant for the future. In Ku Kuei, my future was behind me. And Father was trying to die.

I realized it on the second day of our lessons with Man-Who-Knows-It-All. Saranna and I were lying in the grass, our eyes closed, paying careful attention as the teacher spoke softly and sang occasionally and tried to help us feel his own timeflow as it enveloped us. I don't know what aroused me from the trance (and I roused unwillingly, I'm sure, since Man-Who-Knows-It-All has the gentlest timeflow I ever shared), but I looked over at Father and his eyes were open, staring straight into the sky, and the track of a tear ran down from his eye to his hair.

At the time I put the worry out of my mind. Surely Father had plenty to feel bad about; no reason to try to force him to imitate cheerfulness he didn't feel.

But because of Father, I found it progressively harder to involve myself in the happy-go-lucky mood that unflinchingly gripped the Ku Kuei. Unflinchingly gripped? That was my attitude. Though at times I felt relaxed, felt loved, felt *good*, I was never wholly at peace. Mostly because of my worry about Father. But partly because in all my growing up, I had never had lessons in breaking loose and not caring. I had just survived a very difficult year, and its effects were slow to fade. Besides, it's impossible to be uncaring after having heard the music of the earth.

"You're too intense," said Man-Who-Fell-on-His-Ass (the name I eventually gave to the leader I had given several pratfalls to—he loved the name and several of his friends picked it up). "Man-Who-Knows-It-All says you're not making very good progress. You have to learn to laugh."

"I know how to laugh."

"You know how to make silly sounds with a tight belly. Nobody can laugh with a tight belly. And you're too thin. It's a sign of worry, Lake-drinker. I'm telling you this because I think you want to learn timeshifting. You're trying too hard." For once Man-Who-Fell-on-His-Ass looked deadly serious, very concerned. The expression was so foreign to his face that I had to laugh, and he laughed back, thinking he had achieved something. But he had achieved nothing.

Because Father was not paying attention. Even in easygoing Ku Kuei, one had to pay attention to survive, and Father didn't care. He fell down a lot, once from a rather high hill. That time he ended up with two broken arms. They healed in a few days, but as he lay under a tree during a rainstorm, while I practiced elementary time control by slowing the two of us down a little (very little) so the drops fell with less apparent force, he suddenly held my hand very tightly, which surely caused his arm to hurt worse, and said, "Lanik, you have the power of the Schwartzes. Can you change me?"

"Into what?" I asked, trying to keep the mood light because a light mood was getting ingrained in me.

"Take away my Muellerness. Take away the regeneration."

I was puzzled. "If I did that, Father, that fall might have killed you. And it would take months for these arms to heal."

He looked away from me, his eyes full of tears, and I realized that the fall from the hill might not really have been an accident. It worried me. Father had had reverses before, but this one, admittedly the worst by far, was holding him far too tightly.

Saranna caused me another kind of worry. It began when I found her making love to Bug-killer, so named because he thrashed around so much during sex. She was laughing as he flung out his legs, and she kept laughing even when she looked at me.

Sex under the trees was a common enough sight in Ku Kuei, and I wasn't under any delusion that I had been confining my lovemaking to Saranna because of any overconcern with faithfulness. I just found Ku Kuei women too fat to enjoy. I was a little jealous, I'm sure, but overriding that was my realization that Saranna seemed no different from any other woman in Ku Kuei—amused, detached, easy.

It was Saranna who had begged me to take her with me when I first left Mueller; Saranna who had gashed herself deeply when I refused to let her continue as my lover after I found out I was a rad. And she had been intensely in love with me from the time I came back. Yet now—

"Saranna is a good student," said Man-Who-Knows-It-All.

"I know," I answered. "I can sense her timeflow now almost as well as I sense yours."

"You're unhappy," said my teacher.

"I imagine so."

"Are you jealous because you are the poorest student I've ever had while Saranna is as good as one of our own more gifted children?"

I shrugged. That certainly was part of it. "Maybe I'm more worried because she seems to care less about the things that I care about."

Man-Who-Knows-It-All laughed. "You care about *everything*! How can anybody care about so much!"

"My father cares even more," I said.

"On the contrary, Tight-Gut, your father cares as little as we do. It's just that he tends to despair, while we are full of hope."

"I'm losing Saranna."

"That's good. No one should own someone else." And he went on explaining why it was that my time-sense was no good and I needed to *relax* before I got as stiff and hard as a tree.

I wasn't worried all the time, of course. That would be impossible in Ku Kuei. If there weren't the games in the lake or the mad expeditions through the forest, there would be enough to engage a man for a century just walking through the city, pausing to taste the timeflows as people lived at their own pace.

For instance, Man-Who-Fell-on-His-Ass was almost constantly in a very fast timeflow. I was so inept at timeshaping that I almost automatically joined the timeflow of anyone nearby; in contrast, even Ku Kuei of ordinary skills could hold onto their own timeflow even standing right next to someone else. When I was with Man-Who-Fell-on-His-Ass, the rest of the world seemed utterly stopped. We walked and talked and the sun never moved in the sky and the people we passed were frozen or (if they had a fast timeflow) they moved sluggishly. No one moved as quickly as Man-Who-Fell-on-His-Ass.

"My friend," I finally said one day, when I felt he was my friend, "you speed through life so quickly. What's your hurry?"

"I'm not in a hurry. I never walk fast."

"I've been here for maybe a month or so—"

He interrupted by giggling. "I don't know how you keep track of the days, as if they meant anything!"

"And you've grown older in that time."

He touched his hair. "Grey, huh?"

"Grey. And wrinkles."

"Laugh wrinkles!" he said triumphantly, as if that answered everything.

His fey attitude was growing in Saranna—but it held her differently. She slowed down. It was not a sudden decision—"today I'll be slow"—it was gradual. But after she mastered timeshaping I began to notice that when I was with her, caught up in her flow, everything around us moved quickly. Unbearably fast, the Ku Kuei who passed us dancing madly, racing out of sight, jabbering for a moment and going on. When Saranna and I talked, she kept looking over my shoulder, from side to side, watching as people sped by. Now and then she'd smile, an expression unrelated to our conversation, and I'd turn to see the scene that had amused her already gone.

When I met her once early in the morning and after a short conversation found that it was nearly night, I asked her why she slowed down so much.

"Because they're so funny," she said. "Racing along like that."

That would have been reason enough for the flighty girl I had first fallen in love with, but it wasn't reason enough now. I insisted. She balked. "You're too intense, Lanik. But I love you."

We made love, and it was as good as ever, and her passion for me was still warm, not the laughing, amusing affairs she had with the Ku Kuei. I knew I still had a hold on her, yet not enough of one to persuade her not to make the world race by without taking part.

She became notable. The Ku Kuei took to calling her Stump for another reason now; to most of them she was as immovable and dead as a cut tree. She wouldn't change her timeflow for anyone, and so I, the chameleon who changed times with every friend, was the one who could most easily talk to her. Most of the time she stood, frozen impossibly in midstep, and from a distance I watched sometimes for hours as she would complete a step and shift weight to the other foot.

Once for three days every time I saw her she was in the middle of making love to Man-Who-Knows-It-All. The caresses and strokes were as slow, the movement as infinitesimal, as if they were distant stars, and I felt as if I had never known her, or worse, as if she were merely a pornographic statue under a tree on Ku Kuei Island.

Saranna and Father were both finding their own way to retreat from life. While I was unable to escape.

The day that Father died he came to me and lay beside me under a tree as a thin drizzle fell. "Play no games with time today," Father said. "You always concentrate so hard that I don't think you're listening to me." And so I lay there and Father put his arm around me and pulled me close as he had when we were on maneuvers when I was a child. He was saying I love you. He was saying good-bye.

"I was a builder," he said, writing his epitaph in my mind, "but my buildings crumbled, Lanik. I have outlived all my works."

"Except me."

"You've been shaped by stronger forces than I can muster. It's a shame when an architect lives to see the temple fall."

No one had built temples in Mueller for centuries.

"Was I a good king?" Father asked.

"Yes," I answered.

"No," he said. "Wars and murders, conquest and power, all so important for so many years, and then all undone. Not undone by the inexorable forces of nature. Undone because men who live in trees happened to win the game and get the prize faster than we, and it unbalanced us, threw us to the ground. Chance. And it was as much chance when we got iron from the Ambassador, and so I wasn't an empire builder after all, was I? I just used the iron to kill people."

"You were a good ruler to your people," I said, because he needed to hear it and because, on the relative scale by which monarchs must be measured, it was true.

"They play games with us. A dose of iron here, a dose there, and see what that does to the playing field. I was a pawn, Lanik, and I thought I was the king."

He grabbed me fiercely, clung to me, whispered savagely in my ear, "I will not laugh!" To prove it he wept, and so did I.

He drowned himself that day. The body was found floating in the tall rushes of the shallow side of the island, where the current had carried him. He had jumped from a cliff into a shallow part of the lake and broken his neck; his body could not regenerate quickly enough to stop him from drowning as he lay helpless on the bottom. The pain I felt then still comes back to me in sharp memories sometimes, but I refused to grieve. He had beaten the regeneration, and I was rather proud of his ingenuity. Suicide had been beyond most of the Müellers for years, unless they were mad and could lie down in flames. Father was not mad, I'm sure of it.

With Father gone, some things were better. He no longer worried me, and when I was finally able to forget the empty feeling, the sense of loss, when I stopped turning around, looking for someone that it took me a moment to remember would not be there, I improved as a student. "You are still terrible," Man-Who-Knows-It-All told me, "but you can at least control your own timeflow." And it was true. I could walk within a meter of someone on a different flow, and not be changed. It gave me a measure of freedom I hadn't had in this place before, and I took to changing my flow to a very fast rate when it was time to sleep, so that my nine hours took only a few minutes and to others I seemed to be awake all the time. I saw every hour of every day, and like a Ku Kuei, I found they all amused me.

But I wasn't happy.

No one was happy, I realized one day. Amused, yes. But amusement is the reaction of very bored people when nothing entertains them anymore. The

Ku Kuei had all the time in the world. But they didn't know what to do with it.

I had lived with the Ku Kuei for half a year of real time (the seasons, by and large, were unaffected by their games) when I heard that Man-Who-Fell-on-His-Ass was dying. "Very old," said the woman who told me. And so I went to him, and found him, still in his quicktime, racing madly toward death as he lay in the grass under the sun. I sped up to his time, which few Ku Kuei were willing to do, particularly since there was nothing amusing about death. I held his hand as he wheezed.

His body had grown thinner, though he was still fat. The skin sagged and drooped.

"I can cure you," I said.

"Don't bother."

"I'm sure of it," I said. "I can renew you. I learned it in Schwartz. They live forever in Schwartz."

"Whatever for?" he asked. "I haven't been hurrying all this time just to be cheated now." And he giggled.

"What are you laughing at?" I asked.

"Life," he said. "And you. Oh, Tight-Gut. My Lake-drinker. Drink me dry."

It occurred to me that I was the only person in Ku Kuei who would grieve for him. Death was ignored here, as it had been when my father died. Man-Who-Fell-on-His-Ass had had many friends. Where were they? Finding new friends who hadn't rushed through life and finished up before the others were through.

"It had no meaning for me," he said. "But it means something to you. We say that we are happy because we have hope, but it's a lie. We have no hope. You're the only person I've known in my life who had hope, Lake-drinker. So leave here. This is a cemetery, leave here and save the world. You can, you know. Or if you can't, no one can."

I noticed with surprise that he wasn't laughing.

"You mean this, don't you?" I asked.

"I like you, Lake-drinker," he answered, and then he died. Enough of his timeflow lingered that he had largely decomposed in a few minutes of real time, and so no one moved his body from the place. His corpse just crumbled and dissolved into the earth.

I also sank into the earth, letting it close above me and listening again to the music of the earth. The war was over; the screams of the dying were isolated now, constant but isolated in space, the deaths all in the random patterns of peace. Yet I did not believe the world was at peace. The world had never been at peace.

Save the world? From what? I had no illusions. I couldn't even save myself.

I could, however, savor the world, and here in Ku Kuei the flavor was thin and bland. With Man-Who-Fell-on-His-Ass dead, and Father dead, and Saranna frozen in time, and Man-Who-Knows-It-All convinced that I would never learn any better control of time than I had now, it occurred to me that it was time to go.

"Don't," Saranna said when I told her.

"I want to and I will," I said.

"I need you." The look in her eye was frightened. So I stayed a little longer. I stayed with her in her timeflow for another day, another night, and another day of real time and we made love and said many gentle things that would make good memories later and would soften the pain of parting. One thing that was said was, "I'm sorry," and another was, "I forgive you," though I am no longer sure whose remorse was purged that way. I doubt it was mine.

When I left, she did not cry, nor did I, though both of us wanted to, I believe. "Come back," she said.

"All right."

"Come back soon. Come back while you're still

young enough to want me. For I'm going to be young forever."

Not forever, Saranna, I thought but did not say. Young only until the planet is old and is swallowed by a star. Then you will be old, and the flames will wither what time could not. And because you've chosen to hide from time, the flames will burn you infinitely before you die.

I thought when I left her I would never see her again, and so, once out of her timeflow, I looked back and memorized her, a single tear just starting to leave her eye, a loving smile on her face, her arms reaching out to bid farewell—or perhaps reaching out to catch me and bring me back. She was unbearably lovely. The pretty girl had lost her land, her family, all her loves, and it had hurt her into womanhood. I fleetingly wondered if I was yet old enough to truly love her.

Then I left, bidding good-bye to no one else because my leaving would not have particularly amused anyone. I set out into the forest with my timeflow sliding naturally along in real time, so that at night I got tired and slept, and I woke in the morning with the sun. Normality was refreshing, for a change.

I was a day out of the city when I felt a faster timeflow nearby, and adjusted myself to fit it. I found three Ku Kuei, young girls who were still adolescently thin. They were harrying a stranger who had ventured into the forest. Whatever direction he had been traveling, he was now going south, following the Forest River that flowed outward into Jones. One of the girls left the others and explained to me that they had been with the poor fellow for days. He was nearly insane with worry about why he couldn't seem to travel more than an hour by the sun before he had to sleep. "That's one man that'll never come back to Ku Kuei," she said, giggling.

"You never know," I said. "Someone did that to me my first time through, and I came back."

"Oh," she said. "You're Tight-Gut. You're different." And then she started to undress, a sure sign that a Ku Kuei expects to make love, and I made her laugh uproariously when I told her I didn't want to. "That's what they said, but I didn't believe it! Only that white girl from Mueller, right? Stump, right?"

"Saranna," I said. That made her laugh all the more, and I left her and settled back to real time so that they would go quickly away from me. It was true, though. When I first reached puberty, I had spent countless hours plotting to sleep with every girl I could find who was willing. And there were few who were unwilling to sleep with the Mueller's heir. Yet without ever being conscious of deciding, I had somehow chosen to sleep with no one but Saranna. When had I decided that, and why?

Faithfulness had taken me by surprise. I wondered how long the phase would last.

When you walk in it without fear, the forest of Ku Kuei is beautiful enough. But I was bred to farmland and the riding range. When the Forest River broke out of the trees into the high hills of Jones, a tumble of land that led down to the great Rebel River plain, I sat for an hour on a hilltop, looking at the fields and trees and open land. From here I could see smoke rising from kitchen fires nearby; on the Rebel River far to the south there were sails; but in the great sweep of land men had made little difference after all. I felt philosophical for a few minutes, and then realized that one of the nearby orchards was filled with apples. I wasn't hungry. But I hadn't eaten food in so long that my teeth seemed to tingle just to think of chewing. So I walked down the hill, forgot philosophy, and joined the human race again.

Nobody was particularly glad to see me.

9 JONES

The town had a name, but I never knew it. Just another of the villages astride the great highway between Nkumai and Mueller. Once this had been one of the many small roads that let Jones trade with Bird, Robles with Sloan, but the Nkumai empire had made it a large road, heavy with traffic. The locals said you could stand beside the road and some party of travelers would come by every five or ten minutes all day. I saw no reason to doubt them.

It was only a year since my father and I had disappeared into the Forest of Ku Kuei and never returned; already we were legend. I heard stories that I had murdered him, or that he had executed me, or that we had killed each other in some terrible duel; I also heard the prophecy that Father would return one day and unite all the nations of the western plain in a great rebellion against the Nkumai. Of course I said nothing of Father's plunge into the lake in Ku Kuei, though I couldn't help wondering if he would have chosen death, had he known the great reverence the people of the plain had for his name.

It was ironic, too, since they had once feared him, before they knew how much harder a master was Nkumai than Mueller. Or was it? I had no way to compare. We of Mueller had no particular program of mercy toward those we conquered, back when we went out a-conquering. The people would have groaned under the heel of Mueller as surely as they complained about the oppression of Nkumai.

Talk of rebellion was all dreamwork, anyway. Supposedly, Dinte ruled in Mueller, but it was well known that Mueller's independence was all show. On paper, Mueller was even larger and stronger than it had been under my father, but everyone knew that Nkumai's "king" ruled in Mueller as surely as he ruled in Nkumai. Harsh as the Nkumai might be, the whole Rebel River plain, from Schmidt in the west to the Starhigh Mountains in the east, was at peace. At peace because it had been conquered, yes, but peace brings security, and security brings confidence, and confidence brings prosperity. The people complained, but they were content enough.

The king of Nkumai? I heard much of this king, but I knew better, and so did others who had reason to know. Like the innkeeper in the town, a man who had once been Duke of Forest-edge but made the mistake of holding back some of the huge conqueror's tax the soldiers of Nkumai came to collect. After they stripped him of land and title, though, he still had enough money cached away to buy the inn and stock it, so perhaps it wasn't a mistake after all— now that he wasn't of the nobility, he was pretty much left alone.

"And now I work here day in and day out, and I make a good living, but boy, I tell you cause you'll never know it, there's nothing like chasing the hounds after a cossie fleeing through the forest-edge."

"I don't doubt it," I said, particularly since I had hunted down many a cossie, too. We surplus armigers made up in memories for what we had lost in station.

"But the king says no more hunting, and so we

eat beef and mutton mixed with horse manure and call it a stew."

"The king must be obeyed," I said. In those days, it never hurt to add a plug for the king. There's nobody here but us loyal supporters of Nkumai.

"The king must be screwed," said the innkeeper. I liked him better instantly. Had there been any other customers at the moment, of course, he surely would have been more circumspect. But he could tell by my speech, I suppose, that I was educated, which meant that I, too, was fallen from high station. "The king of Nkumai is about as common these days as starships."

I laughed. So he knew, too.

"Everyone knows the real power behind the throne is Mwabao Mawa," he said.

The name brought back floods of memories, ending on a dark night when she tried to make love to a sweet young girl in her treehouse. Oddly, the memory stirred me and I thought wistfully of what might have happened if we had made love. Wouldn't she have been surprised.

"And what I know but not everyone knows is that the scientists are the power behind Mwabao Mawa," he said.

I smiled. How had the Nkumai been careless enough to let that secret slip? But again I pretended not to know. "Scientists? They're nothing but dreamers."

"Do you think so? Do you think because I've fallen on hard times that I don't have supporters and friends in high places? The same's true of Mueller. The geneticists are running things there—Dinte's just there to keep those that love royal blood from rising up in rebellion. It's a sad day when those born to rule are keeping inns while self-appointed wise men oversee things they were never meant to handle."

He went into the back room, then, and didn't come

back out until I had finished drinking the ale. I didn't need it, but every now and then it just felt good to drink. And afterward it felt good to piss. People who do these things every day never realize how much pleasure they involve. So I drank, and then I got up to leave.

"Don't go yet!" he called out, and he strode back into the common room. "Sit back down, and give me your word you'll not tell anybody what I tell you now."

I smiled, and he foolishly took that for assent. He smiled back. "I knew in a minute," he said, "that you're not a common boy. It's not just your white hair, though sure enough that places you in Mueller or Schmidt. You've got the look about you. Even though you're alone, you've known how it was to command men."

I said nothing, just regarded him. I had made no attempt to disguise my bearing, so I wasn't terribly impressed that he had realized all this.

He grinned and quieted his voice. "My name's Bill Underjones. Understand that, so that you know that I'm not just a dreamer." *Under-jones* made him only one step removed from royalty. "There are those who still oppose these inkers. We aren't many, but we're smart, and we're stockpiling old Mueller iron south of here, in Huss. It's a backwater country, but that's the best place to hide. I'll tell you who to see there, and he'll be glad to take you in. It doesn't matter who you are, one look at you and he'll want you. His name is—"

"Don't tell me his name," I said. "I don't want to know."

"You can't tell me you don't hate these inkers as bad as I do!"

"Maybe worse," I said. "But I break easily under torture. I'd give away all your secrets."

He looked at me slantwise. "I don't believe you."

"I urge you to try," I said.

"Who are you?"

"Lanik Mueller," I said.

He looked startled for a moment, then laughed uproariously. I often used my own name—it always brought that reaction.

"Might as well claim to be the devil himself. No, Lanik Mueller was swallowed up—what a joker. His father killed him. Might as well claim to be the devil!"

Might as well. He was still laughing as I walked out onto the street.

The inn faced the main highway, and as I stepped from the inn's wooden frontwalk, a beggar child ran past me, jostling me as he went. I was annoyed, and watched the boy as he ran on, finally to collide head-on with a very important-looking man with clothes whose price would have fed and clothed a beggar family for a month or more. The man had been talking to several younger men, and when the child struck him, he gave the boy a vicious kick in the leg. The child fell to the ground, and the man cursed him soundly.

It was foolish of me, but this seemed at the moment to be the crowning injustice of all the million injustices I had seen and perpetrated in my life. *This* time, I decided, I would do something.

So I pushed myself into quicktime, and the people on the street slowed until they were nearly stopped. I threaded my way carefully through the crowd until I stood in front of the man who had kicked the child. His right foot was descending to the ground as he walked along, still in animated discussion with his young friends. It was a simple matter to have the soil of the road sink a decimeter directly under his foot, and to have a puddle of water form there, extending a full two meters on in front of him. With my hands I took one of the large stones used to chock wagon wheels and placed it so it would impede his left foot.

Then I walked to the stable where my horse was being fed and groomed, and leaned against the door. I felt more than a little silly to have gone to such lengths to effect such a small thing. It was more a desire for the prank, I think, than any moral principle that inspired the act.

However, now that I was in quicktime among the crowd, I took a moment to relax. In quicktime I had no need to be wary in case I met someone who *would* recognize me, instead of know-nothings who laughed when I mentioned my name. Instead I could survey the crowd at my leisure.

Since I was already being childish right then, I even toyed with the idea of picking pockets, not because I needed any money, but because it was possible to do it and never get caught. There is something about knowing you won't get caught that could tempt the most honest man, and I have never claimed to be unusually honest.

I looked over the crowd to see who might be a likely target. A little way down the road a large wagon was coming—an Nkumai coach, and judging from the large contingent of mounted Nkumai soldiers, it contained somebody important. It was a warm day; the carriage was open; the sole occupant was a middle-aged man, rather stocky and thoroughly bald. To my surprise, he was white. I immediately supposed he was a Mueller returning from a visit to Nkumai. But the Nkumai don't give mounted escorts to foreigners who are leaving. Either this man deserved unusual honor (in which case, why didn't I know him?) or the Nkumai were letting foreigners high in their own government.

Wondering about him put the idea of picking pockets out of my mind. I slid back to real time, turning to watch the result of my prank. Exactly as I planned, the self-important stranger stepped into the rut I had made and fell headlong into the puddle. The splash was formidable, and he arose sputtering and cursing as all the people nearby laughed at him. Even his coterie of admirers couldn't hide their amusement as they solicitously helped him up. And, for all that the gesture was small, I felt a certain satisfaction, particularly when I looked at the laughing child the man had kicked.

The moment passed. People moved to the side of the road to let the Nkumai troop and carriage pass. I glanced at the carriage and was shocked to see, not the middle-aged man, but Mwabao Mawa.

She seemed only a little older—it had scarcely been two and a half years—and she held herself very importantly in the carriage. I briefly wondered why I hadn't noticed her in the carriage before, and where the bald white man had got to. But at the moment that thought was pushed aside, partly because it didn't admit to any ready explanation, but mostly because I let myself remember my days in Mwabao Mawa's house. It seemed impossible to me now that I had once had breasts and passed for a woman. *Been* a woman, rather. And for a moment as I involuntarily reached up to my chest I expected to find softness there, and, for that moment, I was surprised to find it gone.

I glanced down, realized the old habit I had fallen into, cursed myself for a fool, and then looked up to see Mwabao Mawa staring at me, at first in mild interest, and then, as the carriage pulled farther away, with recognition and surprise and, yes, fear. The fear was gratifying, but the recognition could be disastrous.

She turned to give instructions to the driver. I used that moment to step back into the stable and get out of sight. I also pushed into quicktime again—I had to think, quickly. There was no way I could take my horse in quicktime, since Man-Who-Knows-It-All, despite all his efforts, hadn't been able to teach me to extend my bubble of time control outside myself. In quicktime I could walk faster relative to the rest of the world than a horse could possibly carry me at a full gallop.

I went to my horse, a huge, stupid beast with all the instincts of a hog but with a price I could afford, and unloaded the saddlebags, selecting as much as I could carry, and taking anything that might give a hint as to my identity. There was little enough of that—I had never been one for embroidered kerchiefs or blazoned leather. Then, carrying the bags, I slipped out a back door into the corral.

When Mwabao Mawa didn't find me quickly, she would forget the search and figure she had only seen someone who reminded her of me. I didn't think I had made myself so remarkable that anyone would remember me, except perhaps the innkeeper, and he had reasons of his own for not cooperating with the Nkumai.

I tossed the bags over the fence of the corral, climbed after them and walked off down a side street. I'd have to stay in quicktime for several days. Which irritated me, because in quicktime, of course, I aged more quickly relative to the real world. I wouldn't end up like Man-Who-Fell-on-His-Ass, but I resented losing days or weeks off my life. How old was I now, anyway? I had gained days and weeks when I was with Saranna in slowtime; I had lost many more days and weeks in quicktime among the Ku Kuei. Was I anywhere near my calendar age of eighteen? Hardly, even if my body seemed that young and strong. I had been through enough, I figured, to have a middle-aged man's memories. As I strode off through the back roads and started on my way to Robles in the south, I decided that quicktime didn't matter anyway. I had no particular desire to live to be old.

Still, I had no intention of letting the Nkumai catch me and realize who I was.

The worst thing about quicktime was the loneliness. No one is safer than a man who moves so quickly that he can't be seen. But it's a bit tough to carry on a conversation with someone who won't even know you're there unless you stand in the same place for a half hour.

I crossed the Rio de Janeiro into Cummings before I let myself back into realtime. No matter how alarmed Mwabao Mawa was, she wouldn't send troops more than a thousand kilometers to look for someone she had seen only a few meters off that very day.

Why did I go south? I had no particular object in mind. Except that I had lived in a dozen towns under Nkumai control in Jones and Bird during the past six months, and I wanted to get to a place where the enlightened empire of the physicists didn't rule. I didn't want to link up with any rebels gathering in Huss, so I went southeast over the da Silva pass.

There I found that there was no escape from the imperial committees. A few dozen scientists in Gill ruled from Tellerman to Britton, and no one was free.

I might have given up and gone right back to Schwartz then. Or, had my despair been even deeper, I might have gone back to Mueller and faced down Dinte. But I hadn't the weariness yet for retirement from the world, and I hadn't the passion for a dramatic death, and so both Schwartz and Mueller I reserved for the future. Instead I wandered from da Silva to Wood, from Wood to Hanks, from Hanks across the sea to Holt, and finally to Britton, where I found my true home, my true people, and learned what I had to do to keep them.

10   BRITTON

The district of Humping was wild country on the borders of a calm sea. In good weather the steep cliffs and jumbled rocks of the coast were met, not by crashing waves, but by ripples that lapped against the stone as gently as aging dogs greet their master. Stones sprouted from the earth, it seemed, on the steep hills and narrow valleys of Humping. A river hunted for a way to the sea, and found it over a forty-foot fall; sheep looked nervous as they picked a safe way to unshorn pastures; and here, a few thousand Humpers tended their sheep and scratched vegetables from the stony ground and lived as independent a life as human beings can live when they still need human company and still must eat.

I didn't need to eat, but the human company was good, for the Humpers asked no questions and gave no answers. It was hard even to find a town in this most isolated section of Britton, for the people tended to congregate in family groups of two or three simple sod houses with thatched roofs. I never found a gathering of more than twenty families within a kilometer of each other.

The isolation was forced by nature, for the meager land could not support many; only the uniformity of want made the people think they were not poor.

Despite the distances between them, however, they clung to each other's company grimly, wordlessly coming to the help of the family whose house was blown over by the storm, anonymously leaving a young he-goat among the herd whose sire died the day before, and occasionally gathering at each other's homes for a night of tall and terrible tales or songs of loneliness and silent longing.

I also had another impression, subtle but strong: when I came to Humping, as I had come to so many other places in the past year, I immediately felt comfortable there. Or if not comfortable, at least willing to bear the discomforts because they fit the awkward places in my heart.

The people viewed me with suspicion, of course, for I came over the hills from the west, where more civilized folk in easier farms had nothing but contempt for the Humpers, using the name as a mockery for slow-witted children. But I lived in these hills for a week, speaking to no one, until at last my loneliness struck a sympathetic chord. I was standing on the crest of a steep hill, watching as a shepherd far below tried to get his sheep to climb a slope to a saddle that led over to an uncropped valley. The man had no dogs, which was unusual, and the sheep kept breaking to left or right rather than climbing. When the man finally stopped and sat on a rock to watch his victorious sheep hunt for forage in an already-overgrazed valley, I came down the hill and stood a few meters off from him, watching the sheep. I didn't speak because I had nothing to say; my offer was intrinsic in my presence.

The shepherd accepted. He stood and began prodding the sheep and uttering the low, guttural cries that the sheep could hear clearly but that were inaudible from a good distance off. The sheep began to move, but this time when they broke left there I was, crying them onward; when they broke right, there was the shepherd, grunting. Finally the sheep gave in and shambled up the slope and over the saddle, rushing downhill to graze in the thick grass.

I stayed in the valley with the shepherd all the rest of the afternoon, staying pretty much on the other side of the valley from him, but watching his sheep, and sending back the few that strayed in my direction. He seemed not to notice me and said nothing, so that I wondered if by ill-fortune I had stumbled on a Humper who couldn't talk, but when the sun came close to the horizon he stood and began herding the sheep along a fairly easy route home. I did not follow, but when the shepherd crested a rise, after making it plain he didn't need my help on *this* journey, he turned and watched me for a moment, then beckoned. I was to come home with him.

I followed him for several kilometers before we came to a cluster of three low, thatched houses. They looked like small hills, the roofs the color of the summer-yellowed grass, but inside they were warm against the cold night. The sea wind came heavily from the north, even during the summer nights, and the deep current that flowed through the Humping Sea was icy—though Britton was as far south as Wong, which sweltered in the summer, no night in Humping was ever warm, and the winters, while usually snowless, killed any fool who was caught out of doors after sunset. Except, of course, someone like me, who could sink into the earth if I desired; or just as easily draw heat from the air around me, no matter how cold it was. They could not have known this about me, however; to them I was a man alone, inviting death each night I spent in the open.

That may have been part of the reason the shepherd invited me home. It was well-known to the Humpings (for news of any kind travels quickly in lonely places like this) that no one had taken me in;

I spent night after night in the hills, yet was still alive. That made me somehow holy and powerful, and they were in awe of me; yet when I proved my intentions were kind by helping the shepherd with his sheep, I was accepted, not as one of them, but as one they would willingly share their small homes and tiny larders with.

Dinner was a stew, and since the wife had not known I was coming, the pot was meager. Since I needed no food at all, I took the smallest portion I dared—large enough to accept hospitality, but no more. And when the pot had been passed around and scraped clean by the shepherd's wife on her own dish, the shepherd looked at me.

For what? Did these people pray? Or was there some custom a man had to follow when offered food? I didn't know, so I smiled and said, "My name is Lake-drinker, and what good I can do you, I will always do you."

The shepherd nodded gravely, and turned to his wife. She laid her hands on the table, closed her eyes, and intoned:

> Sun on wheat,
> Baking bread,
> Making meat
> From the dead.
> Good we give
> That we live.

Then, reverently, the three children, none older than five, watched as their mother took a spoonful of stew from her own plate and gave it to her husband, who solemnly chewed the bit of meat and swallowed. Then the husband took stew from his own dish and gave it to me, and I also ate. I was unsure what to do next, but the ritual made a kind of sense, and so I took from my dish and gave to each of the children, who looked wide-eyed and surprised, but ate.

The shepherd looked at me with tears in his eyes, and said, "You are welcome here forever."

Then we fell to and the stew was gone in a few minutes.

They made a place for me in the largest bed, a frame filled with straw and covered with blankets. I knew it was the parents' bed, and indeed they were preparing to sleep on the floor of packed dirt. I had slept on the earth during many a field maneuver in Mueller, long before the earth taught me another kind of welcome in Schwartz; I had no need of comfort when I slept. So I ignored the offered bed and curled up on the floor by the door. A cold draught slipped under the door, but my Schwartz-trained body coped easily, and the parents, wonderingly, went to bed in the straw.

In the morning, I was one of the family, and the children chattered freely in my presence.

"Glain," said the shepherd, and then, glancing at his wife, "Vran." From then on, though conversation was never lush, what needed to be said could be said.

His dogs had died in the same week nearly a month ago, and since then he had lost nearly a dozen sheep from random strays that he could not pursue. At first I herded with him while he trained a pup from a neighbor's litter; later I stayed at home and tended his vegetable garden while his wife was sick because the fourth child was coming.

It disturbed me at first to pull so many living stones out of the soil and put them in dead piles; I had gone so long now without killing anything that it even bothered me to know that the plants I planted there would grow only to be killed. In the night I asked the earth, and received only indifference. The billion deaths of plants together made a powerful sound, but that sort of death was necessary for life. For the first time I realized that for all their genius, the Schwartz obsession with avoiding killing was as unproductive, in the long run, as the selfish way the Ku Kuei used their power over time. The Schwartz kept themselves even purer than the earth required, and in doing so, kept all other human beings from becoming pure at all.

What agonized the rock was the cry of unnecessary or unmerciful death, the howls of the murdered. I heard all the sounds, and all hurt, but I decided that in the world outside Schwartz, death was the way of things; even killing, as long as it was done for need, was a part of nature. I had eaten dead plants and animals all my life, and yet the sand had accepted me when I plunged from the pinnacle. So no matter what the Schwartzes said, I knew there must be no murder in farming, and I worked hard and did well for Glain and Vran.

Over time the other shepherd families came to visit, and eventually got over their shyness in my presence. I knew that the story of my nights on the hill and my habit of sleeping on the coldest part of the floor were known to everyone, and while they called me Lake-drinker to my face, I overheard references to Man-of-the-Wind, a legendary creature who comes either to kill or cure, brought by the cold wind and taken, eventually, by the sea.

Yet because they were unused to people of prestige or power among them, they did not know how to show me honor, except to treat me as they treated each other. In a place where all men lack equally, the only reward is trust, and I received that. I learned to handle sheep, to shear wool with glass blades without cutting the skin, to help with the foaling, to know when the sheep were nervous and when they were sick. I learned the soil, too, not in the personal way I had known in Schwartz and Ku Kuei, but as a reluctant ally in the war against starvation. Though I never felt hunger myself, I knew the faces of the children when they were hungry, and so I worked hard.

Vran went into labor a week early; it happened when I was alone with her and the children. It soon became clear that the child would not come easily. She was in the house screaming, while the children stayed outside with me. Humping mothers bore their children without help, alone—it was forbidden for a man to come into the house while they were bearing. But as the children sat by the garden, frightened, I lay on the earth and listened to Vran's screams as the earth heard them, and I knew her death was near.

There are times for tabus and times to ignore them, and at the end of a particularly terrible scream that signaled a new plateau of pain, I got up and went into the house.

Vran was squatting nude over the straw of her bed, the blankets removed. Her hands were buried in the hard sod wall, where she gripped at the clay and roots in her agony. She looked at me with terrified eyes, and I saw the blood coming in a continuous stream, trickling onto the straw.

I came to her and eased her into a lying position and, as I had done with ewes at lambing, I reached in to see what way the baby was presenting. A hand and a foot were in the birth channel.

With a ewe, it would be simply a matter of pushing and pulling. On a woman, that kind of treatment could kill. But no treatment at all would kill, too, and so I forced the child to a different position, breaking its back in the process, and pulled it out. Somewhere in the operation, Vran fainted.

Work on the genetic level was beyond me, but curing wounds and fractures had been simple enough work in Schwartz. It was no great feat for me to restore both Vran and the infant boy, and when the sun was setting, Glain came home to find his wife and child in good condition. Better condition, in fact, than Vran usually was in after a delivery.

What she told him I don't know—she had slept through the worst of it. But word spread, and I began to be brought sick animals and injured children, and women would ask for my advice. I had no advice. If there was a problem, I had to come and see it for myself. I was uncomfortable with the awe they held me in, but better that than let them suffer pain I could prevent. Thus the Man-of-the-Wind story passed from legend into reality.

It was inevitable, I suppose, that even as close-mouthed as the Humpers were to outsiders, word would eventually get out. One day I was planting in the garden for my second spring in Humping when a man came up on a horse. The mere possession of such an animal made him important; when he identified himself as Lord Barton's servant, Vran immediately rushed out of the house, called for me, urged me to come quickly. "It's a man from the cliff house," she said, afraid. I came.

"My master wishes to see you," said the mounted man.

"When the planting's done," I said.

"Lord Barton is unaccustomed to waiting."

"Then he should rejoice, for he'll learn something new today." I went back to the garden. Soon the servant left.

It was hard to concentrate on gardening that afternoon. For nearly two years I had lived in Humping, and while joy was limited here, so was grief. I had found a place where my talents were useful and where I was accepted. No one regarded me as an enemy; I had hundreds of good people I could count as friends.

But could I afford to meet this Barton? I felt my good life in Humping slipping away: I couldn't afford not to meet him. If I resisted, it would only cause trouble to the Humpers, particularly to Glain and Vran. If I went, it might lead to trouble for me. Almost certainly *would* lead to trouble. The only other alternative was to slip off in quicktime and find another place to live.

I didn't want to find another place to live.

And, in fact, as I pushed the wooden spike into the earth and dropped in seeds after it, I realized that I was excited as well as disturbed by the prospect of change. Two years, and what had I done? Saved lives, made some people happier, come to love many, given some of my life to a harsh land. All worthy ways to have spent my time. But I was raised to be the heir of the Mueller, and either that or a drive born with me as my father's son insisted that I must do something that would shake the world or admit that my existence did not matter.

Two days later the planting was done, and, as if he had been watching from a distance, the servant came that afternoon, this time leading a second horse.

"Will you ride?" the man asked, more humbly this time.

I said nothing, but mounted the horse.

The children gathered silently in front of the house. Vran looked at me expressionlessly. I raised a hand in farewell. And Vran, violating every custom I had seen among the Humpers, burst into tears in front of me and fled into the house. It frightened me to see how much such independent people could come to lean on someone who offers even the slightest power linked with kindness.

The servant followed no road—there were no roads in the Humping Hills but one, which led from the lord's house-by-the-sea to the city of Hesswatch a hundred or more kilometers to the south. Our journey would end where that road began. The servant instead seemed to find his way by riding east to the sea and then following the shore from a respectful distance until the cliff house was visible on a virtual pinnacle that rose considerably above the hills of Humping.

The sky darkened over with clouds, and the rains came as we approached, the wind driving swiftly, with the sea, usually so placid, suddenly forming huge swells coming in from the north to break their faces on the rocky coast. The wind whipped at us and the horses became unruly, so we dismounted and walked. The servant seemed unsure of himself. He was not a Humper, and he cast his way inland, away from the sea, which would seem daunting to any who saw breakers only when the wind was high. Unfortunately, he did not lead us to the road, but instead managed to end us up at a ravine, and in the darkness it seemed impossible to tell north from south.

He looked at me, his eyes still confident, but the question quite clear: What can we do, now that we're lost? So I led my horse up away from the ravine and found shelter under a steep cliff, where the wind from the north would, at worst, allow only spray to strike us. Then I tied the horses to each other and the servant helped me as I hobbled them.

"I'll keep watch at first," I told him, and he nodded gratefully and curled up to sleep, looking tall and gaunt in the dark red cape that he wrapped around himself.

I was more tired from the day's exertions than I thought, however, and I decided to catch some sleep in quicktime, so that I would be able to stay awake through most of the realtime night.

I slept easily, and awoke after a long time, feeling refreshed. I lay a moment in quicktime, watching how the drops came crawling down from the sky to hover over the horses' backs, finally striking and breaking instantly into pools and splashes. As I slipped into realtime, I glanced at the servant and was startled to see him looking much shorter and wearing a shabby blue cape that barely covered his knees.

The illusion passed immediately. I was in real-time, and he looked as he had always looked. I laughed at myself for having let my vision be fooled by the darkness and my sleepiness, and I watched well throughout the rest of the night, taking another short nap as the clouds cleared just before dawn. The horses stirred occasionally, but were usually docile, and we got under way almost as soon as the sun was up.

The cliff house rose in a jumble of stone from the promontory, and up close it was even more dramatic than its height made it seem from a distance. It must have been constructed in bits and pieces over centuries; there was no clear architectural style, though some of the earliest constructions seemed to have been designed for defense. Now the place seemed brooding and forlorn, and the still-high seas cast spray up to the level of the lower stories, seeming to say that it was only a matter of time before the sea claimed the house.

The servant led me to the stable, where a single groom put the horses into stalls and ignored us as we left. Inside the house, the rooms were cold, and we passed no one. It was plain the place was designed for large companies; the emptiness made the cold penetrate even more.

But coldness was not Lord Barton's manner, and when we appeared unannounced at the door of a large study, I was struck by the contrast. In *this* room, a huge fire burned; in *this* room, the walls weren't stone, but rather were lined with books rising dizzyingly to the ceiling ten meters from the floor. Ladders were strategically placed and their treads were well worn, implying that the books were read often, though the ladders also gave the room rather the look of a building still under construction.

Barton, an aging man with a smile that overwhelmed his face frequently, welcomed me with a handshake and pulled me into the room. "Thank you, Dul," he told the servant, and we were alone.

"I've heard of you," said Barton. "Heard of you and wanted to meet you for some time, some time. Sit, please, I've moved the softest furniture up here, where I live. It's shabby and old, but so am I, and it all fits nicely when you consider that I'm the decaying remnant of a decadent line. I only have one son." That amused him, and he laughed.

I did not laugh. I looked at the titles on the spines of the books. Habits of the Humpers did not disappear overnight, and when I had nothing of importance to say, it was hard to say anything.

Barton stared at me penetratingly. "You are not what you seem."

That amused me and awoke my old manner of speech. "So many people have said that that I'm beginning to think that's precisely how I *do* seem. What is it I seem to be that you have now discovered that I'm not?"

"A sharp tongue, even when speaking to a lord, and a man who refuses to come when bidden until the planting's done. You seem to be a rebel, sullen and silent. But the people say you're the Man-in-the-Wind, and you save mothers in childbirth and heal lame sheep and help simple children find their minds. Miracles, yes?"

I didn't answer, regretting my outburst of Muellerish speech. Enough of that. I was done with that.

"But the reason I asked to see you has little to do with that," said Barton. "Legends come and go among these superstitious folk, and I don't call every passing healer in to speak with me. What intrigued me was white hair like wool, as the Humpers say, and a man who seeks out hardship. A man who seems young in years but old as I am in experience. Whatever became of Lanik Mueller?"

The last question was so ridiculous, so out of place—so dangerous—that I couldn't hide my surprise. Barton laughed, obviously feeling very clever. "Tricks and traps. I play them even on the wise. There are rewards, you know, for seeming to be a foolish old man. Lanik Mueller has always fascinated me, you know. It's been what, four years now since he and dear old Ensel Mueller vanished into the forest of Ku Kuei, never to be seen again. Well, I don't put much stock in legends. They always seem to have a perfectly natural foundation. And I don't think people who go into Ku Kuei necessarily die. Do you?"

I shrugged.

"I think they come out again," said Barton. "I think that Lanik Mueller, the scourge of the Rebel River plain, I think he lives."

He looked at me intently. "I met you, boy, when you were eleven."

That forced me to look at him again. Had I ever seen that thin old man before?

"I was a traveler in the old days. And a bit of a historian. I picked up tales and genealogies wherever I went, trying to discover what had happened to the world in the days since the Republic set down our ancestors and their families on this paradise of a world as a punishment for their sins. And when I met you, I thought, 'Here's a boy bound to do something important.' They say you burned and ravaged and raped and killed anything in your path."

I shook my head, trying to decide whether to admit the truth of what he was saying or pretend not to know any more about Lanik Mueller than any other man might know. Ironic, that no one recognized me on the Rebel River plain, where my double had made my face well known, while here in the most obscure corner of the world I was recognized.

"But what intrigued me most was something that strikes very close to home, Lanik Mueller. I have learned that your younger brother, Dinte, is now ruling where you would have ruled."

"A figurehead, thank God, since the bastard couldn't rule an anthill with any efficiency," I said, admitting what he obviously knew.

"The child of your mother?"

"Incredible as it may seem, yes. I never saw you, Lord Barton."

"I was younger then." He got up from his chair and strode to a ladder, climbed it slowly, and reached down a book that must have weighed five kilos. When he was back to the floor, he gave it to me. "I bought this from your father, who was reluctant to part with it. But he had another copy, and when I explained how important genealogy was to me he became convinced I was a doddering idiot. He let me buy the book, though he charged me five times what he thought it was worth."

That was my father.

I opened the book. A genealogy of Mueller and a history, kept as a kind of chronicle in the handwriting of a herald. I didn't recognize the hand at the end of the book, but sure enough, the account and the genealogy ended when I was eleven. It was amusing to see what the herald had thought was worth recording. I must have been someone's delight—every clever thing I said as an infant was there.

The expectancy of Barton's silence was pressure enough that I skimmed and rushed through to the end.

"Genuine?" he asked.

"Of course," I said. "Do you doubt it, when you got it the way you did?"

"Not at all. I just wanted your opinion before I point out an omission, a simple but very important thing left out of the book. So obvious it wouldn't occur to you to notice it was missing."

I waited.

"Your brother," he said. "Dinte."

Of course Dinte was mentioned. So many of my childhood memories were tied to him. But I glanced back to the time when Dinte was born, and there was no mention. Nor was there any mention of him for the entire duration of the journal.

"Well, maybe the herald didn't like Dinte any better than I did," I said.

"The herald didn't meet Dinte."

"He led a sheltered life in the palace, then."

"Lanik Mueller, I want you to think back to a memory. An unpleasant one, preferably. I want you to picture it in your mind."

I smiled. "No one takes psychology seriously anymore."

"It's not psychology, Mueller. It's survival."

So I thought back to the time I lied about who had lamed Rurik, the horse I was given after I had learned to ride like an adult. I had jumped him stupidly, and he had been injured, and then I walked him home and told my father that the stableboy had lamed him and that I had noticed it as soon as I was away from the stable. The boy lost his job and had a good thrashing in the bargain, particularly since he had "lied" about it and claimed the horse was healthy when I took it out. I remembered the expression on the boy's face when my father made me accuse him to his face. I remembered clearly how ashamed I felt.

"I see from your face that you've thought of something that mattered. How clearly do you remember it?"

"Clearly," I answered.

"Now, think of your clearest memory concerning Dinte from the time you were, say, seven or eight, and both learning from tutors. Did you have the same tutor?"

"Yenwi."

"But did he have the same tutor?"

I shrugged.

"Think of a childhood memory of Dinte."

Easy enough. Until I tried it. But all my memories of Dinte were of the time when I was older. When I was twelve and thirteen and fourteen and fifteen. I simply could not remember Dinte before that, though the unshakable conviction remained that he was *there*.

"Just because I can't remember details," I began, and then saw that Barton was laughing.

"My own words," he said. "Just because I can't remember details. But you're so sure. Haven't the slightest doubt."

"Of course not. If I could have made the little bastard disappear, I would have done it years ago, believe me."

"Let me tell you a story, then," he said. "Settle down in the chair, Lanik Mueller, because it's a long one, and being old I shall undoubtedly lace it with details that were best left out. Try to stay awake. Snoring puts me off my form." Then he began to recount the story of his son, Percy. When he mentioned the boy's name, I immediately recognized it.

"Percy Barton? Lord Percy of Gill?"

"The same. You're interrupting."

"But he's the ruler—or should we say, figurehead—over the so-called East Alliance. And he's your son?"

"Born and raised in this castle, but I shan't ever finish if I can't begin, Mueller." I let him begin.

"It's my penchant for traveling, you see. I made a journey, not all that many years ago, one of my last before travel became out of the question because of my health. To Lardner. You may know Lardner—a land of cold that makes Humping look like paradise, but it has the world's best physicians. If ever I were sick, I'd want a doctor from Lardner. While I was there, I chanced upon a doctor whom I had known when I was a young man, just married and barely into my own as lord—lord of more than I have now, too, I assure you. Not just Humping, but of the whole east peninsula. I suppose that doesn't matter now. This doctor, Twis Stanly, was a specialist of sorts, women and women's problems, but he was also a damned fine archer and we'd bend the bow together and have the grandest time on hunts and holidays in the Spine Mountains. Good friends, but I remembered he had treated my wife only a month after we were married for a rather odd infection. This was, of course, some time before Percy was born."

He paused a moment, as if unsure how to say what came next. "He inquired, of course, after my wife, and I had to inform him, quite sadly, that she had died only two or three years before, at a ripe but not old age. She was over fifty, and it stunned me that it had been near thirty-five years earlier that Twis and I had brought down two harts of the same herd with a single arrow each, practically in unison. I mentioned the fact, and then commented on how my son, Percy, had hardly a notion that his father was once handy with a bow.

"We shared a bit of a laugh at that and the foibles of youth, and then he said, 'Well, Barton, you remarried then?'"

"The question seemed odd. 'Of course not,' I told him. 'What made you think so?'"

"'Then you adopted the boy? Your son?' asks he, and I deny it. 'A true born son of my flesh,' says I, 'not two years into marriage.'

"He went a bit white then, as we old men are prone to do, and he took down a notebook from his interminable shelves of trivial records, and looked up a particular entry, and had me read it. It recorded the hysterectomy he had performed on my wife a month after our marriage.

"Can you imagine what a shock that was to me? I was sure he was mistaken, but he was a methodical man, you know, and I couldn't shake his surety. He took everything, womb, ovaries, and she damn near died in the process, but it was that or a cancer to destroy her life within the year. So she was doomed to childlessness in exchange for life.

"It was a blow. I insisted I could remember the childbirth, but when I tried to recount the circumstances, I couldn't remember a bit of it. Not the day, not the place, not whether I went in or stayed out, nor even how I celebrated the birth of an heir, nothing. Nothing. Like you, when you couldn't remember anything about your brother just now."

I might doubt many men, but in this case I couldn't fathom a reason for Barton to lie. And now the book of genealogy in my lap weighed heavier, and I struggled even as I listened to try to remember something, anything about Dinte from our childhood together. A blank.

"That's not all my story, Lanik Mueller. I went home. And on the way home, I somehow forgot the entire conversation. Forgot it! Something like *that*, and it simply slipped my mind. It was not until I was out of Britton on my very last journey, this time a visit to Goldstein because of the warmth in the winter. While I was there, I got a letter from Twis. He wondered why I hadn't been answering his letters. Ha! I hadn't known I had been receiving any. But in his letter he said enough to refresh my memory. I was shocked at the lapse that had occurred, appalled that I could have forgotten. And then I realized something. It wasn't old age, Lanik Mueller, that made me forget. Someone was doing something to my mind. When I was at home, something *made* me forget.

"I came home, only this time I thought, steadily, continuously, of how my son was a fraud, a total mountebank. I've never had such a struggle in my life. The closer I got to home, the more familiar sights I saw, the more I felt that Percy had always been a part of me, a part of my home. Everything familiar and dear to me had been tied to Percy in my mind, even though I had no specific memory of him in that place. I clutched Twis's letter to my bosom and reread it every few minutes all the way home. I would finish reading the letter and have no idea what it had said. The closer I got to Britton, the harder it became. I've never suffered so much anguish of mind. But I kept saying, 'I have no son. Percy is a fraud,' and never mind wondering how anyone could come to a childless man and pass himself off as his son. Suffice it to say that I made it. I came here with my mind and memory intact. And behold, on this very desk, four letters from Twis, opened and obviously read, which I had utterly no memory of receiving. Now I could read them, and each one of them referred to the matter of Percy being an impossibility.

"In the other letters, Twis gave me comments from friends who had come from Lardner to stay with him during his days in Britton, friends who had met me. I remembered them well. All of them had clear memories of the fact that I was childless and that my wife and I knew perfectly well that we had no hope of having children. He quoted my own witticism to the effect that at least now my wife had no time of month when she could beg off from her duties in bed. All at once, as I read Twis's mention of that occasion, I remembered it. I remembered saying that. It was as though something snapped inside of me. I remembered everything. I had no son. Until I turned forty or so, and then, suddenly, I had a nineteen-year-old boy, eager to rule, passionate for opportunity. I made him governor of my northernmost holding, and it was all he needed. In five years he was, incredibly, overlord of all of

Britton. Eight years ago he rose from there to the head of the alliance and turned it into a dictatorship."

I shook my head. "Not a dictatorship, Barton. A figurehead for a committee of scientists. The self-proclaimed wise men rule in Nkumai and Mueller, too."

"It's always wise, when looking for figureheads, to be certain who is manipulating whom," Barton said with a bite that made it clear he thought me unclever in holding that opinion. "Don't you understand what I'm telling you? Dinte and Percy are alike. Children who appeared out of nowhere, but no one questions them, no one doubts them in their own family, in their own country, and now they have both risen to the highest position of authority in very powerful countries, and everyone is convinced they're mere figureheads."

It did sound rather odd.

"I shall help you be convinced," he said. "When I spoke to you once about how it felt to be heir to the throne, you said, quite bluntly—your father was proud of your bluntness, as I remember—you said—and you were a little boy then—you said, 'Lord Barton, I can only be comfortable as heir because father has no other sons. If I had a brother, I'd have to be more careful how I behaved, for then if they got rid of me there'd always be a spare.' I remember the words because your father made me recite them to five or six different people during my visit, as evidence of your precocity. Do you recall this?"

I did. I recalled the words. I recalled the moment. I even remembered old Barton, younger then, of course; he was much amused and slapped his thigh, roaring with laughter, repeating fragments of the remark. I had felt much impressed with myself at having won laughter from such a man.

I remembered, and at that moment I knew that Barton was right. I had no brother. I was an only child.

And I remembered something else. I remembered Mwabao Mawa. Not in Nkumai, but riding into Jones in an open carriage.

The servant who had brought me to the cliff house came in with toddy in a pitcher.

I had seen a middle-aged white man in that carriage. And then a moment later, coming out of quicktime, I had seen Mwabao Mawa in the carriage in precisely the same place. She saw me; I fled; and yet in all that time since then, I had never wondered why the man would have left the wagon in the midst of the streets of Jones to let Mwabao Mawa get on. Where had Mwabao Mawa been till then? Where did the white man go?

It fit the pattern. A seemingly powerless figurehead, run by the committee of scientists—but when viewed differently, perhaps the very person who ruled.

The servant poured toddy for me first, at Barton's insistence, and was now carrying another to Barton.

I had been in quicktime when I saw the bald white man. Then, in realtime, I had seen Mwabao. Was that the difference, then? In quicktime, I saw the reality? In realtime, I was fooled like everyone else?

The servant leaned over Barton and I remembered having caught a glimpse, that very morning as I came out of quicktime, of a blue cape on a shorter man turning into a red cape on the gaunt servant who now bent over Barton, who now watched as Barton took the toddy to his lips.

"Don't," I said to Barton. "Don't drink it."

Barton looked surprised for a moment, while the servant stood, blankly looking at me. Then, suddenly, the servant crumpled and Barton leaped to his feet, ran agilely out the door. I was startled. I was put off. I was slowed down. It took several precious moments before I looked again at the servant lying in a tumble on the floor and realized it was not the servant at all. It was Barton.

How had I seen the servant fall and Barton leave, and been in error? They had never changed places, not that I had seen. And yet there lay Barton, his head had been nearly severed from his body, held in place only by the spine. It must have been done in a single strong whick of a very sharp blade. But when had this happened? Why hadn't I seen?

An iron blade.

No time for speculation, of course. I knelt by Barton and pressed the head against the neck and did the kind of thing I had done for so many Humpers and their animals. I connected blood vessels, I healed torn muscles, I linked the skin together without a seam, I made the body healthy and whole. Then, because I was already doing the work and because I cared for the man and because it was easier to do something I *knew* how to do than to think about what to do next, I even found his rheumatism and his feebleness and his lung disease and his dying heart and fixed them, renewed them, made him healthier than he had been in many years.

He was conscious, looking at me. "Man-of-the-Wind," he said, smiling. "The stories are true."

"The servant was one of them," I said, though of course I had no idea who *they* were, except that somehow they had come to rule the world.

"That much I guessed as the blade passed through my throat. Dear Dul. How do they carry off their disguise, Lanik? I distinctly remember believing that Dul was born in this house, the child of my housekeeper. It never occurred to me to question the memory. He overheard our conversation, of course. I suppose he meant to poison us. You warned me not to drink—tell me, how did you guess?"

I had neither time nor inclination to tell him about

Ku Kuei and the manipulation of time. "I just guessed," I said. "You had made me alert."

He looked at me doubtfully, then probably decided that if I had wanted to tell the truth I would have told it already. He got to his feet. He arose so suddenly, in fact, that he startled himself and nearly lost his balance forward. "When you heal someone, you don't go by halves, do you?" he asked. "I feel like a thirty-year-old."

"A shame. I meant for you to feel twenty."

"I didn't want to brag. Lanik, what are you? Never mind. Never mind. The question that matters is, What is Dul, what is Percy, what is Dinte? I doubt we'll find Dul, at any rate. Even if we chased him, he'd probably seem to be an old woman and then slip a knife into our backs as we passed."

"We?" I asked.

"I was waiting to see if you confirmed my theory before I acted," Barton said. "I was still—in the back of my mind, I was still more than a little worried that I was going mad and had made it all up. But now, of course, I know I'm right and so do you, and since I'm also now in excellent youthful vigor, it's time to confront Percy and kill the little bastard."

Kill? "You don't seem the type," I said.

"Perhaps not," Barton answered. "But there's a sort of rage a man feels when he's been deceived where he most trusted. It compares to no other anger. He made a fool of me, and not over something small, but over my own self, over my own wife, over my own hope of a family. He became my heir, he used me as a springboard to power, and all by pretending, by illuding me into thinking he was my son. I'm very angry, Lanik Mueller."

"He'll also think you're dead, once Dul gets back to him. Is it wise to disabuse him of the notion so soon?"

Barton paused at that.

"Besides, Barton, what good will killing one of them do? We already have evidence of four of them—Dinte, your son Percy, Dul, and the woman from Nkumai, Mwabao Mawa."

"So now you're sure of her, too?"

"I saw something once that I didn't understand till now. Four, but surely there are others ready to step into their place. If we're to solve the problem, we have to find out where they're from."

"Does it matter?" he asked.

"Doesn't it?"

He smiled. "Yes, it does. It occurs to me that they've gone a long way toward taking over the entire planet. And Nkumai and Mueller both had iron, yes?"

"And now these people, whoever they are and however they do what they do, now they control the source of that iron."

Barton shook his head and laughed bitterly. "For thousands of years all the Families have competed murderously for something to sell offworld through the Ambassadors in order to be the first to build a starship and get out of here. Now they'll be first, no matter who wins. Now they'll control it all. And no one but us even realizes they're doing it."

"It's not your normal swindle," I pointed out.

"You've taken all this so calmly."

"I'm used to seeing strange things in this world. I'm going to Gill, Barton, but I urge you to stay here. Here, at least, you'll be safe. And I think I have a way of recognizing them. Easily and safely. Recognizing them and getting around their illusions."

He didn't ask how I could do this, because I think my manner made it clear I wouldn't answer anyway. Oh, I thought of telling him, but there was no need to have someone else, even a good man like Barton, know what I could do. Not yet. Not until I knew what I was going to do about it.

He promised to stay at the cliff house, though he

wasn't happy about it. I went down to the stable, saddled a horse—the best Barton owned—and set out for Gill. It's a measure of my stupidity that I did not walk in quicktime. There with Barton I had stepped back into my oldest role as armiger heir of Mueller; I had spoken like a lord, and now without thinking I mounted a horse so I could travel like one. Such is the power even an ancient, long disused habit can have. I had ceased to be heir of Mueller years before, but that role was still embedded in me, ready to come forward and control my actions. It nearly killed me.

As I sat astride the horse walking briskly but not frantically down the road toward civilization and eventually toward Gill, I saw a Humper driving his flock north, toward the less-civilized and therefore more inviting part of Humping. It seemed incredible to me that just the day before I had finished Glain's and Vran's planting; that I had seriously thought of spending the rest of my life there among the Humpers. The memory, only a day old, was like a terrible ache, a realization that I was not, after all, ready for goodness and peace and happiness, but instead still felt a sense of mission. If there is a purpose to fulfill, I will fulfill it, I thought bitterly (and yet with some pride, for up to now all my purposes had come to nothing), and this time—this time, because in quicktime the illuders stood revealed to me, I was not just a person who could stop them, I was the *only* person outside Ku Kuei who could even find them. And apathetic as the Ku Kuei were, there was no chance I'd have any help from them when it came time to destroy the illuders.

Destroy them. Did I already, so casually, plan murder? But it's war, I insisted to myself, and wondered then who had declared it and why I thought I was on the good side. I need not ask the earth on this one, I realized. This time it wasn't a matter of eating vegetables. I meant to kill men, kill them in cold blood, kill them for a noble cause, but kill them just the same.

Was the cause really noble? Was I striking a blow for Mueller's independence? From what? Perhaps these illuders were actually doing something valuable for our miserable planet. They were ending the bloodshed, weren't they? Ending the competition among Families, unifying the planet to achieve a common purpose.

No. Wrong. They were not ending the competition. They were winning it by fraud, and that was a different matter. It struck me as being unfair.

Which is, after all, the only way any man decides what is right and what is wrong—how it seems to him. To me, this was *wrong*. Other men's minds were solving the problems of the universe. Other men's blood and genes had gone into winning the iron Mueller had taken from the Ambassador. And those minds and that blood were being stolen without anyone's knowledge that the crime was even taking place.

I remembered being a radical regenerative. I remembered standing at the window, observing the pens, imagining myself among the monsters of many legs and arms who were fed from troughs and denied even the slightest shred of humanity. It was cruel, though how else rads could have been treated God only knew. Still, even that cruelty might have been bearable, or at least partly bearable, because the rads knew that they were doing it for Mueller. Doing it to ensure that their families and their families' families would be the ones to sell offworld, would be the ones to make the starships and go out into space and be free.

If that hope had helped keep them sane, it was a

terrible thing to turn it into a lie and have their suffering and loneliness and loss of humanity be for a race of strangers who insinuated themselves into families—

I hated Dinte. I had despised him before, but now I hated him. I pictured myself going into the palace at Mueller-on-the-River and walking up to him and going into quicktime and seeing the man who really was Dinte, the man pretending to be my brother, the man who had destroyed my father and robbed me of my inheritance; and when I saw him, I could picture myself killing him, and the picture gave me pleasure.

(I could remember the earth moaning with the cries of dying men, but I shut out that memory. Not that memory. Not today. I had blood to shed before I was ready for that memory again.)

But first, Percy Barton, Lord Barton's "son." I had to learn from him where he came from and who his people were, and then I'd destroy them all. If they *could* be destroyed. Was there any way to make an end to people who could appear to be something they were not, who could trade places with a man before your eyes and never have you notice, who could pretend to be your brother for years and never give you a clue?

How did they do it? How could I fight it?

As I descended from the hills of Humping, I felt a terrible sadness, because I knew I was leaving my truest home in order to go out and destroy my peace of mind and cause agony to the earth. I remembered the spokesman of the Schwartzes telling me, "Every man who dies at your hand will scream into your soul forever."

Almost I turned back. Almost I went back to Glain and Vran. Almost.

Instead I rode on for twelve days until I came to Gill, the capital of the Family of Gill, and also the capital of the empire called the East Alliance. In my days of travel, I had figured nothing out and knew no more than I had known before. I hadn't even taken elementary precautions, didn't even have the sense to arrive in quicktime, which is why they caught me in Gill and killed me.

11   GILL

Lord Barton's servant, Dul, had reached Gill ahead of me. That had been predictable. What I had forgotten was that if Dul heard enough of our conversation to want to poison us, he also heard enough to know that I was Lanik Mueller.

Did they believe him? Did they suspect that Lanik Mueller had survived, had reemerged from Ku Kuei after two years? Perhaps they doubted it at first, but once word reached Mwabao Mawa, there would be no more doubt. She would remember having seen me in Jones a year ago, and they would be certain.

It was an academic question at the moment, however. Whoever I was, Lanik Mueller or Lake-drinker or Man-in-the-Wind, I had discovered the existence of the illuders and I had to be destroyed. They had my description, and when I came to the gate of Gill, the soldiers took me, dragged me from my horse, and held me while the captain compared me with a written notice that he had some trouble reading. "He's the one," he finally said, but there was a little doubt in his voice.

"You're wrong," I said. "I just look like him, whoever he is."

But the captain shrugged. "If somebody else comes in who fits the description, we'll kill him, too." The soldiers put me in a cart, blindfolded, and dragged me off through the streets.

I was concerned. If they believed that I was Lanik Mueller, and if they knew—as the illuders surely did by now—that Muellers regenerated, they would kill me much too thoroughly. I might really die from beheading or burning. It would be beyond my ability to save myself, and so I would have to escape before they performed the execution; and the only methods of escape I had were too demonstrative of my abilities to fail to raise a real alarm among the illuders.

I was lucky. Dul, whoever he was, was not bright enough or well-enough informed to realize that if I really was Lanik Mueller, they couldn't kill me in the ordinary way. Executions in Gill were by squads of archers. Arrows are easily taken care of by any Mueller, unless there are too many of them all at once, and to a rad like me, they didn't *have* enough arrows to destroy me beyond my body's ability to heal.

The soldiers were very businesslike. In Mueller every person—stranger, slave, or citizen—had the right to a hearing. In Gill, apparently, strangers were exempt from that particular formality. I was arrested, carted off in a wagon through the streets of Gill (the people apparently disposed of rotten fruit and vegetables by casting it as a parting gift into the executioner's wagon), pulled out of the city through a back gate, dragged from the wagon, and placed in front of a large pile of straw, so that misses wouldn't result in a lost or damaged arrow.

The archers looked bored and perhaps a little irritated. Had this been their day off? They lined up casually, selecting arrows. There were a dozen archers, and all looked competent. The captain of the guard, who had escorted me to the place of execution, raised his arm. There were no preliminaries, no last words, no final meal (a waste of food, of course), no announcement of what I was supposed to be guilty of. When he lowered his arm, the arrows loosed in a commendably uniform and accurate flight. All the arrows landed in my chest, and though two were stopped by ribs, the others all penetrated, with four piercing my heart and the rest wreaking havoc with my lungs.

It hurt. I knew that I didn't need to breathe, knew that my brain could stay alive far longer with scant oxygen than most people's; and while the arrows had stopped my heartbeat, as long as they were still in my body they also partly stanched the flow of blood from my heart. Still, the wound was serious enough, the pain sudden and drastic enough, that my body decided that it was dying, and collapsed.

They didn't rush over and pull out the arrows, unfortunately, so my heart couldn't yet begin to heal; and it would not be politic, I decided, to reach up and pull the arrows out myself. So I went into slowtime—a mild slowtime that left me stiff to them, while their handling of my body left painful bruises, but that was nothing my Mueller body couldn't heal on its own. I figured they'd probably be rid of my body within fifteen minutes—they showed no tendency to wait around—and that would be about five or six minutes of subjective time, leaving me a few seconds to remove the arrows and heal before my body started hurting for lack of blood. I could live for some time without breathing, but the blood had to flow.

They cut it close, and for one terrible moment as they carried me by a furnace I was afraid they practiced cremation, in which case all bets were off. Instead they dumped me in a hole in the ground and yanked the arrows out of my chest, tearing open my heart where it had started to heal around the arrowheads, but allowing it, at last, to start healing properly. As soon as they had quit shoveling on the dirt,

I went into realtime, muscled the dirt out of the way enough that I could remove the arrows, and lay there healing for a while. Once I was in reasonable health again, I went back into slowtime—no point in trying to endure hours of being shut up in a grave if you can avoid it—and only came out when I estimated it would be evening.

It was nearly dawn. I woke the earth around me, and it raised me gently to the surface. I spread my arms, and the earth took its firm shape under me. I looked around to see if I had been observed. I had not.

The graveyard, like the place of execution, was near the southern edge of the city, outside the wall. The sea was nearby, and festering garbage on the shore, mixed with the smell of the normal number of clumsy crabs that couldn't remember which way the water was, made the place unforgettable to my nose, if not to my other senses.

I refused to be stupid the same way twice. This time I would enter the city more subtly.

I pushed into quicktime and made my way among the hovels clustered around the walls until I found what I dubbed "garbage gate" and went inside. I saw only the seamy side of Gill. In the years since then, I've seen many cities, but for slime and sludge Gill is queen of them all. Their position at the isthmus between Landlock and Slashsea won Gill a role as the largest merchant Family in the East. Yet the wealth didn't show up in the city of Gill itself— people with property moved east into the mountains, building wood or stone mansions that would make princes in other Families jealous.

In Gill, poverty and business made an uneasy division of the town. Warehouses and manufactories and wholesale houses made way for slums and whorehouses and gaming rooms. In the nighttime, the gaiety must have been something to see; in the early morning, the city seemed weary. And still a little drunk.

There were corpses on the roads leading to the garbage gate. I passed a wagon loaded with dead bodies, stopped in the middle of the road. Several men who looked little healthier than their cargo wearily hoisted another piece of human flesh into the cart for the trip to the graveyard. There are few places where life isn't cheap, but this was the first place I had found where even the poor (especially the poor, who are often kinder to their dead than the rich) had so little regard for the dead that they were cast like garbage into the street.

The palace of the governor of Gill, now the headquarters of the East Alliance, rose from the warehouse district like a wart among moles: there was no attempt at grace, only a great grey block of stone brooding among smaller and yet somehow more inviting structures that stocked cloth, salted meat, and leather.

Gaining entry to the palace was difficult. The doors were all closed, and guards stood with their backs against them. There would be no subtle way to enter, even in quicktime—not through the doors. It attracts too much attention to knock over a guard. And the force of my passage, in quicktime, might well kill him.

I would have to wait until later in the morning, when people were passing in and out. So, for nostalgia's sake (and probably with an unconscious plan for petty vengeance) I sought out the gate where I had been taken the day before. As I walked along the streets I became more and more depressed. I wondered if Gill were really exceptionally vile, or if all cities, even Mueller-on-the-River, were this bad to those who had no money. The harsh hill country of Humping was kinder to its residents than this artificial desert of stone and dirt.

I saw in the distance as I neared the gate that the executioner's cart was already in business. What a busy day it had ahead of it! I toyed with the idea of breaking an axle, but decided it wasn't worth the time or trouble. Instead I went on to the gate, hardly glancing at the cart and the hooded prisoner as I ran past, and found what I was looking for. The captain who had so silently taken me to my death the day before was in a guardroom whose door was latched. I unlatched it and walked in. Placing myself directly in front of the captain, who was alone, I slipped back into realtime. I had seen the effect often enough in Ku Kuei—from his point of view, I simply materialized out of thin air.

"Good morning," I said.

"My God," he answered.

"Ah, first question answered. You can speak. It was quite irritating not even to be greeted yesterday before you took me off and killed me."

His look of terror was delightful. "I am not a vengeful man, but now and then this kind of thing does wonders for the soul. I won't bother you long. I'm just checking up on this murder business you have here. For instance, who decides who's going to die?"

"P-Percy. The king. It isn't my fault. I don't decide anything—"

"Never mind all that, I don't do the judging around here. How many people a day do you take from the city gates straight to the graveyards?"

"Not very many. Honest. You yesterday, Lord Barton today, and I can't remember anybody for months before that. And usually they're taken as they're leaving, not as they arrive."

I tried not to look shocked. Barton! He'd ignored all my advice and come here anyway.

"You handle it very efficiently," I said.

"Thank you," he answered.

"What happens to you if something goes wrong?"

"Nothing does."

"But if it did?"

"I'd be in trouble," he said. He was beginning to act a bit more confident with me, and I suspected that in a moment he'd reach out a hand to see whether I was solid or spirit.

"Then you're in trouble," I said. "Because Barton isn't going to die. And if you should succeed in killing him, I'll be back for you within the hour. No matter how much trouble you get in for his failure to die, just remember it's better than what you'll get if you actually kill him. Now have a wonderful morning." I slipped into quicktime, pausing before I left to turn an inkwell upside down on his head.

I ran down the streets in earnest, and soon found the executioner's cart. If I had looked closely before I would have recognized Barton's clothing—he was dressed as he had been that day in the cliff house. I climbed into the cart, then slowed to normal time long enough to say, "Don't worry, Barton, I'm with you." Then I was back in quicktime and out of the cart. The driver hadn't noticed me, and if any passerby saw me, he'd only blink and wonder whether the alcohol from the night before was still in his blood.

I got to the place of execution and waited out of sight among the stacks of straw. It took a half hour for the cart to arrive, and then the routine of the day before was followed—the archers lined up, very casually, and their leader, not the captain from the gate, raised his arm. I slipped into quicktime and walked out into the space between Barton and the archers. I paced back and forth (I become visible when I stay in the same place too long) until the leader's arm fell and the arrows were loosed. Then I collected the arrows in midflight, took the hood gently from Barton's head, and stuck the arrows through the hood into the straw directly behind Barton's chest. Then

I walked back to my concealed observation point and watched.

It took a second in realtime before the archers realized that Barton's hood was off and no arrows were sticking into his chest. Then, angrily, the leader of the archers told them to go collect their arrows, furious that they had missed. When they found the arrows sticking through the hood in the straw, however, even the leader became a little less outspoken. There was no natural way those arrows could have ended up directly behind him.

Barton was smiling.

"I don't know what kind of tricks you're pulling," the leader said furiously (yet there was fear behind his voice), "but you'd better stop 'em."

Barton shrugged and the leader formed up his archers for a second try. I slipped back into quicktime. In order to put an end to this quickly, I took the arrows in midflight and this time shoved them through the pulling wrist of each of the archers. For good measure, I took a few more arrows out of one archer's quiver and impaled the leader's hand, fastening it firmly to his thigh, while similarly sticking the three men lounging around watching the execution. Then I was back to my observation post and into realtime.

A howl of pain from a dozen throats told me that my work had been effective. The archers dropped their bows, clutching at the arrows in their wrists. The pain was nowhere near as bad as the shock. It isn't every day that you fire an arrow and have it turn around and hit you.

Barton's presence of mind was astounding. He haughtily said, "This is your second warning. There won't be a third."

"What's going on!" shouted the leader.

"Don't you know me? I'm the emperor's father. I'm Lord Barton of Britton. And it's a crime for commoners to shed royal blood."

"I'm sorry!" cried the leader. Several of the archers chimed in—most were too preoccupied stanching the bleeding.

"If you're sorry, you'll go back to your quarters and cause me no further trouble today."

They were sorry. They went back to their quarters and caused him no further trouble that day. As soon as they were gone, he looked around for me and found me lying against a pile of straw, laughing. He came over looking a little upset. "You didn't have to wait until the last minute, did you?"

"I told you not to worry."

"You try not worrying with a dozen arrows pointed at your heart."

I apologized profusely, explaining that I wanted to spread a little fear of the supernatural among the people of Gill. He agreed at last to overlook the matter, since I *had* saved him and since he *had* disregarded my order that he remain in Humping. We headed out of the place of execution, toward the city. "The one thing they won't expect us to do," he said, "is come into the city after they've tried to kill us both." Then he laughed. "It *was* funny. I wouldn't like to be the soldier who has to report this to my dear son Percy. What *are* you, anyway?" he asked.

"Man-in-the-Wind," I answered.

"I don't know what's going on in the world," he said. "Everything seemed so reasonable and scientific until I discovered my son was a fraud with the ability to hide my own memories from me. And now you come along. The captain at the gate told me you were executed and buried yesterday."

"He spoke to you? He didn't say a word to me," I said.

"Don't change the subject, young man. I'm accusing you of violating the laws of nature."

"Nature's virtue is intact. I just know some different laws."

By then we were at the garbage gate. The guards weren't too bright, and, not surprisingly, no alarm had yet gone out. However, we looked conspicuous if only because of the contrast between us, Barton in expensive clothing and I dressed like a Humper, quite countrified. I had to get Barton off the streets while I carried out my original intention of paying a visit on Percy. So I led him to a whorehouse I had noticed on my earlier trek up the street.

The manager was a crusty old man who looked more than a little irritated at being disturbed in the morning. "We don't open until afternoon," he said. "Late afternoon."

Barton had money—quite a bit of it. I was surprised the executioners hadn't removed it. Maybe they had planned to wait until he was a corpse, so he wouldn't know he was being robbed. It was a touch of delicacy I hadn't previously suspected the soldiers of having. The money, spread on the table, served to open the house for business a little earlier than usual.

"Full service?" the manager asked.

"Just a bed and silence," I said, but Barton glared at me. "I feel like a nineteen-year-old, and you expect me to sleep all day in a place like this? I want your youngest girl who doesn't have any foul diseases," he said. Then he caught himself and said, "But of course she must be of age." The manager looked as if he were trying to figure out what age he meant.

"Over fourteen," I said helpfully.

"Sixteen," Barton said, horrified. "Do they really offer them younger?"

The manager rolled his eyes heavenward and led Barton off. As soon as they were gone, I pushed into quicktime and made my way back to the palace.

When I arrived someone was just passing through the door. It was tight, but I skinnied through beside her without jostling her—it would bruise her painfully. I passed on into the palace. I followed the path which the most guards impeded and soon found myself in an impressive throne room. Then I made my way to an unobtrusive corner and looked over the people assembled there. I tried to look carefully at every face in the room, so that if any of them changed I'd know it. And then I slipped into realtime.

The old woman sitting on the throne became a youngish man with a remarkable resemblance to Barton. Most of the officials around him remained unchanged, but I recognized Dul among the crowd. He had been a smallish young man in a plain brown tunic. A few other faces changed, too. I passed back and forth from realtime to quicktime several times to make sure I had spotted them all. There were eight.

I had come with the full intention of killing them after finding out where they came from. Now I wondered how I'd manage either. I couldn't talk to them in quicktime, which meant exposing myself to the dangers of a realtime confrontation. And how could I kill them without attracting the attention of all the other illuders? Warned against me, they might be able to defend themselves.

At least I knew that I could spot them by switching from realtime to quicktime and back again. But killing them in quicktime—that would not be easy. Oh, of course, it would be simple enough to perform the act itself. But it would be a far different thing for me to plunge a knife into the heart of an unaware man than to do the petty tricks I had played in quicktime up to now. I was trained for battle; I had fought and killed before. But always my enemy had a chance to defend his life. I had no stomach for striking when a person was utterly helpless.

The Ku Kuei had killed animals by hitting them on the head in quicktime. And I had condemned them for it. But they were right—you don't cut off your feet just when you're starting a race. If they were not to take over the world, I would have to use my acquired advantages to kill the illuders. There was no hope of treating with them—they had already proved their determination to get and keep power at any cost. Justice would not be offended by their deaths. And if the only way to kill them was to creep up like a coward. . . .

It was an unproductive line of thought, and anyway, Dul was moving away from the crowd in the throne room. I waited until I saw which door he was headed toward, then pushed into quicktime and passed through the door ahead of him. Murder was not on my mind—only information. As he walked through the door, I, in realtime again, stepped out and took him by the arm. "Dul," I said, "what a pleasure to see you."

He stopped and looked at me, his face registering only mild surprise. "I thought you were still in Britton," he said, and then, though I could clearly see both his hands at his side, I felt a knife plunge deep into my chest. My poor heart would have to regenerate again, I realized. I also realized that there were going to be difficulties about dealing with illuders face to face. When a man can kill you without you seeing that he's moving his hands, he poses some unusual problems in a fight.

Quicktime, of course, and I saw him just pulling his hand back from the knife sticking in my chest. I took out the knife, stepped away, lay down on the floor, and waited in quicktime while my heart healed well enough to let me go on. It was a clean wound, but I dared not push myself too hard—there were limits to what my heart could take without rebelling and insisting I spend a few hours in bed. Finally, though, I could go on. I got up and came back to Dul, who had brought back his hand; his face was beginning to register surprise that I was gone. I took the knife and, in order to convince him that I was serious about the need for his cooperation, pushed the knife-blade (iron of Mueller manufacture!) deep into his arm. Then I slipped back into realtime, watching him transform at the last moment from the young man I had stabbed into the tall and taciturn servant Dul. The stolidity didn't last long, however. He looked startled, gripped his arm, and in that moment the illusion flickered, faded; he changed back and forth before my eyes, until finally he resolved as himself, the smallish young man.

He leaped at me, dragging me to the floor. The knife was already out of his shoulder, was slicing toward my throat. I stopped it, and wrestled him for control of it. He was strong and young—I was younger and a good deal stronger. Also, he was quite unskilled in the use of the knife. He probably had never had to use it in a situation where his enemy could see it coming.

I had him pinned to the floor and was demanding that he tell me where he was from before I killed him when I heard a sound from the door. I looked and saw no one—but the door was still swinging open. If the illuders could do all I had already seen them do, they could probably make me think I saw no one: I was sure someone else was in the room. Interrogation would be impossible with an audience of illuders, and now they were warned. I had had one chance, not a very good one, to find out where they were from. Now I had lost it.

I pushed into quicktime and arose from where my erstwhile opponent lay on the ground. Not one but three illuders were already heading toward where I had been, knives ready. It was pointless, but I took the knives out of their hands and brought them with me into the throne room, where the old lady who was pretending to be Percy Barton sat on the throne looking bored. I placed the knives in her lap, blades pointing toward her, and then walked out of the palace. The message would be clear—she could have been killed. But it was only a message, only a could-have-been, and I didn't know what to do next.

Kill them all? Pointless, utterly wasted if I didn't know where they were from. They would only be replaced by fellow illuders, and the plot would hardly be thwarted, only mildly delayed. As it was I did have some time to plan my next move, in quicktime, at least—it would be a week before riders could get from Gill to another capital of any size, and with a week in quicktime I could accomplish a lot.

I left the palace. They would hardly leave records lying around saying, "The impostors in this palace come from the following Family." I would have to use reason alone to determine their homeland. And when it came to reasoning, I had learned to respect Lord Barton.

"You weren't gone long enough," he said after I sent the girl out of the room. "You impose on our friendship."

"I need your advice."

"And I need solitude. Or dualitude. Do you realize that I was on the verge of accomplishing something that I haven't achieved in thirty years? Twice in a row. Twice in ten minutes."

"There'll be other opportunities. Listen, Barton, I've been to the palace. I've met your son. He's a woman, your age or older, and she's surrounded by fellow illuders, including your former servant. But I can't get anything out of them. They're a bit alarmed, in fact. They know that I know them; they've had a taste of what I can do. Within a week they'll be able to notify others, and I'll never be able to stay ahead of them. Do you understand the situation?"

"You bollixed it up."

"I took a chance and it missed. So now, since you

were stupid enough to come here after you promised to stay in Humping—"

"Humping," he said wistfully.

"You might as well make yourself useful. I need to know where they come from. I need to know their homeland. Because unless we strike there, first and hard, we'll never stop them."

He began thinking at once.

"Well, Lanik, it's plain enough that we can't just pull numbers out of a hat and hope to find them. There are eighty Families—it could be any one of them."

"There are ways to narrow it down. I've got a theory, a good one, I think, about what the Families are doing. In Nkumai I found a history of sorts; it listed what the different Families' founders specialized in. Nkumai, for example, was founded by a physicist. Their export product is physical and astronomical theory. In Mueller we exported the product of genetic research—the first Mueller was a geneticist. You see?"

"How constant is that?"

"I haven't visited that many countries and been informed what their export product is. But it held true for Ku Kuei and Schwartz."

"A philosopher and a geologist."

I must have looked startled.

"I don't know why the information should surprise you. Britton was founded by a historian. Not a very likely field to turn into a viable export product, but we're fanatics about keeping records. The list of the original eighty traitors from Anderson to Wynn is memorized by every schoolchild, along with brief biographies that include their occupations. We're very thorough. I can also recite my genealogy from Britton himself to me. I haven't done so up to now because you haven't asked me to."

"I never will. You're a man of iron, Barton."

"The question is, what occupation could possibly

have led to a Family becoming illuders? Psychologists would be most obvious, wouldn't they? Who was a psychologist? Drew, of course, but they live in their hovels in the north and have dreams of killing their fathers and sleeping with their mothers."

"That could be an illusion," I said.

"Only last year they attacked Arven across the mountains and were humiliatingly defeated. Does that sound like our enemy?"

I shrugged. How could we tell anything about the illuders?

"Besides, they've made little secret of what they've been working on for centuries. Somewhere along the line, the people we're looking for would have to have become secretive. Don't you think? Another psychologist, the only other one, was Hanks. I know nothing about them except that they rebelled against the East Alliance two years ago and my loving son went in with an army and burned the whole country to the ground. The stories said that only one in three people survived, and they lived by getting over the borders and living on charity in Leishman and Parker and Underwood. There *is* no charity in Gill. Again, it doesn't seem to be a likely spot for the illuders' homeland."

Again, he was right. "No more psychologists?"

"No."

"What other professions then?"

"Maybe they're an exception to your theory, Lanik. Maybe they came up with something new."

"Go through the list. We've got to try to find the most likely prospect, anyway."

So we went through the list. It was tedious, but he wrote it down in a beautiful script that gave me even more respect for his education, though I could hardly read it. Our guesses were long shots. Tellerman was an actor, but that Family was well known to have literary pretensions. The Ambassador had rejected every book and play and poem they had offered in three thousand years. Their persistence was remarkable. There had been no illusionists or magicians among the original group exiled here, of course—that was too crass a profession, since the rebellion had been a revolt of the elite against their exploitation by the democratic tyranny of the masses. With a few exceptions, the exiles on Treason were the cream of the cream, the prime intellects of the Republic. Which meant that except for the psychologists and a few other peripheral ones, probably involved in funding the revolt, most of the rebels were experts in a science.

When we had spent more than an hour exhausting, as we thought, every possibility, the answer suddenly seemed so obvious I couldn't believe we had overlooked it until now.

"Anderson," I said.

"We don't even *know* what he did," Barton said.

"As a profession, we don't. And yet he was head of the rebellion, wasn't he?"

" 'Of traitors, traitor most foul,' " Barton intoned.

"Leader of the intellectuals, and yet not an intellectual himself."

"Yes. One of the inscrutable facts in history."

"A politician," I said. "A demagogue who got himself elected to the Republic Council, and yet the same man was able to win the trust of the finest minds of the Republic. Isn't that a contradiction?"

Barton smiled. "You have something there. Of course he wouldn't have any ability like our current enemies. But he was able to make people think he was what he wanted them to think he was. And, except that they're better at it, isn't that what the illuders are doing now?"

I leaned back on my chair. "You at least admit that it's plausible then?"

"Plausible. Not probable. But none of the others

are even possible, so far as I can see. Which makes Anderson the best bet, at least to try first."

I got up and started out the door.

"Isn't this a bit rude? Aren't you going to invite me along?"

"I'll only be gone a couple of days," I said.

"It's at least a week's ride across rough country in Israel till you get to the shore, and then you have to get a boat to cross the nastiest bit of water in the world, the Quaking Sea—unless you're fool enough to try the Funnel. That's at least a fortnight's absence—and you'd probably kill a couple of horses doing it that quickly."

"It won't take me that long. Trust me. Have I let you down yet?"

"Only when you sent the young lady out of the room. Don't worry, though. I won't try to follow you. If you say two days, I'll wait two days, or even more. A man who can make arrows turn in midflight can fly to the moons, if he wishes."

I had another thought. "Maybe you ought to wait somewhere else," I said.

"Nonsense. It's more risky to go out on the street. Besides, I have unfinished business. I want to set a record for myself. Three times within one hour. Send her back in here."

I sent her back in when I left.

It was infuriating that I arrived sooner when I walked the distance in quicktime than when I rode it in realtime on a horse—all because I hadn't learned how to extend my bubble of time in Ku Kuei. It took me nine long days' worth of walking to get to the coast of Israel in the quickest quicktime I had ever attempted since leaving Ku Kuei. There had been a time in my life when solitude and exercise had been invigorating. Now I was weary of being alone, even wearier of endlessly walking from place to place, seeing people like statues in the fields, all so unaware of how they were being subverted by the illuders. I was out to save them, and they didn't even know they needed to be saved.

I was weary to the bone when I reached the promontory of Israel overlooking the Funnel, the narrow strait between Anderson and the continent. The waves of the sea were frozen, of course, in the middle of their furious rush northward into the slightly lower Quaking Sea. The crests of the waves reached nearly to the level of the promontory where I stood, like hills rising from a cataclysm of the earth.

There were few things I hadn't done in quicktime, but swimming in a realtime sea was one of them. In Ku Kuei, when I swam in quicktime I was always with someone whose timeflow was strong enough to carry a portion of the lake, not to mention me, along with it.

I gingerly stepped into the water. While air caused me no resistance at all in quicktime, the water was sluggish and bore my weight much better than it did in realtime. In fact, my passage across the Funnel was not properly swimming at all. I crawled, after a fashion, up the slope of a wave as if it were a muddy hill after a rainstorm. Then I slid easily down the other side. After a while it became exhilarating, if exhausting. It was still afternoon when I reached the other side and scrambled out of the sea onto the rocky shore of Anderson Island.

Once out of the reach of the giant seas, I looked around. The land was grassy, strewn with boulders, and sheep grazed here and there—it was settled land. But it was also hot and dry and bleak. The grass was not thick, and each sheep that was moving at all had a small cloud of dust around it, which from my point of view seemed to hang in the air.

I walked along the crest of the slope leading down to the rocky coast, wondering how I would now go about discovering if this were indeed the home of

the illuders. I couldn't very well go up to someone
and say, "Good afternoon, is this where the bastards
who are trying to take over the world hail from?" I
had to have some plausible reason for being there.
Remembering the sea I had just crossed, shipwreck
seemed a likely possibility. All I had to do was make
sure to struggle ashore conveniently near some shepherd's house. From there I could, I hoped, play it by
ear.

When I came to a house only a few meters from
the beginning of the rocky littoral, I scrambled back
down the rocks to the sea. Recognizing how high
the waves really were and how violent they must be
in realtime, I prudently climbed to the crest of the
first wave away from the shore. And then I slipped
back into realtime.

I should have stood on a rock and let the spray get
me wet.

12   ANDERSON

The wave didn't wait around for anything. I was immediately dropped sickeningly toward the rocks of the coast as a new wave came after and slammed down on top of me. I met the rock with a sickening crunch of bone and then was lifted again to be slammed down again.

The pain of my shattered right leg was excruciating, which distracted me, and my body refused to let me use it in my swimming. For the first time in quite a while I had met up with a force of nature I couldn't cope with, and I feared for my life. My father had died by breaking his spine in water. As I sank rapidly toward the rocks a second time, my urge for survival took over and I scrabbled through the water toward the shore and caught at a rock. But the wave that hit me tore loose my grasp and pulled me out again.

The third time I was able to keep my hold and drag myself farther from the waves. I was still soaked by spray every time a wave came to shore—which seemed to be every second or two—but I was relatively safe. I waited for several minutes for my leg to begin to heal enough that, if necessary, I could walk on it. When I was satisfied that it could bear my weight, I began calling out.

"Help!" I bellowed. It was hopeless—I couldn't possibly be heard above the din of the waves. I had to get closer to the hut and farther from the sea. I clambered less than nimbly among the rocks. It was then that I saw her, a girl who couldn't have been older than twenty, dressed in a simple garment that didn't come to her knees. She was winsomely beautiful, and the light breeze tossed her black hair. This was hardly the moment to feel amorous, but I was immediately attracted to her. Seriously attracted to a woman for the first time since leaving Saranna in Ku Kuei.

I called out again and she came delicately down among the rocks until she reached me. She smiled; I smiled back, but let the pain I still felt show clearly in my face. I stumbled often—not hard to manage —as she helped me up to the plateau. While she led me to her house I burbled out a story of getting caught in the current heading up the Funnel, my father and I in a fishing boat; how I was sure he had been drowned, since the mast when it broke struck him in the head. She, in turn, told me how the sea had snatched her old father from the rocks not three years ago, and she was struggling to keep a flock of sheep and retain her independence.

"Surely you don't lack for marriage offers," I said.

"No," she answered shyly. "But I'm waiting."

"For what?" I asked.

"The right one, of course," she said playfully, and then led me to her cottage.

From a distance, when I had first seen her house, I hadn't noticed the flowers growing around the walls. They made a pleasant contrast in this land of desolation, and I found myself liking her. She offered me food, showing me a cold stew that she could soon heat up.

Before I could say anything the earth began to shake and I was thrown to the floor. I knew enough about earthquakes to know that indoors was not a good place to be during one—I scrambled on all fours to the door and watched as the earth visibly heaved and a crevice opened in the ground not ten meters off. It was wide, and the earth groaned as it opened and closed again.

Then the quake was over. I got up, sheepishly, and dusted off my clothes. They were still wet from the sea—mud clung to them. I remembered to limp, though my leg was nearly healed now.

"I'm sorry," she said, and I realized she seemed more vexed than terrified by the quake. "We have such inconvenient weather here, between the earth, the sky, and the sea." As if to prove her point, the sky, which up to a moment ago had been cloudless, suddenly began to pour down rain as clouds roiled from one horizon to the other.

The flowers were quickly drenched—but they seemed to stand a little straighter.

"Your clothes," she said. "I can wash out that mud, if you want to take them off. And the salt from the sea, too."

I trust my blush was convincing—*I* was convinced, anyway. She seemed so innocent that it was impossible not to be shy with her.

"I'm not wearing anything under these," I admitted.

"Then go into the back room—I have two rooms —and pass them to me through the curtain."

I didn't have to be urged. I stripped off the trousers and shirt, reminders of Glain and Vran and Humping, and handed them to her, then lay on the bed, which was surprisingly soft—luxury like Mueller, here in sheep country! I sank into the bed, naked, spread-eagled, to dry out and relax. It felt good, after a month of relentless travel and a grueling few hours with the sea.

I slept.

What woke me, I'm not sure. I couldn't have slept long—the sky was virtually unchanged, still dark with clouds but not with night. The smell of the stew was strong in the house. Then the door opened.

She stood in the doorway, naked. Her body was young; it reminded me achingly of Saranna's body when we were children in our teens, before I left Mueller too many years ago. I was still in my teens, wasn't I? But it felt too long ago for me to believe it. I wanted the girl. Or perhaps I wanted my youth again. Whatever my own motive, from her nakedness, from her smile, it was plain she wanted me to want her.

Wanted me to want her. Was this the shy woman who made me blush?

Something didn't fit. Many things didn't fit. As she came into the room and knelt on the bed, I realized how terribly unlikely it was that such a creature as this could live unmolested in such isolation, so near the coast. I realized how odd it was that the rainclouds appeared from nowhere, that she hadn't been bothered by an earthquake that nearly shook her house down, and that as sweet and shy as she was, she now knelt straddling my body, her arms crossed over her breasts.

I pushed into quicktime. The knife was only a handspan away from my throat. The nude young girl was now a vile, ugly old man, with perhaps the most vicious, hate-filled expression I have ever seen on a human face. His eyes were deepset and watery, his face gaunt with poverty. I had no doubt what he was after. His skeletal body cried out for meat. By comparison to him, I was fat.

The bed I was on was not soft, either—it was a board, and so hard and ungiving that when I slid awkwardly out from between his legs, he hardly bounced. I stood there for a moment, wondering what to do. The door to the kitchen was still open. I went in and found that the stewpot, far from being full of cold stew, was actually dusty from nonuse. None of the interior finishing that had made the place look homey and inviting was real—it had made way for rough sod walls, a dirt floor, and filth everywhere.

The dirt, in fact, was indescribable. It was as if, because the man could choose to live in illusion, he didn't bother to make his real surroundings even tolerable. Did his illusions really fool him? Perhaps. Yet, I realized, he had already put on my clothes, and I could find no trace of his own. Had he been naked then, before? The poverty was appalling. I had never seen a human being live in such relative savagery outside of Schwartz, and there the poverty had dignity, since the Schwartzes were truly clothed in sunlight and air.

Outside, even the flowers turned out to be brambles and dusty grey grass. The hut was tilting, slipping toward collapse. There was no trace of any crevice in the earth, and the rain, like the quake, had been an illusion.

There could be no doubt, then, that Anderson was the place I was seeking. And no doubt that my decision was correct. If there was an opposite to what the world should be, Anderson was it: all seeming beautiful, but in truth vicious and squalid and murderous.

I went back into the house, back to the tiny lean-to that in the illusion was a bedroom, and took the knife out of the old man's hand. Then I slipped into realtime. He turned into the girl again, but suddenly she pulled up and held one hand with the other because of the pain of my having pulled away the knife so quickly. She looked to where I was, and her face registered shock. I kicked her squarely in the groin, and suddenly she was an old man lying on the floor, writhing.

"Who are you!" he demanded. "Whose dream are you!"

"Yours," I said.

Recovering somewhat from the pain, he nastily said, "I come up with better dreams in my sleep. I thought you were real, the way that quake scared you."

I reached down with the wooden knife and stroked his throat with the tip. Then, suddenly, hands were around my throat from behind. I cursed myself for a fool and shoved into quicktime. The man disappeared from the floor in front of me and now leaned over my back, trying to strangle me. I broke his hold, then got behind him. As soon as I was in realtime again, I picked him up and pushed him from the bedroom and into the kitchen. He screamed all the way—I had broken all his fingers in getting him loose from my neck in quicktime.

But illusions extended even to the sense of touch, and suddenly he was behind me again, this time with the knife, this time stabbing through my back to my kidneys. By now I was tired of pain, and so instead of trying to fight him, I ran out of the house. An earthquake began instantly. It took tremendous force of will, but I walked right across a crevice that yawned in front of me. It was solid ground. Then, a few dozen meters from the house, I lay on the earth and as quickly as I could forced an earthquake that swallowed up the house in a huge collapse of land.

I was lying on the surface of the earth, and it shook beneath me. But it was not the quake that swept through me like a harrow through fine soil. It was the scream of death. Not the scream of a man murdered by a weapon in battle, nor the scream of the countless men and women and children taken by disease or famine or fire or flood. It was the scream of someone murdered by the earth itself, unwillingly, and the cry was amplified a thousand times until it filled me and I, too, screamed.

I screamed until my voice could no longer fill my ears. The pain was not physical. When it ended, there was no residual aching in my muscles or tension that would not release. The pain was in that part of me which had been in communion with the earth, and as it shattered me I wondered, briefly, if I would die from it.

I did not die. But when my own scream fell into silence and I looked and saw that the earth had closed again, leaving no trace of the house and its sad, non-existent flowers, I wanted to call it back, call back the hideous old man, let the life of him continue even though the self of him could not live. He deserved to die except that nothing deserves death, and I might have gone mad at that moment, needing the house and the man and the life to return and knowing that it had to be destroyed, except that for some reason I thought of my father bloated by the water of the lake; I thought of the thousands of soldiers and civilians of the Rebel River plain killed or left homeless as the Nkumai, led by an Anderson illuder, ravaged and ravished their way across the earth. I thought of the million deaths they had caused and would still cause, the billion lives they would grind down in misery, and this balance, this sense of the utter rightness of the destruction of Anderson, preserved my sanity and let me get up from the ground and weakly, wearily walk back to the rocks leading down to the sea.

Yet the questions were not so easily resolved. I had heard the scream of the earth at being forced into complicity in a killing—even a just killing. It would strip the structure of my soul forever. I had never believed I had a soul until then, when it laid bare a hurt more deep than any part of me could bear.

I grieved all the way across the water; all the way in quicktime back to Gill. I stopped only once, to replace the clothing that got swallowed up in Anderson. I was careful to steal clothing from a house that looked like its owners could afford the loss. These long walks in quicktime left me nothing to do but think, and my thoughts were not comfortable ones on this journey. This time, for once, I could look forward to the relief of talking to someone to whom I didn't have to lie, someone who might be able to understand what I had done, who might not condemn me for it. At last I came to the whorehouse and mounted the stairs and found Lord Barton's body cut into dozens of small pieces, already rotting in the heat coming through the south-facing window.

13   TREASON

How they had found him I didn't know, but it couldn't have been hard. The integrity of the manager was suspect at best; stories of our odd midday arrival might have circulated up through the symbiotic chain of criminals and police until it reached the attention of someone who was aware of Barton's miraculous salvation from the archers. The mutilation of his body was probably because, having seen me again after I seemed thoroughly dead, the illuders and their unwitting assistants wanted to make sure there was no chance of error. And they left him in the whorehouse so I'd be sure to find him.

I was still in quicktime as I surveyed the destruction of my friend. It had been, to me, ten "days" since I left Anderson, nineteen "days" since I had left Barton. In realtime, however, it was early evening of the day after I left. I couldn't help wondering if I could have saved Barton by coming back a little faster, or by not leaving him quite so soon. But as I gave him grief, I realized that the guilt I felt because I might have saved him was a trivial thing compared to the pain of the earth's scream in Anderson. The earth did not hold me responsible for Barton's death, and after the illuders had added Lord Barton's murder to their list of crimes, I couldn't bring myself to feel guilt for the killing of that hideous man in Anderson. So I was able to shrug off the blame for this and remember only that I loved the man, that he was good, and that I had to stop others like him from dying at the illuders' hands.

With Barton gone, I had no reason to delay the next stage in my journey; I had every reason to hasten it. None of the illuders would escape. No matter what it took, Treason would be free of them before I was through. Any doubt I had about the rightness of my intended killings was gone. I was beyond thought, and intended only to carry out the decision I had so reluctantly made, yet was now grimly glad to fulfill.

There was a matter of priorities. Before moving against the Andersons who were running things in other Families, I had to see to it that the home island was depopulated. No replacements, no angry and deceptive and irresistible army from Anderson, should be able to rescue the rulers. And the population of Anderson could be as much as a million; certainly it was no less than a hundred thousand. That would be long and weary work in quicktime, with me armed only with my iron knife and forced to go from person to person. It would use up my lifetime before I was half through. Their destruction required a cataclysm they could not resist, that would kill them all at once. It was not something I knew how to do.

I needed help, and there was only one place I could get it. But could I persuade the people of Schwartz to kill, even when that killing would save other lives—and, perhaps more importantly, make millions of lives more worth living? There was little room for making value judgments in the Schwartzes' thinking, I knew too well. Life was life. Murder was murder. And I, who had left them still innocent, was coming back to them with blood on my hands, asking them to help me with my killing.

For weeks I had lived utterly alone in quicktime, neither eating nor drinking, neither speaking nor hearing another human voice except that of the beautiful girl in Anderson. Yet I had no time to waste. So for another thirty days I traversed the whole southland of the continent, from Wood to Huss. The trees gave way to lush grassland. The grass gave way to brush that could survive the low rainfall. And finally the brush gave way to endless sand and sunbroken rocks.

I stopped, in quicktime, by the last bush I could see, and there slipped into realtime. I could not find the Schwartzes. They would have to find me. And find me they would, I knew.

For a moment I toyed with the thought of turning back. My reunion with them would not be happy. They couldn't possibly kill me, but when I had lived with them I had known the kind of love they give. I had depended on it. It would not be there now.

I had walked into the desert for half a day when the first Schwartz began paralleling my path, visible from time to time a few dunes away, or at the crest of another rockpile. By afternoon there were three others, and by evening, when I stopped in the shadow of a rise of rock, there were nearly a hundred all around me, more than I had ever seen at one time when I lived among them.

They were silent, all watching me. I did not eat, of course, but sat before them and in my mind reached into the sand, found the water far below, and pulled the water to the surface. It glittered in the reflected light from rocks that still caught the sun. I leaned down to drink. The water withdrew, sank away from me. They had judged me, just as I feared.

I stood, then, and spoke to the Schwartzes.

"I need your help."

"You'll get nothing from Schwartz," said an old man.

"The world needs your help."

"The earth needs nothing but life." And someone murmured, "Killer."

"I didn't say the earth!" I answered, sharply. "I said the world. Men. You know what men are—they're the ones who still have to eat to live, who still worry about dying."

"Who still fear murderers," said the old man. "We heard the echoes of that scream, Lanik Mueller. You performed the act, so only you heard it clearly, but we know what you did. We taught you, and you used the knowledge to kill. You forced the earth itself to be your sword. If we ever longed to kill, you would be the one whose death we'd seek. Can I say it more plainly? Leave us. You'll get nothing from Schwartz."

"Helmut?" I asked, recognizing him, though I didn't know how.

"Yes," the old man answered.

"I thought you wanted to remain young forever."

"A friend betrayed me, and I grew old."

Then he turned his back on me, and so did the others. Yet none of them left.

The darkness came in then, swiftly as it comes to the desert once the sun is down. But soon Dissent passed through the sky, casting little light but at least providing a reference point so that the vertigo of utter darkness did not overtake me. The silence was unbroken, however, until at last I could stand it no longer. My memory of my months among the Schwartzes was too acute. I had been one of them, and now they hated me; I had a task to perform and now I would fail; there were people I cared for, and they would not be freed. I took off my clothes and pressed myself into the sand and wept.

I wept for myself, who had betrayed the trust of the rock and killed. I wept for Barton, whose wit and courage in trusting a stranger had cost him his life, even as he opened up the possibility of saving the world. I wept for the thousands of people I had passed in my journey here, none of them even suspecting that their fate was passing by, that their future would soon be hanging in the balance.

And I wept because I knew that in the end it would be largely futile. Even when the Andersons were gone, if I could destroy them, how free would anyone on Treason be? The Muellers would again make iron swords and attack their neighbors; the Nkumai would again descend from the trees and overrun those who fought with wood and glass. Killing the Andersons would open up a flood of death on the earth. Unfree as the world was, they didn't really know it, and they were at peace.

Who was I to think that this peace was worse than war?

The real enemy was not the Andersons. The real enemy was iron. Not iron for starships to escape from Treason and return to the rest of the human race. Iron to bring blood from soldiers and make them die—that was what was destroying us. Because what choice did anyone have? If they had something, anything that could be sold to the Ambassadors for iron, then a Family had an advantage over all the others. And so it was necessary for a Family to protect its independence by striking down all other Families that might develop or had developed something the Ambassadors would buy.

As I lay in the sand, my head resting on my arms, I realized that killing the Andersons would accomplish nothing, unless I also destroyed the Ambassadors. As long as dead iron could be sent from other worlds to shed blood on this one, the dying would go on.

"You taught me," I said, "that there is iron in the earth."

They didn't answer me, had not turned even when

I wept, supposing, probably, that I wept the tears of the guilty and the damned.

"Why is none of this iron on the surface?"

No answer.

"There was some iron on the surface, wasn't there? That's why the first Schwartz came here, wasn't it? The geological survey showed that there weren't any easily accessible iron deposits. But there was iron *here*, wasn't there?"

Helmut spoke: "No one will ever find iron in Schwartz."

"But it *was* here, wasn't it? It was here, and you knew, or your ancestors knew, what iron could do, didn't they? They knew the iron would kill. They knew that in the scramble for supremacy, so much blood would be shed that any victory would be meaningless. Didn't they!"

Helmut turned to me, a strange, twisted expression on his face. "No one has ever left Schwartz believing that."

"You had the iron! And you decided not to use it! Didn't you!"

Helmut stood, angry. "Don't you know anything? Haven't you seen the mountains? Why do you think we never let it rain here? If we let the rain fall in Schwartz, the rust in the rocks would be visible for miles! We'd have no peace, not here, not anywhere in the world! We have kept the iron hidden, and you will *not* bring the world in here to take it and kill with it!"

Others were facing me now, and they looked angry, too.

"You don't understand. I don't want to tell anyone about it. I want to finish the work your fathers started. You live here in Schwartz protecting mankind from iron, but out there iron is shedding blood anyway. Don't you know that?"

"Of course we know that," said Helmut. "But we haven't the power to change men's hearts. We're not responsible. It isn't our fault."

"Your hands are clean, aren't they? Out here where the sun keeps everything pure. But you're not pure! Because if you can stop the suffering and dying, and don't stop it, then you *are* guilty. It *is* your fault."

"We kill no one. We do not let them kill us. We have nothing to do with them."

I had the thread of an argument, though, and I pursued it. "If you help me, I can stop the iron from coming here. I can completely stop the flow of iron from the Republic, and I can end the fear and competition that has been causing these wars. But I can't do it without your help."

"You're a killer."

"So are you!"

Helmut's eyes widened.

I pressed the point. "In Hanks, hundreds of thousands of people died at swordpoint or from the famine when the land was scorched by the armies of Gill. On the Rebel River plain, hundreds of thousands died when the armies of Nkumai destroyed every living thing in their path. Had any army ever done that kind of thing before? Ever?"

"The sound of it was terrible," Helmut said faintly.

"The reason that kind of war was waged was because of iron. Was because Nkumai and Mueller were both getting iron, and it seemed inevitable that one of them would become supreme among the Families. But there was another Family, one that had a product they could never export. The Ambassador would never give them iron. But what they *could* do, what they *have* done, is go out and take the iron the other Families got."

"What do we care what happens to Mueller and Nkumai?" Helmut said scornfully.

"Nothing at all. But you should care what happens

to humanity, for the sake of the rock if for no other reason. The Family I speak of is Anderson, and their power is to lie. Not just to tell someone something that isn't true, but to make them believe it, against their will, to make them so sure that the lie is true that it never occurs to them to question it." I told them about Dinte, about Mwabao Mawa, about Percy Barton.

Helmut looked concerned at last. "These are the people who have been killing so many?"

"They are."

"And what would you do? Kill them all?"

My pause was answer enough. Helmut's look changed to loathing. "And you want *us* to help. You were never my friend, not if you can believe we would do it."

"Listen to me!" I shouted, as if sheer volume would make him open his mind. "The Andersons are irresistible. No man can fight them. They've come subtly this time, insinuating themselves in governments and ruling people who don't know they're ruled by them. But if they're aroused, they can come from their island in force, and no army could resist them, because they would come appearing to be terrible monsters; or they would come invisibly in the night; or they would fight openly, and yet when a man struck at them his enemy would no longer be where he seemed to be, and every soldier would be killed before he ever put his sword to good effect."

"I know what warfare is," Helmut said contemptuously, "and I reject it."

"Of course you reject it. Who can kill *you*? You'll never die. But out there are millions of people who *can* die, and when someone comes up to them with a sword in his hand and says, 'Obey me or I'll kill you and your wife and your children,' what does he do? He obeys. Even if he's a hero, he obeys, because he knows that anyone who has the power to kill and is willing to use it will defeat all enemies unless they are just as eager to kill. The power to steal life is the ultimate power in this world, and before that power every other man is weak."

"We aren't weak."

"You aren't men. Men are mortal. You can laugh at a soldier and throw up a wall of rock that will keep him out forever. You can stand on that wall and watch as he and his children and his grandchildren grow old and die, and you'll never understand why it is that they're so constantly afraid. They're afraid because the rain might not come and if their crop fails they'll starve; because floods or earthquakes can snatch away their lives without warning; but most of all because in the night another man can come and lift a sword and cut them off completely from the world. They're afraid of *death*! Can you at least imagine what that means?"

"We fear death, too," Helmut said.

"No, Helmut, you resent death. You regret death. But as for your own life, you know perfectly well that no one can threaten it at all. Death is something that happens to someone else."

"And because of that you want us to kill people? You want us to do the same thing?"

"No, I don't. I want you to help me stop everyone on this planet from having the power to be irresistible. I want to destroy the Ambassadors so that no Family will ever be able to raise iron weapons against wooden ones. And I want to destroy the Andersons because they, like iron, kill wantonly and cannot be withstood."

"How would we be different from them, killing those whose actions we don't like?"

"I don't know! Maybe there's a measuring rod somewhere in the universe where men's acts are judged, and those who kill other men for the sake of power will be judged more harshly than those who kill those power-hungry men for the sake of freedom. But if there's no place in the universe for a man to resist the thieves of freedom and still be called a good man, then I don't think there is any good or evil in the universe, and if that's true then it all means nothing and it wouldn't make any difference then whether you kill or not but that can't be true, it can't be that way, it *does* make a difference, there comes a time when you have to take lives in order to— listen to me—in order to—"

But there was no way to convince them. I saw that now. They watched me impassively, and I despaired. "All right. I can't compel you. Nobody can force you to do anything." Bitterly I hurled insults at them. "You hold freedom like a prize, and it's in your power to help others be free, but you're too selfish to reach out and give them freedom, too. Keep your freedom, keep your immortality, but somewhere along the line I hope you figure out what you're living forever *for*. What noble purpose you mean to achieve. Because you're no good to anyone here, not even to yourselves."

I turned and walked away, back the way I had come, toward Huss and civilization and hopelessness. I walked for hours, and then I realized that someone was close behind me. It was Helmut, and he looked different. It took me a moment to realize why, but it was because his hair was no longer white with age.

"Lanik," he said, and his voice was younger. "Lanik, I must talk to you."

"What for?" I asked, not daring to believe that my words might have had an effect on him after all.

"Because you love me. Hearing you talk like that, I realized that I love you, too. Despite everything."

So I stopped and sat in the sand, and so did he.

"Lanik, you have to understand something. We aren't deaf to other men. We heard you. We understood. And we *want* to achieve the goal you set out. We *want* to destroy the Ambassadors. We hate the Andersons and their murders and their deceptions as much as you—nothing is worse to us than those who murder, not for anger or hurt or revenge or because they believe it is their duty, but for profit. Do you see that? We hate what you hate. And we long for it to be destroyed.

"But Lanik, we *can't do it*. Did you think our hatred of killing was just an opinion, just an emotion, just a wish that no more suffering take place? We *cannot* kill. It's that simple. We suffer from the song of death among the rocks even now. But you heard the scream of the earth when you made the earth kill that man in Anderson. You *heard* it. What was it like?"

I answered honestly. "It was the worst thing in the world."

"Well, Lanik, you have more ability with the earth than any one of us. We told you that years ago, before you left. And so you heard that scream more clearly than any of us could ever hear it.

"But if we were to destroy Anderson, we'd have to swallow up the island in the sea and the earth, take it completely from the surface, and you know as well as I do that there isn't one of us, alone, that could do that."

I nodded. "I hoped the council—"

"That's the problem, Lanik. The council is a collection of individuals. Weak ones, like me. Together, we can twist and turn the earth in ways you couldn't imagine. We could sink Anderson into the sea in moments. We could build a mountain range from one end of the world to the other in an hour. We could, if it were ever necessary, take this entire planet and twist it in its orbit until it was cooler or warmer, farther from or closer to the sun.

"But if we should kill everyone on Anderson by

sinking the island under the sea, the scream you heard from one man would be magnified hundreds of thousands of times. Can you comprehend that? And those hundred thousand screams would be borne by a mere three or four hundred of us. Each of us would bear a scream hundreds of times more terrible than what you heard. And worse, because we would be the council, we would have penetrated deeper into the heart of the earth than you could ever pierce, yet we would still be individuals, and there where the rock's voice is loudest, we would be individually less able to resist. The scream would penetrate us deeper, and we would be drowned in it as surely as the sea would drown the people of Anderson.

"Do you understand, Lanik? To do that would destroy us. And who would control the anger of the earth then? Who would absorb the hatred of the rocks? Who would cool that burning? No one. We would destroy the earth because we would no longer be able to contain his wrath. That's why we can't agree to what you propose."

I hadn't known that. I hadn't understood the price they would have to pay. "I'll do my best without your help."

I got up to leave. Helmut got up, too, and after looking into his eyes a moment, I turned away.

"Lanik," he said.

"Yes," I answered.

"They asked me to tell you the way."

"The way to what?"

"The way to do what you want to do."

I studied him, unsure of what he meant. "You said that it's impossible."

He shook his head, and tears came to his eyes. "I said it was impossible for us. But there's another way. I didn't want to tell you, Lanik, for fear you'd accept it, because it would destroy you and I love you and I don't want you destroyed."

"If there's a way, Helmut, I'll take it, even if I die. God knows every alternative means death one way or another. I never planned to live forever, anyway." Even as I said these words, I wondered if I meant them, if I would really choose to die, or if instead I wouldn't prefer to find a place to live, a quiet place like Humping, or a hidden wood like Ku Kuei, or even here on this desert with the beautiful strange people of Schwartz. I could hide, and I could live, so whyever would I choose to die?

Helmut put my own doubts in words. "You have so little love for your own life?"

And in answering him, I answered myself. "Helmut, you don't know, you've never been alone like I have, but in my solitude I've discovered something. That I'm passing through the world invisibly. Even when people see or speak to me it's as if I didn't exist, as if I had no right to exist. I tread across their land and they don't see me. I act and act and act and nothing makes any difference in the world. But they touch *me*. There's a family in the hills of the poorest part of Britton, and they needed me, and their very need became the most important thing in my life. There's a woman frozen in time by a lake in Ku Kuei, and she needed me, but we've been torn apart and if I could do anything to take her from the eternal death she's consigned herself to I'd do it. A man who wasn't old enough to die killed himself in Ku Kuei, and when he died I realized that half of me was him, and that half died with him, and the other half will never stop mourning. I'll do what it takes, Helmut, so no one else will choose to die rather than live in this world. I'll do what it takes."

At other times and on other days, both before and since, I couldn't have said those words. Heroes and victims are the product of the mood they were in when opportunity came or when circumstances were at their worst, and had I not walked three thousand solitary kilometers only to be met with refusal and despair, I don't know if I would have said so easily, "I'll do what it takes."

But I said it, and I meant it, and Helmut embraced me and explained. "When we act together, we don't all have to go into the earth. We can send one, and he lies among the rock and sings all our songs with his voice, and he hears all the earth's song with his heart. It can be joyful, and we honor our greatest men by sending them for us on such occasions. It can be painful, and we also honor our greatest by entrusting them with the pain for all of us. But there's not a man among us who could bear this. And so we can't send any of us into the earth. You, however, are stronger than any of us. How much stronger, we don't know. But if you went into the earth for us, we could hope you might survive. And if you died, and the fury of the earth continued, we would still be alive to contain it and keep the world safe."

We lay together in the sand, all with our arms spread; I lay in the middle, curled into a ball, and as I sank into the sand I felt them join me, one by one, until all their songs were singing in my mind as the sand swallowed me up and bore me down.

Always I had stopped at bedrock before. But now the rock softened and flowed out around me, like cold mud, closing again over my face. The deeper I sank, the warmer the rock became and the faster it seemed I fell, until the heat was as much as I could bear and even when I stopped sinking, the rock seethed and twisted around me.

With the knowledge of the hundreds of Schwartzes above me, I easily found Anderson Island, this time not an aberration of the surface but instead the leading edge of a plate of rock floating on a sea of molten granite. The flow was incredibly slow, but once I found the island I began to draw the magma out from under it.

The settling seemed slow where I was working, of course, but the damage began on the surface from the first instant. The rock sank abruptly, and every building and living thing on the island tumbled to the ground. Then, as the island continued to sink, the sea rushed in from both sides and met in a great wave in the middle of the island, along its length from north to south.

Because of the interruption of the plate of rock, hot magma surged up to the surface, striking ocean and leaping still higher until it shot into the sky, throwing hot ash and steam and mud and lava out of the sea. The water boiled, and anything left alive in that part of the sea was killed as thousands of hectares of the ocean turned to steam.

All this happened because I, with the strength of all the Schwartzes to sustain me, had forced the earth to act. And the earth, ignorant of time and so of consequences, obeyed. It was not until the screams of death began that the earth rebelled, and in that moment the Schwartzes left me. Now they had to work to keep the earth from tearing apart, to keep the crust of the earth from shrugging off the irritating life that had caused it so much agony and so little joy. They had to stem the tide of molten rock that seethed to escape and win its way to the surface at every point that had felt the trembling when the island fell.

I, however, knew nothing of their work. There were other matters at hand, because the earth was screaming at the murder of half a million men, and I was the only listener.

So many of those who died were innocent. These were the ones that would haunt me from then on—

the fishermen innocently casting nets in Britton's Bay when the huge wave struck the shore; the people in tall buildings in Hess and Gill and Israel who were killed when the structures couldn't bear the shock wave riding out from Anderson; and however many people of Anderson who, even though they were il-luders, were not murderers and meant only good to other people.

As for the earth, however, there was no distinction between the innocent and the guilty, between those whose deaths achieved no purpose and those who had to die if mankind on Treason was to mean any-thing. The earth knew that this was not like the reaping of fields; it could not comprehend the human logic that had brought us to this point. The earth only knew that we who had gathered there in Schwartz had commanded the earth itself to murder people who were so far away that in no sense could we call our act self-defense.

The rocks groaned horribly as if to say, "We trusted you, we gave you power, we obeyed you, and you used us to kill!" The rocks screamed "Traitor!" as the heat swept back and forth across my body.

In a moment I lost all moorings, all connections with reality, all sense of time, and where the scream of the man I killed in Anderson lasted for seconds, the scream of the earth this time lasted forever. It had no end because there was no time, and for an infinity I felt an agony of infinite magnitude and I longed for only one thing. Not to die, because death would only add to the scream of the stone, but rather to be annihilated, to have never existed, to have never lived because my life had reached this point, and this point was unreachable, unendurable, impossible.

"Treason," screamed the earth forever.

"Forgive me," I pleaded.

And when at last time returned and infinity was

over, the rock spewed me out, the sand vomited me up, and I was thrown into the air and rushed head-long toward the stars.

I rose, and then the rising stopped, and I fell back toward the earth. It was the same feeling I had had when I stepped off the precipice in the darkness be-fore Dissent rose, and I wondered whether the sand would receive me after all, or whether this time I would strike the surface and simply stop, broken and spread out for my blood to soak into the sand and for the sun to dry my flesh to leather and then to dust.

Yet even in the air, I exulted. Even if I died now, I had done the first and greatest work; I had lived through it, if only for a while; I had heard the most terrible scream of the earth and had lived.

Then as I fell I listened and realized that the scream was not over. I could still hear it, even in the air, unconnected with the earth. If I lived, I would hear it forever.

I reached the sand and it gave, it bore me up, it let me sink slowly, and at last I lay on the earth's surface again, at rest, though never to be at peace again. The earth would never (the rock *could* never) forgive me for having betrayed its trust. But while it did not forgive, it could still endure me. It knew my heart, and it would bear my life. As long as I wished to keep on living, the earth would permit me to live.

The Schwartzes lay around me. After a long time I realized they were weeping. Then, strangely, I re-membered Mwabao Mawa singing morningsong from a perch high in Nkumai. The melody played end-lessly through my head. For the first time I under-stood the haunting beauty of the song. It was the song of a killer who longed to die. It was the song of justice yearned for but not yet done.

We lay there, all of us, exhausted beyond move-ment.

Hours later—or was it a day later, or days?—the vast cloud of vapor from the sea that had poured into the sky above the sinking of Anderson came over Schwartz, and for the first time in millennia it rained there, and water touched the iron-rich mountains and water bled into the sand and cooled it and water mingled with the tears on the faces of the people of Schwartz and erased and washed away their weeping and Helmut arose and walked to me in the rainstorm and said, "Lanik, you lived."

"Yes," I said, because he was really saying, "Lanik, I love you and you still live," and I was really saying, "Helmut, I love you and I still live."

"We've done what we've done," Helmut said, "and we won't regret it because it was necessary if not good. But even so, we ask you to leave. We won't thrust you out because without you worse things would have happened, but please, Lanik, leave us now and never come back."

"You'll still hear of me. I have more work to do. I'll cause you more pain."

"Do your work," he said. "I hope that someday the blood will wash from your hands."

"Guard your iron. Keep it safe. Don't let it rust."

He smiled (a grisly thing at the moment, and yet more surprising and refreshing than the rain) and he embraced me and he said, "I thought you had betrayed me when you left before. I didn't understand, Lanik. I thought that when I trusted you, that meant you would always act the way I wanted you to. I think perhaps I'll be young again after all, and let someone else be spokesman. I've had enough responsibility for a lifetime."

"And I for ten," I answered. He kissed me and embraced me and then sent me away. I walked eastward toward Huss. Somewhere along the way I found my clothes, neatly folded and placed in my path, and on top of them my knife. It was the Schwartzes' benediction, absolution in advance for the murders I had yet to commit.

I put on the clothes and held the iron knife in my hand and shoved myself again into quicktime, and for the next three years of my own time I spoke to no man and heard no man's voice, and spent my days walking between murders, listening to the cry of the dying and dead and hearing the earth's scream and knowing that someday I would have found them all, they would all be dead, and I would never have to kill again.

Percy Barton I killed willingly, for that old woman had deceived and murdered my friend. But her death scream harrows up my soul as loudly as that of Mwabao Mawa, even though she (no, *he*, a bald white man ruling a nation of proud, unknowing blacks) had sung the beautiful morningsong. There was no distinction. The hated and the loved died the same, and in the end my knife went no more easily into Percy Barton's throat than into Mwabao Mawa's.

Destroying the Ambassadors was easier, for the earth made no protest at their death. They were machines, already lifeless. All I had to do was break the seal where it said, "Warning, tampering will result in the destruction of this machine and the death of anyone within 500 meters of it," and then walk away in quicktime faster than the explosion could follow.

I killed along a path radiating outward from the ruins of the lands bordering Anderson, visiting every capital of every Family to make sure I found all the Andersons and killed every one, and to make sure that no Ambassador survived. Because I was in my fastest timeflow, all this took a week of realtime. I was ahead of every messenger. So far as the people of the world knew, a sudden scourge removed the rulers from their world, and the Ambassadors as well.

I wondered what the people thought when they found an old woman's corpse sitting on Percy Barton's throne. Would they make a connection? Or always wonder who it was they found, and never know why or where their king had disappeared?

There was no point in keeping a calendar during my long journey of assassination. By the end of it, a week after it began, I was, as closely as I can guess, about twenty-four years old. When my father was twenty-four I was already alive, and he had played with me in the morning and gone out and led his men into battle in the afternoon. I had no child, but neither could my murders weigh as lightly on my soul as my father's did. He knew no better, and thought the killing would make him a good king. I hadn't even the faint right of kings, and I knew exactly how much murder cost. I was twenty-four in years, but at heart I was unbearably old, and my body was weighted down and weary.

There was one place, however, where I had not yet gone, and when all the other Andersons and all the other Ambassadors were dead, there was one yet to kill: the one who had been my brother Dinte; the one who had destroyed my father; the one who had robbed me of my inheritance; the one that I had hated and rivaled and resented in all our years together; the one who, inexplicably, was still my brother regardless of how much I knew he was really not.

Could Lord Barton actually have killed the man he once believed was his son? Could I really kill Dinte?

That I would find out when the time arrived. And so I came at last to Mueller-on-the-River, and for the first time in years I entered a city, not hidden by quicktime, but openly. I was Lanik Mueller, and this place had been my home, and whether I was welcome here or not, I would come in proudly and declare, at last, when all the Andersons were dead, the work that I was doing and the work that I had done. The world thought of Lanik Mueller as a monster back when I still wasn't one; now that I was, I wanted them to know it. Even those regarded as evil want their deeds to be known.

I walked into the court where Dinte sat upon the throne and strode firmly to the middle of the room. While many there did not recognize me, for even those who had known me had last seen me as a fifteen-year-old boy, enough did recognize me that the whisper "Lanik Mueller" ran through the room. Every eye was upon me and, for a moment, everyone feared to act.

My brother Dinte arose from the throne and held his arms stiffly out, and in an unnaturally loud voice he said, "Well, brother. Have you come at last to take your throne?" He stepped aside to let me sit where by right I should sit. He commanded the people there to kneel as I mounted the dais. They knelt. Dinte waited for me, smiling, welcoming.

14 LANIK IN MUELLER

In all the possible versions of this scene that I had imagined, this one had never occurred to me. Yet for one long moment it seemed exactly right. The usurping brother, confronted by the wanderer who has at last come home, willingly steps aside in order that the more lawful heir may take his rightful place.

I had planned to come in, name Dinte as a traitor and a murderer, and in front of everyone in the court stab him to death. Nothing secret: This was not to be Lake-drinker, Man-in-the-Wind, or the Naked Man performing justice on an Anderson illuder. This was to be Lanik Mueller performing justice on his brother Dinte, the usurper who drove his father into the forest of Ku Kuei where he died.

Now Dinte had robbed me of that. Having so willingly (though I knew it was a lie) stepped aside for me, if I killed him now, openly, it would only add to the legend of Lanik Mueller as Andrew Apwiter come to life to re-create chaos and end the world. So, reluctantly, before the Anderson who hid behind Dinte's face could kill me unaware, I pushed into quicktime and stepped forward, which meant that to all intents and purposes I disappeared.

But Dinte did not turn into the Anderson I expected, the crusty, middle-aged man or woman I had supposed waited for me in quicktime. Instead he turned into a creature with four arms and five legs; two sets of male genitals contrasted absurdly with the three breasts that dangled in middle-aged sags. If I had seen such a being in the pens, I would not have been surprised. But I had been expecting an Anderson, and this was either an incredible monster or a radical regenerative from Mueller. And who from Mueller could ever have become an illuder?

Then I looked into the creature's face, frozen, staring at the spot where a moment ago I had been standing. And I recognized the monster, and everything changed.

The face was mine. Lanik Mueller's head topped the bizarre assortment of limbs and protuberances. Despite the ears and eyes and noses growing out of place, I recognized myself. It was I who stood beside the throne; not the Lanik Mueller who was cured in Schwartz, but Lanik Mueller the radical regenerative, the monster, the child.

It was my double, who was born in the forest of Ku Kuei.

Impossible! my mind cried out. This creature didn't exist until after Dinte had lived with us for years. This creature could not possibly have been Dinte.

At first I tried to tell myself that he was obviously a secondary illusion; that this Anderson had found a way to fool me in quicktime, too. But that was nonsense—if an Anderson could have fooled me, another would have done it long before.

So I walked in quicktime to the throne, sat down, and slipped back into realtime.

The effect was one I had rarely been able to show off before: suddenly I disappeared in one place and appeared in another. The murmur of the crowd was frantic. But Dinte (now with the normal number of arms and legs, as I had always known the little bastard) did not seem surprised.

"Dinte," I said. "All these people are startled to see me sitting here, but you and I know that Lanik Mueller has been sitting on this throne for years."

He looked at me a moment, then nodded slightly.

"And so, Dinte, I will meet you, privately, in the room where I kept my snail collection when I was five." I pushed back into quicktime and left the throne room.

I had kept my snail collection in a long-unused attic in one of the older parts of the palace, a place never locked but, because it was accessible only by ladder and winding corridors, rarely visited. I headed there in quicktime, then slowed down nearly to the flow of realtime, and waited. I kept just enough edge of speed that if Lanik/Dinte had ideas of treachery, I could react faster than he could attack.

If he was a fraud, if he was not truly me, he would not know what room I meant.

I waited for fifteen minutes. Then he came along the dusty attic walkway and sat before me on the floor. It was hard for him to walk, with his awkward arms and legs, and sitting was ludicrous, but I didn't laugh. I remembered my struggle up a not-too-difficult slope in Schwartz after I was set off the Singer slave ship. It had taken him three years in realtime to reach the condition I was in after my months of confinement on the ship. But I remembered; I had been inside that body. I knew exactly who he was and how he felt.

In realtime now, I spoke softly. "Hello, Lanik."

"Hello, Lanik," he answered, his smile ghastly on a twisted face.

"Last time we met, I tried to kill you," I said.

"Many times since then I've wished you had succeeded."

We sat in silence for a few moments. What do you talk about when you meet yourself after so many years?

"How did you come here?" I asked, though I already had guessed much of the story. "How did you learn to be an illuder?"

He told me. How he had lain half-dead as his already weak body tried to regenerate the skull and skin and keep the brain tissue from degenerating. How he had been found by the huge search party the Nkumai had sent after me. "If they hadn't found me," he said, "they would certainly have kept searching until they found you. When they finally realized what had happened and tried to follow you again, they traced you right to the seacoast. You were easy enough to find; if they had followed you at once, you wouldn't have escaped." He smiled. "I saved your life."

Then he told me of days and weeks with Mwabao Mawa in her treetop house. My body, in constructing him, had given him my memories; or perhaps in my delirium as we traveled together in the forest I had poured out into him all that mattered, all that made me who I was. It took Mwabao some time before she realized that he was only a duplicate of me. "By then she had learned enough that she was certain I was from Mueller—I had spoken Dinte's and Father's names in my madness, and her fellow Andersons were already here, as you seem to know."

She immediately seized the opportunity my double represented and fanned his hatred of me, his feelings of worthlessness because he would always be the monster, the horrible one, the creature that had no right to exist. It didn't take him long to consent to lead the Nkumai armies and their allies into battle against Mueller.

He exacted a price, however, that Mwabao was only too willing to pay. He asked for training in the

Anderson deception, and Mwabao Mawa taught it to him. While I was in Schwartz learning to control the earth, he was learning to control men's minds.

"People's beliefs don't exist in isolation," he explained. "Everyone's firmly held beliefs exert an enormous pressure on everyone else. Not opinions, of course—*beliefs*. We—they—could make anybody think the sun was blue and had always been blue. But, of course, the farther you got from the place where other people believed intensely in the deception, the less you would be influenced. However, by then the work would have been done. Once someone honestly believes something to be a fact, he'll never doubt it without pretty convincing evidence." Which is why Lord Barton was able to learn the truth separated from Britton by a thousand kilometers, but had to struggle to remember it when he returned to his home, where others were also in thrall to the lie.

He had not consented, he told me, to the wasting of the land by the Nkumai army on its passage through the Rebel River plain. I could never have done that —and so neither could he.

"And then you reappeared," he said, "and we didn't know what to do. Until, of course, you and Father escaped to Ku Kuei. Then it was clear that I had to disappear so that the monster they had made of me would color other men's perception of you, ruining your effectiveness. At the time, Lanik, I was glad of it. You can't know how much I hated you. You had hated me, not for who I was, but because I *was* at all."

At first they didn't know what to do with him now that Lanik Mueller was officially an exile in Ku Kuei. "Until word reached us that Dinte had disappeared. Mwabao Mawa panicked. How could anyone have known about Dinte and killed him—and yet not publicly raised the cry about who he was?

Whoever killed him would surely have seen him change before their eyes from the young heir to a much older man."

Then I realized what should have been obvious to me long before.

"I killed Dinte," I told my double. "I slit his throat as I left the palace. I assumed he would regenerate."

He smiled at me. "So you got your wish, didn't you? You killed Dinte, and in the process you saved my life. Because I was the only one who knew Dinte well enough to impersonate him without making waves. The Andersons aren't omnipotent. They can't fool the whole world all at once. So Mwabao Mawa sent me home to Mueller. I appeared to them as Dinte. I claimed that you had captured me and left me for dead after torturing me, but I had regenerated and come home. Who could doubt me? I've played the role ever since."

His voice grew soft (as mine always grew soft when I was afraid I would show fear or pity or grief) and he said, "You know—*you* know how much I hated Dinte. And yet I had to *be* him, and talk to his covey of traitors who had plotted your death and Father's death and—God, Lanik, how I survived that time I'll never know. But always I kept telling myself, 'I am Lanik Mueller, not his monster child,' and I endured the sycophants and the traitors and the petty criminals and Ruva and all the rest. Because it was common knowledge that you had gone with Father deep into Ku Kuei and would never come back. Father was dead, you see, and I loved him, just like you. The more people here in Mueller abused his memory and yours, the more I felt free to identify with you, to become you in my heart. I stopped hating you long ago. I just longed for you to come back and set me free.

"Lanik," he said, "I go from time to time, I go into the pens and have these limbs cut off. They always grow back, and more besides. I'm almost due now. The doctor never knows I'm me, never remembers that he performs these operations until it's time for the next one. No one ever sees my monster shape, but *I* see."

He looked at me, at my body. "You," he said. "You're whole. You're right and normal. You haven't lived this sick deception for these long months, these years. Let's go back out to the throne room. I'll appear in my true form and tell them all the truth, tell them that you're not the monster you were believed to be. You can take your true place, and I'll be free."

"What will you do then?"

"I'll plead with you to kill me. I've lived for years now as a radical regenerative. It doesn't qualify as life. If you won't kill me, I'll drown myself."

I shook my head. "I came here to kill you."

"Did you know who I was, then?"

"No. I came to kill the Anderson who controlled Mueller, the one pretending to be Dinte."

He was shocked. "You knew before you came? Then the Andersons' secret is out?"

"The Andersons," I told him, "are dead. A rainstorm reached you"—I groped for the real time—"a few days ago. A drenching rainstorm. And the sky is still overcast." He nodded. "That rain was caused a week ago when Anderson sank into the sea."

He was surprised. "Just like that? Sank into the sea?"

I heard the scream still ringing inside me. "Not just like that. But they've disappeared from the earth. Not just the ones on the island. All the others, too, in every Family. You're the last one alive who knows the Andersons' technique. You and any who worked with you here."

"How did you do it?"

"Never mind how. What matters is why." And I explained to him.

"So the Ambassadors are gone, too," he said. "No more iron. Do you realize what you've done?"

I laughed. "I have a good idea."

"We—the Andersons knew every secret in the world, Lanik! Do you realize what was being achieved on this world? Incredible things. Things to make you proud to be on this godforsaken prison planet! And you've stopped it. Without the Ambassadors, do you think that level of invention will continue?"

I shrugged. "It might. The Andersons didn't know all the secrets in the world."

"Stupid! Shortsighted and stupid and—"

"Listen, Lanik!" I shouted back, and the act of using my own name in reference to another person surprised me. "Yes, Lanik. You are me, aren't you? Me as I should have been. Me, captured by the Nkumai and induced to learn Mwabao Mawa's tricks—and I would have learned them, just as you did. I would have let myself become their tool, to a point; and there you sit, as I would have sat, a monster in a body trapped inside an even more monstrous illusion. No, Lanik, you're not the one to judge me as shortsighted or stupid. And I'm not the one to judge you. You called this a godforsaken planet, but you're wrong. Thousands of years ago the Republic decided to be God. They decided to put the finest minds in the universe on a hopeless, ironless planet, to punish them and their children forever and ever, as if we were born with the guilt of their crime upon us. They cruelly held out in front of our ancestors a reward: The first Family to build a starship and come out into space would receive unheard-of riches and power and prestige. For three thousand years we believed that, and spent our souls working to do what—to give to the bastards who keep us here the best we could develop. Our own flesh! The finest products of our minds! And what have we had in return? A few tons of a metal that's cheap everywhere but here."

"So we can build a starship," said my double.

"We'll never build a starship with Republic iron, never. And if we did, do you think they'd let us all come out and take part in human life? Don't you realize the miracle this planet is? If they realized what's *really* going on—if they could spend a few days in Ku Kuei, or a week in Schwartz—if they understood what our potential really is, Lanik, they'd be here immediately, they'd bomb this planet out of existence, wipe us out of the universe. That's the only hope and promise we have from them.

"And what would we do if we joined them? Persuade them to be nice? If they were going to be kind, they wouldn't be keeping the hundredth great grandchildren of traitors imprisoned on a hopeless planet like this."

"I know that," he said. "I've often thought about the hopelessness of it, too, Lanik. Dissent accomplishes nothing. It's something I told a young man who had been arrested for protesting against a law. I took him out by the river at night, without his guards, and I pointed out some facts to him. That if he kept his mouth shut, the law would leave him alone and he'd be free. 'I don't want to be free,' he said, 'while that law exists. I will dissent until you take it away.' 'No,' I told him, 'you'll dissent until you die in prison, and what will you have accomplished?

" 'It's like the moons,' I said to him. 'See how Dissent moves so quickly and brightly? The most spectacular thing in the sky. But it's spectacular because it's so close to Treason, and so small. Freedom is a much larger moon, much farther away. It doesn't make half the show. But Freedom makes the tides go,' I said. 'Freedom raises and lowers the sea.' "

I was filled with a strange feeling. Recognition. This deformed man thought as I did; and though it was only logical that he would, still it was a surprise to me. No one ever meets a man who thinks exactly as he does, not normally. But now it was as if I could say his words—my words—along with him.

"With Anderson gone, and the Ambassadors," he —I—said, "we're cut off from the Republic. We're free. And when the universe hears from us again, we'll be making the tides."

Silence. Then I realized that I had said the last few words, not he. He smiled at me. We understood each other. Not everything, but the thought, the *way* we thought was clear to both of us, and, so help me, I felt affection for him. If the ability to communicate well has something to do with love, there is no one a man can love quite so well as himself.

"Lanik," we said in unison, breaking the silence together. We laughed. "You first," I told him.

"Lanik, please take the throne. If you know me, you know how I feel in this body. You know from what I've told you that I've done unbearable things. Set me free."

Unbearable things. I didn't tell him, didn't try to explain the unbearable things I had done, didn't try to communicate the scream that underlay every thought I had. Instead, I closed my eyes and began to do for him what the Schwartzes had done for me.

It had taken only a handful of Schwartzes to change me, to cure my radical regeneration, and so I hoped I could do it alone. I had nothing like their knowledge of the carbon chains, but I could sense them well enough to compare. Any difference between his DNA and mine I changed in him until we matched, perfectly. It meant that not only would his regeneration be cured, but also he would have the gift of never hungering and thirsting again, of being free of the need to breathe, of taking his energy directly from the sun.

But I couldn't give to him the abilities that I had learned, and wouldn't have if I could. He was the real Lanik Mueller, not I. He was Lanik Mueller as I should have been: ruling in Mueller, and ruling well; lonely, but living where he ought to live. Now, without the curse of radical regeneration, he would be free to achieve a measure of happiness that would always be beyond me.

It took hours. When I was through, he lay asleep on the attic floor, his body whole and correct and healthy. He was naked—there were no tailors to clothe the deformed bodies of radical regeneratives. I looked at his body as I have never been able to look at my own. The skin was young and smooth—for he was younger than I—and the muscles were good and the body well-proportioned. For a moment I saw myself as Saranna must have seen me, and for all that I have no love or longing for other men, I understood why she so often told me that my body was sweet. It had irritated me—an adolescent boy does not aspire to sweetness. But she was right.

It was the face that made me ache inside. He thought he had known pain, and he had, to a degree greater than many men. His face showed maturity beyond his years, and kindness, and compassion. But I had seen my own face in mirrors, had studied what time and my own acts had done to me, and my face was not kind or compassionate. I had seen too much. I had killed too often. There was no sweetness left in me, not to look at, and I yearned to be as innocent as he.

Impossible, I reminded myself. That choice was made years ago in the sand at the border of Schwartz. And I began to suspect that the ultimate sacrifice isn't death after all; the ultimate sacrifice is willingly bearing the fullest penalty for your own actions. I had borne it, and I couldn't hope not to have the scars show in my face and my body.

He awoke and looked at me and smiled. Then he realized what had happened to his body. He touched himself incredulously and wept and kept asking me, "This isn't an illusion, is it? It's real, isn't it?"

Yes, it's real, I told him. "And when I've destroyed the Ambassador, there'll be no more need to keep rads like cattle. So do this for me. Make it a law that rads be sent to Schwartz, all of them, as soon as they're identified. Have them go into Schwartz and when the desert people come to them, have them say they come in Lanik Mueller's name. The Schwartzes will know what to do after that. They'll send them home, whole. Or if they don't come home, it's because they freely chose to stay."

"What about you?" Lanik asked.

"I don't exist," I answered. "In the forest of Nkumai it wasn't you who became the extra Lanik Mueller, it was I. You're the real one. Over the next few years, Lanik, change the illusion. Gradually make Dinte's face become your own until you can end the deception. You want to anyway, I know that much. End the lie, except for the name, and live and rule with your own face."

"And you?"

"I'll find another place to live."

Then I pushed back into quicktime and left him in the attic and went back to the court, where quite a few people still milled around, chattering about what had happened. It took me only a few minutes to spot the Andersons among them, the last of their Family to survive. I had left Lanik feeling sad and yet better than I had felt in a long time. But that didn't stop me from killing the last of the Andersons.

In quicktime I carried their bodies to the Ambassador and laid them where the explosion would leave them unrecognizable. Back when I first set out to destroy the Ambassadors, I had decided that when I blew up the last one, I would die with it. But now I realized that that decision was unmade. I think it was because I knew that the real me was still a sweet-bodied boy who would make a good king, and though he wasn't the me-that-I-am, he was the me-that-ought-to-be, and I gained a little respect for myself, and no longer wanted to die.

So I stayed in quicktime to break the seal on the Ambassador, then walked off to a safe distance before slipping back into realtime to watch. It took a few moments as the Ambassador waited metallically, unknowingly, as it made its own death. I felt wistful for that instant. All our history, all our purpose for far too many years, had been shaped to try to win our return to the Republic, to the kind of civilization that could make machines like this. They knew so much that we could not know once I destroyed this last Ambassador. I found myself slipping into quicktime, so I could rush to the fuse, stop it before the Ambassador died.

But I did not move. If our years of slavery had taught us anything, it should have taught us this: that the Ambassador was not the key to our freedom, it was the chain that bound us. Our freedom would only come when we forgot our dead ancestors and our distant enemies and discovered who and what we had actually become in these centuries on Treason.

I did not move, the Ambassador finished its self-immolation program, the explosion destroyed it from the inside, the lights of the machine went off, and I wondered for a frightening moment how I dared to make such a decision for the whole world, without consulting anyone else.

Then I laughed at myself. It was a little late to wonder if I ought to play God. The game was already over.

The dust from the explosion cleared. My work was done. I had decided to live past the end of my work after all, and it meant I had to make decisions I had thought never to make again. Where would I go? What did I want to do with the rest of my life?

As I walked through the fields east of Mueller-on-the-River, I knew where I would have to go. On an island in the middle of a lake in Ku Kuei, Saranna had said, "Come back soon. Come back while you're still young enough to want me. For I'm going to be young forever."

I wasn't young anymore, not by any definition of the word. But I wanted her. Perhaps I only wanted the innocence of the children we had been, making love beside the river, oblivious to the pain that could and surely would come to them. Still, I wanted her more than I wanted anyone else in the world, not because my passion was so overwhelming, but because all the other things I wanted were either painfully accomplished or so hopeless that I had given up on them. Only she was left. She and a strange and quiet land of poor yet kindly people who tended sheep among the rocks by the Humping Sea.

15 MAN-OF-THE-WIND

       I came to Ku Kuei in realtime and laughed a bit when several of the young ones, not knowing who I was, tried to play quicktime games with me. I easily coped with their timeflows and stayed in realtime despite all they did. They must have got worried then, and called on someone older and more skilled. Which is why Man-Who-Knows-It-All came to greet me.

"Lake-drinker," he roared as he came into view, laughing and holding out his arms. "Gone forever! My worst student, the bad example I hold before all the children who come to me to learn. You stayed away so long, however long it's been, who can keep track of time? But it's been a long time, you old bastard, and come on, come on, come on, hurry!"

We hurried, the fat Ku Kuei leading the way briskly. I drank in the air of the forest. Forest wasn't the kind of land I called home, but this forest was my father's cemetery and the last place I had been when someone still loved me as a son and as a lover.

"Saranna," I said, and Man-Who-Knows-It-All looked puzzled. "Stump," I reminded him, and he laughed. "Oh, her. Her, what an incredible thing. A good student, for an outsider. We don't call her Stump anymore, you know. It's Stone now, Lady Stone, because there she stands in the slowest damn slowtime anyone's ever done. Do you want to see her?"

Did I want to see her? I didn't know how much until I stood there and realized that she was standing just as she had stood when I left, six subjective years and three real years before. Her hands were still reaching out to me. Her lips were still parted with her last words. The tears in her eyes had overflowed, and yet the first drops hadn't reached her chin.

I gazed at her and the last six years fell away and it was only a moment ago that I had left her. I walked close to her, slowing my time; I slowed beyond anything I had ever experienced before, slowed until even the trees seemed a blur, and then, at last, her tears began to move, and her eyes saw me, and her expression changed to hope, and she said, "Lanik. I've changed my mind. I don't want to be young forever. Take me with you."

She embraced me, and I embraced her, and I kissed her cheek where it was wet. "I've been away for six years," I said.

"Hush," she said.

"I've done terrible things."

"I don't need to know it."

"I'm not a good person," I insisted.

She only kissed me, and whispered, "Good enough for me." And she smiled and I smiled and gradually we slipped out of slowtime and the world ceased to be a blur and we were in Ku Kuei again. There were hundreds of people gathered around us. I recognized none of them.

"Why are you watching us?" I asked.

"Because," one fat man said, "people told us the Stone Lovers were speeding up to realtime, and we had to come to see."

"Stone lovers?"

"People have been born, grown old, and died, and only seen the two of you move an inch or two, or smile or seem to speak a single word. You looked so intense. Whatever you were saying, you seemed to mean it, and it wasn't amusing at all. Started quite a fashion. People keep looking for purpose now. Complicates everything."

"How long?" I asked.

"Two, three hundred years, I figure," he said. "But now I expect you'll be just ordinary people."

"I hope so," I said, and Saranna smiled.

We left the forest and traveled east until at last we reached Britton, and in the easternmost part of Britton's east peninsula, we came to Humping. In the last few centuries nothing had changed. A new lord ruled from cliff house, but he called himself by the hereditary name Barton. Glain's and Vran's house was now a garden and someone else's house stood a few meters off, but the house was full of children and nothing had been changed. The people were still poor, still taciturn, still good to the heart.

Saranna and I built a sod house near the sea, where I began at once to teach her all that I had learned. After a time a shepherd came to see what we were up to. I healed his painful joints and Saranna cured his sick lamb, and then they all knew who I was. "Man-of-the-Wind," they called me, and Saranna became the "Man-of-the-Wind's Lady," and soon just "Windlady," and though the people of Humping loved us, they couldn't have loved us as we loved them. The legend of Man-of-the-Wind was well known—how he had come from nowhere and lived with Glain and Vran, healing and doing good for everyone until someone told the lord in cliff house and Man-of-the-Wind went away and never came back again. This time, they vowed, it would be different. And in all the years we've lived here, the lord in cliff house has never sought us out.

The Humpers aren't surprised that though they grow old and die, we don't grow old. We have lived to cure the ills of children whose grandparents' broken legs we fixed. It's a quiet life, but a good one, and sometime soon Saranna and I plan to have children. When we have children, though, we will stop changing ourselves, and will grow old and die when our grandchildren are growing up, just like anyone else. Children don't need their parents to live forever.

But we're not quite ready for that now. Life is still sweet enough for us without children, though I look at Saranna and see that it won't be too long now; and I look at myself and see that I'm nearly ready. And that will be good, too. Even death will be good, I think, not because it ends old bitterness, but because I believe it will come as the last of the many sharp tastes that have taught me I am alive.

Under everything I still hear the scream of the earth, but it no longer taints the things I see and do. Instead, it heightens my pleasures, and sunrise is brighter because of the dark place inside me, and Saranna's smile is kinder because of the cruelty I have known, and healing the animals and children and adults that come to me is sweeter because once, against my own instincts but because of my own sense of right, I killed.

Whether Treason is a better place to live now I'm not the one to judge.

Whether we are progressing as well as we did before the Ambassadors were destroyed I don't know. It's not up to me to evaluate how well we've done with the opportunity I made.

Sometimes I marvel that I accomplished it at all. "You don't exist," Saranna often says after we make love, "you can't be real." She means it one way, but I believe it another, and for all the planning and plotting that I did before I acted, I know that I was shaped more by circumstance than by my own will. I wonder sometimes if I'm not, after all, a piece in some other player's game, following blindly his grand designs without ever knowing that my path along the board is only a feint, while the important matters are played out elsewhere by other men.

But whether there's some grand design really matters little to me. My only hope was this: To see what might be, to believe that it should be, and then to do all I could to bring it to pass, whatever the cost. When a life spins out as joyfully as mine has done, then the price, once paid so painfully, is now recalled in gladness. I have received full value. Here among the shepherds, my cup is filled with the water of life; it overflows.

The manuscript of this novel was composed using WordPerfect on an ALR 386 computer with an NEC Multisync monitor; it was printed out on an Epson GQ-3500 using a Glyphix font, and duplicated on a Canon NP3525-EF.

At last I realized that my only hope, thin as it was, was to escape, not as a woman, but as a man. But could I get past Mwabao?

Not so simple. I couldn't kill her—I liked her. She had breached diplomatic protocol, but she had done me no real harm. So I wouldn't kill her. A knock on her head, a breaking of bones, that should be enough. All that remained was to hide who I was.

I began searching quietly through the boxes, hoping to find a knife. I would need it to disfigure myself in escaping.

But I didn't find a knife. Instead I found several books. One book was a history of Treason.

I had read *our* history of the planet, of course, but this book was more complete in some ways. In some very important ways, and I began to realize that I had been almost completely fooled . . .

PRAISE FOR THE WORKS OF ORSON SCOTT CARD

"Beguiling . . . robust but reflective."
—*Publishers Weekly*

"A tribute to the art of storytelling . . . highly recommended."
—*Library Journal*

St. Martin's Paperbacks titles are available at quantity discounts for sales promotions, premiums or fund raising. Special books or book excerpts can also be created to fit specific needs.

For information write to special sales manager, St. Martin's Press, 175 Fifth Avenue, New York, N.Y. 10010.